LONGSHOT

ASH FITZSIMMONS

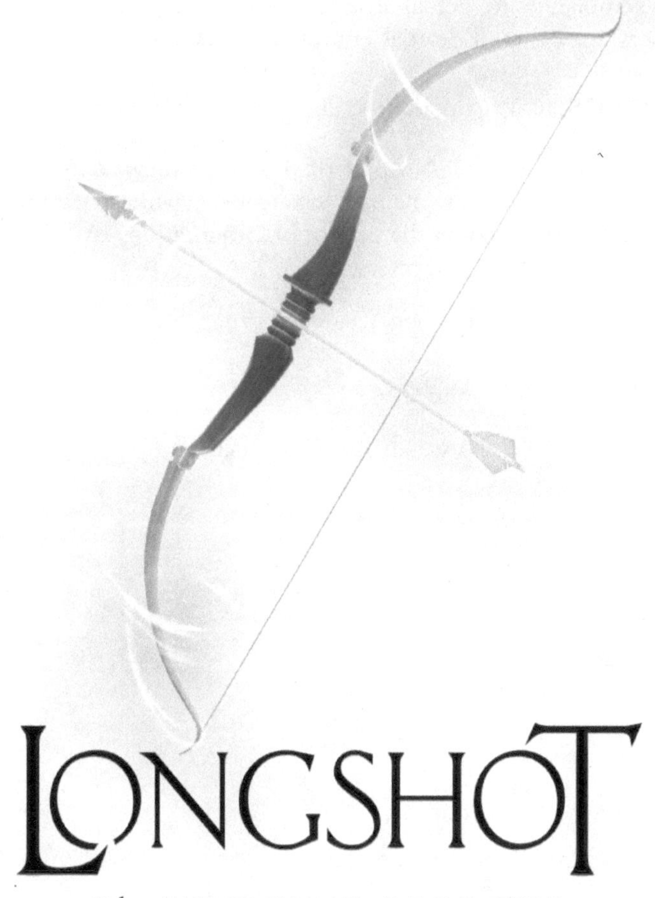

LONGSHOT

The WILD HUNT, BOOK TWO

This is a work of fiction. Names, characters, places, and incidents are products of the author's imagination or are used fictitiously and are not to be construed as real. Any resemblance to actual events, locales, organizations, or persons, living or dead, is entirely coincidental.

Print Edition ISBN: 978-1-949861-57-0

Cover design by MiblArt.

www.ashfitzsimmons.com

CHAPTER 1

As a private investigator, even in my short time in the profession, I'd grown accustomed to missing persons cases. The ones I'd seen generally involved desperate parents and a teenager or twenty-something who'd skipped town. I hadn't dealt with that many teens—cops tended to pay attention when a minor vanished—but the police were less inclined to sound the alarm when a taxpaying adult stopped returning Mommy and Daddy's phone calls. That's when the parents would seek out a PI, someone who could be hired to snoop around when a gut feeling insisted that the situation was *very* wrong.

Jack Schwartz, the PI who'd hired me fresh out of community college and trained me up, was a thirty-year veteran by the time I came aboard, and he looked the part: silver hair, neat moustache, partial to red suspenders and black suits. He'd lean against the wooden desk in his small but tidy office with his shirt sleeves rolled to the elbows and talk to the parents while I took notes, and they always seemed to leave feeling more hopeful about their lost kid. There was an art, Jack taught me, to dealing with the families of missing people. You wanted to maintain your objectivity but not come across as an unfeeling bastard. "You've got to leave that space, Annie," he used to tell me. "You sympathize, you promise what you can deliver, but you stay back a pace and keep your eyes open. Sometimes, people who go missing have their reasons why they don't want to be found."

Professionally, then, I knew how to handle folks who

were worried sick when a loved one seemingly vanished off the face of the earth. But now that I'd joined their ranks, all I could do was stare into space and beg my scattered thoughts to focus.

"Hey," said Maya, my roommate, stepping into my field of vision. "I'm putting water on. Want a cup of tea?"

"Sure," I mumbled. If nothing else, holding a mug would give my hands something to do.

As Maya walked off toward our kitchen, her diaphanous wings fluttered in agitation. After spending nearly a year with them stuck growing out of her back, she'd mastered basic control of her novel appendages, but I'd found that they often betrayed her mood. They weren't good for much beyond trapping her with me in the Pactlands, though at least people didn't panic when she walked by. My antlers, however, the result of the same potion that had left Maya looking like a fairytale illustration come to life, gave me a resemblance to a member of the feared and poorly understood Wild Hunt, and when I ran errands around the city, strangers crossed the street.

The *fucking* Hunt.

They'd taken Wylan. I'd mentally processed the scene a dozen times that day, and I couldn't come up with another explanation that made sense. Sure, Wylan was gentle around me—and handsome, awkward, and occasionally goofy, but someone whom, in only a few short months, I'd grown to accept that I'd like to find beside me every morning for the rest of my life. Still, the guy was a Huntsman, and I had every confidence that he could defend himself against just about anything short of a mob of angry trolls. With preternaturally keen senses, a well-toned physique, and decades of weapons training, Wylan could take care of himself—and that was without factoring in his own rack. Unlike me with my late-acquired antlers, Wylan surely knew how to employ his for defense. Hell, he could even teleport in a pinch.

But he was gone, leaving no trace but blood and a

broken prong. *Something* had overpowered him.

His father had to have figured out that Wylan had been in on our operation to rescue Fellora ti'Mal. That was the only conclusion that made sense to me.

But *how* had the Hunter guessed? Wylan told me he'd never been alone during his last trip to the Hunt's hidden lodge, and I'd crept in with him, de-scented by a potion and rendered invisible by a ring I'd just as soon forget for the side effects. I couldn't have been spotted—the Hunt would never have let me trudge off into the woods with a wolf slung over my shoulders if they'd sensed me. Surely Wylan hadn't spilled the plan to any of his brothers…

Whatever it was, we'd screwed up, and now the Hunt had kidnapped their wayward youngest brother from his shitty little apartment in Beukal.

The kettle whistled, and a moment later, Yven brought me a steaming mug. "Decaf. Maya's orders," he said, his English accented but otherwise perfect.

I was grateful for the touch—while I'd been speaking Pactish for most of the last year, my brain was barely processing that night without throwing translation into the mix.

He sat on the edge of the coffee table as I sipped the minty brew, regarding me as if I were an unexploded bomb, potentially bad news and quite probably unstable. "You can't stay up all night, Annie. Watching the clock won't help anyone."

I shot him my best *don't fuck with me* glare and sipped again. Under ordinary circumstances, I liked Yven just fine. The elf was slightly fastidious and way too invested in his orchid collection, but he'd been kind to Maya and me, and there was no denying his love for Rose. If he was good enough for my friend, he was all right in my books. That night, however, I wasn't about to take orders in my own damn den—not when the Division of Laws could call at any moment with an update.

The first twenty-four hours were the most important in

any missing person investigation, or at least that's what had been hammered into me back in Richmond. Surely the detectives at DOL understood that. They'd be working this case, exploring leads, making calls, rushing to process evidence…right? And that, I concluded, trying to reassure myself, was why no one had called me all day.

Any minute now, my phone would ring.

Any minute.

I'd wanted to surprise Wylan with breakfast that Sunday morning. After a night in my own bed, I was feeling leagues better than I had upon waking in the Division of Plants and Potions' on-site medical unit two days before. Given my condition when Fellora and I had been found—dehydrated and with a massive rash, my back raw from the blisters that had broken beneath the weight of Fellora's body, and on the verge of renal failure—I probably would have been sent to a hospital, had I been anyone else. But the people who best understood Roulette, the potion that had rendered me a freak of nature and left me stranded in the Pactlands, were the research team at DPP, and so I'd been kept in the agency's tower while the healers worked on me and the specialists trying to find an antidote catalogued my adverse cross-reactions. *Nothing* magical functioned quite like it should with me, thanks to Roulette, but if my body's freakout pushed the researchers closer to an antidote to the potion, then my pain would be worth it in the end.

But there had been no "eureka" moment before the healers had released me to my apartment with some pain-numbing potions and a stern admonition to rest, so I'd tried to make the best of it. Fellora and I were alive and mostly intact. Wylan had ridden with the rest of the Hunt and returned to the city with none of his brothers the wiser. The Pactlands' weather being as mild as it was, surely a walk on a brisk morning in early October wouldn't land me flat on my back. So I'd picked up a couple of to-go breakfasts and headed for Wylan's place, a virtually unfurnished fifth-floor apartment in a building that had seen far better days. I'd imagined his surprised pleasure at finding me there with food—heck, maybe he'd even come to the door shirtless, a little bonus for me—but he hadn't answered the buzzer. When his neighbor had let me in, I'd found Wylan's door open, and the apartment…

I wasn't a cop, but I was sufficiently savvy to recognize a crime scene.

The details remained burned in my mind's eye like an afterimage. The den furniture—the wooden crate Wylan used for a chair and the pine end table that only served to make the setup sadder—had been tossed. The end table had landed on its side by the wall, while the crate had splintered on impact. Wylan's bedroom had fared marginally better, but then he slept on a mattress atop a metal frame, not the sort of furniture so easily moved or broken. The bedclothes were rumpled, which suggested he'd been sleeping when the commotion began. The bathroom was untouched, and when I took the hidden closet staircase to the roof, there was no sign of disturbance above. But the den, the bedroom, the connecting hallway, and even the edge of the kitchen were streaked and spotted with blood: splashes on the bedroom window shade, drips on the blankets, stains on the ancient carpeting, a half-formed handprint on the wall beside the front door. A broken antler prong had been kicked to the wall beside the fallen end table, and something in me *knew* it was Wylan's.

He'd fought so hard.

I hadn't screamed like a horror-movie blonde or run from the apartment—my training had kicked in enough to keep me in place—but my hands had shaken while I'd pulled up the one contact in my phone who might help me.

Syvin Deop was the chief deputy at DPP, a veteran

agent of long tenure. Surely she'd know who to call.

The first of the DOL agents arrived not ten minutes after I hung up from Syvin, evidence technicians who shooed me out of the apartment and left me dazed in the lonely hallway. Wylan lived in 5B, and the neighboring apartment appeared to be either vacant or inhabited by a deaf tenant, as no one came out to question the ruckus next door before Syvin and a green-haired nymph reached the top of the staircase. Spotting me, Syvin told the nymph, "That's our girl. Annie, come down with me. You need to give a statement."

I don't know what I said in that moment, stunned as I was—hell, I hadn't yet realized that I'd left our breakfast on the floor of Wylan's den. The nymph, perhaps having had more experience with shocked witnesses, took over. "Annie Humphries, yes?" he—or she, maybe, it was almost impossible to tell with nymphs—asked. "It's all right, dear, you're safe. Why don't you and Chief Deputy Deop go to the manager's office for now? We've already commandeered it for you." When I stammered, the nymph gently gripped my arm and held my stare. "Annie, you need to allow us to do our job. Are you hurt?"

I shook my head.

"That's good. Go downstairs, please. We'll talk later."

By then, I'd begun to process details about the nymph: sandstone-colored skin, the typical willowy build and long, pointed ears, and a simple black uniform bearing DOL's insignia, an eight-pointed silver star with a violet circle around the agency's name at the center. Clipped to the nymph's belt was a holster holding a black-handled pistol—probably a semiautomatic, based on what I'd seen around the capital. Nymphs wielded elemental power, but as agents and officers, they carried backup of a far more mundane variety.

"Annie," said Syvin in a no-nonsense tone, "Detective

Venanu has been spearheading the investigation of Fellora's case. He knows what he's doing. You need to come with me."

Unable to formulate a decent protest, I followed Syvin, who, even with her short stature, made surprisingly quick work of the staircase. Then again, the woman was a faun, and weren't goats supposed to be nimble climbers?

Something cautioned me against making this comparison within Syvin's hearing, evidence that my wits hadn't completely deserted me that morning. I liked her, but Syvin had spent the last four hundred years at DPP, and she'd earned her reputation as a force to be feared. Trolls twice her size called her "ma'am" and moved out of her way—possibly because one good blow from her curling horns could send a grown man to his knees. Syvin's head was built like a tank.

In the manager's office, Syvin helped herself to the coffeemaker, thrust a cup into my hands, and told me to start from the beginning. Once I'd taken a few bracing gulps of the cheap, bitter brew, she pulled up a chair beside me and plopped a notepad on her shaggy lap. She listened as I recounted everything I could recall, nodding in the right places and interrupting me with the occasional question when my mind skipped around.

Distantly, I recognized this dance, though I'd grown accustomed to being the leading partner.

As Syvin wrapped up the interview, Detective Venanu rapped on the door and let himself in. "Thoughts?" asked Syvin.

He grunted and folded his arms. "Damned strange crime scene."

"How so? What do you have?"

The detective arched a thick green eyebrow.

"The Huntsman's on our payroll, Kov, and you know your director will answer my questions if I pry."

With a huffed sigh, he relented. "Preliminary scene testing suggests the blood isn't from a known Pact species.

I've got a specialist sorcerer on the way."

"Does DOL actually have blood from a Huntsman on file?" Syvin asked.

A quick shake of his head answered that. "I'd be surprised."

"It's Wylan's apartment," I pointed out. "He doesn't have a roommate…"

"And I'd be inclined to believe it's his," Detective Venanu replied, "but for the fact that we've got a multiple donor situation." His mouth twitched as my eyes widened. "Donor 1 is all over the bed, and that handprint by the door is theirs. One of my techs is looking for a match in the bathroom, but my initial assumption is that Donor 1 is your Huntsman. But we've got spatter from at least four other donors in there, which tells me that whatever happened, he gave as good as he got, know what I mean?"

My oh-so-helpful mind's eye conjured the scene: Wylan, awakened by an attack from his brothers, lashing out in the dark as they mobbed him.

"What about the broken antler?" I asked.

"Still being tested…" His voice faded as his phone beeped, and the detective pulled it from his pocket to read the message. "Never mind. Antler scraping matches the profile of Donor 1 *and* the profile from the bathroom trash. Looks like we have a winner."

Seeing his phone sparked a desperate idea. "Wylan's got a cell phone—I bought it for him last Monday after I interviewed Fellora's family. Did you find it? Maybe his call log—"

"We found it," said Detective Venanu, "or what was left of it. Smashed. It's going back to the office for analysis."

That, I mused as my rational brain tried to reassert itself, was probably a waste of time. If Wylan had no phone before coming to Beukal, then what were the odds that his brothers were carrying them? And what did I expect, that they would have called to warn him to prepare for a rumble?

"So you've got Wylan bleeding in his bedroom," Syvin remarked, "and then his blood by the door, which was open when Annie arrived."

The detective's eyes, the color of new leaves, fixed on me. "You're certain?"

"Absolutely," I told him. "I don't have a key to his place, so how would I have gotten in?"

"Fair." He frowned as he slotted that information into his calculations. "The locking mechanism wasn't broken. Who else had access to that apartment? What do you know about his friends?"

I laughed at the absurdity of the question. "Wylan works with me at the café, and of late, he worked with me on Fellora's case. He's never mentioned other friends in the city."

"Nor would he be likely to have many, all things considered," Syvin muttered.

"As far as I know," I continued, "the only other person who can get in his apartment is the manager here."

"Where *is* the manager?" Detective Venanu asked Syvin.

She pointed over his shoulder toward the street. "One of your techs thought to call him before they arrived. He got out of bed to let them in, and my understanding is that he was being taken down the road to get a cup of coffee for his 'nerves.' The little darling doesn't like blood, it seems."

They rolled their eyes.

"So you don't think the manager was prevailed upon by a group of Huntsmen to give them access to the apartment?" he pressed.

"I think we'd have found him a twitching mess in that scenario," she replied. "Considering his reaction to—"

"You know they can teleport, right?" I interjected.

The detective's head jerked back toward me. "Come again?"

"Teleport," I repeated. "Or whatever you people call it. Here one second, somewhere else the next. It's weird and disorienting as hell, but Wylan seems pretty blasé about the whole thing."

"*You* have—"

"That's how he got me to Fellora," I told him. Prudence counseled that I not mention that one *teensy* little hunting trip Wylan and I had taken outside the Pactlands.

Syvin nodded. "I saw them off. Something else to add to the file on the Hunt. But assuming Wylan's not an aberration, then it's possible his assailants didn't need the door."

"Huh," Detective Venanu grunted, rubbing his forehead. "Then why was the door open?"

"Because Wylan was trying to run."

The others looked at me in query, but I saw the solution as clearly as if I were watching it play out in the manager's office. "Whatever Wylan is touching goes with him when he teleports—clothes, gear, me. Maybe he was being grabbed. He was attempting to break free long enough to get out of there…"

Syvin lifted a finger to stay the detective's interrogation while I took a few deep breaths, then murmured, "How would the Hunt have found him? You don't think he left an address, do you?"

I shook my head. "No clue. I know that *he* knows when the Hunt is riding, so maybe they have some deeper connection he hasn't told me about. Or they could have smelled him."

"Oh?" Detective Venanu asked.

"He says his sense of smell is close to a troll's. I watched him at Green Lake—he tracked Fellora days after she was snatched, and he didn't break a sweat. If he left his scent anywhere in this city, it'd be here and at the café."

Silently, I thought of the other places he'd been of late: my apartment, my van, Yven's apartment, the DPP tower…

"Good to know," said the detective, and awkwardly patted my shoulder. "Why don't you go home, Ms. Humphries? We'll be in touch."

Syvin would have given me a lift, but her sedan couldn't accommodate my antlers. Instead, she insisted on walking me back to my apartment, then escorted me upstairs and quietly explained the situation to Maya while I stood with my shaking hands braced against the kitchen counter, trying to remember how to make coffee.

I knew what the Hunter was capable of. Seven feet tall without factoring in his rack and built like a bear, the guy was an ambulatory red flag to the ancient part of my brain that warned me against predators. I hadn't fully understood the phrase "aura of menace" until he walked into the room where I was hiding…and that was before I knew that he'd had a woman abducted, turned her into a wolf, and was planning on hunting her in the morning.

Swell guy.

Had I been able to get to the lodge, I'd have run to find Wylan as soon as Syvin's back was turned. I'd have swigged the sent neutralizing potion that left me with a full-body rash and begged Teolm ti'Cren to re-loan me the invisibility ring that made the rash burn. The healers would have killed me if the cross-reactions didn't, but I'd have risked it to pursue Wylan.

Slight problem, though: no one outside the Hunt knew the way to their hidden lodge. Still, I had to do *something*, so once Maya settled me on the couch with a whiskey-laced cup of coffee, I tried to casually broach the idea with Syvin of taking DOL's fancy rotor-less helicopter up to the place where they'd found Fellora and me, then backtracking to locate the lodge. She quickly shot that down.

"Forget Laws. *Intelligence* has already been snooping around, and they've found nothing," she told me, perching on the edge of her chair so that her hooves could reach the rug. "The area is nothing but grasslands and scrub forest. You appeared from thin air."

"But—"

"And you are *not* going back to poke around. I don't care if DOL lands in the street and offers you a ride. Is that clear?"

"I can't sit here and do nothing," I protested.

"You can stay out of trouble for now," she said, holding my stare. "Don't make this more complicated than it needs to be, Annie. I don't want you to disappear, too." With that, she rose and nodded to Maya. "Keep her home today, hmm? I'll tell DOL to call with updates."

By eleven that night, I'd heard a whole lot of silence from Detective Venanu and his crew, and Syvin had nothing to offer me when she checked in at dinnertime. At least I wasn't alone with my thoughts. Maya, ever the trooper, had stuck around the apartment to babysit me, leaving me alone only for the odd smoke break on the balcony. When she'd called Rose and Yven to spread the news, they'd hurried over to keep watch with us. Yven had made dinner, which was a lovely gesture, but Rose had flopped onto my bed to put her skills to use. Possessed of her family's wild talent, farsight, Rose tranced periodically throughout the day, looking for any clue as to where Wylan might be. Unfortunately, just as when she'd sought Fellora, she saw nothing but blackness. The good news was that this meant Wylan wasn't dead—her vision wouldn't kick in at all if that had been the case. The bad news was that he was almost certainly at the Hunt's lodge, where Rose's farsight couldn't reach, and I could only imagine what his father had in store for him.

While Rose worked, Maya and Yven had tried to reassure me. Maybe the Hunter just wanted all his sons back. Maybe this was some sort of Huntsman hazing ritual. Maybe Wylan had managed to hurt himself sleepwalking and went home to get patched up. I appreciated their effort, but we all knew they were grasping at straws.

As Maya joined Yven and me with two more mugs of tea, I heard the floorboard creak and whipped around, stupidly hoping I might find Wylan there. Instead, I saw Rose emerge from my room, weary and frustrated. She pushed her mussed auburn hair from her face with a swipe of her hand, and her gray eyes landed on our impromptu tea party. "Any more hot water?" she croaked.

"Sit down, I'll get you one," said Maya, pointing to the couch, and Rose sank onto the cushion with a soft groan.

I knew better than to ask if she'd had any luck finding Wylan. While Rose had an incredible gift—and an incredibly rare one—much of her technique was self-taught, and extended sessions wore her out. Yven was quick to wrap a blanket around her shoulders, and she smiled up at him in thanks as Maya hurried back with her tea.

"So what now?" Rose asked us. "Short of tracking down this detective and demanding answers, I mean. Assault's probably not the wisest idea tonight."

"Seconded," Yven muttered, and glanced at me. "Annie, get some rest. Rosie needs sleep, and so do you. If DOL calls and the phone doesn't wake you, I'm sure one of us will hear it."

I didn't want to go to bed. Admitting that this wasn't going to be solved in less than a day meant facing the reality that something truly wrong had happened to Wylan, and I still held out a sliver of hope that he'd come walking in at any second. But before I could pull together another half-assed rationale for why I needed to maintain my vigil, I heard a sharp knock at the door.

The four of us jumped, then looked at each other, suddenly unsure.

"Stay here," Yven whispered, motioning Rose down as he stood, and quietly padded to the double-locked door.

He pressed one eye to the peephole, then drew back in surprise, hastily undid the latches, and cracked the door open. "Um…yes, sir?"

Glancing past him, I saw a youthful-looking man on the doormat, an elf who seemed no older than I was, thirty at most. He wore a black turtleneck sweater over dark jeans, and a charcoal duster disguised some of the details of his form. But his face was one I knew well—not from personal interactions, but rather from the occasional televised shot. Slightly hooded gray eyes beneath coppery brows, barely upturned nose, thin lips, red hair falling loose over his shoulders…and despite the differences in their individual features, a look that reminded me strongly of Rose. To the untrained eye, he could have been her older brother, but I'd been in the Pactlands long enough to know better.

That Diriem ti'Dana, the director of the Division of Intelligence, was at my door so close to midnight boded nothing good.

"*Pop*?" Rose asked, frowning as she put down her tea. "What are you doing here?"

He seemed unsurprised to find her at our place, but then again, Diriem was a future-oriented farseer of high repute. I suspected he'd known *exactly* where to find his great-granddaughter.

"You need to come with me," he said, quickly eyeing us in turn. "All of you. Right now."

"What's going on?" Rose asked.

"The less said here, the better. Do you have anything important at Yven's place?"

"No…"

"Good. Perhaps you could help him pack, then," he suggested, and glanced back at Yven. "You'll want your work computer. Maybe a decent robe in case you need to appear long-distance. Toothbrush."

Yven barely balked. If one were wise, I'd gathered, one did *not* tell Lord ti'Dana no. "Pack for how long, sir?"

"Unclear as of yet, unfortunately," he replied with a slight scowl. "But don't worry about economizing your luggage. Can you be back here within an hour?"

"If need be—"

"It does. Go. Rosie—"

"On it," she interrupted, grabbing her purse. "I'll call when we're headed back."

As she slipped past Diriem, he stepped into the apartment and locked the door behind him. "Sorry to intrude like this, girls, but you're not safe here. Pack quickly."

Maya headed straight for her room, but I paused long enough to note the tension in his shoulders. "Can you at least tell us where we're going?" I asked.

He nodded. "My place. Hurry, now."

CHAPTER 2

Once upon a time—actually, about five hundred years ago—the elven Halls swore fealty to one of two thrones: the southern, based along the Mediterranean, and the northern, tucked in a remote corner of present-day Norway. From what I'd gathered, the southern king had viewed signing on to the Pact and running off to its shiny new pocket world as conceding defeat to the ever more numerous humans, and he and most of his vassal Halls had declined the offer. But the northern throne was held by Hall ti'Dana, and Diriem, who'd been king for less than a century at that point, decided that survival was a better option than waging a war that his people wouldn't win. A few of the southern Halls defected and ran off to the Pactlands with him, but those who remained were wiped out.

While Diriem had technically surrendered his throne in signing the Pact, elves in particular still approached him with deference. Putting aside the matter of his farsight, a talent that left many unsettled, the man had saved his species from extinction. Small wonder, then, that he'd headed DOI since the agency's inception and served the occasional term as a representative to the Forum.

The other Halls squabbled among themselves for prominence, and their members' misdeeds fed the gossip mill. Hall ti'Dana remained the undisputed first among alleged equals, ignored the jockeying, and seldom made waves. And when word of a scandal within that Hall arose—for instance, that Diriem's only child had taken the death draught to run off with a human, and that the only remaining descendant of that disgraceful union was not only a farseer in her own right but *acknowledged* into the Hall as the heir apparent—well, the gossips mostly kept their mouths shut. Some targets were simply off-limits.

Though Hall ti'Dana no longer had a *throne*, per se, the family manse was palatial, a stone edifice with towers and stained glass and graceful arches and acres of lawn that would surely have been a tree-festooned park if the Pactlands' weird soil could support trees taller than hip-high without a complicated connection to the outside world. I'd never seen it in person, but Rose, who had an apartment within the hall, had shown Maya and me pictures. She claimed that Hall ti'Cren's mansion was larger still, but as far as I was concerned, once you started counting your bathrooms in the dozens, the actual square footage didn't really matter.

The ti'Dana mansion was in Viratta, a small district not terribly far from the capital. Had the Pactlands collapsed, Beukal would have landed close to Richmond, while Viratta would have appeared in central Pennsylvania, but the Pactlands' system of internal portals made short work of the drive, especially past midnight. We drove out in a convoy, Diriem leading in what appeared to be a black Porsche 911, Rose in her blue Outback (recently modified with a few select magical upgrades), Maya and me in our DPP loaners, and Yven bringing up the rear in his beloved red Mustang. As we neared the house, I noticed only a few lit windows, mostly on the upper floors. There were no lampposts along the winding private driveway—rather, the road itself glowed with a pale aqua phosphorescence, illuminating like a blue tide as our vehicles approached.

My van's headlights offered a poor view of the mansion, and I didn't realize we'd reached the far side until I saw enormous garage doors rising up ahead. Diriem pulled in and parked, and Rose and Maya followed in turn. When I crept into the garage, I saw that the ground level offered room enough for two dozen vehicles, and a down ramp suggested an additional subterranean level. I grabbed a free space between a silver sportscar of unfamiliar markings—a Pactlands original, I assumed—and a shiny black vintage Phantom. My well-used van had *no* business being in that spot, but I eased the door open, focused on skinny thoughts, and managed not to ding the small fortune on either side of me.

Eleven months before, back when I was just a green PI in Richmond, I would never have dreamed of rolling up to the home of a seven-hundred-year-old elf with an expansive car collection in the middle of the night, running from some unknown danger, but here we were. Things could have been worse, I told myself while I grabbed my bags from the back of the van. Wylan could be dead.

I could be dead.

I tried not to ruminate on that distressing possibility as I shouldered my loaded tote bags—I had no luggage—and followed our pack toward a disappointingly institutional metal door at the far end of the garage.

The door led into a hallway with polished oak floors and stone and plaster walls, a space illuminated by a crystal chandelier and decorated with subdued landscapes. The runner on which I stood looked far too close to a silk carpet for comfort, and I hastily checked the soles of my sneakers for mud. We might as well have stepped into a luxury resort, perhaps the sort of boutique property housed within a renovated castle where the nightly rate started at my old apartment's monthly rent.

Before I could get my bearings, a reedy, gray-haired man in a plaid bathrobe and matching pajamas hurried around the corner. "Success, sir? Ah, Miss Rose. Good evening."

"Morning, more like," Rose replied, stifling a yawn. "Hi, Scel. Don't you ever sleep?"

"She has a point," said Diriem with a weary smile. "I'm afraid I've kept you late. We can manage from here."

I surmised that the man in the bathrobe, Scel, had to be a sorcerer. He looked like any other middle-aged human—judging by the wrinkles around his blue eyes and his mouth, I'd have put him in his sixties had I seen him back home—but given their lengthened lifespans, I guessed that Scel was around two hundred years old.

He regarded Diriem with deep suspicion. "Are you certain, sir? I don't mind—"

"I know, and I appreciate that, but I'd rather you not sleepwalk through the day tomorrow," he said. "Have our other guests arrived?"

"All but the ones you said were coming late. I've sent the rest to their rooms."

"Perfect. Get some rest, eh?" Diriem suggested, and pointed to the ceiling. "I'll see you after breakfast."

"Oh, *no*, sir—"

As the two of them gently bickered about the overtime situation, Rose leaned close to me and whispered, "Scel Curain. He's been Pop's house manager for, like, a hundred and fifty years. His dad did it before him."

"So...the butler?" I whispered back.

"More than that. Pop says Scel runs this place, and he just lives here." She waved goodnight as Scel was finally convinced to retire, then turned to Diriem and folded her arms. "All right, now what's going on?"

"One moment more," he said, then focused on a spot in the distance and made a complicated series of gestures. The lights briefly flashed green, and he nodded curtly. "And that should protect us against unwanted visitors. Follow me, if you will," he told us, and headed off in the direction Scel had gone, casually flicking his fingers to flip on the lamps in the next room.

"What was that about?" I asked Rose.

"Beats me," she said with a shrug, then followed after our host.

The mansion didn't shout its price tag—Diriem didn't seem to be the type to invest in, say, golden bathroom fixtures—but the décor hinted at old, understated wealth. Nothing I saw in the corridors through which he led us suggested he gave a damn about what was on trend. The furnishings I noticed were of dark wood with brass accents, a far cry from the particleboard flatpack tables I'd assembled back in Richmond. Though the stone and plaster walls continued throughout the ground floor, the construction felt almost airy, with tall, arched windows and high ceilings. And Rose's photos hadn't lied: interspersed among the ordinary windows were stained glass pieces, their details difficult to discern by night but nonetheless an evident touch of luxury.

We emerged into a grand foyer, complete with a wide wooden staircase at the rear that split in two before it reached the second floor, and then we turned down another hallway, passed a series of closed doors, and finally stepped into an office. The home's overall aesthetic continued within—antique cherry desk, heavy couch in supple navy leather, oriental rug—though the painting with pride of place behind the desk was a view of the James River that I recognized from Rose's Carytown gallery. Fleetingly, I wondered how many of her canvases had found their way into the mansion in the last four months since her acknowledgement.

Once we and our bags had crowded the room, Diriem waved toward the door, which shut behind us, then gestured to the couch and chairs in invitation as he leaned against his desk. "I'm sorry about the cloak-and-dagger summons," he began. "But I didn't know precisely who would be within earshot tonight, and certain information needs to remain out of the public consciousness for the time being."

"Want to elaborate?" Rose asked, folding her arms.

"Impatient, aren't you?" His brief smile dulled the retort. "Short version: the Hunt's on the move, so I'm relocating anyone I consider to be at risk tonight, especially you four and the ti'Mal bunch."

Maya's dark eyes widened. "They're coming for *us*? Why?"

He grimaced. "Unfortunately, I haven't seen every detail, including the Hunter's true motivation. I'm as blind to whatever goes on in his hideout as Rosie is," he admitted. "But I *do* know that Huntsmen will be visiting your apartment before dawn—and eventually yours, too," he added, turning to Yven. "None of you are safe in the capital right now."

"Is Wylan going to be okay?" I blurted.

Diriem's expression softened when he looked back at me. "I'm sorry, but I don't yet know how this plays out. There are…moving pieces. Possibilities, probabilities—"

"Is he *likely* going to be okay, then?"

"Annie, I understand your concern," he replied, holding my anxious stare, "but I *cannot* give you that information."

Late as it was, strung out as I was, I gave no thought to propriety. "Why the fuck not?" I demanded. "I've *seen* the Hunter, all right? The guy's huge, and he's some sort of unstoppable killing machine. If he'd wanted to chat with Wylan, do you really think there'd be blood all over the apartment? And now you're just going to leave me here to *guess* about Wylan's safety?"

From the corner of my eye, I saw Yven step back a pace, as if he feared a crater in the wake of my anger, but Diriem waited while I got it out of my system. "I'm not doing this to grieve you," he finally said while I fumed. "Rosie can share with you anything she sees because she perceives events as they're happening, but I can't because much of what I see is potentialities. We know from *long* experience that giving too much information, or giving the proper information in the wrong fashion, can prevent the best outcome. Now, I assume that you'd like to see Wylan alive and unharmed."

I nodded.

"Good. As would I. So believe me, child, I understand

that this is frustrating, but you need to trust me."

When I held my silence, he blew out a long breath and absently tucked his hair behind his ears. "In general, farseers try not to meddle to excess, but I wasn't about to stand back and let the four of you face the Hunt."

"But why us?" Maya asked again. "How would they even know who to look for? Annie was invisible at the lodge, and they couldn't smell her…right?"

"They'll smell me in the city," I muttered. "I've been to Wylan's apartment, and with all the times he's walked to the café…"

I saw the pieces fall before me like dominoes. If Wylan's brothers didn't notice my scent at his place, they'd surely smell me when they followed his trail to Mangia Due—and Maya's scent, too. That would lead them to our apartment…but where else had we gone of late? Who had crossed our paths? Dinners at Yven's place…my scouting trips around town during my search for Fellora…

"The substitute crew at the café," I said, almost jumping off my chair. "Director Erenani's niece and her friends. If the Hunt looks for us there, they'll pick up those trails—"

"I've already spoken with Kabno and Pateme," Diriem soothed. "Syvin is passing the word to that foursome. They'll be here before dawn."

"What about—"

"Fellora?" he finished. "Already here, as is the rest of the family and her fiancé."

"But shouldn't we spread out?" I protested. "If we're all concentrated—"

"You're here together because I can protect you in this house." He smirked as my brow furrowed. "I've engaged the security measures. At this moment, no one can enter except by the doors, and only Scel and I can give permission."

"Unless the Hunt decides to ignore your pesky doors and teleport," I countered.

"My security measures block that as well. What," he asked as my expression shifted, "did you think this was my first encounter with the Hunt? I *have* headed an intelligence agency for quite some time, you know." Glancing at Rose, he added, "Caradin designed the counter-teleportation feature, in fact. Your grandfather downplayed it, but he was brilliant. Anyway," he continued, addressing the rest of us, "I asked Scel to have rooms prepared, and you should try to sleep. These matters always seem clearer in the morning, do they not?"

Had I not been so preoccupied with the tiny matter of Wylan's safety, I'd have pitied Yven. Hall ti'Ansha was one of the old northern families, but as elven aristocrats went, they landed near the bottom of the ladder—respectable, but not a prize for most climbers. From the little I'd gathered, most of the Halls tended to intermarry with the families of relative social proximity, with only the odd child straying too far above or below. Within a matter of months, Yven had gone from surreptitiously seeing an unacknowledged woman of partial human extraction—a scandalous relationship forbidden by Pact law—to finding himself engaged to the heir to the most prominent of the Halls, which had to have left him feeling whiplashed. Adding Rose's great-grandfather to the mix—farseer, director of DOI, freaking former *king*—made Yven skittish and far quieter than usual, as if he feared calling down wrath upon his head if he so much as breathed improperly.

Rose, who stayed in the mansion when she was in the Pactlands, had no such hang-ups. If Diriem made her nervous, I never saw a hint of it. Then again, she was the great-granddaughter upon whom he doted, and while Rose had insisted to me that "Pop" had no problem with Yven, I had to imagine that her poor fiancé felt utterly intimidated.

Judging by the way Yven kept looking around as we climbed the staircase, I assumed it was his first time in the mansion, too. Once we reached the second floor and he awkwardly searched the landing for a hint, Rose steered us down a long corridor into the southern wing of the house—or so she later informed me, as I was in no condition that night to pay attention to residential geography. The corridor terminated in what my frazzled mind first interpreted as a cul-de-sac before I realized we'd stepped into a circular tower. Rose showed Maya and me to adjoining rooms, then pointed back down the hall from which we'd come and said, "Balcony doors are right there, and the balcony's covered. If anyone needs a smoke, Pop asks that you just take it outside."

Maya nodded. "I think I can wait until morning."

"Sure. Tell me what brand you like, and I'll put them on the shopping list." With that, Rose opened a third door, revealing another staircase, and gently nudged Yven upward. "You're staying with me," I heard her say as he started to climb.

"I really don't mind—"

"Pop's neither stupid nor a prude. We're bunking together."

Maya snorted once the stairway door closed behind them, then gave me a long hug. "I'm here if you need to talk, okay?" she said, rubbing one hand over my back. "And if DOL calls, you'd better come get me."

I promised I would, and she released me to investigate my guest room…which, I discovered once I flipped on a lamp, was more opulent than any hotel room I'd ever rented. The wide bed had been turned down, revealing cream-colored sheets and a mattress at least twice as thick as the one in my DPP-furnished apartment. It had even been moved away from the wall, making room for my antlers beyond the pillows. Facing the foot of the bed was a stone-framed fireplace—mostly unnecessary with the Pactlands' mild climate but still a nice touch. Someone had laid a fire, which had burned down to warm embers. A flat-screen television wide enough to make a frat boy proud hung above the slate mantel. The curving outer wall featured a trio of windows, plain glass below and stained above my head, and before them sat a round wooden table and a pair of plush chairs. A leather couch nicer than anything I owned had been pushed against the side wall as if it were nothing more than an afterthought. As I dropped my bags on the wooden floor near the bed, I looked at the table again and realized that what I'd originally taken for decoration in the dark was in fact a tray bearing two bottles of water, an ice bucket—still perfectly chilled despite the open fire in the room—a pair of weighty tumblers that had to be crystal, and several foil pouches of nuts and sweets.

Whatever else could be said for Diriem, he hadn't skimped on his guest accommodations.

As tempting as the single-source chocolates looked, it was closing on one in the morning, and my body begged for rest. I didn't bother digging out my pajamas, or even turning out the lights—off went my shoes, and with a groan, I collapsed onto the mattress that would spoil all other beds for me for the rest of my life. Physically, I was exhausted. I hadn't yet been forty-eight hours out of the DPP healers' custody, and despite the seeming gallons of potions I'd consumed since Friday, I was still very much on the mend from my fun-filled field trip to the Hunt's lodge. The new skin on my shoulders and back tugged like a too-small shirt being stretched, and while the worst of my scarring had begun to fade, I knew how to trace every line in the harsh bathroom light. I *needed* sleep.

But my brain wouldn't turn off. Between showing me its latest unpleasant ideas about Wylan's whereabouts and fate, it led me along the routes I'd taken through Beukal in the last days. How long would my scent trail be trackable for a Huntsman? Would they go after the nice couple who ran my favorite hole-in-the-wall restaurant, which I'd last visited to pick up breakfast that morning? The owner of the bookstore I frequented? Fellora's friends? Unsuspecting museum patrons? Rose's great-uncle, Pateme ti'Tam, who ran DPP? Syvin?

For the first time since I was carted off to the Pactlands, I was grateful that I hadn't been able to visit my parents in eleven months.

After an hour of staring at the ceiling, I surrendered and slipped out of my room. Truth be told, I could have used a map of the mansion before I went exploring, but I told myself that if I got lost, at least I'd be good and tired by the time I found my way back.

And so I wandered. I climbed up and down the spiral tower stairs, hoping I wouldn't wake Rose and Yven, then backtracked toward the middle of the house and the grand staircase. I peeked past open doors, finding libraries and parlors and shapeless furniture covered with dust sheets, and tried not to imagine Wylan bleeding in his apartment. I'd made it to the fourth floor when Maya's band of substitute café minions arrived shortly after three, and I heard Diriem admit them from the garage. They seemed subdued—whether due to anxiety or the hour, I couldn't say—and I stuck to the shadows as our host escorted them toward the tower where the rest of us had landed.

By seven that morning, I was no closer to sleep, but the light beyond the mansion's many windows had begun to brighten toward dawn, and I'd stumbled across the massive kitchen. While I didn't have a world-class nose, even I could smell the dark-roasted beans sitting between the espresso machine and the coffeemaker on the marble counter, and a quick search produced a grinder. Months of making lattes at Mangia Due had left me equipped to start a pot of coffee on autopilot, and I didn't stop to think twice about *whether* I should be helping myself to a stranger's stash.

The brew cycle was gurgling to a close when I heard Diriem's voice behind me: "Cups and mugs are in the cabinet to your left, by the sink. There should be sugar in the cannister in front of you."

I wheeled around, caught red-handed, but he flashed a weary smile and leaned one hip against a clean expanse of counter. "Please tell me you made enough for two."

"Yes, sir," I mumbled, and pulled out a clean pair of mugs. "Sorry, uh, I—"

"It's all right, Annie. And forgive me for saying so, but you look like hell, kid."

I grunted and poured. "Had better nights."

"I'm sure." He waited for me to finish with the sugar, then pointed to a line of chrome barstools parked beside yet another bit of the enormous counter. Honestly, the kitchen was one walk-in freezer away from restaurant quality. "Join me?"

There wasn't a good way to decline that invitation, and so I pulled up a stool and sipped.

I was halfway through my coffee before he spoke again. "If you'd like a sleeping potion, I keep some on hand. Insomnia only worsens with age."

"Would it turn me green and give me feathers?" I muttered into my mug.

He chuckled. "Probably not. I suspect you were kept sedated at DPP last week without ill effect."

Last week. Shit, he was right—it was Monday all over again, though I barely knew what planet I was on. I'd begun my investigation into Fellora's disappearance just last Monday…had it only been a week?

"I'm sorry," I said, "I'm—"

"A mess," he finished, not unkindly. "Someone you care about is missing, probably hurt. I'd have been shocked had you slept through the night."

I eyed him over my coffee, but his small smile raised as many questions as it answered. "What do you know about—"

"I know that your feelings for Wylan are veering in what most here would consider to be a dangerous direction, and the same is true for him. That's not common knowledge," he assured me, "and Rosie certainly hasn't mentioned it, but I would imagine that Syvin suspects, if no one else. That woman is *sharp*. I've tried to poach her, oh, half a dozen times, but she's loyal to her agency. Can't condemn her for that," he said, and drank his coffee.

My stomach clenched. "You haven't told her about…you know…"

"Of course not—I'm the last person who would expose something like that," he replied with a hint of reproach. "But I'm not blind, and neither is Syvin. Your body language the night you two left from DPP was difficult to overlook. Anyone with eyes and a little experience could tell you're far more than mere colleagues."

"Then you know I can't just sit here and hope he shows up again," I said, putting my mug aside. "I…I know there are rules about farsight, but can't you tell me what to do?"

He sighed. "Annie—"

I reached out and grabbed his free wrist, and he quickly slid his coffee to safety on the counter. "Lord ti'Dana, I am *begging* you. Help me."

He didn't so much as flinch. "I am," he said calmly, "and I will. What you need to understand right now is that I don't clearly see the best path forward. Sometimes, it's like a spotlight, but this isn't one of those situations. And as I've already mentioned, I can't give you everything I see unfiltered. That route almost always ends in disaster." He twisted his arm until he could grip my wrist in turn. "What I *can* tell you is that you need to step back and try to be critical about the situation. Assess it dispassionately. You're scared, you haven't slept, and the caffeine you just drank will do nothing to help. That's a dangerous recipe on its own, and if we add to it your feelings for Wylan…" He grimaced. "Love, more than anything else, will make you act rashly. You know that."

He wasn't wrong.

"I'd like to keep you alive, if it's all the same to you. Now, let's be realistic: if you were to go to the Hunter's lodge this minute, guns drawn, and demand to have Wylan back, you'd probably be ripped apart. You can't fight him on his own turf and win."

"No chance of that," I grumbled, releasing my hold on his arm. "We don't even know where the lodge is…" A sudden thought darted across my mind, and I stared at Diriem. "Unless *DOI* knows something. Can you get me there?"

Before he could answer me, an insistent chiming began around his pocket, and he rose from his stool to pull his phone free. With a soft grunt, he took the call. "Early for you, Kabno. What's happened?"

My heart leapt into my throat. That had to be Kabno Erenani, the director of DOL, and I struggled against the urge to rip the phone from Diriem's hands and demand an update about the investigation. Instead, I drummed my fingers on the countertop, waiting and hoping for crumbs.

Diriem said little, and his face betrayed nothing. After a brief conversation consisting mostly of monosyllables on his end, he said, "I assure you that Dili is safe. I saw her to bed four hours ago, and she has yet to emerge. Put that from your thoughts." He listened for another moment longer, then said, "Of course. Do keep me informed, yes?"

Once he hung up, he took his seat before I could jump off of mine and retrieved his cooling coffee. "Well, I'm glad you listened to me last night. Your apartment was broken into sometime before six."

"*What?*"

He nodded. "I asked Kabno to have the building checked. An agent reported finding your door open half an hour ago. The place seems to be intact, by his estimation, but all the closets were disturbed."

"Hiding places," I murmured.

"Precisely. And that's not all. Kabno says the security cameras outside the DPP tower caught motion inside the café around four. Since the lights were off inside, it's difficult to make out who was in there—not trolls, not gnomes, and probably not centaurs, but there are many possibilities within that range."

"They broke into the café?"

"Kabno says that per DPP, no entrances were forced. They appeared in the café, moved around for a few minutes, then vanished. No alarms were set off in the tower."

I groaned and rested my forehead on my fingertips. "Shit. They really are tracking me."

"Or Wylan," Diriem replied. "Still, as long as you're here, you're safe."

"Not to be rude, but are you sure about that?"

He smiled briefly, revealing a glimpse of sharp elven teeth. "Quite," he said, and sipped.

Hearing the creak of footsteps on the wooden floors, I turned to glance through the kitchen door and found the substitute Mangia Due team—who, by then, probably regretted ever taking the job—lurking in the hallway. Kabno's niece, Dili, had pulled her pink hair into twin buns above her ears and sported a crop top and lounge pants. Looming over the three-foot gnome was Frog, an eight-foot troll whose black mohawk had flopped over due to lack of gel. His baggy sleep shorts could have fit two of me, while his tight white T-shirt left little doubt about the advanced state of his abs. Noticing the red enamel caps atop his tusks, I vaguely wondered if he slept in those or popped them on by instinct. Lurking behind Frog were Makera, a violet-skinned water nymph who appeared to have thrown on white leggings beneath a silky nightgown, and Korek, a dark-haired faun. I had yet to see a faun in pants, and Korek didn't break the streak, though he'd had the presence of mind that morning to tie a green bandana over his curly hair. With his single gold hoop earring,

Korek looked primed for maritime plundering.

"Uh...good morning, Lord ti'Dana," said Dili, who appeared to be the foursome's spokeswoman. "Sorry to interrupt. Um...since you put us up last night, we were wondering if, uh..."

"We could make breakfast," Korek finished. "We did the culinary track in school."

"They're recent graduates," I added. "It should all still be fresh."

Diriem, stifling a yawn, lifted his mug in salute. "Generous of you, but don't trouble yourselves on my account. I'll be asleep by noon if everything goes according to plan. But I did give my cook the morning off, so if you're hungry, please don't be shy."

I watched them quickly take in his setup, which put Maya's to shame. "Seriously?" Dili squeaked.

"I mean, try not to start any unintentional fires, but otherwise, have fun..." His voice faded at the sound of the distant doorbell, and he glanced at his watch. "Ah, good. Right on time."

"Who's that?" I asked.

He finished his coffee and stood to unkink his back. "The last of my guests. I'll—" His phone beeped, and he glanced at the screen with a flicker of irritation. "I *told* Scel to sleep in. Honestly, that man acts like he's still a hundred years old."

CHAPTER 3

The beep, as it so happened, had been Scel informing Diriem that he would admit the visitor. When the house manager found us in the kitchen, he looked a little baggy-eyed but was impeccably dressed in a burgundy formal robe over a black shirt and dress trousers. "Good morning, sir," he said to Diriem, and gave the rest of us a quick nod. "Your guest, as expected."

I'd anticipated someone connected to the café or to Fellora, someone who might find himself at the wrong end of a scent trail. Instead, bafflingly, Diriem had invited a sports reporter to swing by the mansion at dawn. Oh, I knew *him* on sight—there were only a handful of trolls on the local news shows, and Moonless Night was a fixture. He'd been on the air since the first of the Pactlands' nascent television stations decided that they needed someone to talk about the previous day's sporting events, and he'd become something of an institution in the decades that followed. Moonless Night had an incredible recall for statistics, a carrot-colored strip of hair atop his gray scalp, and effortless charm in front of the camera. The young agents who caught his updates on the café TV reminisced about the occasional visits he'd make to the capital's schools to report on junior championships. Winning your game was great, but to be interviewed by *Moonless Night*, who treated student athletes with the same professionalism he showed the major stars…well, you never forgot *that*.

I had only a few seconds to take him in—perhaps a

hair under eight feet tall, built like a tank, unadorned tusks, sporting a brown sweater over jeans—before Frog started fanboying. He ran up to the newcomer, almost knocking Scel aside in his haste, and began an excited, rapid, and wholly unintelligible conversation in Trollish.

Of all the languages spoken in the Pactlands, I'd been given the most common tongue via potion, which wasn't a pleasant experience but beat the hell out of fumbling through immersion in Pactish. As far as I knew, most species maintained a language of their own—elves actually had two—but with enough education or potion-swigging, one could learn to speak almost anything but Trollish. For starters, the language was tonal, and some of those tones went so low that the average non-troll vocal cords couldn't replicate them. The syntax was just bizarre, my DPP customers informed me, and even the trolls among them concurred. Heck, there wasn't a single troll in the agency who went by his full name. Trolls bestowed upon their newborns long, complex monikers evocative of the natural world and unpronounceable to virtually every non-troll in the Pactlands. To outsiders, they generally offered a translated nickname. Frog, for instance, was The Sound of the First Frog to Herald the Spring—or rather, that was an approximation of how his true name was rendered in Pactish. He hadn't bothered telling me his real name, and I'd learned well enough not to ask.

Though I couldn't understand a word of Frog and Moonless Night's conversation, something about the reporter struck me as odd. Maybe it was the early hour, or maybe he was uncomfortable finding himself in Diriem's kitchen, but he seemed less like his self-assured TV persona. I noticed that he kept rubbing a large silver ring on the third finger of his left hand—a nervous habit, I guessed. But more troubling to me than the question of what was on Moonless Night's mind was the more basic question of what he was doing there. I'd never met the guy, I could almost swear than Wylan hadn't, and unless he was Fellora's super-secret lover—*really* unlikely—I couldn't fathom his connection to our band of surprise houseguests.

And while he was talking to Frog, he kept staring past the younger troll at me. Nothing unusual there. People who didn't know me assumed I was part of the Hunt and generally gawked as they tried to get out of my way. That there were no female Huntsmen in existence didn't matter—I knew that factoid only through Wylan, making me an expert in comparison to the average Pactlander on the street.

Once Frog came up for air, Diriem slid into the brief silence. "Good morning, Moonless Night. Thank you for coming so early. Might I have a word with you in private?"

"Of course, sir," he rumbled, cutting his eyes around the kitchen. "Uh, here?"

"My office. Scel, get some rest," he chided the sorcerer, then pointed to another door and told the troll, "This way, please. Annie, join us."

Leaving the culinary grads to play, Moonless Night and I followed Diriem through the corridors in silence. The stained glass windows had begun to glow, abstract geometric flourishes interspersed with scenes of mountains and meadows, but I was in no state for art appreciation.

Diriem closed and locked his office door behind us as I plopped onto the leather couch. "I doubt you two have been introduced," he said as Moonless Night gingerly took a seat beside me. "This is Annie Humphries, one of the Roulette victims," he told Moonless Night, nodding to me as he pulled a chair closer. "You know about the ti'Mal girl's abduction?"

Moonless Night grunted. "It's been in practically every show for the last week and a half. We're not *that* sheltered on the sports desk," he added, barely grinning around his tusks. "Why do you ask?"

"This doesn't leave the room, understood? Everyone in this house is aware, but I don't want to hear this mentioned on the evening news."

"Of course."

"Good. Last Thursday night, a Huntsman sneaked Annie here to the lodge. She carried Fellora out before the next day's festivities. The Hunter had trapped the girl in the form of a wolf and intended to use her as prey."

The couch creaked as Moonless Night leaned back against the padding and rubbed his chin. "I thought such was forbidden by the terms of the Pact."

"Oh, no, that hasn't changed. Anyway, the Huntsman—"

"Wylan," I interjected.

Diriem nodded. "*Wylan* was apparently abducted sometime before dawn yesterday. The preliminary assessment suggests he was taken by his brothers."

Again, I wondered why Diriem had brought in Moonless Night. Was he thinking of a manhunt? The trollish sense of smell was unsurpassed in the Pactlands—those who worked in DPP's research lab could identify potions in blood by scent alone. If we took Moonless Night up to the place in the wilderness where DOL had found Fellora and me and backtracked, maybe he could smell a way into the lodge…

"Annie," Diriem continued, gesturing toward the troll, "this is—"

"The Sound of Deer Running Through the Forest on a Moonless Night," he interrupted, offering me his hand. It swallowed mine like a catcher's mitt cradling a baseball when we shook.

"Nice to meet you," I offered. Though I had questions, tired as I was, I went with the default response.

But Diriem crossed his legs and propped his head on his fist, then murmured, "Don't you think it's time to drop the mask?"

Moonless Night stiffened, but Diriem held his stare.

"I know," our host told him. "I've known for a long time, and I will say nothing to your employer. But we want that boy back alive, and we need your help."

The troll began to fidget with his ring again, and my stomach clenched as I realized what it was.

Only two of the Pactlands' peoples could mask without assistance, elves and sorcerers. Everyone else who needed or wanted to alter their appearance resorted to masking jewelry. The agencies kept loaners around for those who needed to venture into the outside world but didn't want to incite a panic. These pieces being government issue, they were fairly basic in their function, so folks with cash to burn or more frequent business outside the Pactlands invested in custom jewelry. Syvin, for instance, wore a gold pendant that could make her look human with a touch and a few whispered words—a useful trick for when one needed to visit a DPP grower beyond the Pactlands but didn't want to make the drive with faun's legs.

I'd borrowed a masking necklace from Teolm ti'Cren just a week before so that I could investigate Fellora's disappearance in peace—an *expensive* necklace, as Teolm had tried to find one that wouldn't interact with the Roulette in my system. He knew his father's stock, and the necklace had worked beautifully, hiding my antlers without a trace…well, for about ninety minutes at a time. Anything longer gave me a miserable scalp rash. I'd left the necklace in the jewelry dish on my dresser back in the city, and I hoped the Hunt hadn't disturbed it. Teolm and I hadn't exactly settled on the duration of the loan, and I knew I couldn't afford to replace the necklace if it walked away.

Masking didn't have to be a major affair. For elves, it was easier than applying cosmetics and safer than plastic surgery. That Moonless Night, who appeared on camera at least five days a week, would want to touch up his appearance didn't strike me as odd…but that didn't explain his evident anxiety.

He glanced at me, then back at Diriem, and sighed. "I'd wondered if DOI suspected."

"Far more than suspect," said Diriem with a soft

chuckle, but he quickly turned serious again. "It should be obvious that we have no quarrel with you. If I could see a better option, I'd let you go about your business unbothered. But Wylan helped save a life when no one else could, and we owe it to him to try to help him now."

Moonless Night hesitated, as if hoping for a reprieve, then pressed his thumb against the ring and muttered under his breath.

When his mask fell away, I gasped in spite of myself.

The troll was *gone*. In his place, swallowed in his clothing, was a man who looked much closer to human on first blush: olive skin, a clean-shaven square jaw, dark hair falling halfway down his back. But when he glanced my way, I noticed the familiar hue of his amber eyes, and I saw the tip of one ear barely peeking out from his hair.

"Could I offer you some wardrobe assistance?" asked Diriem.

"Thanks," he replied, his voice still low but an octave higher than it had been seconds before. With a few quick gestures from Diriem, his clothing shrank until it seemed tailored to his body, and I got a better sense of his size: a little smaller than Wylan but broad in the shoulders, with a bulk suggesting a disciplined gym routine.

"You're a Huntsman," I whispered.

His mouth twisted into a wry smile. "What gave it away?"

"You and Wylan have the same eyes. But, um…"

He cocked his head. "Spit it out, girl."

I didn't want to be rude, but I lacked the mental capacity for finesse that morning. "What happened to your antlers?"

"Short answer, I annoyed my father. But I take it you want more than that."

I nodded. "And I take it you're not really named Moonless Night."

"It's a name I've worn for a long time. Who's to say it's not mine?" he countered. "But if it would satisfy DOI…"

Diriem gestured for him to continue.

"My father called me Morial," he said, and folded his arms. "What did you want to know?"

"Broadly speaking, everything," replied Diriem, "but let's begin with the basics. Where is—"

"Why didn't you ever reach out to Wylan?" I demanded. "He's been here for a couple months, he's living in a crappy little apartment, he couldn't get a job for weeks, and you never even offered to show him around?"

"No."

"He's your *brother*!"

"I've never met him," Morial protested. "Never met many of them, actually. Father cast me out centuries ago. I'd heard rumor of a Huntsman in the capital, certainly," he continued, "and I saw him from a distance back in July. He came to the station to ask about a janitorial position, and I was driving up when he arrived. Hid in my car until he left."

"Mighty big of you," I muttered.

Morial remained unabashed. "I take no chances with my cover. Now, what's your interest in…Wylan, was it?"

"He's my friend," I replied, which wasn't untrue.

The Huntsman cut his eyes to Diriem, but our host maintained his poker face. "You seem rather invested—"

"Wylan and Annie have been working together," Diriem smoothly interjected, seizing control of the interrogation again. A sharp glace in my direction warned me to cede the floor. "You said your father threw you out of the Hunt? Why?"

"As I told you, I annoyed him." Morial locked his hands behind his head and leaned deeper into the couch. "The Hunt was riding one night—an autumn night, as I recall, but unseasonably warm," he said, staring at the ceiling. "We came across a village. Humans. Their young men were gone, and the women and old men couldn't defend themselves. The ones who could scatter did so." He paused but continued to gaze at nothing, as if watching the memory replay. "One of the women ran with a child—a boy, I think, more than a babe but small enough to be carried. Father shot her in the back, and she fell. He dismounted to finish the job—the child," Morial clarified—"but when I saw the little thing crying while his mother gurgled her last, something in me...*snapped*, I suppose."

"What did you do?" asked Diriem.

"Stepped between Father and the child. I told him to stop. There was no sport in hunting a creature who couldn't run, no glory in a kill like that. He told me to move aside. I refused. So he shoved me out of the way, stabbed the boy in the heart, and dragged me back to my brothers. He told them I'd defied him, and to let this be a lesson to them. Forced me to my knees. I thought he was going to kill me, too."

"Why didn't he?"

"I don't know. Perhaps he'd had enough for the night. But he ordered two of the others to hold me still, and he broke off my antlers. Snapped them like dry twigs. Then they rode away without me. Took my horse, my weapons, everything but the clothes on my back."

At that, he sat up again, pushed aside his thick hair, and leaned toward me, revealing smooth nubs protruding from his scalp. "Not much left, see?"

"You keep cutting them off for work?" I asked. "Doesn't the ring mask them?"

"No. They never grew back. I ground down what was left, evening them out and taking off the jagged edges. Easier to go about like this than it would be if I couldn't cover them," he explained, absently patting his hair into place as he withdrew.

"Wylan never mentioned one of his brothers being tossed out of the Hunt," I told Morial. "He said a couple had died before his time, but—"

"Close enough. Two of us have been expelled—well, that I know of," he amended. "One of my younger brothers similarly annoyed Father a few years later, but he couldn't accept banishment. After a decade with me, he said he was going to confront the Hunt when they came riding and beg Father to take him back." Morial's mouth tightened into a thin line. "I found the fool's body three days later, and I would know the arrows that killed him anywhere."

As I mulled over the implications of *that* grim bit of Wylan's family history, Diriem enquired, "You've been masking all this time? I took a peek at the records and saw Moonless Night on the registry with one of the troll clans at the time of the Pact, but what did you do before then?"

"I got by," said Morial with a shrug. "Shortly after my idiot brother died, I came across a family of sorcerers. Women and children, not a hunter among them, and a bitter winter. They'd lost their men to some sort of pestilence—they couldn't name it, and I have no idea what it might have been. They offered me shelter, and I fed them. Drove off a few bandits as well. In the spring, the matriarch presented me with this," he said, lifting his hand to show us the masking ring. "To make matters simpler for me."

"A fair bit of silver for a starving family," Diriem remarked.

Morial grunted. "When the ground is frozen and the autumn's stores are a memory for every home within a week's walk, silver and gold are useless. Can't eat them." His lips barely curled. "You know something of true winter, yes?"

"Too well, but we managed to avoid the starving times. Farsight does have its advantages," he admitted. "But what became of your sorcerers?"

"The expected: they died. The older ones, at least. I remained with the family until the younglings were able to fend for themselves, then took my leave. Too many humans around, too many questions."

Diriem nodded.

"Eventually, I made camp near a troll clan," Morial continued. "Unintentionally—I hadn't realized how far their territory extended. But they made good neighbors, and we assisted each other on occasion. After a time, they invited me to their fire, and I began to learn their ways. Their tongue," he said, quietly laughing. "*That* was the work of years, and I could only speak it properly when I used the ring to change my voice. The low tones, you understand."

"I'm quite familiar with the problem," said Diriem.

"I'm sure. Anyway, I came to live among them. Began to mask as one of them, and their chief adopted me into the clan. And I'd have remained with them had they not been ambushed by a damn human mob. I fought until our defenses fell," he murmured with a slow shake of his head, "and then the chief told me to run. He wanted *someone* to escape. So I did as he ordered, and when I returned to look for survivors, there was nothing but ash and stinking flesh."

Morial's jaw clenched, and I tried not to imagine what he was seeing in his mind's eye.

"I settled in with another clan eventually. Called myself by the name my first clan gave me, and as far as I know, they never realized I was an imposter. Trolls have a superior sense of smell, but the ring helps," he said, wiggling his finger. "It's an exceptional piece of sorcery. But as I was saying, I lived as one of them, and I'd only been there for a few years when the Pact was forged. I entered under my assumed name, and that was that."

"But why hide out as a troll?" I asked.

"Why not?" he retorted. "Some of them were the best family I've ever had. More importantly, I can smell well enough to pass as a troll. Can't pretend to be a sorcerer if you can't cast spells, am I right?"

"And the short lifespan would be a pain," Diriem offered.

Morial nodded emphatically. "Starting over every three

centuries—no, thank you. I said I was only about fifty when I entered the Pactlands, so I've got a few hundred years to go as Moonless Night. Not sure what I'll do after that, but for now—"

"Can you get me to the lodge?" I blurted.

The two men stared at me, Morial with surprise, Diriem with consternation.

"Annie," Diriem began, "what did I say about acting rashly?"

"Don't worry," Morial told him, then flicked his gaze back at me. "No, I can't get you there. I have no idea where it is. Never been there, remember—I was banished long before this place existed."

I frowned. "Wylan told me your family can find the place—"

"What part of 'banished' was unclear? I have no map. Unless Intelligence knows something…" he hinted to Diriem.

For a brief second, hope flared within me. Diriem hadn't given me an answer before Morial arrived, so maybe—

"If we knew the way," Diriem replied, "we'd share it with Laws. They're considering how best to initiate proceedings against the Hunter, and being able to find him to serve papers would be a plus. Alas."

Morial's eyebrows rose. "What sort of proceedings?"

"Well, I'm no counselor, but I would think charges could be brought for the kidnapping of the ti'Mal daughter. Perhaps attempted murder. You would have to ask Director Erenani for the specifics."

"So how do we find the Hunter?" I demanded, leaning toward Morial. "Or contact him, anything?"

"You *don't*."

"That's not acceptable."

He laughed in disbelief, but when he saw that Diriem wasn't joining in, he sobered. "You're seriously asking me, girl?"

"I intend to find Wylan alive," I shot back, "and that means finding your father. How do I do it?"

"There are far easier ways to die," he muttered, then closed his eyes and rubbed his forehead. "If you want to confront him—which I *absolutely* do not recommend, considering his general invulnerability—your best bet would be to find him when the Hunt rides."

Which, unfortunately, had taken place just a few days before. "How often does it happen? Wylan got twitchy before it kicked off," I continued, recalling his odd behavior. "He felt it coming on, even from Beukal. Did you?"

Morial reluctantly nodded. "Yeah, I feel the call. Tells me when to lie low and where to avoid. If I showed my face when the Hunt was riding, they'd kill me."

"So you know where the Hunt goes, then?"

"Once they're riding," he admitted, "but are you not hearing me? If you want to live, stay away from the Hunt."

Diriem cleared his throat. "Regrettably, that may not be an option."

"Are you *mad*?" Morial goggled at the two of us as if we'd suggested a Sunday stroll through a lava flow. "Do you not understand what I'm telling you?"

"I understand you well enough," said Diriem, "and I don't like this, either. But what I can tell you is that while my farsight is imperfect and the way forward is still unclear, the impression I'm receiving is that Annie will likely need to locate the Hunt if we want to recover your brother. Perhaps she'll be able to ask the Hunter for information, or perhaps she could bargain for his return. I don't know the specifics yet—"

"What you're suggesting is incredibly dangerous. And what would you have me do, place her in the Hunt's way and retreat?"

"No," he replied, and Morial relaxed only a degree before Diriem added, "I'd like for you to train her to ride as a Huntsman would, weapons and all."

"Wait, *wait*," I said, jumping in, "that seems like overkill. Why can't Morial just drop me off and run away? Give me a good rifle, a .45, and ammo. It's only the Hunter who's unkillable, right?" I asked Morial.

But Diriem was firm. "If you intend to walk this path, then you need training. *This*, I'm sure of." Looking back at Morial, he asked, "When will the Hunt ride again?"

Morial, who appeared less comfortable with the plan by the second, chewed his lip as he thought. "Soon, I would think. If Father intended to hunt an elf and she was taken from him, he's probably still sulking. I'd expect the Hunt to ride again before midwinter."

"A do-over," I murmured. "You think he'll snatch someone else?"

He grimaced. "Hard to say. I wouldn't wander off alone."

"I realize that this request is an inconvenience to you," Diriem resumed, drawing Morial's attention again, "but can you train Annie? We have no better expert on the Hunt."

Morial's amber eyes narrowed. "What you're asking can't be accomplished around my work schedule."

"Which is why my agency will happily provide your employer with an excuse for your absence."

"And what, pray tell, does DOI need with a sports reporter?"

"Who at the station is going to ask too many questions if I sign the letter?" Diriem countered. "Stay here, work with Annie, help us try to save your brother. If it's a matter of compensation—"

"I don't need the money," said Morial, giving me a long look. "I just don't like being a party to the kid's suicide."

"Precisely why I'm asking you to train her." With that, Diriem rose and extended his hand to Morial. "Please."

Though Morial sighed, he shook on it. "One slight complication," he added as Diriem released him. "*Where* did you want this training to occur? In my experience, arrows and windows mix poorly."

"You'll have the run of the estate," he replied. "The grounds behind the house are protected against intruders...and should the worst happen, I can repair a damn window," he added with faint reproach. "Now, there's one other matter we should settle before you bring your luggage in—you did pack for a few days, did you not?"

Morial nodded. "I got the memo, yes..."

"Splendid. My question: can Moonless Night train Annie, or is this a task better suited to Morial?"

He glared at me, then at Diriem, but grunted, "Morial."

"As I suspected. So," said Diriem, "how would you like to break the news to your fan club in the kitchen?"

CHAPTER 4

By the time Diriem released us from his office, the kitchen had become a scene of controlled chaos. I stopped in the doorway to take it all in: the rich scent of espresso, the result of Korek's handiwork with the machine I'd purposefully avoided that morning; the sizzling of batter on the griddle that Dili superintended with the aid of a stepstool; the laughing camaraderie as Makera and Frog washed and cut up fruit at the sink, his dropping into a deep bowl for raw consumption, hers into a copper saucepan for what I presumed to be a compote in the works. If they were worried about the developments of the last twenty-four hours, they seemed to have lost themselves for the moment in the rhythms of the kitchen.

"I should host them overnight more often," said Diriem, coming up behind me. "And I may have rediscovered my appetite. Think they'll share?"

Dili glanced our way and grinned briefly before returning to the business of flipping pancakes. "More than enough here, sir, and since these were your groceries to begin with…"

"Smells like you're doing them far better justice than I could. Ooh, *yes*, thank you, young man," he added as Korek lifted an espresso cup in query. "Dili, your aunt said you were still seeking permanent employment."

"Hoping for a restaurant of my own one day," she replied, standing on tiptoe to turn the pancakes at the rear of the griddle, "but for now, we're all looking. Mangia Due is great, don't get me wrong," she hastily amended, meeting my eyes, "and I'd gladly stay on"—the others nodded vehemently as they worked—"but now that you're back, Annie, I think our fill-in time is over. If Maya has any suggestions—"

"Hold that thought," Korek interrupted, and pointed to me. "What are you drinking?"

I leaned against the door frame and sighed. "How about a doppio?"

"*Just* a doppio? You look like you haven't slept." His earring flashed in the morning sunlight as he cocked his head to study me. "Triplo?"

"Sure," I replied, and he turned to his work. Only about five feet tall, Korek had pulled the espresso machine close to the edge of the counter, and his hooves clicked on the slate floor as he moved. "Your Italian's pretty good."

He glanced over his shoulder and smiled. "It only extends to coffee, I assure you."

"As I was saying," Dili resumed, "Annie, if Maya knows anyone in need of kitchen help—"

"Let's be real: *Maya* is in need of kitchen help," I said. "I'm mediocre at best, and I'm not going to be around until Wylan's safe—and even then, I'm pretty sure she'd rather have the four of you over the two of us any day."

"That's kind of you to say," Makera interjected, pausing in her inspection of a pint of beautiful raspberries, "but I doubt DPP would be willing to employ us in the long term. We're making a dent in the café's budget, I'm sure."

The conversation paused briefly as Korek finished Diriem's drink, and Diriem closed his eyes and groaned in satisfaction as he sipped. "Tell you what," he said, "if Pateme tries to dismiss you, I'll have a word with him."

The foursome brightened. "Really?" asked Korek.

"There's a balance to be struck between fiscal responsibility and keeping your people happy," Diriem replied. "DPP has never been known for its employee comforts, the last few months notwithstanding. If something were to happen to the café, Pateme might actually have a riot on his hands."

Korek chuckled, then squinted into the shadows over my shoulder. "Is someone else out there? I'm taking orders."

A few seconds later, Morial slunk into the kitchen and folded his arms. "Hot and strong, if you would. I don't care what else goes into it."

The rest of the kitchen crew turned at his voice—though higher, it still bore Moonless Night's cadence—and frowned bemusedly. "Can do," said the faun. "Sorry, I'm Korek, and you're…"

"Complicated," he muttered.

Diriem drank his espresso for a moment, waiting for him to elaborate, then said, "This is Morial, Wylan's brother."

Dili's spatula slipped from her hands, and she swore as she hurried off her stool to retrieve it. The others simply turned to stare.

"Morial was banished from the Hunt some time ago," Diriem continued. "And for the last five hundred years or so, he's been Moonless Night."

I looked up in time to see Frog's jaw drop. "But…*but*…" the troll stammered, "but he…"

Muttering under his breath, Morial touched his ring, and his voice dropped into its more familiar register as he spoke to Frog in Trollish.

After a moment, with the two of them still deep in their incomprehensible conversation, I muttered, "Any chance of a translation?"

Dili offered an exaggerated shrug.

"If I may," said Diriem, and the others fell silent. "Morial will be working with Annie to prepare her to pursue the Hunt. In the meantime, no word of his other identity is to leave this house. Should you find yourself hard-pressed to maintain your silence, I'll have *zero* qualms about fixing your memory to remove the necessary information. Is that perfectly clear?"

They mumbled their agreement and quickly turned back to their stations.

Shortly thereafter, Korek passed Morial another perfect espresso, and he nodded his thanks. "Sorry for the shock," he said, then turned his vocal mask off again. "This wasn't my idea."

Frog risked another peek in his direction. "I still can't believe you speak so *well*."

"What, Trollish? It's not impossible to learn, just challenging," Morial replied. "And I've had considerable practice, kid. How old are you?"

"Uh...thirty-six in January."

He grunted. "I've got scarves older than that. But thirty-six...let me think...you were born shortly after Leaping Trout's third heavyweight title, weren't you? Around the time of her title bout against—"

Frog said something long and unintelligible, and smiled around his tusks. "My parents were there."

"*Were* they?" Morial's eyes lit. "I've never seen a fight like that one. When he tried to gore her—"

"And she almost broke his neck," Frog finished, warming to the subject. "I've watched that replay *so* many times."

"You wrestle?"

He made a face. "Not well. Much better with a blade," he added, jokingly raising his paring knife. "But what's Leaping Trout like in person?"

"All business until she's had a few drinks," said Morial between sips. "Then she's hilarious. That woman has a wit as a dry as a desert when she chooses to employ it. At the party after that bout, the beer started flowing, and—"

"Wait," Makera ordered, her sloppy blue ponytail flipping over her shoulder as she turned from her compote. "I'm sorry, but *what* was that about Annie pursuing the Hunt?"

Morial shrugged. "Ask Lord ti'Dana. This isn't my doing."

"Call it a hunch," our host offered.

Korek, having been momentarily distracted by Morial, finally put a triplo in my hand. "No offense, sir," he said, giving me a fresh once-over, "but that seems like a terrible idea."

"It wouldn't be my first choice, no," said Diriem, "but I see what I see."

"Annie, do you, uh…do you need help?" Makera asked.

I could hear the anxiety in her question, and I suspected it wasn't entirely due to concern for my safety. The nymph had about as much business going in search of the Hunter as I did.

"Thanks, but we'll be fine," I said, trying to inject unwarranted confidence into my voice. "Though I wouldn't say no to breakfast first, if that's on offer."

Maya heartily concurred with Korek's assessment of Diriem's plan, as did Rose and Yven when they stumbled to the table and were brought up to speed. But as no one could offer a better idea than listening to the farseer—and as Rose, the only other farseer on hand, could still see nothing but blackness when she sought Wylan—I ate up and drank as much coffee as I could stomach, hoping to trick my body into believing I'd rested.

It didn't work. Desperately in need of a bath, and with teeth that felt fuzzy, I retreated to my room to clean up and almost fell asleep on my feet beneath the warm, pounding spray of the shower jets. Once I'd toweled off, I considered the hairdryer beneath the sink—a nice touch for less magically gifted guests—then caught sight of the lovely bed I'd abandoned the night before.

I told myself a quick nap while my pancake breakfast digested wouldn't hurt anything.

Three hours later, Rose came knocking to check on me, waking me from a deep sleep. I untangled my damp hair from around my antlers, threw on my sweats, and followed her to the spacious den where the rest of our party were lounging.

Diriem, who'd taken an armchair in the corner, looked up from his computer as I slouched in with a knowing smile. "Feeling better?"

"Something like that. Sorry," I mumbled, spotting Morial sitting alone nearby with his own computer.

"No harm," Diriem replied, then straightened as the sound of the doorbell. "And I think I know what *that* is."

Scel beat him to front door, but when I joined them in the foyer, I found a pair of elves and a troll in DOL-marked black clothes lurking on the staircase. "Sure, you can bring it in here," Diriem told them as I drew closer. "I'll handle it from that point. Do you need assistance?"

They declined the offer, and a moment later, the trio lugged in several lumpy canvas bags, strapped and padlocked at the zippers. Bemusedly, they deposited their burdens in the ornate entryway—from the way the elves were staring at their surroundings, I doubted they'd ever made Diriem's guestlist—and the troll handed Diriem a tablet. "Sign here, please," he rumbled.

Diriem read the screen, then did as he asked. "Your director doesn't trust me, eh?" he joked.

The elves looked mortified, but the troll replied before they could start falling all over themselves. "Nothing personal, sir. We prefer to know the whereabouts of the contents of our armory, you understand." He paused, considering the bags, then gave Diriem a curious stare as he handed over the keys. "Not that it's any of my business, but if the armory chief were to ask why Intelligence needs these particular items…"

"Interagency training purposes," he replied with a smile that suggested no further answers would be forthcoming.

"Understood, sir. Have a nice day," said the troll, and ushered his colleagues out of the mansion.

Scel closed the door behind them, and I arched an

eyebrow. "Interagency?"

Diriem shrugged. "Well, technically, you work for Plants and Potions…"

"That's a stretch of a technicality if I've ever heard one."

"Then clearly," he said, patting me on the shoulder, "you haven't spent enough time in an executive wing. And you can stop skulking now, they're gone," he said to Morial, who'd hidden himself around a corner.

While Diriem crouched to unlock the bags, Morial considered the delivery and frowned. "Seems excessive."

"Kabno can be generous," he said, and opened the first of the bags, revealing a bundle of black gun cases. He pulled one out, a case large enough for a shotgun, and nodded. "Laws does pack their toys carefully. Before we unload, did you want to start with these or something else?"

"Bows," Morial replied without hesitation.

"Classic. I like it." Diriem quickly unlocked the remaining cases, then stood and pointed to the back of the house. "All yours. I'll set up targets for you on the lawn."

I'd hoped that Morial would begin with the compound bows DOL had sent over, a little different than the ones with which I'd hunted in the Appalachians but still familiar. Instead, as I'd feared, he pulled a simple bow from the bag—Wylan's weapon of choice—added a couple of quivers, and led me outside to my fate.

Diriem's targets were of the concentric circle design, placed at various intervals around the grassy expanse. Unburdening himself, Morial pointed to the closest and said, "All right. Whenever you're ready."

I tried, I really did, but the bow was too big for me, my aim wasn't Olympic-worthy to begin with, and only about half my shots hit the target. Morial accepted my successes and failures with equal stoicism. "Again," he said once my arrow had struck the paper or landed somewhere in the grass, pausing only once I'd exhausted my ammo and needed to collect the leavings. *Again*, *again*, *again*, an infernal drumbeat that left my arms shaking and my fingers cramped.

After permitting me a few minutes for a sorely needed water break, Morial unpacked and loaded one of the pistols. "Try something smaller," he said, and gestured toward the arrow-torn targets.

My performance that time was far better. I knew guns decently well, having spent my share of quality father-daughter bonding time at the range, and I could consistently hit the closer of the targets, if not always the bullseye. Still, Morial made me shoot for hours, switching me to larger pistols, then to rifles.

As twilight descended, Scel emerged from the house with a folding table and a pair of covered plates floating before him. "Dinner," he said, then set up the table with a few whispered directions. When I regarded him questioningly, he explained, "Lord ti'Dana assumed you wouldn't be joining the others this evening."

"That's correct," said Morial before I could answer him, and Scel nodded before returning to the house.

We ate on a pair of stools that had unfolded from the table, neither of us saying much at first. Just forcing my hands to close around my utensils made me ache, and I was about to get up and go in search of a painkilling potion when Morial said, "You're not terrible."

"Thanks," I mumbled.

"Not nearly good enough, but not terrible. You've been trained?"

"My dad and I go hunting. Or we did before Roulette," I amended. "I've been stuck here for the last year."

His brows knit. "You're a prisoner?"

I tried to be political in my response. "Not in so many words. Maya and I have been treated really well, but let's just say that no one's giving us portal credentials back to

Virginia any time soon."

"Why not? Surely you could mask—"

"For short periods. I get a bad cross-reaction when I use masking jewelry, and God only knows what it would do to Maya. So no, we're stuck here until DPP figures out how to fix us." I stabbed at my dinner—fish of some sort, herbed and flaky—and smiled to myself. "Well, I *have* been out once this year. Wylan took me hunting back in September, and—"

"He *what*?"

Morial made no effort to disguise his shock, but I shrugged and kept eating. "Yeah. He surprised me one morning. Took me to Montana, I think. He knew the area, but he didn't know what it was called."

"He took you hunting," said Morial, sounding as if he couldn't believe the words coming from his lips. "A Huntsman took *you* hunting."

"Sheesh, am I that bad?"

"If he's anything like the brothers I know, then you aren't nearly in his league. Why would he waste his time with someone who couldn't keep up?"

"Because I was homesick," I murmured. "Missing the start of the season with my dad. Wylan loaned me a bow, helped me quite a bit. And he was nice enough not to insult my shooting," I added.

But Morial's confusion only deepened. "That's such a risk, going out there without the rest of the Hunt…"

I let that hang for a moment, unsure of how much I wanted to confess, then looked up at him in the fading light and said, "I've got feelings for Wylan, all right? And I'm pretty sure it's mutual."

He straightened on his stool, his mouth moving in a silent *Oh*. "Well, um…I suppose you're reasonably attractive, all things considered, but I still don't see why he'd do that."

"He obviously enjoys hunting," I pointed out. "I do, too. It was something to do together, and he wanted to make me feel better." I smirked at Morial's continued consternation. "You're not much of a romantic, are you?"

"Not at all." He popped a bite of fish in his mouth and chewed slowly, studying me while I ate. "Some of my brothers enjoy copulation," he said after an awkward moment. "Not always with their chosen partner's consent."

"We call that 'rape' where I'm from."

Morial grunted. "I'm not condoning, just stating a fact. What I was about to say is that it's never done much for me."

"Never met the right person?" I asked.

"Frankly, I'm not sure there *is* one. I've been one of Beukal's more notorious bachelors for much of the last century—among trolls, at least," he said with a little smile. "Don't see that changing."

By the time we finished eating, the stars were twinkling overhead, and I grabbed my dishes to head into the house.

"Where are you going?" Morial called after me.

I turned and peered at him in the gloom. "Inside. Unless Lord ti'Dana has floodlights out here, it's too dark to shoot."

"What do you mean?"

Right. "Human, remember? All that potion did was give me antlers. My senses aren't any better than they were a year ago."

"Oh." He sounded surprised. "I thought perhaps…never mind," he said brusquely. "But you truly can't see?"

"I mean, I can see basic shapes—my eyes have adjusted somewhat," I said. "And the light from the house helps. But, say, the targets?" I continued, gesturing toward the vague lumps in the darkness. "I can barely pick them out, let alone aim."

"You do realize that the Hunt often rides by night, yes?"

"That…had occurred to me," I admitted.

"Good. So we'll keep practicing, then. Bows again, I think."

When Morial finally called a halt that night, the waning gibbous moon was climbing over the horizon, and my arms felt like gelatin. Leaving me to carry the weapons and ammo, he picked up the table and stools—neither of us could figure out how to collapse the set—and started for the back of the mansion.

At least Diriem had moved the weapons bags close to the rear door. As Morial brought the dishes into the kitchen, I knelt to pack everything away—unless forced, I wasn't about to clean the guns that night. When I finished and dragged myself toward the kitchen to hydrate, I found him pulling a crystal lowball glass from one of the cabinets. A half-full bottle of Pactish-labeled whiskey waited on the counter, golden brown in the glow of the light above the sink.

"Helping yourself?" I asked.

"He won't mind." Morial poured himself a generous double while I filled a glass at the tap, then closed his eyes against the burn as he sipped.

"After that many years passing as a troll," I said, "I'd think you could handle a little liquor."

He snorted. "Moonless Night does not partake. *Ever.* The mask doesn't equip my body to handle troll-strength spirits, and I don't need prying questions or accidents."

"Sounds like someone speaks from experience," I replied once I'd drained my glass.

"Learned that lesson an age ago, before the Pact. If a troll tells you it tingles, avoid it like death." With that, he took his glass and headed for the hallway. "I smell a fire laid in the sitting room," he said, then glanced back at me before I could follow. "You should bathe and sleep. We'll resume at dawn."

"Do you, uh…want company?" I asked.

"That won't be necessary."

Honestly, I wasn't upset at the dismissal. I climbed the stairs and retraced my steps to my tower room, then stood beneath the shower until my aching shoulders began to unknot. Drugs. I wanted painkillers *so* badly, or at least a decent potion. I doubted Maya would have anything on her, but maybe she'd know exactly where Rose's room was, and maybe Rose could raid Diriem's stash for me. Or ask Scel to do it…she could make that sort of request, couldn't she? Sure, he was Diriem's employee, but wouldn't he do a favor for a member of the family? Unless it was super late. I hadn't bothered to look at the clock…

By the time I emerged from the shower, pink and smelling of bergamot, I was too weary to work out the steps necessary to acquire a potion. Being horizontal seemed like a decent alternative, however, and so I threw on pajamas and collapsed, grateful for the silky sheets in which I cocooned.

It didn't last long. Anxiety nagged me awake—concern for Wylan, guilt about the others camping here with us, the sudden realization that I'd forgotten to set my alarm—and once I accomplished that, it was only midnight, and I was wide awake and hurting. Deciding not to go hunting for Diriem's medicine cabinet, I opted to limp to the kitchen in search of the whiskey Morial had left on the counter. If nothing else, at least a few shots would help me sleep.

But when I wandered in, I found the bottle open and waiting, and I wasn't alone.

The blonde sitting on a stool at the counter raised her head at the sound of my footsteps. While the lone light over the sink kept the room dim, I could make out the general features of her face: a porcelain complexion, high elven cheekbones, a natural pout, dark eyes beneath well-groomed brows. But her eyes appeared sunken and shadowed, as though she hadn't slept in days, and her hair, always so perfectly coiffed in the photos the television stations used, hung against her scalp in oily tangles so flat that they did nothing to hide her pointed ears. Her forest green terry bathrobe had seen better days, possibly decades. While she only looked about twenty-five to me, I knew she was sixty years old.

She might not have been stuck as a wolf any longer, but Fellora ti'Mal had surely passed more restful nights.

She stiffened at the sight of me, then pushed her glass away as if she could hide it on the spotless counter. "Uh…hi," she mumbled, reddening.

"Hi," I echoed. "Is that whiskey reserved, or do you mind sharing?"

"It's not mine. I just, um…"

"Morial found it earlier tonight. If Lord ti'Dana didn't want us drinking his booze, he should have seen this coming and locked it up."

Despite her embarrassment, she chuckled while I procured a clean tumbler. "Can't sleep either, eh?"

"Not really. My friend was kidnapped, the fucking Hunt is after me, and everything hurts like hell, so…" I poured and raised my glass. "Cheers. Also, it's nice to meet you properly."

"I am *so* sorry for what you went through last week," Fellora mumbled.

"Don't be. We're both alive, right?"

"Only thanks to you." She retrieved her glass and gave it a little swirl before sipping. "I swear, if my mother knew I was sitting up like this, stealing Lord ti'Dana's alcohol…"

"I won't say a word about it if you don't," I offered. "And I'm guessing that's for medicinal purposes, right?" I added, cocking my glass toward hers.

She sighed. "Since my parents cut me off the sleeping potions, this is the only way I can relax enough to doze. I'm sorry, I'd intended to have pulled myself together before meeting you again so that I could thank you—"

"*Fellora*," I interrupted, and waited until she met my stare. "I'm no expert, but you're probably a *little* traumatized right now. Just a tad."

She flashed a weary smile. "Perhaps a touch."

"Nightmares?"

"That's part of it," she replied, and drained her glass.

As she poured herself another round, I asked, "Why'd they stop the sleeping potions? I didn't think those were overly addictive…"

"They're not," she said bitterly. "And the healers sent me home with enough for two weeks. But if you listen to my dear mother long enough, you'd think I was embarrassing the Hall for being so weak."

I thought of my own parents, who'd tended to me after my wisdom teeth extraction and carefully monitored my meds. The oral surgeon had given me a prescription for oxy, and while my parents had treated the pill bottle like it might explode, they'd made sure I was comfortable and on the mend before weaning me off the good stuff.

"That's some bullshit right there," I declared, and stuck out my hand as I pulled up the stool beside her. "Since we're drinking together, I'm Annie."

She met my handshake with a surprisingly firm grip. "Fell."

"Not Fellora?"

"You know," she replied with a smirk, "I can't say how far you hauled my furry ass, but I think we're *definitely* past the 'Fellora' stage."

We clinked our glasses and nursed our bedtime tonic.

After a moment, she said, "You look much better than you did that night. Your skin, I mean."

"DPP brought in a dermatologist and, like, *all* the potions. Nothing ever works quite as it's supposed to with me," I explained. "Roulette screws everything up."

She winced. "Is that what caused your skin to—"

"Yeah. The potion that removed my scent left me with the rash, and once the invisibility ring kicked in, everything started to burn and blister."

"*Everything?*"

I nodded. "Just about."

"Your shoulders?"

"That, too," I replied, deciding not to show her the scarring where the weight of her body had rubbed my back raw. Her guilty expression spoke volumes. "But hey, I'm on the mend. What about you? I noticed blood on you when—"

"Just cuts and bruises. A few healing potions took care of the physical effects."

"And a few good meals, I'm sure."

"Haven't had much of an appetite lately, to be frank." She finished her drink and pushed the glass away. "My parents said you were some sort of detective. You're with DOL?"

"No, just a volunteer. I'm a private investigator—or I was before Roulette. A fairly *new* private investigator," I admitted, "but most of my career to this point has been finding missing people. When you disappeared and Rose couldn't find you, I offered to pitch in."

Fell's brow furrowed. "Rose…"

"Thorn," I finished, then quickly corrected myself. "Ti'Dana, sorry. She's a farseer, yeah?"

"I'd heard as much, but I didn't know she'd been involved. My parents never mentioned that."

"I think her work was off the books, too. Intelligence doesn't seem to make a public fuss about anything, and Laws was trying to keep the investigation about you quiet."

"Yes," she muttered, "I heard."

There was, I deduced, a lot to unpack in those few syllables, and neither of us had the mental bandwidth to accomplish it that night.

As Fellora reached for the whiskey again—I sure as hell wasn't going to tell her to slow down—she said, "I don't remember much from the transport. They sedated me pretty quickly. But I do remember the healers panicking once they did a system scan on you. Something about your kidneys?"

"They're better now. Another cross-reaction," I said,

and drained my glass. "Pass that when you're finished, please."

She poured for me instead. "I'm sure it's not coming through as clearly as I'd like, but I'm *very* gratefully, Annie. I don't know how I can ever repay you—"

"Don't worry about it," I interrupted, patting her hand. "I'm just glad we got you out of there in one piece."

"As am I, though that doesn't stop the nightmares. This, however…" She closed her eyes and drank deeply, then sighed. "I find that I don't dream as vividly when I pass out. A little trick I learned back in school," she added with a slight grin.

"Yeah, well, *I* learned never to drink anything that's mostly grain alcohol."

"*Oof.*"

"Only made that mistake once. God, the hangover…"

We drank our refills in silence for a moment, and then Fell said, "The Huntsman who's missing, um…"

"Wylan."

"Yes, him. Is he the one who helped you find me?"

I nodded. "He figured out where you were and got me up there. Couldn't have done it without him." I paused, considering her face. "Did no one tell you that?"

"I've heard bits and pieces over the last days," she replied. "No one's sat me down with a firm timeline, and frankly, I think my parents would prefer to say as little as possible about this mess. Keef, uh, my little sister—"

"We've met."

"See, news to me. Anyway, she said my mother wouldn't leave DOL until everyone who'd glimpsed me before I was *fixed*"—she rolled her eyes—"had been sworn to silence. Can't have word getting out that a ti'Mal's running around like an animal, now can we?"

"But your fiancé's not upset, right?" I asked. I'd only met Camun ti'Grell once, but the accountant had seemed like a decent sort of guy—maybe a little nerdy, but definitely in love.

Fell's smile showed no warmth. "He doesn't know everything. He knows I was kidnapped and that you sneaked me away from the Hunter, but the details have been left nice and vague. We mustn't risk having the wedding ruined," she muttered.

"I thought it was postponed."

"Oh, yes, but Mother wants to reschedule it for the spring. She's concerned that Camun might bolt if he knew everything, and he's been awfully quiet in the last few days. Distant." She sipped, then put the glass on the counter with a sigh. "I'm sorry, I shouldn't complain—"

"Uh…you're allowed," I said incredulously. "Believe me, I understand having your life upended over something out of your control. Complain away."

"You're kind. I just…I can't put a label on how I'm feeling right now—besides a little looser, I mean," she added, cocking her head toward the whiskey—"and I don't know how I'm *supposed* to be feeling."

I reached my free hand toward her, and she clasped it. "Look, I'm no therapist, but I really don't think there's a right answer to that. If you're honest with Camun and he's half the man he seems to be, then he'll wait for you to get your head on straight. You don't want to rush into marriage when you're not even feeling like yourself, and I bet he'd understand."

"You've never had to consider Hall politics, have you?" she replied, then gave my hand a squeeze and released me. "But enough about my problems. This Wylan—why did he help me, and why was he taken? All Lord ti'Dana said was that we weren't safe, and it has to do with the Hunter."

I picked up my glass again and stared into the amber liquid. "Wylan's the youngest of his family. He wanted to see the world beyond the lodge, so he came to Beukal last summer and started hanging around the café. Got *super* confused when he saw me," I added, smiling to myself. "No one would hire him, so Maya—she's the one with the wings," I explained, catching Fell's blank look.

"This is my first time out of our apartment since we arrived," she said apologetically. "Mother insisted that the four of us and Camun stay together, and a servant has been delivering our meals."

"Scel? Sorcerer, gray-haired…"

"I haven't caught his name. So forgive me, but I don't know who else is here."

Introductions seemed like a task for the morning. "Well, uh…Maya's the other Roulette victim in town. We share an apartment, and it was her idea to open Mangia Due—she was a restauranteur back home. But anyway, she convinced Director ti'Tam to let Wylan work with us, and when I offered to help find you, he insisted on coming along. His dad's apparently less than thrilled by his actions of late."

"Sounds like a decent friend," Fell offered.

"Yeah, he's…" I paused, gnawing my lip, then met her curious stare. "Can you keep a secret?"

"Sure."

"I…*really* like him," I admitted, emboldened by the hour and the booze. "We've only known each other a few months, but we've seen so much of each other already, and I…I'm *happy* around him, you know? I've dated my share of guys, right, and there have been some good ones and some terrible mistakes, but I've never been with someone who makes me feel like Wylan does. And," I concluded, lifting my glass, "that's a *major* problem."

"He doesn't feel the same way about you?" she guessed.

"No, I think he does. But this is just a potion side effect, remember," I said, pointing to my antlers. "Take away the Roulette, and I'm a pretty average human."

She frowned briefly in thought, and then, even with the whiskey in her system, the tumblers fell. "It's illegal," she muttered.

"Exactly."

"Well, *shit*."

I laughed in spite of myself. "Slight problem, that. I've tried to tell myself he's too old for me, but it hasn't worked yet."

Fell returned to her drink. "What's the spread? I've heard some strange ones. Camun and I are only about two and a half years apart, which is pretty rare for us, but I've known elf couples with centuries between them. My parents have sixty-three years' difference," she offered.

I sipped, then made a face. "We'd be close to that. Wylan's eighty-nine, and I'll be thirty next month, so—"

"*Thirty*?" she echoed, aghast, and slammed her drink onto the marble beside us. "You're only thirty?"

"Almost thirty. We age a hell of a lot faster than you do—"

"Stop." She held up one hand and kept it raised while she finished her drink. "Let me…let me make *sure* I have this straight, all right?"

"Okay…"

"I'm kidnapped in broad daylight to be run down and murdered," said Fell, counting off on her fingers. "My parents pressure DOL into not launching a major search for fear that I've broken my engagement. And instead of conducting a reasonable investigation, DOL and my idiot parents sit back and let a *child* almost kill herself?"

"I'm not a child," I protested, bristling slightly at the last. "Age of full majority is twenty-one in my part of the world. I actually had an apartment and my own business before all this, you know?"

"Fine, but you're still of school age by Pact standards. Closer to my baby sister…"

The look of horror that crossed her face wasn't just the booze talking.

"And you don't have any actual talent, right?" Fell pressed. "I mean, you're human—you can't do anything with magic, can you?"

"Not a blessed thing…oh, no, don't cry," I hastily added as her eyes began to well.

She sniffed and swiped at them. "Sorry, I..." she managed, and shook her head. "Sorry. I don't know what's worse, that I mean so little to my family or that they would happily endanger someone so *helpless*."

The part of me that got its dander up when strange older men called me "little lady" wanted to object that I was a capable, independent woman, but I let it go. "People make dumb decisions when they're desperate," I told Fell. "And I don't know everything your parents said to DOL, but I did interview them and Keef last week. They were worried sick about you."

"About me, or about the situation?" she countered.

I didn't have a good answer for that. Instead, I slid the whiskey bottle away and gingerly pushed myself off my stool, wincing at my deep aches. "Want to try to sleep? I've got training in the morning, so..."

"What training?"

"Lord ti'Dana says that if I'm going to try to find Wylan, I need weapons training first. Apparently, my shooting isn't quite up to snuff."

Her dark eyes widened. "You...you're not going back to the *lodge*, are you?"

"Can't find it," I replied. "Wylan's probably there, and he may be hurt, but I can't get to him, so it looks like I've got sunrise target practice until a better idea presents itself."

Fell didn't complain when I carried our glasses to the dishwasher, but when I turned around, I found her standing behind me. "I'll go to the Forum on your behalf," she murmured. "If you find him and you want to stay here. Least I can do."

My mouth quirked. "Pretty sure Lady ti'Mal would have thoughts about that."

"Yeah, well, I've had some *thoughts*, too, of late. Good night, Annie."

I watched her head toward the staircase, swaying ever so slightly, then made my own way back to bed.

CHAPTER 5

Despite my nightcap, shortly before my alarm Tuesday morning, I gasped myself awake from a nightmare in which Wylan was plummeting off a cliff, having slipped through my sweaty fingers. I staggered into the bathroom with a groan to make myself presentable. As usual, I checked to see if my antlers had spontaneously disappeared overnight, and when, as usual, I found them still perched atop my head, I unsnarled the worst of my tangles, then pulled my hair back in preparation for the work to come.

Never had my weary body been more grateful for the shortening daylight hours than it was that morning. The sun wouldn't rise until a little after seven, giving me a chance to rummage for sustenance before training commenced. Fortunately, Yven had risen before me, and he'd put an oversized pan of cinnamon rolls in the oven by the time I wandered into the kitchen. "Here," he said, handing me a mug of perfectly serviceable drip coffee, then mopped a splash off the counter with the corner of his brown flour-dusted apron.

He hadn't slept well, he explained, and neither had Rose, who'd awakened intermittently throughout the night and tried to locate Wylan. Her farsight remained stymied, however, and Yven, unable to doze off again around four, had decided to bake instead of stare at the ceiling.

"How many people in this house turn to cooking as a form of stress relief?" I mumbled into my coffee. "I feel like I'm slacking."

"Hardly. I watched you and Morial yesterday—how are you doing after that?" he asked.

"Honestly? Everything from the waist up hurts."

Yven's mouth tightened. "I was afraid of that," he said, and headed out of the room.

"Where are you going?" I called after him.

"Back soon."

A few minutes later, he returned with a black tacklebox in hand, which he plunked onto the marble counter and flipped open. Craning my neck, I saw small vials and packets cluttering the top tray—potion ingredients, I gathered. He lifted the tray free, then pulled out a vial of pale green liquid. "Here," he said, handing it to me. "Painkiller. Swig that and give it a few minutes to kick in."

I took the potion from him but eyed the tacklebox. "Did you make this?"

"Nah. Standard field kit," he explained as he reassembled it. "I'll get another the next time I'm in the office. Really, it's fine," he insisted, seeing me hesitate. "Drink up, Annie."

Too sore and groggy to pry more deeply, I braced myself for a nasty shock and sipped. The potion tasted of honey and vanilla, however, making it far easier than I'd anticipated to finish the dose. By the time Yven's cinnamon rolls emerged and he began to ice them, the sharpest edges of my pain had begun to dull, and even the coffee seemed to be kicking in.

As I waited for the amateur chef to finish fussing over his work, the chiming of the doorbell echoed through the ground floor. "Who the heck is that?" I asked, glancing at the kitchen clock—barely six a.m.

Yven shrugged and began washing up while the rolls cooled. "I didn't hear that anyone else was expected…maybe another ti'Mal?"

"The immediate family is just the parents and two daughters—who are all hiding in their room, incidentally. I bumped into Fellora last night."

He smirked at me over his shoulder. "Perhaps the company's not up to standards."

"I don't think you're wrong," I said, but quieted at the sound of approaching footsteps. Two people, I gathered, one shod, the other hooved. The click of a faun's feet was unmistakable. Assuming that Korek and one of his friends had come downstairs to wrest back control of the kitchen from Yven, I was surprised to instead see Diriem escort Syvin into the room.

Unlike our host, whose morning ensemble was business casual at best, the chief deputy had dressed for work in an elegant purple formal robe over a thin lilac sweater, and her golden eyes narrowed as she spotted Yven at the sink. "Ti'Ansha?"

He jerked at her voice and turned, straightening. "Ma'am?"

Syvin gave his pajamas and borrowed apron a once-over, then grunted. "Is that coffee fresh?"

"She takes it black," I offered, and Yven quickly handed her a mug.

"I thought you'd be working remotely, ti'Ansha," she hinted.

His eyes slid to the clock and back. "Yes, ma'am, but I'm not on schedule yet…"

"And it looks like Yven's made breakfast, so let's not beat him too severely, eh?" Diriem suggested, and gestured to the open stool beside me. "Will this do, or would you rather go elsewhere?"

"This works," she replied, hoisting herself up with far more grace than I'd expected, then turned to me as Diriem pulled out a third seat at the counter. "I came by to check in. How're you feeling, Annie?"

"Fine," I lied. "How's everything at DPP? I heard there were Huntsmen in the café…"

"Briefly," she muttered, "but yes, we've got them on surveillance. Tell Maya the café is intact. The agency is collectively going through caffeine withdrawal right now, but we'll survive, and Pateme is glad you're safe."

"Anything new from DOL?" I asked hopefully. "Have you heard from Detective Venanu?"

She shook her head. "Not yet, and he doesn't report to me. If we've had no update by tomorrow, I'll ask Pateme to speak to Kabno, but as of right now…"

"You think he's holding back?"

"Doubtful. If they had a strong lead, I'm sure I would have heard of it." She cut her eyes to Diriem and asked, "Can DOI give us a nudge? Happy to pass it along."

"Regretfully, no," he replied. "And I expect Rosie would say the same…"

Hearing the hint, Yven nodded as he dried a mixing bowl. "No luck overnight, sir."

Syvin sighed. "I was afraid of that. Well, I'll inform Pateme. Any chance of getting this to go?" she asked, lifting her mug. "I should head back to the city before the inbound traffic snarls."

Diriem kept disposable cups on hand, and soon, Syvin was on her way. I saw her to the door, and when he latched it behind her, I quietly asked, "Does DPP know about Morial?"

"They do not."

"Why didn't you tell her?"

He started back toward the kitchen and beckoned for me to join him. "Because as much as it pains me to admit this, we don't know what the Hunter knows or how he knows it. Obviously, he has an unusual connection to his sons, and there's no one in the Pactlands who can teleport the way the Hunt does—not without significant preparation and a salve made of certain plants that are *particularly* difficult to grow. That's an expenditure made only in case of emergency."

"Have you done it?"

"Once, and that was more than enough. I couldn't keep a damn thing in my stomach for three days following that trip." He glanced at me and barely smiled. "Slightly easier when you go with Wylan, I trust."

"Yeah."

As we passed the staircase, a brown-haired young man in a blue work shirt and khakis came running down, almost tripping over his shoes in his haste. "There's no fire," Diriem told him. "Don't fall, now."

"I'm sorry, sir," he panted, smoothing his cowlick as he slowed. "Forgot to reset my alarm, I'll have breakfast up in a few—"

"It's been handled," he said gently. "And you may find yourself pushed out of the kitchen until some of our guests leave. Don't take it personally, Ranarma."

The reassurance didn't set him at ease. "Really, sir, it won't happen again."

"Hear me: I'm not upset," Diriem insisted. "Catch your breath. Perhaps you could refresh the coffee—that would be nice."

Ranarma nodded and scurried off, and once he'd rounded a corner, Diriem whispered, "Scel's little nephew. I hired him as my cook about a year ago. He's quite good, but I'm not sure how he's going to cope with so much competition in the kitchen." He paused, frowning in thought, then grunted to himself and started onward again. "But you were asking why I haven't told DPP of Morial. As we don't know the full extent of the Hunter's abilities or whether he has any sources within the agencies, the only way to protect Morial right now is to keep knowledge of him out of the official channels."

"You really think the *Hunter* has a mole at DPP?" I asked.

"It's unlikely at best," Diriem allowed, "but I prefer not to gamble with lives when possible. And I'll tell you this," he added, lowering his voice. "We need Morial."

I hesitated. "Is that farsight talking?"

He nodded. "That, and common sense. He's the only person available to us who will know when the Hunt rides again."

When we reached the kitchen, Yven's lonely vigil had turned into a team effort, complete with huge skillets of bacon and eggs sizzling on the stove and Ranarma sharing counter space with Korek and the espresso machine. My mouth was watering after a couple deep breaths, and I was almost feeling good about the morning until I spotted Morial sitting at the long oak table with a glass of water and one of Yven's cinnamon rolls. "You're awake," he said, noticing my arrival. "Good. Eat quickly."

"It's not quite dawn yet," I pointed out.

Morial glanced out the window at the lightening sky and shrugged. "Close enough, I should think."

My lessons that morning were a painful recapitulation of the previous day's tutelage. My arms, overworked by the constant shooting, protested when I drew the practice bow again and again, and when Morial finally let me switch to the rifle, my tender shoulder throbbed where the butt pressed against it. I tried not to complain—after all, I wasn't going to magically improve just by watching Morial, whose marksmanship made me look like a Girl Scout at her first camp by comparison—but I'd had better days.

As the sun climbed, my confidence waned. My dad had taken me hunting since I was a kid, and I'd always thought I was a decent shot. By the time I hit my teens, I was able to keep pace with him and his buddies, and while I was never a prodigy, I'd taken down my share of deer and turkeys. But the familiar aluminum compound bow I'd left in my closet back in Richmond was far easier for me to manage than the longbow DOL had sent over, which required greater upper body strength to use effectively. Sure, I'd played with a longbow and a recurve at the range, but I'd never been as accurate a shot with the more traditional weapons as I was with a compound. Since the loaner was barely above "Robin Hood reenactor" in terms of tech, I felt like an utter novice as I fumbled with my arrows, and Morial wasn't exactly the encouraging type.

While I shot, my mind wandered to the next step. Diriem had said that this training was important, but I couldn't see *how.* Assuming Morial could get me close to the Hunt, my archery skills wouldn't be useful—if I shot the Hunter, he was practically invincible, and all I would accomplish would be to annoy him. But even if I ran up on the Hunter and convinced him to listen to me with an arrow pointed at his face, what then? The odds that he'd free Wylan if I asked nicely seemed pretty abysmal. An exchange, then, a tit for tat, something he'd want more than Wylan—but *what?* It wasn't like I was going to offer Fell in trade.

When Ranarma slipped outside at noon with the previous night's folding table and lunch for Morial and me, I could have kissed him for the break. Morial allowed me to sit and eat, and I wrapped my cramping fingers around my cold water glass, trying to soothe them as I chewed. After a few minutes, I looked up from my plate at the sound of the door opening again and spotted Yven emerging with another vial of green liquid in his hand.

"Time for a fresh dose," he told me, giving the potion a slight shake. "You're in luck. Lord ti'Dana keeps a stash around the house."

Though I could have swigged a pint of the stuff, I forced myself to say, "I don't want to use up all his potions…"

"He insisted," Yven replied, and grinned as I popped off the top. "How're you feeling?"

I tossed the potion back and sighed. "Still alive."

Morial frowned as I passed the empty vial back to Yven. "Painkiller?"

"Yeah. Something wrong with that?" he asked.

"Pain is a good teacher," said Morial. "One of the best—it sears lessons in the memory. Beyond that, it's a useful warning against bodily damage—"

I couldn't contain my laughter at that, though Morial's

glare should have been sufficient to silence me. "I'm hurting. The damage is happening," I told him. "So if you want to continue this today, I'd like a little something to dull the worst of the pain."

His face screwed up in confusion. "You haven't said anything about pain to this point—"

"Annie almost *died* last week," Yven interjected.

"What?"

"Rescuing Fellora from your father. Or did no one tell you?" he snapped. "Bad potion cross-reactions, and she carried Fellora on top of everything else. For *hours*. By all rights, Annie should still be in bed. Incidentally," he added to me, "Fellora and Camun have emerged."

"How are they?" I asked.

"He's perfectly pleasant. She seems slightly hungover—"

"Excuse me," Morial muttered, rising from the table, and stalked inside.

Yven and I waited until the door slammed behind him, and I shrugged. "He's never this touchy on television."

"I suppose he's paid not to be," he replied, and plopped onto Morial's vacated seat. "How badly are you hurting, really?"

"I mean, I've been worse in the last few days…"

"*Annie*."

"I'm fine. If this helps me bring Wylan back alive, I'll make it," I said, resuming my lunch. "Anything from Rose?"

"He's not dead yet."

Could have been worse. "I'll take it," I muttered, and prayed for the potion to kick in.

To my surprise, Diriem came outside as I was finishing and announced that he'd given Morial the afternoon off. "You need a second tutor to work on skills he's less equipped to teach," he explained. "I've put in a call, and your new tutor should be here within the hour."

"*What* other skills?" I asked, regarding Diriem suspiciously.

He pointed to the bow and rifle in the grass. "There is more to combat than weapons training, you know. And considering your present condition," he continued as I groaned, "I thought someone other than Morial would be better suited to work with you."

Forty-five minutes later, after I'd grabbed a quick shower and liberally applied the numbing gel Rose had left in my room, the doorbell rang. I made it to the foyer just as Scel admitted a hulking giant of a sorcerer with a brown crewcut, trim moustache and chinstrap beard, twisted nose, and deep-set dark eyes that scanned the room with faint trepidation. His black uniform and muscular seven-foot frame suggested he was the sort of person who easily ended arguments with violence, but his sparkly silver nail polish belied his bruiser's appearance—and I knew for a fact that he took his coffee with vanilla oatmilk and hazelnut syrup when he was feeling fancy.

"Hi, Pars," I said, waving to draw his attention. "What are you doing here?"

"*Annie*?" His heavy brow knit briefly before he grinned and hoisted me off my feet in an oversized hug. "Hey! Glad to see you! I heard the healers cleared you on Saturday—"

"Getting better," I managed, gasping in his embrace, and he released me with a mumbled apology. "Are you my other tutor?"

Pars made a face. "I have no idea. My chief just told me to get my ass out here, so here I am."

A wise move. Intimidating though Pars might be, the Interdiction chief, Gentle Breeze, was a troll who'd have given Moonless Night a run for his money. I liked her well enough, based on her trips to the café, but I wouldn't have wanted to *cross* her.

"Ah, good," said Diriem, coming around the corner.

"Welcome. You must be Agent Mera," he added, extending his hand.

Pars gingerly shook it. "Yes, uh, sir. I'm sorry, I wasn't informed—"

"That was my doing. I apologize for the short notice and the lack of detail, but certain matters are being kept quiet at the moment as a safety measure. I do hope you haven't been overly inconvenienced."

"No, sir…um…"

Diriem patted Pars's arm. "Relax, young man, you're not in trouble. I asked Pateme to have you sent here on Rosie's suggestion."

He perked slightly at the mention of her name. "She's here?"

"Upstairs, trying to make her farsight cooperate. A futile effort, I fear, but she's a stubborn little thing," he said fondly. "Now, have you heard about the Huntsman's abduction?"

"Who," Pars asked, glancing at me for assistance, "Wylan?"

"Sunday morning," I replied. "I'm trying to get him back, but he's probably with the rest of the Hunt right now."

He whistled low. "No, this is news to me. Does this have anything to do with Yven's absence from work?"

"An unintentional vacation, I assure you," said Yven, hurrying into the foyer with his formal robe flapping behind him. "And I've got a conference call in half an hour, so I'm not exactly lounging around."

"Why don't we take this to my office?" Diriem suggested before the two of them could get into it, and I smiled to myself. According to Rose, Yven and Pars had been best friends since they were ten—a true odd couple, the slightly built horticultural nerd and the bodybuilder with dyslexia so severe that he kept a reading aid nestled in one ear at all times. Pars was one of Mangia Due's most loyal regulars, a guy who could drink half a dozen shots of espresso with nary a heart palpitation and always tipped. The nail polish was the result of letting his little girls play beauty parlor in his off hours.

After a *most* insistent swearing to silence and a rapid but thorough explanation, Pars regarded me with incredulity from Diriem's office couch, then turned his attention back to our host. "So, just to be clear, sir, you want me to train Annie in non-magical combat?"

"If you'd be so kind," Diriem replied.

"She's in no condition—"

"I've already had two painkilling potions today," I interrupted. "I can handle it."

"You need *healing* potions and rest," Pars retorted. "I cannot, in good conscience, beat you up right now."

"Precisely," Diriem interjected. "Agent Mera, Rosie speaks very highly of you. She says you're a welcome counterpoint to Agent ti'Mal's particular style of tutelage."

"*Agent* ti'Mal?" I asked.

Pars nodded. "Emarae. He's Gentle Breeze's second. You'd probably know him if you saw him—long black hair, blue eyes, dresses like me."

"He's not a main-line ti'Mal," Yven offered. "A cousin. He's been training Rosie off and on since last November."

"Glad *someone* can keep the Halls straight," I muttered.

Diriem quietly snorted. "It's a practiced skill."

"And Emarae's something of a hard-ass—oh, uh, sorry, sir," Pars mumbled, but Diriem brushed the apology aside. "Anyway," Pars told me, "he tends to get excited with Red and forgets she doesn't have the background to really spar with him yet, so I step in sometimes. Better for her to practice with someone closer to her age, yeah?"

"Which is why you're here," said Diriem. "Annie needs an instructive breather, as it were. Are you willing?"

Frowning, Pars glanced at Yven, then back to Diriem. "I…have a choice, sir?"

"You don't work for me," he replied, "and if I've misjudged, I'm happy to tell Pateme as much and ask for someone else. But if you're willing—"

"Oh, no, I am," Pars hastily cut in, "I just, uh…I don't typically have instructions framed as optional."

Diriem's lips twitched. "Something you will realize after a few centuries at your job is that people are far more likely to do what you want when you don't stand back and bark orders." He pushed himself off his desk, and the rest of us quickly stood. "I have a gymnasium on the third floor with plenty of mats. Doable?" he asked Pars.

The answer to that was a resounding *yes* from my new tutor, who stood inside the doorway and stared at the mansion's cavernous workout space with undisguised envy. In fairness, between his machines and his free weights, Diriem had a setup to rival my neighborhood gym, and even with that, at least two thirds of the room remained vacant. The floor was padded with thick blue mats, but the stone walls were worryingly bare, and the unprotected stained glass windows left me a little skittish.

"This is his *personal* gym?" Pars mumbled once we were alone.

"It's good to be the king, I guess."

"Damn."

I eyed the treadmill and elliptical, both of which seemed marginally more appealing than an afternoon of shooting, and prayed that Pars didn't have chest presses in mind. "So, um…what do we start with?"

He looked down at me a skeptical gaze. "Two painkilling potions, you said?"

"So far."

"Could you do with a third?"

"Are you offering?"

"Not quite yet, but that tells me what I need to know. We're starting with stretches. Come on," he said, heading for the open mats.

"What kind of stretches?" I asked.

"The kind that don't overtax you," he replied, settling onto the floor as a joined him. "If you're in pain, you're damaged. Let's see if we can limber you up a little without making matters worse."

I've never been the most limber of people, and Pars was certainly no yogi, but he knew a surprising number of ways to bend and guided me through breath counts while I held nameless poses. "There's a game we played when I was in school officially known as 'melee,'" he said while helping me hoist myself into an ungainly backbend. "Unofficially, we called it 'deathball.' It's a sport for the young and stupid."

"How do you play?" I asked, closing my eyes against the upside-down view.

"Get the ball across the field and into the other team's goal by any means necessary—and I do mean *any*," he replied. "Technically, we weren't supposed to use lethal moves, but each team had at least one healer on the sidelines. You could stack your team in different ways—some liked to go troll-heavy for the sheer clobbering ability, some favored nymphs, mine had a special team of fauns that could take out a line of defenders before they realized what had hit them—but the important rule was to prepare for *anything* on the field. Our coach was a big believer in limbering up beforehand. Said we were less likely to hurt ourselves when we fell if we could do so with a modicum of grace. All right, deep breath, arch your back a little higher…"

I did as he ordered and exhaled on the release signal. "Did Yven play with you?"

Pars's response to that was a rumbling chuckle. "Hell, no. You've seen the man, yeah?"

"Sure…"

"It's the rare elf who goes far in deathball. If you've got a kid who can cast quickly enough to defend himself, then maybe—Emarae said he played when he was a boy, and I'd believe it. But in general, elves aren't built to be repeatedly trampled, and Yven will be the first to tell you that he's lousy at defensive magic."

I let myself flop onto my back and stared up at Pars. "I'd probably suck at deathball, too. The antlers might do a little damage, but I don't think Roulette gave me the reinforced skull and neck muscles to use them effectively."

He jokingly rapped on my forehead with his knuckles. "You're probably right. Wylan, now—I bet he'd be a force to be reckoned with."

"They can teleport. Just pass him the ball, and he'd show up at the goal. But they come into being as adults," I added, sitting up, "so I think your youth league is safe for now."

Pars's brow furrowed. "They're born *adults*?"

"According to Wylan, strictly speaking, they aren't born. They just…start existing. *Poof.* I mean, we could ask Morial when we finish, but I don't think Wylan was pulling my leg."

"Hm. Speaking of which, cross your legs, get comfortable, and start to slowly turn your torso to one side. We're going for a deep stretch, but let's ease into it." He waited until I was twisted halfway around, then said, "This Morial fellow."

"Yeah?"

"How long have you known him?"

"Do you want that answer in hours or days?" I asked, wincing as my back cracked.

"That's what I thought. Hold it there, breathe…two…three…okay, other direction." Watching me groan into the stretch, Pars asked, "How are you sure that Morial won't run to Daddy and offer you up as a way back into his good graces?"

"Beyond the fact that he doesn't know how to get to the lodge?"

"That *could* be a problem, yes," he allowed. "But how do you know he won't turn on you? If he's been exiled from his family for centuries and you could be his ticket home…"

Pars let that thought hang, but I just kept deepening

my twist. "I don't get that feeling from him. Frankly, I don't think he *wants* to be Morial. He only dropped the mask because Lord ti'Dana talked him into it."

He grunted. "You may be right, and I hope you are. But don't get so focused on your goal that you forget to notice danger signs around you. And hold…"

When he released me, I sighed and shook out my torso. "I know you all think I'm young, but I'm not completely naïve."

"Never said you were," Pars replied. "I just want you to remember that desperate people do desperate things."

"Like trying to track down the Hunt?"

"*Precisely*. Now brace your feet against mine and give me your hands. Let's see how far you can go."

If Pars was nervous about being in the Intelligence director's house, he was far more nervous about getting home late. "My wife is picking up the kids as we speak," he told Diriem once we finished in the gym. "If I leave her alone with four children after a full day of work, she'll kill me."

Not wanting Pars's blood on his hands, Diriem thanked him, and we walked him to the door. "A suggestion," said Pars before he took his leave. "Annie's recovering, but she should probably still be under a healer's supervision. My wife is a DOL healer, so if you're worried about confidentiality, Canna's got all sorts of clearance. If you're comfortable with it, I could ask her to come out tonight and check Annie's progress."

Diriem smiled at that. "Once the little ones are in bed, I trust."

"I'm not crazy, sir."

Pars hit the road and promised to send word. Shortly after eight that evening, a blue minivan pulled up outside the mansion, and I hurried to the foyer as Scel showed a pretty brunette inside. She was tall for a sorcerer, maybe a hair under six feet—dwarfed by Pars, no doubt, but able to look Diriem in the eye. She carried a utilitarian brown purse on one shoulder and had slung a black nylon case onto the other, and I caught a flash of white teeth as she shook my hand. "Canna Nerin," she said. "I've heard a *lot* about you lately, Annie."

"I thought you were at DOL," I replied.

"Interagency communication," she replied with a slight grin. "When you showed up as battered as you must have been last week, the DPP team started calling around for second opinions." Glancing at Diriem, she asked, "Do you have a decently large bathroom around here? I'd rather do some of this over a sink."

The restroom nearest the foyer—a true guest bathroom, designed with stalls and sinks for four—was larger than my apartment bedroom in Richmond and decked out in pale gray marble. Canna took a moment to size up the place, then had me sit on the counter between two basins while she ran diagnostics. "Kidney function looks good," she announced when a small box in her hand beeped, "but I'd go easy on anything handling filtration for the next week or so. Have you been drinking?"

"Water?"

She arched a brow. "You know what I mean."

"Just a little to dull the pain last night," I replied, fudging the truth.

"Well, knock it off. I'll give you potions, honey, but no alcohol for now."

When Canna finished the internal exam, she rooted around in her black case, a bag neatly packed with potion vials, and extracted a tube of salve. "Your skin looks like it's cleared up—I heard about your blisters," she explained.

"It's a *lot* better."

"How about your shoulders?"

I made a face. "Getting there."

"Thought so. Take your shirt off, and let's get some of this goop rubbed in. We use it for burn victims, great stuff, very gentle."

I pulled out a padded bench from beneath the counter, stripped off my shirt, and took a seat. Canna hissed when she saw the condition of my shoulders—the scarring wasn't exactly pretty—and she tried to warm the salve in her palms before she started working it into my new skin. "You poor kid," she murmured. "I'm leaving the rest of this with you, and if Director Erenani has a problem with that, I'll tell her to jump in a lake. Have you seen a specialist for this?"

"Yeah, a dermatologist came in to work on me," I began, but paused as the door opened.

"*Oh*," said Morial, freezing on the threshold. "I'm sorry, I didn't realize—"

"The important bits are covered," I interrupted, grateful for my sports bra. "Go ahead."

"No, that's all right, I'll find another…" His voice faded, and I watched in the long mirror as he stepped closer and stared at my back. "What happened to you?"

Canna turned and gave him a look suggesting that a quick egress would be the safest option, but I said, "Cross-reaction last week. I told you I had a bad one when I used masking jewelry, didn't I?"

"Yes, but…"

"Blistered pretty badly. Carrying Fellora over my shoulders made it worse. This is a *great* improvement."

"And I'm sure Annie could tell you more details, but let's wait until she has her shirt on, hmm?" Canna hinted.

"Of course," said Morial, hurrying out, but I caught his troubled expression in the mirror as he slipped away.

"Honestly," Canna muttered once the door had slammed, "you'd think people could learn a little *tact*. And there, that should do it." She waited until I'd dressed, then gave me the salve, two tubes of green painkiller, and a tube of the expensive burgundy healing potion I'd lived on while I recovered. "Take that tonight," she instructed. "The painkillers are for tomorrow. Salve after you shower, while your skin is nice and soft. Now, to bed with you."

I could have protested. It wasn't even nine o'clock, and my friends were hanging out in one of the mansion's dens, watching a movie. But I was physically exhausted, and Canna had an *excellent* mom voice.

"Yes, ma'am," I said, then thanked her and shuffled off to my room to collapse.

CHAPTER 6

I ran.

Despite the darkness, my eyes could just make out the contours of the forest around me: hardwoods denuded by the autumnal chill, bracken between the trunks, the laden branches of the tall pines blotting out the moonlight. My freezing bare feet pounded over the detritus of the forest floor—twigs, fallen acorns, pine needles, desiccated leaves that crumbled into dust with every rapid footfall—as my lungs strained for breath, an undersized bellows struggling to keep a furnace glowing. I couldn't give a precise name to what was chasing me through the woods, but I knew with every fiber of my soul that if it caught up, it would destroy me.

For now, though, I had the lead. It was still tracking me, still following the trail I left through the undergrowth, but those precious yards between us were my salvation…

Until my antlers caught in a low-hanging snarl of branches.

Panicking, I yanked and twisted, trying in vain to free myself, but the branches seemed to tighten their grip, and the pine needles cut my feet, and then I felt *it* behind me, its breath hot and fetid, its teeth closing on the back of my neck—

I jerked awake with a cry and flailed at the blankets until I recognized the bed beneath me. Rolling over with a groan, I checked my phone for the time: a little after four in the morning.

Good enough.

Thus, when Morial found me in the kitchen at five-thirty, slumped over a cup of coffee and glowering at the world, I was dressed for the day if displeased to be conscious so far before dawn when I didn't have a coffee shop to run. "You're early," he said, opening the refrigerator.

"Nightmare," I muttered. "Another one."

"Oh?" He rummaged for the jam, then headed for the half loaf of bread tucked into its box on the counter. "You know dreams can't hurt you, right?"

"They can dissuade me from going back to sleep for the sequel."

"Fair. Do you want toast?"

"If you're offering."

A few minutes later, he slid a plate in front of me and passed the jam. "Eat up. You'll want your strength today."

"Thanks," I grunted, and started fixing my breakfast.

Just as I raised the first piece of toast to my mouth, Morial said, "I was somewhat hasty in my assessment of you."

I bit off a chunk. "How so?"

"You're stronger than you seem on first impression. I…" He paused as if wrestling with the words, then said, "I, uh…I didn't realize the extent of your injuries."

"My back looks worse than it feels. And I got some good stuff for the scarring last night—"

"Beyond that. I'd thought Yven was exaggerating yesterday when he said you'd almost died last week, but I made further enquiries, and…well."

I ate more of my toast, letting my full mouth excuse my silence.

"I've not had much contact with humans in recent centuries, you understand," Morial continued. "And I'd forgotten how slowly you heal."

I swallowed and sipped my coffee. "The potions are helping."

"Sure, but considering your state when you went to the

healers—oh, Maya was *most* descriptive," he explained when my eyebrows rose. "As was Fellora."

That took me by surprise. "You spoke with her?"

"Passed her on my way to bed last night. I believe she was self-medicating," he replied with a faint smirk. "But yes, I asked for her impressions of your injuries. She was blunt."

"I drank another healing potion last night, so I'm coming along. What are we starting with today, the bow?"

"Yes. But…" Again, he struggled with his words, then managed, "He must mean something to you. Wylan."

"Uh…"

"For you to be pushing as you are in your condition, you've got more than mere *feelings* for him," he pressed, leaning across the counter toward me. "I may not play the game, Annie, but I know what it looks like. What's truly between you two?"

It was far too early in the day for me to be having this discussion with Wylan's brother, of all people, but I realized there'd be no escaping it. "I'm pretty sure that he likes me," I mumbled into my coffee, "and I like him."

"*Like*?" Morial echoed.

I sighed, then drank to stall for time. "Look, I'm not going to pretend to know how Wylan feels. I do think there's something there—"

"Because he took you hunting?"

"Actually, the bigger tell was after we got back to Beukal."

His amber eyes narrowed. "Meaning?"

"I mean Wylan kissed me like he meant it," I said, and raised my mug to avoid Morial's stare. But I couldn't gulp coffee forever, and when I lowered it again, I found him still regarding me like one might consider a curious specimen on a pin. "What? You think he's toying with me?"

"No," he said simply. "Doubtful. But what you're feeling—do you think it's genuine, or might this be infatuation?"

I didn't answer him until I'd gotten up, fixed a second cup of coffee, and drunk half. "Let me put it like this," I said, reclaiming my stool. "I carried Fell for hours through the woods while my skin felt like it was on fire and the bit underneath her was a sticky mess. I walked until I collapsed and couldn't force myself off the ground. I barely had energy to lick the dew off the grass, for God's sake. So I'm lying there, basically trying to die, and I started thinking that maybe the last year had just been one long, weird dream, and the Pactlands didn't exist, and I was home on the couch and going to wake up at any moment. Comforting, right?"

He nodded.

"Well, in the middle of all that, I realized I didn't *want* this to have been a dream because I wanted Wylan to be real." Shrugging, I said, "Do with that what you will."

Morial said nothing for a time while I finished my toast and coffee, then cleared his throat. "You haven't know Wylan long."

"Nope."

"And you realize that under Pact law, you cannot be together."

I hesitated to answer him.

"You do know that, right?" he insisted. "If he wanted to pursue a legal relationship with you, then his only option would be the draught."

"Does that even work on Huntsmen?" I asked.

"I can't imagine it's ever been tried. But once DPP finds an antidote to the potion that's stranded you here, they'll send you home—they'll have no choice. The whole point of this place is to keep the people here safe from your kind."

"That doesn't change my feelings," I murmured. "And there might be an alternative. Fell said she'd go to the Forum for me…"

My voice petered out as Morial chuckled and shook his

head. "You did a good deed for that girl," he said. "A brave deed. No one can deny that. But I've been here since the beginning of this place, and I'm telling you now that the Forum won't allow you to stay, no matter how much she advocates on your behalf."

"*Rose* gets to come and go, and she's partly human—"

"And not only acknowledged ti'Dana, but the ti'Dana heir apparent," he countered. "She has a claim to the Pactlands. You're just an unfortunate castaway."

As my shoulders tightened, Morial nodded toward the window and the twilit yard. "Perhaps you could vent your temper on a target instead of waking the house with an argument you won't win, hmm?"

"You're an asshole," I muttered, but stalked toward the door.

He caught me by the shoulder, and I glared back at him. "I'm not going to baby you, Annie," he replied. "You deserve better than that."

It really is amazing what a healing potion will do for you. A little sleep-deprived but feeling better than I had in a week, I tried to focus and not complain that morning as Morial relentlessly drilled me. He never raised his voice, nor did he berate me for my imperfect form or my wilder shots, but he remained insistent until the lunch break: *again…again…again.*

Morial didn't nag me when I downed a painkiller after eating, nor did he object when I took a few minutes to stretch as I digested. Once the potion had kicked in and my aching arms had quieted, I sucked it up and returned to work, shooting arrows and bullets by turns until the sky darkened. To my surprise, Morial didn't push me to keep going after sundown, instead releasing me to clean up and eat dinner with the others.

I didn't know how much of the meal was Ranarma's doing and how much was the result of boredom among

Maya's crew, but I could have inhaled everything on the long table. The culinary end of the room kept up a lively critique of the dishes, alternately praising and suggesting tweaks, and by dessert, Ranarma had pulled up a chair to join them as they bickered about the best way to roast a pork loin. At the other end, far from the "help," sat the ti'Mal family and Camun, who said little as they ate and quickly excused themselves. Diriem served to buffer them from the less savory midsection: Rose, who was sporting bags under her eyes from the hours she'd spent trying to push through the block in her farsight, Yven, who kept coaxing food down her, and me, sore again, wet-haired, and eating like a linebacker. Morial kept his own company in the kitchen.

After dinner, I pitched in to help with the dishes—a surprisingly brief task, as Ranarma cleaned the worst of the pans with a few muttered words—and reluctantly turned down a proffered beer in favor of my remaining pain potion. While Maya gathered her minions and the young sorcerer for an evening class on the wonders of fluffy cheesecake, I wandered the halls of the mansion for a while, stretching my legs and trying to shake off my nervous energy. Worn out and well fed through I was, I was too alert to go to bed just yet.

I was completing a lap and heading toward the den in search of the television when I passed Diriem's office. The door was cracked open, and as I neared, padding along the thick hallway runner, I heard Morial's voice from within: "I can't do it."

Under ordinary circumstances, eavesdropping was frowned upon. Eavesdropping on a conversation including the head of the Pactlands' intelligence agency was *definitely* a bad idea. But seeing as a decent chunk of my career had been spent surveilling people, I pushed my manners aside and stopped in my tracks, trying not to betray my presence as I listened in.

"I didn't think she was inept…" Diriem began.

"She's not. If she'd never held a bow before, this would have been a simpler matter. Judging by what I recall of human archers, she's a decent shot."

I held my breath and strained to hear them.

"Has she improved in the last days?" Diriem asked.

Morial sighed. "Some. She's teachable. She's not particularly complaining, though I suspect the potions have much to do with *that.* But even if I were to drill her morning and night, I *couldn't* raise her skills to the level they would need to reach. Not in the time we have, anyway."

"And how long is that?"

"I can't give you a day and hour, but I'd be shocked if the Hunt didn't ride again before winter sets in. There's no way I can prepare Annie to face Father in time."

A chair creaked within the office. "Perhaps," Diriem began, "if there are particular skills she could hone—"

"She would require years of training to match the level of the youngest of my brothers," Morial interrupted. "And even if she had that, she lacks our reflexes and senses. Her night vision is pitiful."

"You're familiar with the concept of night vision goggles, yes?"

"Of course," he replied testily, "but that's only one example. I know she's willing, but her limitations are simply too great to overcome."

"Put the bow aside," Diriem suggested. "Focus on the rifle. It's probably easier for her."

Morial's soft laughter gave way to a groan. "You're not hearing me. She doesn't have what it takes. And beyond that, say I could make her an expert marksman in a matter of days. How would you like her to intercept the Hunt, eh?"

"You know where they go—"

"It's usually rugged, often heavily wooded, and their mounts seldom touch the ground, remember? What do you want Annie to do, get a van, drive it through the wilderness, and hope for the best? She'll never catch up, let alone come within shooting range. And supposing she did," he continued before Diriem could offer another idea, "what could she possibly do against Father? She can't kill him, she wouldn't be able to take on the rest of the Hunt by herself, and she has nothing to offer in exchange for Wylan, *if* he's still alive by the time the Hunt rides, which I can't guarantee."

My chest clenched.

"She's in love with that fool," said Morial.

"I'm aware."

"And *I'm* now aware of what she did for DOL and the ti'Mal girl," he retorted. "They hid at home where it was safe and sent a child to steal from the Hunter."

"Annie's young, but she's not a child—"

"She's not fully of age, either," he countered. "So what's the plan? Let the lovesick human kid do what DOL won't attempt? Or is it DOI that wants Father more?"

Diriem kept his voice low even as Morial's rose. "Laws wants to bring him to justice. I can't fault them for that."

"No, but I can fault them for using the girl as bait. For using her feelings for Wylan to draw her into this mess. I don't suppose you could offer her citizenship if she were to deliver my father to you in chains, could you?"

"That…would not be my decision," he admitted.

"I didn't think so. Thus, even if she were to succeed—and I can't see that happening—she'll be out once DPP finds an antidote. And since she *won't* succeed, the research team will soon be free to focus on another project, especially once Father finds Maya. Well," said Morial, "do what you will, but I won't be a party to Annie's suicide. I'm returning to work in the morning. Destroy my cover if you must, but I'm not staying here."

Leaving?

An image of Wylan's broken body flashed before my mind's eye, and I could hold my silence no longer.

I marched into the open office, gratified to see the

men's twin looks of surprise. "Give me another chance," I said to Morial. "The potions are working, and I'll shoot better once I'm not hurting—"

"Annie?" He pushed himself from his chair, taking the two-inch advantage he had over me. "How much did you hear?"

"Enough," I replied, folding my arms. "I can do more—"

"You can't." His answer, though firm, wasn't harsh. "You're unequipped for this, and I cannot give you what you need. I can't make you other than what you are."

"And *I* can't sit back and just hope Wylan reappears someday," I snapped. "Unless you can guarantee that he's perfectly safe right now…"

Morial said nothing.

"I didn't think so. Will you not help me?"

"Annie," Diriem tried, but I kept my stare fixed on Morial.

After a long moment, he sighed and rubbed his stubbled chin. "I…appreciate that you don't view this situation with perfect objectivity. Having considered the variables with *slightly* more clarity, however, I'm telling you that you can't win. If this were only a matter of courage or stubbornness," he pressed on before I could object, "I would bet on you. You're stronger than I'd first imagined, and I say none of this to diminish that. But kid, this isn't your fight."

"Then whose is it? You won't make it yours," I replied, and glanced at Diriem. "Neither will you or DOL. *Someone* has to try."

The tough thing about trying to shame people who measure their age in centuries is that somewhere in that span, they seem to learn how to throw together a decent poker face. Neither Diriem nor Morial flinched, but I held my ground. "Walk away, if you insist," I said to Morial, "but I'm not throwing in the towel yet."

"She has heart," Diriem murmured.

Morial turned to him with an impatient glare. "*Heart* is a wonderful quality to discover in the middle of a match against a better team. Here, it will get her killed." Looking back at me, he continued, "I'm going to be plain with you: as you are, you're nothing more than an annoyance to my father. You have nothing he needs, and he has no reason to hear you, much less return Wylan. Since the Hunt has sought you in Beukal, you would be best served by staying here until DPP finds a solution to your problem, then getting the hell out of the Pactlands. The Hunt could follow you there, but it's less likely to do so."

"That's it, then?" I said, fighting against the sudden constriction in my throat. "You're done? Washing your hands of all of this?"

"And if the Hunt's pursing Annie in the capital," Diriem interjected, "why do you think you'll be safe there? If they can track her scent, then surely they can follow yours."

At that, Morial bent and lifted his phone from the coffee table—an oversized phone designed for troll hands, too large for most pockets. "I have an excellent security system, internal and external motion sensors, the works. Want to guess what hasn't been triggered since I left town?"

"That doesn't mean they *won't* seek you out," Diriem replied.

"Ah, but I've given them no cause to do so. Keeping a low profile is the key to survival," he told me. "And you need to remember that you're not the hunter here—you're the *prey*. The sooner you internalize that lesson, the longer you'll live. Well, that lesson," he amended, "and one other: don't put your life on the line for people and organizations who don't give a damn whether you live or die."

With that, he tucked the phone under his arm and nodded to Diriem. "Thank you for your hospitality. I'll be taking my leave in the morning. Now, before I show up at the station tomorrow, should I assume that Moonless

Night will be unemployed?"

Diriem shook his head. "You have my silence. Be careful," he said, and stood by his desk as Morial swept from the room.

I watched Morial leave the mansion around four a.m. from my perch at the top of the foyer staircase. If he knew I was there, fresh from another nightmare—and in fairness, he almost certainly did—he didn't acknowledge me, and he didn't look back as he headed toward the garage with his bag. A few minutes later, I saw the headlights of his troll-sized SUV cross the front windows, and I opened the front door to watch the driveway illuminate ahead of him, a blue wave receding through the darkness.

The asshole had really given up, I realized, and slammed the door. Fine, I told myself, I didn't need him. I'd rescue Wylan without his help, and then I'd rub it in his stupid, smug face.

And that's why Diriem found me in the backyard at five in the morning, shooting arrows at the one target I could decently see by the lights I'd left on in the house behind me. He quietly strolled across the manicured grass to join me and watched as I emptied my quiver, then said, "I'd have thought you'd opt for the rifle, all things considered."

"Not before dawn," I replied, slinging the bow over my shoulder as I walked off to retrieve my arrows. "That'd be pretty fucking rude."

"Fair." He waited while I pulled the bunch free of the target, his hands shoved into his pockets against the morning chill. "You're still resolved to locate Wylan?"

"What do you think?" I muttered.

"I think you need a sleeping potion and a few more days of bed rest, but something tells me my opinion doesn't matter in that regard. So." Stepping in front of me before I could resume shooting, Diriem said, "You overheard quite a bit last night. Let's clear the air."

I lowered the bow before I could accidentally loose an arrow into his chest. "What's there to clear? Morial's out, no one with any actual power gives a shit about Wylan, and so I'm the lousy last hope. Something I missed?"

"Kabno wants him found alive," said Diriem. "And if it matters, so do I."

"Then why is no one doing anything?" I demanded. "Huh? Why isn't there a DOL SWAT team gearing up to go after him? Or…whatever it is your people do," I said, momentarily thrown off my rhythm. "Why am I the only one making an effort? *He* helped save Fellora, too, and—"

"That hasn't been forgotten. Come with me."

I wanted to refuse, to tell Diriem that I didn't have time to sit around and talk about how inept I was for this job, but something in his tone suggested that I shut up and follow him back into the house. Once we'd reached his office, he locked the door and watched as I plopped onto the couch, then leaned against his desk. I wondered if it was a psychological move, maintaining the ability to loom over everyone else in the room, or if Diriem just became restless when forced to sit and placate people who hadn't seen hints of how the next few centuries would play out.

"Laws is working on a strike team," he said without preamble, staring me down. "Some of the best minds in that agency are putting together a plan to bring in the Hunter. You know as well as I do what problems they face."

"Finding him and getting cuffs on him," I murmured.

He nodded. "Difficult to accost someone if you can't reach him, potentially deadly to attempt to subdue him when he's backed up by approximately four dozen well-armed men with advanced weapons training—particularly in ranged weapons—heightened senses and stamina, and lest we forget, teleportational abilities. Now," he continued, folding his arms over his sweater—a surprisingly ratty thing, but appropriate for the early hour—"I want you to understand that Wylan hasn't been forgotten. Laws' interest in his safety has nothing to do with what he did last week. He's a citizen, and he's presumably been abducted—that's all the reason the agency needs to involve themselves. But when you're dealing with an agency, with teams of people and oversight and checks and balances, sometimes your plans come up against a difficult calculus. The same calculus that explains why Kabno didn't insist on sending a full team to the lodge to fight their way in and demand Fellora's return."

"You've got lives on the line."

"Mm-hmm. This isn't a drugged-up troll or a sorcerer who refuses to surrender. The Hunter is, by all accounts, virtually unkillable, so he has less reason than most to come quietly. And say they were able to bind him—how do they stop him from disappearing?" Leaning toward me, Diriem lowered his voice and said, "We know their teleportation can take them beyond the Pactlands. The Hunt continues to ride outside our borders, but they don't use the portals."

I held his gaze. "Can confirm."

"Where did he take you?"

"I have no idea what you're talking about," I replied, deploying my own poker face.

"You know we employ backward-viewing farseers, yes? I could ask someone to look."

"Go ahead," I said with a shrug. "To which I'll remind you that I was brought into the Pactlands without my consent, and I've been denied portal credentials. I'm a prisoner here."

One corner of his mouth twitched. "And how long do you suppose you would last out there in your current condition?"

"Long enough to tell the right people what happened to me and where I've been."

He studied me for a moment more, then grinned as he straightened again. "Good, Annie. *Very* good."

That wasn't what I'd anticipated. "Huh?"

With a subtle flick of his fingers, a ring of brilliant white flames erupted around us, and I shrank from them in alarm. "The *fuck*—" I yelped, then noticed something odd: while the fire looked and felt real enough, it wasn't burning the rug or spreading.

"You're defiant in the face of a better-equipped opponent," Diriem replied. "That will either serve you well or get you killed, but I'm hoping for the former."

"This is all just illusion," I said, pointing to the flames. "You're trying to scare me."

"I assure you," he said dryly, "it is not. Well contained, yes, but hardly illusory. Don't burn yourself."

Another quick gesture extinguished the blaze, leaving nothing but a glowing afterimage in my vision. I waited for that to clear while I caught my breath and my heartbeat slowed from a frightened gallop, and then I stood to look Diriem squarely in the face. "What the hell was that all about? You're…what's it called, a pyromancer?"

"Hardly. Most of us figure that out in time. Give Rosie a century or two, and you'll see."

"So you're just playing mind tricks? Really? Trying to get under my skin and freak me out?"

"Yes," he admitted with a slight dip of the chin.

"*Why*?"

"I have my reasons."

"Well, that's just fine and dandy, then," I retorted, laying the sarcasm on thick. "You've got *reasons*! Any chance you'd like to share with the class?"

His little smile returned. "What are you feeling right now?"

I paused, caught by the non sequitur and suddenly very much aware of that smile. In my eleven months in the Pactlands, I'd acclimated to elven teeth, but I found myself considering their sharpness as I formulated a response. "Uh…pissed, I guess. Frustrated. Annoyed. Why?"

"What else?"

"Why do you—"

"*What else*, Annie?"

I huffed a sigh but rooted below the surface. "Tired. Anxious. Kind of homesick."

"Is that all?"

"No," I retorted, exasperated, "I just watched you set your freaking office on fire for funsies. You tell me, Diriem!"

That was, I reasoned an instant later, once my brain caught up with my tongue, perhaps a step too far. I most certainly did not have the clout to call Lord ti'Dana by his first name. But rather than explode at the slight, he merely chuckled at my red face and slid his hands into his pockets. "You're afraid," he murmured. "Admit it or not, I rattled you. That little display cost me almost no effort, so right now, part of your mind is trying to calculate what I could do to you if I actually flexed my muscles. Am I wrong?"

"No," I mumbled.

"But instead of cower in terror and try to appease me, you start mouthing off. Straighten your spine. Shroud your fear with indignation." His red eyebrows flicked up and down once like punctuation. "Remember that."

He stared at me, and I held it, though my stomach squirmed a bit under his gaze.

"Now, then," he said after the space of a long breath, as relaxed as if the previous minutes had been a product of my imagination, "let's talk about your training."

"Uh…you said that if I was going to have any chance of finding Wylan alive, I needed Morial to train me," I reminded him. "You have a plan to get him back?"

"No," Diriem replied, cocking his head. "And as I recall, what I said was that you needed training—I never specified that it needed to come from Morial. You made that leap yourself. Logical under the circumstances but inaccurate."

My brow knit. "So…you're going to call Pars back out here? Please not Emarae ti'Mal," I added in a rush. "I know he's good for Rose, but I don't think I can handle him right now."

"Patience. You should eat first. You'll think better with a full stomach—I know I always do," he said, then walked around his desk and extracted something from a drawer. "After that...well, what are your feelings on this?"

The object in his hand was a potion tube full of bright green liquid, almost neon compared to the color of the painkillers I'd been quaffing, and I recognized it immediately. "Scent neutralizer?" I asked.

Diriem nodded. "My understanding is that your reaction to this particular potion is a full-body rash, annoying and perhaps unsightly but not painful. Accurate?"

"That's what happened last time. It didn't hurt until I used the invisibility ring."

"Which won't be necessary. I'd like to take you to another location today, but while you're outside of the house's protections, I thought it might be wise to eliminate your scent. Probably overkill," he admitted, "but I'd rather a stray Huntsman not pick up on your trail. So what do you say?" he asked, jiggling the tube. "Want to continue your training?"

I could deal with a damn rash for Wylan's sake.

Before I could think too much about it, I took the tube from Diriem, popped the cap, and muttered, "Bottoms up," before gulping it down.

CHAPTER 7

As I'd anticipated, my rash was in full bloom twenty minutes later when Maya and her minions came down to the kitchen to start whipping up a simple multi-course breakfast. I tried to put their minds at ease—this was Diriem's idea, he'd just gone to make a few phone calls, and I felt fine, really—but my assurances did little to satisfy them. By the time Diriem joined us, Rose and Yven had wandered in, and Rose summed up the general opinion succinctly with a pointed, "What the *hell*, Pop?"

"Annie's okay," he insisted. "A little on the ruddy side, but unharmed. Is there still coffee?"

"Yeah, sure," said Rose, pointing to the half-full carafe, "but this seems reckless. How do you know it wasn't that potion that shut down her kidneys last time?"

"We're kind of partial to keeping Annie around," Maya added, folding her arms over her borrowed apron while the bacon sizzled and her wings fluttered in agitation.

"The experts at DPP believe it was the combination, not the scent neutralizer acting alone, that led to her injuries," Diriem replied calmly as he poured a cup. "And I've already arranged for Ms. Nerin to return this evening—your friend's wife," he said, cutting his eyes to Yven. "Just to be absolutely safe."

"And where, exactly, are you taking Annie?" Rose pressed.

He sipped and smiled at her over the rim. "The less information is shared, the more secure it remains."

"*Pop.*"

"Nowhere dangerous, and we'll be back by dinner. I promise," he said, taking in the uneasy stares ringing the kitchen. "You don't believe me?"

Maya cleared her throat, then pointed to me and what appeared to be my tropical sunburn. "That doesn't exactly inspire confidence, no."

"We'll be careful," he said, and nodded to me. "Eat up, Annie, you'll need it. Find me in my office when you're ready to leave."

I've never been one to drool over cars. My vehicle back in Richmond was a black, secondhand Ford Focus, nondescript and perfect for my needs. Sure, it wasn't flashy—not something I'd want anyway as a PI—but it was paid off, and I sorely missed my sedan. Still, I knew enough about cars to recognize the fortune in Diriem's garage, and I'd have loved to go cruising down the road in a Bentley or an Aston Martin. I mean, when else was I going to get the chance?

Unfortunately, my damn antlers prevented me from riding in anything less than a high-ceilinged van, and as Diriem thought that taking a convertible might draw the wrong sort of attention, we were stuck in my borrowed DPP clunker. The loaner van was the color of a sun-bleached battleship and roughly the antithesis of a sexy ride, serviceable but not the sort of thing that beautified the neighborhood when it was parked by the curb.

I wasn't surprised when Diriem didn't fight me for the driver's seat, but I *was* perplexed when he approached with a spray bottle of scent neutralizer. The mere fact that he was in possession of at least a quart of the stuff was staggering if you considered the expense of the potion, but he carried it like one might a bottle of shower cleaner and told me to wait before getting in. I stood back and watched as he spritzed every surface of the van's interior and exterior that I might have touched, even putting a few squirts down the air vents for good measure, then allowed him to spray my clothing. As I considered the fresh green spots all over my white button-up, he assured me, "The color fades as it activates. The stains will vanish in a few minutes."

Satisfied, I slid into my damp van and eased us out of the garage. "Where are we going?"

"Not too far."

I glanced at him with annoyance. Diriem certainly hadn't dressed for a trip into the capital—he'd opted for jeans and a thin brown sweater instead of a formal robe—but considering my limited knowledge of the Pactlands outside of Beukal, I had no clue where we might be bound. "Going to give me directions, or should I just guess?"

He chuckled as he tucked his loose hair behind his ears. I'd have had to have been blind to miss where Rose got her looks. "Can you get us to the internal portals, or do I need to guide you?"

"Well, since the one and only time I've come out here was in the dark…"

"True. End of the driveway, turn right."

With Diriem serving as my GPS, I navigated the Viratta portals, catching one back to Beukal before quickly turning and taking an outbound portal to another unfamiliar district, Gerentrent. As we drove through the portal, a hole in space that hung over the road and flashed colorful lights like a rave, I asked Diriem, "Where are we?"

"Unless the sign was mistaken, Gerentrent—"

"No, *where*? Like, map this onto the outside world."

"*Ah*. Kentucky, I think."

"Mm." My familiarity with that state being largely limited to bourbon and the Derby, I had little to compare to our surroundings, yet another of the Pactlands' gently undulating prairies scarred with a four-lane road. Fleetingly, I wondered if anyone had tried to import bluegrass. "So…you said we'd be back by dinner, right?"

"If all goes according to plan. If not, I wouldn't worry," Diriem added. "Given the sheer number of cooks in the house, I assume we'll be able to find leftovers."

"And will this be a one-off training trip?"

"Probably not. No offense intended, but I'd be shocked if you ended the day a master." He paused, then asked far too casually, "Have you ever ridden a horse, Annie? Left at the four-way stop."

I made the turn onto a winding two-lane road. Wherever we were, it wasn't a suburb—the few houses I spotted were set back acres from the street and spread out like tiny estates. "Uh…no, I don't ride. The odd pony at a birthday party, and a mechanical bull once at a bar—oh, and I got to ride a camel at a petting zoo when I was ten. Ever been on one of those?"

He chuckled. "Can't say that I have. But you never learned equestrian basics?"

"My folks are way too middle-class for that. Why?"

"Are you allergic to horses, by chance?"

"Not that I know of, and again, why do you ask?"

"Because we're going to a farm," said Diriem, "and there will be horses. You're not afraid of them, are you?"

"No, sir…" I replied, more bemused than annoyed by that point.

"Perfect. Take the next left."

After another twenty-minute drive through the countryside, Diriem directed me off the road and up a long dirt driveway barely wider than my van. Tidy fences of black wood marched along on either side, and I scanned the pastures within the large enclosures until I spotted a few horses grazing in the distance.

Well, the Hunt *did* ride, I mused. If I could handle a horse, then maybe I'd have better luck navigating whatever wild terrain they chose for their next night of fun. But how long would it take to learn to ride? I'd known girls who'd ridden since elementary school, but what could I accomplish in a matter of weeks?

"Park beside the barn, if you please," said Diriem.

I pulled up on the scraggly weeds next to a weathered gray structure roughly fifty feet high and at least as wide as Diriem's expansive garage. As I turned off the van and slid out, I noticed an old man emerge from a side door—a sorcerer, judging by his apparent age, though a far cry from the polished professionals I'd met around DPP. He was only about five and a half feet tall, rail-thin, and sinewy, with a complexion long tanned to the color and texture of leather. A mop of white curls perched atop his head like dandelion fluff, and he sported patched denim overalls, a brown work shirt, and dust-caked boots. I estimated he was close to Scel's age—about two hundred or so—and he squinted at me in turn, sizing me up as I straightened my oversized blouse.

"Hakk," said Diriem as he slammed his door. "Good to see you again. Thanks for fitting us in."

The sorcerer shook his hand and nodded. "You can probably tell how busy my schedule is, Diriem."

That the two men were well acquainted, I had no doubt, though I couldn't see the connection. Diriem didn't exactly keep a stable on his property.

"There's no shame in retirement," Diriem hinted.

He snorted. "I'll retire when I'm dead. This the girl?" he added with a flick of his scruffy chin.

"It is. Hakk," he said, turning to me, "this is Annie Humphries. Annie, this is Hakk Frondan."

Hakk's fingers were callused, and his strong handshake almost made me wince. "Feeling all right, kid?" he asked me. "Are you warm, or are you burned?"

I sighed. "Neither. It's a potion side effect."

He made a face and stepped back. "*What* potion?"

"Scent neutralizer. Annie's prone to unusual reactions due to her condition," Diriem explained. "It's not contagious."

"Looks painful, though."

I pressed one finger against my arm and lifted it to see

the white patch quickly flush red again. "It's mostly a cosmetic problem. So, uh…am I here to learn to ride a horse?"

Hakk peered at Diriem. "You didn't tell her?"

"I was getting around to it."

The sorcerer rolled his blue eyes and turned back to me. "*Yeah*, he asked me to teach you to ride. But since he's springing it on you once you're already here, I take it he didn't give you an opportunity to evaluate the risks."

"It's okay," I assured him. "I went to school with a girl who did show jumping, and she took a bad fall and broke her arm. Considering everything else DPP's pumped into me of late, I'm pretty sure that wouldn't be fatal," I added with a smile.

But Hakk didn't see the humor. "Did Diriem tell you *what* you'll be riding?"

Perplexed, I pointed to the nearest cluster of grazing horses, which, while tall, looked about as ill-tempered as a mall Santa. "Those?"

As Hakk sputtered, Diriem intervened. "The Frondans have been horsemasters to the agencies for several generations. Of course, with technological advances, some of the programs have been…" He paused, thinking. "You have a term I like…*ah*. Mothballed," he said, briefly segueing into accented English. "Still, one doesn't wish to be caught off guard, so Hakk oversees equestrian matters. And while I'm sure he's not keen on loaning a mount to a civilian—"

Hakk interrupted him with a snort. "'A mount,' he says. Like he wants to put you on a parade pony."

"Perhaps we should, uh…show her," Diriem suggested.

Perplexed and increasingly concerned that Hakk was going to slap me atop a homicidal bronco, I followed them past the wide barn and toward a far pasture. But as I rounded the building and caught a glimpse of Hakk's *other* horses, I stopped in my tracks and, to my eternal humiliation, squealed.

Seven-year-old Annie went through a "rainbows and glitter" phase, and many of the accoutrements tailored to little girls with that sort of aesthetic sensibility featured cute animals. Dolphins, baby fur seals, fluffy puppies, kittens, ponies, and the pinnacle of them all…

"Oh, my God," I managed in a high-pitched rush that would have embarrassed even seven-year-old me, "they're *pegasuses*!"

Hakk emitted a strangled noise that might have been laughter, and Diriem turned and stepped into my path before I could run up to the fence for a better look. "Winged horses," he corrected. "Pegasus was the name of a particular horse. As a breed, they're—"

"So. Pretty." I swear, if one of them had been a unicorn as well, I might have exploded.

"It's an ancient breed," said Hakk. "Arose in southern Europe and spread, but their numbers were always low, and they almost died off. Getting foals out of this bunch takes time, patience, and far too much luck, but the lines haven't shown any major defects yet, thank goodness."

"And, like…DPP *rides* them?" I asked, still not quite believing my eyes but suppressing a burst of giddy joy at the sight of the folded feathery wings.

Hakk snarled his lip. "Not them so much. Laws, more than anyone, but rarely of late. Once they figured out mechanical flight, there wasn't much call for the herd here."

"Too bad."

"We stole the tech from you, you know," he replied, eyeing me strangely. "You don't like it?"

"I mean, airplanes are great and all, but…" I gestured toward the fence as if that explained everything. "Can I pet one? *Please*?"

The sorcerer chuckled deep in his throat and clapped a hand on my shoulder. "Kid, you're going to be *riding* one of those. You'll get to touch, don't worry." He paused, considering my expression, then asked, "You really can't ride a horse?"

"Never learned."

Judging by the tightening of his lips, my answer came as an insult to his profession, but Hakk didn't dwell on my ignorance. "Well, Diriem made the call, and Kabno backs him up, so I guess I'll be teaching you. Not a great breed for beginners…"

"The wings get in the way?" I guessed.

"Nah, not really. I was thinking more about how much farther you have to fall from atop one of them," he said, then cocked his head toward the barn. "Come on inside. Let's go over some basics before we get you in a saddle."

Suddenly, the implications of what I'd come out there to do began to hit me. Diriem must have noticed my face, as he said, "Hakk, why don't you go on ahead? Let me have a word with Annie before we get started, eh?"

"Probably long overdue," he quipped, but headed inside without us.

Diriem waited until the door closed, then murmured, "This is the only way you'll ever catch up with the Hunt. Kabno and I have considered other options, but nothing makes as much sense."

"A flying horse without a seatbelt seems safer to you than, like, a helicopter?" I retorted. "Or whatever you want to call that vehicle that picked Fellora and me up…"

"Those are great, but you'd need a pilot—we can't get you trained and certified for a piece of equipment like that in the time Morial seems to think we have. Plus, they're not the easiest to maneuver. Say the Hunt rides down into a canyon. You'd lose them." He paused while I considered that, then said, "If this is more than you're willing to do, I won't think any less of you. Everyone has a limit."

I took a deep breath and slowly released it. "But?"

He smiled, then turned and started walking toward the barn. "There's no one better than Hakk," he called over his shoulder. "Think about it, Annie."

And I did. I thought about how there was a whole herd of creatures out of my sparkly girlhood fantasies standing just a few yards away, but how feeding apples to a horse named Buttercup was a drastically different proposition than climbing onto one and hoping gravity went easy on me.

I thought about Wylan's bloody handprint by his apartment door, evidence of his fruitless struggle to escape whatever fate awaited him at the lodge.

Then I thought about what Diriem wasn't directly telling me. Even with Morial's departure, there was a chance of finding Wylan alive—and if the farseer still had hope, then I had to swallow my fear and try.

I jogged after him to catch up. "One more question," I said before he could open the barn door.

Diriem looked back at me, brow quirked.

"Have you foreseen me falling to a messy death?"

He chuckled and stepped inside.

"Hey, that wasn't a no!" I protested.

"Less jabbering, more listening," Hakk interrupted, beckoning me toward a vaguely equine dummy beside a pile of leather and straps. "Come here, kid. Ever saddled a horse?"

I stepped around a questionable pile of what I hoped was just dirt and drew closer. "Uh…no, sir."

"No time like the present, then," he replied, and patted the dummy's back. "Let's start with the basics."

Two hours later, once Hakk seemed reasonably convinced that I knew what a saddle looked like and had made me put a headstall on the dummy half a dozen times, he led us back to the pasture where the winged horses continued to graze, unbothered by our arrival. I leaned on the fence and gave them a closer look. Most were pure black or white, and all wore silver collars low on their necks. "Why are they collared?" I asked Hakk. "Agency property tag or something?"

"Nope. *That* keeps them from flying off," he explained. "Last thing we remove around here when tacking up. It's either collar them or keep them in the barn, and the girls seem to prefer this option."

"They're all girls?"

"In this pasture." He pointed to a distant patch of field beyond the fence line, where more of the winged horses grazed around a clump of hip-high trees. "Geldings are over there. I've got my stallions spread around, but at least the mares are out of heat. *That's* a fun time at the ranch."

"Oh?" Diriem asked.

"*So* many dropped feathers. And they all keep screaming at each other. Well, maybe we'll get a foal or two this year. No guarantees with this bunch, though they certainly do try." Pointing to a trio of mares to my left, he said, "Sunshine's the biggest of those girls, and I've got hope that she's in foal. Midnight's a likely contender—she's been bred successfully. The little black one is Amethyst, Midnight's daughter, and this was her first time. That bloodline seems particularly fertile, but I won't start scanning for another month or so." Nodding to another group, he continued, "Now, *those* girls are trickier. The black one with the white blaze, Snowflake—she's only ever had one successful pregnancy. Pearl to her left is tied with her, and Diamond there—that's actually Snowflake's half sister—has yet to make it onto the scoreboard. I tell you, I've never worked with a breed so determined to make itself extinct."

I watched the mares for a moment longer—some with their heads down, grazing, some looking around the pasture, a few adjusting their wide wings—then sidled a little closer to Hakk. "So, um…which one can I ride?"

He grinned, then made a series of whistles and complicated tongue clicks. A dappled gray horse a bit smaller than the other mares raised her head and came trotting toward the fence as Hakk reached into his pocket.

"Here," he said, depositing a sugar cube in my palm. "Make friends."

I eased my hand over the top rail, and as the eager mare went straight for the sugar, I rubbed her soft nose and tried my best not to spook her with a fresh squeal. "She's beautiful," I said as she snuffled toward Hakk's clothing, looking for more treats.

"She's good for beginners. Undersized and fairly gentle," he replied, then relented and offered up another sugar cube. "Some of them have *real* tempers, but she's pretty steady."

I leaned against the fence, wishing she would turn so that I could brush my fingers against her silky wings. "What's her name? Misty? Shadow? Raindrop?"

Hakk sighed deeply. "Jimbo."

"*What*?"

"I lost a bet to a buddy of mine at DOL," he explained. "He got to name her. Fair's fair."

"*That* is not a 'Jimbo,'" I protested, patting her neck. "She is a *beautiful* girl, yes, you are—"

"Jimbo," Hakk interrupted, and the horse's ears perked. "Well, kid, I'd say that's her name. She responds to it."

"I am *so* sorry, sweetie," I told the horse, having fully slipped into the kissy voice I used to employ around my neighbor's corgi puppies. "You're a pretty girl. Don't let those mean boys tell you otherwise."

Finally, Diriem cleared his throat. "Hakk, I realize that riding is going to be a challenge in itself, but do you think you can teach Annie to shoot from the saddle?"

The sorcerer gave me a hard look, perhaps calculating the odds that I'd accidentally shoot the horse if given weapons. "Yeah, I can teach her, but not until she can ride competently. And since daylight's burning," he added, clapping me on the shoulder, "let's get Jimbo saddled and see what you can do."

Diriem claimed he was sticking around in case Hakk needed backup, but the cynical part of me suspected he'd come for the show. He found a seat on a bench outside the training ring and quietly worked on his phone while Hakk walked me through saddling Jimbo, who snorted and stamped her feet a bit but took my novice fumbling like a champ. Hakk showed me how to check the tightness of the cinch around her chest, and once the horse's equipment was sorted, he led Jimbo to a post, tied her there, and told me not to stand behind her while he went to get the rest of the gear.

When he returned, he carried a black helmet, plus a bundle of nylon straps. Having been on a climbing wall a handful of times, I recognized the straps as a harness when he shook them out, and I followed his instructions to put it on and secure it. He checked the harness as thoroughly as he'd checked Jimbo's saddle, then considered the helmet and scowled at my antlers. "Suppose I could drill holes in this," he said, "but I'd probably need to split it in half to get it on you, and that would seriously affect its usefulness."

I rapped my knuckles against my skull. "My folks always said I'm hard-headed."

"Not *that* hard-headed," he muttered, but he put the helmet aside and told me to saddle up.

I'm proud to say that I made it atop the horse on the first go, though not without a grunt, a moment of profanity, and a quick shriek when I thought I was pulling the saddle off. While Hakk had warned me that the saddle's horn wasn't meant to be a handhold, my death grip on it kept me from falling on my ass, and Hakk smirked as I made myself somewhat comfortable and caught my breath.

"Which hand is dominant?" he asked me.

"Right."

"Good. Standard placement, then. Look at the area around the horn. See the pair of D-rings?"

I nodded.

Pulling over a stepstool—I was *slightly* miffed that he hadn't offered to share—Hakk clipped what appeared to be a blue bungee cord into the lefthand ring and locked the carabiner, then affixed it to the ring at my waist. "This is the last part of your tack for riding a winged horse," he explained, gathering the extra length of cord and tying it out of the way with a piece of cloth attached to the side of the saddle. "And *crucial*. We're not putting you in the air today, but I want you to get accustomed to this before you actually need it."

It didn't take a rocket scientist to guess to purpose of the cord. "In case I fall?"

"Yep. You take a tumble, the tie holding the slack will tear with the strain, and you should be caught far enough below the horse to avoid her hooves. It's not comfortable, but you probably won't die."

"That's reassuring," I mumbled, imaging myself dangling below Jimbo like a baby carried by an overgrown stork.

"The horses are trained to land if their rider falls," Hakk continued as he climbed off his stool. "And they do…most of the time. Sometimes, it takes them a few minutes—I've got a pair of geldings who are both dumb and incredibly stubborn, and they'll whisk you off on a joyride. But the pressure of the line is usually enough to make the horse realize there's a problem."

I tried to envisage such a landing, hitting the ground and being dragged along as the horse majestically coasted to a stop. "How do you keep from getting banged up when you touch down before the horse?"

He grinned. "Try to land so that you can run diagonally. Clear the landing zone. You'll probably be yanked off your feet at some point, but a few abrasions are better than being kicked in the head." He considered my posture from the ground, then said, "Loosen up, kid. You're tense."

Hakk may have been a touch on the gruff side, but he clearly recognized my inexperience, as he started my lesson by clipping a long lead onto Jimbo's harness and walking her around the ring. As I began acclimating to the sway of Jimbo's back beneath me, Hakk talked about the history of his family's ranch and its various programs, interspersing his facts with critiques of my riding style—too rigid, too far forward, too wobbly, too far back. "There's an art to riding," he said as we completed yet another slow circuit of the dusty ring. "A sweet spot. You'll feel it when you harmonize with the horse's body. That's something I can't just teach you—it comes with experience, with trial and error, and you'll only reach that point once you build up your confidence. Afraid you're going to fall?"

"Is it that obvious?" I joked.

"That was rhetorical. Here's the thing: that saddle's not going anywhere, and your feet seem to be firmly planted in the stirrups. I'm not doing anything more than walking Jimbo, so unless you greased that saddle before climbing up, you're not about to slide out. Here," he said, starting the next lap, "talk to me. Let's get your mind on something other than gravity."

I shifted in my seat, trying to ignore the faint pull in my inner thighs that suggested true discomfort down the road. "What do you want to talk about?"

"Well, for starters, why the hell do Laws and Intelligence want *you* proficient on one of my girls?" He glanced up at me, brow furrowed. "You're one of the Roulette victims, aren't you?"

"Heard of us?" I asked with a weak grin.

"Eh, you hang out with agency types, and you hear all sorts of things. Right?" he asked, raising his voice as he turned toward the spectator bench.

Diriem looked up from his phone with an enigmatic smile.

"Yeah, I got dosed with that crap," I told Hakk. "Hence the antlers. It's been a *fun* year in Beukal, let me tell you."

"I'm sure. But while you're telling me things, let's go back to why you're on my horse in the first place."

As we passed the bench, I cut my eyes to Diriem, who nodded.

"So, uh…" I cleared my throat and brushed my fingertips along one of Jimbo's folded wings, which covered my bent legs like a pair of feathery blankets. "Did you hear about the abducted elf on the news two weeks ago? Fellora ti'Mal?"

"Plenty. Why? I heard she was found…"

"Yeah, about that. Short version, the Hunter took her as prey. One of the Huntsmen, Wylan, started working at our coffee shop over the summer, and he sneaked me into the Hunt's lodge."

Hakk stopped dead and whirled around to stare at me. "You went *where*?"

"They've got a hideout somewhere in the Pactlands. Not even DOI can find it, but the Huntsmen know how to get in," I explained. "Anyway, I got Fellora out of there, and Wylan came back to the city after the Hunt rode, and we thought we'd made a clean getaway. But it seems like Wylan's dad was more observant than we thought, as Wylan was abducted from his apartment before dawn Sunday."

"How did *you* get entangled with the Hunt?" he demanded. "I mean, looks aside…"

"I was a private investigator once. Volunteered to help," I said, and shrugged. "But as for why I'm here, nobody can get to the lodge, and Lord ti'Dana seems to think the best thing I can do for Wylan is ride after the Hunt and—"

"Stop." Stepping past the horse to see the bench, Hakk yelled, "What the hell are you doing to this poor kid, Diriem? You're going to get her killed!"

He put the phone aside and stood. "Annie's more resilient than you might think."

"That doesn't make her fit for a job like this! She can't be more than...what, forty?" he asked me.

"Thirty next month," I mumbled.

"*Thirty*. Damn it all." He leaned to one side and spat in the dirt. "You're sending a child on a suicide mission? This is DOI's great plan?"

"If I thought it were a guaranteed suicide mission," Diriem replied as he walked over, "I wouldn't have Annie here. Frankly, I'd rather she not be involved—she came far too close to killing herself the last time she was anywhere near the lodge. But Wylan was integral to Fellora's safe return, and Kabno believes—as do I—that we owe it to him to try to secure his freedom."

"Sure, deploy whatever *agents* you like," said Hakk, "but the kid is—"

"As I said, more resilient than you might think."

Hakk glared up at him, reddening in his indignation. "You're telling me that no one at DOL is more qualified to go after the Hunt than a human child is?"

"Look, guys, I'm *really* not a kid," I interjected from atop Jimbo. "Grown woman. Pay taxes."

They ignored me. "Tell me," said Diriem to Hakk, "how many DOL agents do you suppose are eager to face the Hunter?"

"Roughly none, I'd wager."

He nodded. "Precisely. Kabno has her counselors preparing a case against him for the Forum, but that still leaves the matter of finding him and bringing him in. We can't arrest him if we can't reach him. But that's a matter of later concern. More pressing is the safety of the abducted Huntsman, and in light of the blood left behind, I don't think the rest of the Hunt will shy away from violence. We want him alive."

"Well...sure," said Hakk, "but how—"

"The current plan is for Annie to follow the Hunt when they next ride, intercept them, and negotiate with the Hunter for Wylan's release. That's why she needs a horse and training in mounted marksmanship."

Hakk stepped back, and I noted the look of horror on his face. "The Hunter will kill her."

"Not if I can figure out what he wants more than Wylan," I said, cutting short Hakk's protestations. "If I can put together a decent trade..."

I glanced at Diriem, but the elf's poker face remained as blank as ever.

After a long moment of consideration, Hakk grunted, then clicked his tongue and led Jimbo onward around the ring. "You're insane, kid," he murmured.

"So people tell me," I replied, trying to find a comfortable position in the saddle without falling out.

He muttered under his breath.

"Sorry, what was that?"

"Nothing. One more time around, and then we'll work on steering."

Diriem wasn't wrong about the day's schedule. By the time Hakk called an end to the training, the October sun was low over the rolling prairie west of the barn, and I was famished. He released me with orders to return the next morning, let me give the sugar-loving Jimbo her fix one more time, then allowed me to stagger to my van on aching legs.

"You did well," said Diriem as I headed down the long driveway toward the road, a cloud of dust blowing in my wake. "How's the rash?"

My arms still looked like I'd been flopped on a beach for days, but my skin wasn't bothering me. "No pain *there*..."

He chuckled. "I asked Ms. Nerin to return tonight in part to ensure that the rash isn't your only side effect from the neutralizer, but mostly because I'm sure your legs are killing you. You walked out of there like a cowboy in a Spaghetti Western."

I cut my eyes to him in silent query, and he grinned. "What? You know we import your films…usually late, sometimes poorly dubbed—"

"Would we say *import*, or would we say *pirate*?"

"Well, since as far as the people responsible know, we don't exist…"

"Technicalities."

"Oh, absolutely. Anyhow, you should have time to eat before the healer arrives. Probably even shower."

I turned onto the two-lane road and began backtracking for the portal. "Thanks again for putting us up. We're a lot of houseguests all at once."

"Not the most I've had in a single span, nor the worst," he replied. "Frankly, the house is far too much for one person, and even with the staff thrown in, it's cavernous. It hasn't seen this much life in a long time."

"That's got to get old, though."

"I have ample retreats for privacy and quiet," he said, shrugging, then paused. "Will you keep this next bit in confidence?"

Something told me that it would be *extremely* imprudent to blab anything Diriem wanted held close to the vest. "Uh…sure."

He shifted in his seat—the van's chairs weren't exactly ergonomic. "Between us, I'm hoping this will serve as a trial run for Rosie and Yven. I know he isn't entirely comfortable with the idea of moving in, but if he realizes that we wouldn't be in each other's way…"

Diriem sounded so earnest about the matter that I tried not to rain too hard on his parade. "I'm not sure it's an issue of *space*, exactly. You, um…you know that look Yven gets whenever you two are in the same room? Like he's about to shit himself?"

He groaned. "It hadn't escaped my notice. Truly, I do not give a damn about his Hall. What matters to me is that Rosie is happy, and since she's happy with Yven, why should I be upset?" Propping his arm on the window ledge, he muttered, "Hall politics are so stupid."

"Um..."

"And I know that's easy to say when one is coming from a position of extreme privilege, but I've watched the other Halls fight for prominence all my life. That might have made sense outside, but *here*, now...what's the point?"

"My experience here is kind of limited," I said, "but from what I've gathered, you're, uh...you're deeply in the minority, there."

"Oh, that's obvious." He waited while I braked for a rabbit crossing the road, then sighed and looked out the window. "I've overseen DOI since its development, yes? I want the best people for my agency, so when I consider hiring and promotion, I don't give my agents' families a second thought beyond anticipating issues with childcare."

"Probably wise..."

"And that includes Halls," he insisted. "The farseers on staff are largely elves—it's the nature of the talent. If I considered Halls in their selection, we'd be the poorer for it. I mean, the best past-oriented farseer I've ever *met*, let alone employed, is a ti'Van."

Though my knowledge of the elven hierarchy was patchy on a good day, I knew Hall ti'Van was near the bottom of the heap, a conglomeration of commoner families that had come together inside the Pactlands.

"He's fantastic," Diriem continued. "He can lock on better than anyone else in that unit, and the *detail* he sees...well, he's peerless. You couldn't give me a dozen ti'Crens or ti'Hars or ti'Grells for him because he's absolutely the best person for that role, and I don't care what his family was like five hundred years ago. Now, as far as Rosie is concerned," he said, angling himself toward me, "the role at issue is 'person who makes her happy.' No one fills that role better than Yven does, so who am I to complain? I have no quarrel with him."

"You say that," I replied, "but not to be overly blunt,

you're still the ex-king with the giant house and the agency and the freaking farsight, and he's just a dude who loves Rose and his orchids. Probably in that order."

"Point," he conceded. "Still, I'd be thrilled if they moved in on a more permanent basis."

"And in the meantime, you've got a *ton* of houseguests," I reminded him. "So thanks."

Diriem waved it off. "It's no trouble. Besides," he said, leaning closer and lowering his voice, "I'm in possession of a large, well-stocked kitchen, and a fair number of my current guests are the sort of people who can't resist a shiny mixer. I can only begin to speculate how many pastries are going to come out of my ovens before this little getaway ends."

I smirked. "Going to have to buy more flour, I think."

"A hardship I'll gladly endure. Honestly," he grunted, leaning back in his seat again, "I could send Ranarma on vacation, and I don't think anyone would notice."

CHAPTER 8

Canna's reaction on seeing me that evening was a groaning facepalm. "Annie," she muttered as Scel locked the door behind her, "what the *heck*?"

"I'm not hurt," I insisted.

"I'll be the judge of that," she snapped, and half-dragged me into the bathroom for a checkup.

To my relief, the scans came back clear. "It's only a superficial reaction," Canna said, consulting her computer. "Vascular dilation. Everything else seems to be functioning within normal parameters—"

"Normal for whom?" I asked, rebuttoning my shirt.

"I got your file from DPP, so normal for you. Blood pressure's good, heart rate is fine, kidneys are functional…" She looked up and shook her head. "There's no explaining the side effect—"

"Roulette."

She flashed an impatient scowl. "What I meant is that there's no reason why *this* potion should have *that* reaction. None of the ingredients are known to trigger skin issues."

I shrugged. "Again, Roulette."

"What a mess." She darkened her computer and began to pack her kit while I untangled my damp hair from around my antlers. "Well, speaking as a healer, I absolutely cannot approve of your continued use of the scent neutralizer—not when you're showing a consistent negative reaction."

"But?" I hinted.

"*But*, since these do seem to be extenuating

circumstances, I'm going to tell you to monitor yourself, call me immediately if you have any new side effects, no matter how minor, and stay the hell away from possible interference." Catching my confusion, she explained, "Other potions and magical items. No taste-testing, no masking jewelry, nothing that might make your rash go in exotic directions. Understood?"

Since I generally liked having my internal organs in good working order, I promised to behave, and she handed me a painkilling potion. "Take this immediately before bed. I want as much of the neutralizer out of your system as possible before you add something else to it."

As I limped with her to the front door, she said, "By the way, Pars told me he's been asked to return here tomorrow night. Any idea why?"

"News to me."

Canna gave me a last once-over in the foyer, then nodded. "I'll tell him to be gentle. Try not to break any bones, eh?"

Once she'd driven off to relieve her husband of solo parent duties, I hid out in the kitchen, nursing a cup of tea while my inflamed skin continued to calm. Chamomile wasn't my favorite brew, but I didn't need the caffeine of Diriem's other offerings, and wisdom suggested that chasing a beer with a potion might be a poor life choice. Sitting at the counter, I listened to the distant sounds of a television and laughter—definitely Maya, probably Rose. Part of me wanted to join them and try to forget the last week, but the other part of me that ached at the thought of motion insisted that the stool was *just* peachy.

Around nine, as I drained my mug, Fell wandered in, took one look at me, and backed away. "Heavens, what happened to—"

"I'm not contagious. Scent neutralizer. As long as I don't try to go invisible, I shouldn't have a repeat of what you saw when we met."

She muttered something unintelligible—Low Elvish, I

gathered—then took the stool beside mine. "Why are you using neutralizer?"

"Because Morial abandoned me, and Lord ti'Dana took me on a field trip to learn to ride a horse."

Her brow knit. "Why a horse?"

"She can fly. *Pretty* girl. Do you ride?"

"I mean, I learned as a child, but on the wingless variety." Fell gave me a long look, then asked, "Is this part of rescuing Wylan?"

I nodded. "Assuming I can get my act together. I've been cleared to drive out alone tomorrow for another day of riding lessons. Can't blame Lord ti'Dana for not wanting to hang out, watching me try to act competent."

"Have you ridden before?"

"Nope."

"And *how* long were you on a horse today?" she pressed.

"I'm still bow-legged, if that answers your question. Got a pain potion for bedtime," I added before she could object to my treatment. "I'm just…winding down, you know? How're you doing?"

But she wouldn't leave the topic. "You're going out there alone tomorrow? What if the Huntsmen find you?"

"Hence the neutralizer. I'm not going any closer to Beukal than the main portal, and if they don't smell me coming—"

"Say they do find you, though. How do you plan to defend yourself?"

Honestly, I hadn't given that much thought. I'd left my weapons at home that day, though in fairness, I'd also been chaperoned by an elf old enough to have learned more than the basics of magical combat. "Bring a gun, drive like hell, don't get caught?"

"That's ridiculous. I'll go with you."

"Fell—" I started to protest, but she cut me off.

"You'll be safer with backup, I'm not doing anything useful…and besides," she added, lowering her voice, "I'm going insane sitting around here, listening to my parents gripe about the situation."

I smirked. "Riding shotgun in my van and watching me fail as an equestrian can't be any more entertaining than staying here with the movie collection."

"I wouldn't know about any movies, as my parents continue to insist that we stick to ourselves," Fell griped. "Come on, Annie, this would be a win for us both. You get a bodyguard, and I get an excuse to leave the mansion."

"That's nice of you to offer," I replied, "and I wouldn't be opposed, but remember that the only way I'm leaving is with neutralizer in my system. That stuff's not cheap, right?"

Her expression veered toward incredulity. "You…really don't know much about the Halls, do you?"

"Bare minimum."

"Fair, I suppose." She patted my shoulder. "Let's just say that I have savings, and money will not be an object."

Friday morning, I bolted awake from a fresh nightmare around dawn, limped out of bed, and prepared for another day atop Jimbo. My clothes had been laundered overnight—the plan was to remove the sweat and grime and hopefully leave nothing but the smell of soap—and I found them in a sealed plastic bag outside my door. Once I brushed my teeth, I downed one of the scent-neutralizing potions Diriem had provided for me, making the previous day's subsiding rash flare anew within minutes. When my skin began to redden, I opened the laundry bag and dressed, trying not to rub up against anything else in the room that might smell strongly of me.

After that, I went down to the kitchen—a quiet place at that hour, as Ranarma seemed to have learned that he wouldn't need to make breakfast while Maya and her culinary minions were around. At least Diriem was right about his houseguests and their baked goods. Stealing day-old croissants from the covered platter on the counter beat the heck out of trying to whip up something fresh. That said, I didn't mind pulling my own shots of espresso that morning, and I put a pot of coffee on for good measure, doing my part to keep Diriem on our side.

Fortified by a doppio and a pair of jam-slathered croissants, I hunted around the kitchen to find lunch foods and a container to put them in. Hakk certainly hadn't offered snacks the day before. I found a jar of cashew butter and made a couple of sandwiches in case Fell got hungry, then poked about in the pantry until I found Diriem's stash: single-serving chip bags, candy bars, trail mix, and even crackers with shelf-stable cheese, much of it imported from beyond the Pactlands. In truth, it was a little disheartening to discover that the aspect of my culture Diriem seemed to like best was Pringles, but I figured he wouldn't mind if I helped myself.

As I carried my booty out of the pantry to pack it, Frog wandered in and squinted at the fresh brew. "Is that to share?" he asked hopefully in a morning bass that sounded like grinding boulders.

"If you'll do me a favor first." Coming close to him, I pushed back my sleeve to bare my red forearm, then held it up toward his face. "Smell me?"

He frowned bemusedly but obliged, bending closer and sniffing deeply. As I watched, his frown deepened, and he leaned even closer to my arm, almost grazing it with his tusks. "Nothing," he declared after a few exaggerated snorts. "I smell detergent, and there are hints of coffee near your hand, but I'm not picking up on you."

"Success." I stepped aside and swept my arm toward the coffeemaker, and Frog helped himself. "Sorry, I know that's awkward, but I figured I'd go to the guy with the most sensitive nose on the premises…"

"Oh, I've done weirder things," he replied with a chuckle. "But I'm not finding your scent, so you should be clear to leave."

"Thanks. Frankly, I can't imagine how you and Wylan go through life with such a sense of smell."

Frog shrugged. "It's what you're used to, I suppose," he said, and took a test sip. "*Ah.* And it's useful in the kitchen, you know, smell and taste being as linked as they are. It's the rare troll in the culinary classes who can't pass a blind taste test." Leaning closer, he confessed, "I caught a cold two years ago before a final and turned into an absolute *terror.* I tried everything to make my nose functional—folk remedies, the foulest potions I've ever tasted...my poor roommate couldn't walk past the kitchen without retching."

"How did you fix it?" I asked.

"Time and a box of pills that my roommate's brother in DOL brought across the border. He said he's never had anything like it for a stopped-up nose, and I agree. *Potent* little red things. Took me half the box, but hey, passed my exam!"

I tried to imagine an eight-foot troll on a Sudafed high and quickly decided I'd rather not.

As I filled a travel mug for the drive, Fell marched into the kitchen with her parents, sister, and fiancé on her heels. "Morning, Annie. Uh..."

"Frog," he offered.

"Good morning," she said, nodding, and pointed to the croissant platter. "Are these free for the taking?"

"If they're still good," Frog replied.

"They are," I said, and hoisted the cloth sack I'd borrowed from the pantry, now heavy with snacks. "I've got munchies for the day. Have you been de-scented?"

Fell pulled a tube of the now familiar green potion from her pocket. "Thought I'd chug this after breakfast—"

"You don't need to be *chugging* anything, young lady," her mother snapped.

I cut my eyes to Fell's parents. Her father, Janon ti'Pon,

stood close to the door, his blond hair tied back and his dark eyes darting nervously between his wife and daughter. Several steps further into the kitchen stood Noiana ti'Mal, visibly furious but well-dressed even with the early hour. Her blonde curls had been swept into an updo but for a pair of ringlets framing her face and skimming the collar of an indigo silk formal robe that surely cost more than half my closet put together—*way* too dressy for the circumstances. Though Lady ti'Mal headed her own Hall, I wondered if she felt the need to up her game in Diriem's house. Considering the robes her husband and younger daughter, Keef, likewise sported, I had a hunch that she had set the wardrobe parameters for the day. Even Fell's fiancé, Camun, had woven his hair into a tidy blond braid and thrown on a navy robe better suited for the office than for a grab-and-go meal.

Fell, at least, had ignored the memo, though she still cut a striking figure in a crisp white blouse and dark-washed jeans. She'd even managed to slip a pair of black boots into her luggage before running away from the capital. If she'd thrown on a bit of turquoise and masked her ears, she could have passed for an affluent horsewoman back home, someone who knew her way around a stable but paid other people to handle the mucking.

The look she shot me as Lady ti'Mal glared at us spoke of a badly fraying rope.

"I'll sip it daintily, if you prefer, Mother," she muttered. "But since I'd rather not make Annie late—"

"There's no reason you need to go out there! I'm sure that, uh...*Annie* can manage without you," she added, giving me a tight-mouthed once-over.

I lifted a hand in a weak wave. "Lady ti'Mal, Mr. ti'Pon...um, hi."

"You look a bit...different," said Janon.

With a sigh and a quick prayer for patience, I said, "I masked when I went to meet you so that you wouldn't freak out. You had enough on your minds without throwing these into the mix," I said, gesturing to my antlers, "and I didn't want to make matters worse."

"Do they hurt?" Keef asked.

Her mother wheeled on her, but I spoke before she could chastise the teenager. "Only if I get them tangled in light fixtures. I mean, they're a goddamn pain in the ass"—the elder elves looked slightly shocked at my profanity—"but things could always be worse, right?"

"I can ride, too," she volunteered. "Do you want more company today?"

"*No*," Lady ti'Mal barked. "And your sister—"

"Is a grown woman," said Fell, turning back to her mother, "who can manage her own outings." She bit off the end of a croissant and cocked her head in silent challenge.

Lady ti'Mal's jaw clenched. "Camun? Anything you'd like to say?"

Camun may have come from a higher-ranking Hall than ti'Mal, but he was a somewhat introverted guy, and his voice was low when he answered. "I, uh…please be cautious out there, Fell."

"*Camun!*" Lady ti'Mal cried, glancing back at him. "Tell her to—"

"I have no right, my lady," he murmured. "If she's willing and Lord ti'Dana believes it's reasonably safe, then who am I to tell her no? Besides," he continued as his gaze slid to me, "considering what Annie went through, I don't think this is unreasonable. Personally, I don't ride," he told me, "but if you would feel better with an additional pair of hands in case of attack, I'm willing to join in."

"Unnecessary," Diriem interjected, striding into the kitchen by another door, "but I'm sure she appreciates the offer. Fellora, you should take your coffee to go."

I caught the flash of gratitude in her expression as she nodded to him. "Yes, sir. Oh, thank you, Frog," she added as the troll passed her a travel mug and held out the carafe.

"Hey, did you make the croissants? They're *buttery*."

"Can't take the credit. It's Maya's recipe—"

"*Diriem*," Lady ti'Mal interrupted, folding her arms. "Please. Our daughter's been through so much lately, and she's perhaps not thinking clearly at the moment…"

One of his eyebrows rose, and he glanced at Fell in time to see her shove the rest of the croissant in. "She seems fine to me, Noiana. And it's nice to see all of you out of your suite. Have you explored the grounds?"

Seizing the opportunity, I grabbed the bag of snacks and hustled out of the kitchen, and Fell followed after with her steaming coffee in hand.

Apparently having been forewarned of my change in chaperones, Hakk just nodded when I parked my van by the barn and slid out. "Thought you might have gotten lost, kid," he said, squinting at the climbing sun.

"My fault," said Fell, and slammed her door. "We had to spritz our clothing and the interior of the van before leaving, and I was, uh…delayed this morning."

He grunted. "You've got enough neutralizer to be *spraying* it?"

She shrugged in reply. "The bottle in the garage this morning wasn't for show."

Muttering about DOI's budget, Hakk waved for us to follow him into the barn. "What's in the bag?"

"Snacks," I told him, shifting it on my shoulder. "So I don't get dizzy and go splat."

"A fate best avoided, splatting," he said, and softly chuckled. "Think you remember how to saddle a horse?"

"I mean, I'd feel much better if you checked my work…"

Hakk turned to me with a look of horror. "Oh, *that* isn't an option. You're not climbing onto anything until I approve the equipment. Honestly, girl," he said, shaking his head as he led the way past the stalls, "don't get cocky on me."

At least Fell was able to maintain her dignity around the back pasture. While she asked Hakk questions about breeding lines and wing care, I suppressed the part of myself that still wanted to squeal at the sight of Jimbo and tried to remember what I'd learned the previous day about saddling her. The mare was calm and tolerant of my fumbling, occasionally stamping a foot and twice nosing around my hips as if I might have hidden sugar in my pockets, and I was proud of myself when Hakk only had to tighten one strap before clearing me to clip on and get up.

Fell took Diriem's seat on the bench outside the training ring and watched with interest as Hakk guided me through riding basics. Every so often, she yelled encouragement from the sidelines. As the morning progressed, she took to leaning on the fence around the training ring, observing my form and offering suggestions, and Hakk grunted his approval.

"Something tells me he's unaccustomed to working with beginners," she told me when we broke for lunch in the barn. "My instructors used to make the older riding students tutor the younger ones. It's easy to forget that *nothing* comes naturally the first time one's on horseback when you've been riding for years."

"Any tips about this?" I asked, pointing to my aching thighs.

She winced in sympathy. "Pain potion and stretching. I could show you a few exercises tonight, if you'd like."

But she didn't get the chance. As soon as I limped back into the mansion that evening, dirt-streaked, sweaty, and not entirely convinced that I wasn't still in the saddle, Lady ti'Mal ordered Fell upstairs for what I could only assume was a lecture. Fell rolled her eyes at me but went, leaving me a couple hours to clean up and shovel down dinner before Pars arrived for the evening's conditioning.

"*Yikes*," he said upon catching sight of me in the foyer.

I glanced at my bare arms, which were still covered in their crimson rash. "It really doesn't hurt."

"That's what Canna said, but…" He hissed, then raised a hand as Yven hurried to join us. "Have you seen Annie?"

"She looks like a tomato. Difficult to miss her," Yven replied, and I punched him in the shoulder for his pains. "All right, sorry, that was uncalled for."

"I'm telling Rose," I deadpanned.

Both men winced. "Could I bribe you with a little something Canna sent over?" Pars asked. "You know, in the spirit of no one being exiled to a couch…"

I snorted and led him upstairs, heading for the gym.

"That was a 'yes,' right?" Yven called after us.

"Whatever," I said, and cut my eyes to Pars's face in time to catch his smirk.

Once Pars had dropped his bag in the corner of the gym, he pulled out a squat plastic container of light blue cream. "Canna says it's an anti-inflammatory," he explained, handing it to me. "Might help with the redness."

I opened the container and sniffed the goop, catching a whiff of citrus with overtones of menthol. "Does this count as a potion?"

"Canna sent along a prescription for it, so yes."

"And she's not worried about cross-reactions?" I asked dubiously.

"She says she's never seen one with this stuff…"

Considering that full-throated endorsement, I rubbed the cream into my forearm as a test…and while the rash did begin to subside, I only had to wait thirty seconds before my skin turned as icy as if I'd been caught out overnight in a blizzard. "Thank her anyway for me, will you?" I said, showing Pars my goose-pimpled arm, and briskly rubbed it in an ineffective attempt to dispel the chill.

He swore and put the container back in his bag, then led me out to the mats. "Stretches first, I think," he said, "and then we can try some hand combat. Have you studied it?"

"Just self-defense basics," I replied. "You know, go for the eyes and the crotch, then run like hell."

"Mm. Well, that's not terrible advice," he allowed, "but we can do better than that. Let's warm up."

I hadn't anticipated a weekend reprieve, so I wasn't distressed when Diriem caught me in the foyer after Pars left that night and told me that Hakk would see me at the usual time Saturday morning. "Fellora wishes to accompany you again, if that's all right," he added.

"You cleared this with her mom, did you?"

The flash of sharp teeth he bared wasn't precisely a smile. "I most certainly did not."

"Mind if I ask a dumb question?"

"I sincerely doubt it's dumb, and no, I don't mind. Shall we take this to my office?" he offered.

In truth, my aching body wanted its painkilling potion and bed, but I figured a few minutes on Diriem's leather couch wouldn't make matters worse. As I settled in, he locked the door, then leaned against his desk and nodded. "Ask away. I don't guarantee answers, mind you, but you're welcome to try."

Sitting on the edge of the cushion, I rubbed my frozen arm and said, "I don't want to get Fell in trouble."

"That's not a question."

"A precursor. Her parents are obviously not thrilled that she went with me today, and I doubt they'll be any happier tomorrow. Fell's grown, but…like, what can her mom do to her?"

"In other words, how much power does the head of a Hall actually wield?" Diriem glanced at the ceiling and made a face. "In some respects, a fair bit. In others, hardly any. I could stop a marriage if I lodged a formal protest, for example, but I can't tell the rest of the Hall, say, where to live or what occupations to pursue. The same goes for

Noiana."

"So Fell's not going to face major consequences if she keeps hanging out with me, then?"

"Major? No, I doubt that. She's the heir apparent, anyway, and Noiana will want to avoid the scandal of a rift with her daughter. Much of what we can do if…*displeased*," he said with mocking emphasis, "comes down to social opportunities. Anger your Hall's lady or lord, and you might not be invited to functions. Now, this is hardly a problem in some Halls—a few of my peers are of the 'live and let live' bent, and I find myself drifting further in that direction the older I get. On the other extreme, you have ti'Cren—well, the former lord, at least. Inade was a despot, but I don't think Teolm particularly cares."

I'd never had the misfortune of meeting Rose's other great-grandfather, but the new Lord ti'Cren was a short, dimpled botanist who, per Rose, favored T-shirts to formal robes.

"I wish Rosie were on better terms with that Hall," Diriem murmured. "Teolm may be the only man who loves his flowers as much as Yven loves his. Perhaps someday…"

"But for now, if you could put my mind at ease," I said, "is Fell setting herself up for backlash if she keeps telling her parents to sit down and shut up?"

Diriem's eyebrows rose. "Are you asking this of a farseer or of a man who's decently acquainted with Hall politics?"

I sat back and folded my arms. "Whoever's willing to answer me."

"Fair. Putting aside farsight, nothing I've seen suggests that Fellora is in danger of making a pariah of herself. If she's old enough to be married, then I should think her old enough to babysit you."

"*Ouch.* Babysit?"

"You're not even thirty, child," he replied, but the twinkle in his eye gave him away. "Call it what you like, but if you, with your deep maturity and wisdom, could tolerate the ti'Mal girl's presence, I think the arrangement would benefit you both."

"Ha."

"I'm serious. She needs to breathe, and frankly, I do feel better sending you out with an escort. So, does that satisfy you?"

"Somewhat," I replied, pushing myself off the couch, the better to hold Diriem's stare. "Will you still not tell me anything about Wylan?"

He had the grace to grimace in sympathy. "You know I can't do that, Annie."

CHAPTER 9

And thus, my life fell into a pattern: wake to my alarm, down a tube of scent neutralizer, grab a quick breakfast, and drive out to Hakk's with Fell, where she could watch from the sidelines while I tried to master the basics of horseback riding. At night, once he'd been released from both DPP and parenting duties, Pars came by for a few hours of conditioning and to deliver the occasional gift from Canna's stores, potions and salves to numb my pain and heal abrasions. Most worked as they were intended, more or less, and Canna assured me that she was sharing the results of our trial and error with the Roulette research team in case anyone could discern a pattern. If they did, no one mentioned it to me, and so I continued to brace myself and hope for the best every time a new bottle emerged from Pars's pack.

On Tuesday, my sixth straight day with Hakk, the old sorcerer had me lead Jimbo to a tethering post in the training ring after a few warmup laps, then secured her halter and told me to wait. When he returned from the barn, a massive coil of black filament barely thicker than fishing line floated along in front of him, and he dropped the pile at Jimbo's feet with a muttered word to break the spell. The horse stamped and nickered, and he rumbled soothingly as he pulled the end of the line from the coil and knotted it through steel rings in her halter. Another whispered spell unwound the bundle and spread it in neat waves across the training ring, and Hakk began tying the free end to a metal post in the middle of the space.

He'd put us on a long line before, but even eyeballing the one on the ground, I estimated it was at least twice the length of a football field. "Uh…Hakk?"

"Mm?" he asked, not looking up from his work.

"What's this?"

He gave the knot a final test tug, then stepped back and dusted off his hands. "This is for your first flight."

"Whoa, now, hang on, I'm not sure about—"

"You'll never learn to ride her properly if you don't get her off the ground," he interrupted, rejoining us. "And Jimbo knows what's going on, don't you, girl?"

A bit of sugar from his pocket ensured the horse was in a fine mood.

"You're decent in the saddle, all things considered," Hakk continued, rubbing Jimbo's nose as I fought the urge to unclip my harness and bolt. "I think you're ready to go up—and if I weren't confident, I wouldn't suggest it," he added before I could protest. "Jimbo's not going to do barrel rolls. I just want you to get the feel for flight and start learning the commands that'll take her up and down. Three-dimensional riding is *slightly* more complicated than the usual version, but you seem trainable."

"But…but I don't—"

"Trust your horse," he said, then quickly untethered her from her mooring post, removed her silver collar, and clicked his tongue.

Jimbo knew *exactly* what that sequence of events meant. I barely had time to tighten my grip before she took three running steps, spread her wings, and jumped.

That first flight was far from my proudest moment. Having left my stomach somewhere in the dirt, I screamed and clung to the poor horse, who ignored my antics as she continued to climb. While I managed not to throw up my breakfast, I couldn't bring myself to look down until Jimbo reached her apparent cruising altitude and flew in lazy circles around the training ring. Hakk and Fell looked like toys below me, and the fact that there was still slack in the line warned me that the situation could worsen.

"What do I do?" I yelled, one hand on the reins and the other buried deep in Jimbo's mane.

Hakk made a twirling motion with one finger, then shaded his eyes and watched while Jimbo continued her flight.

After ten minutes of trying to bond with the horse on a molecular level, I released my death grip ever so slightly and started to consider my steering options. To my surprise, Jimbo reacted to the pressure of my knees and the pull of the reins, and with some trial and error, plus a fair deal of pleading, I managed to get her back on the ground. Trembling, I started to dismount, but Hakk caught me before I could swing my leg out of the saddle. "Oh, no, you don't," he said, then made me reposition myself and sent Jimbo back into the air.

Hakk kept me going up and down until we broke for lunch. By then, I'd started to regain a modicum of the confidence I felt with conventional riding, and Fell reassured me that I was doing fine as I fumbled open my chips and tried not to spill them. At least Jimbo seemed to be having fun. Hakk had replaced her grounding collar while we ate, and she kept pointedly snorting beside her water trough as if asking us what the holdup was.

As soon as we resumed, Hakk had me saddle up and clip in again. "More flying?" I asked.

"Of course. Question for you."

"Shoot."

He patted the horse's neck to still her. "When you're up there, what are you most afraid of?"

I chuckled weakly. "Uh…falling off? I think that's a legitimate concern."

"Oh, sure. And that's why you harness up before you ride," he said, checking the carabiner connecting my bungee umbilicus to the saddle. "What we're going to focus on for the rest of the day is getting you past this fear. I won't be able to work with you effectively until you deal with this."

"Um, okay…so, more laps around the ring?"

"Not exactly. You're going to learn to trust your equipment."

That statement set my mental alarm bells jangling, but I tried not to panic. "What do you mean?"

"Well," said Hakk, "you're going to take Jimbo up, and when she's comfortable, just roll out of the saddle."

"I'm sorry, *what*?"

"The cord will catch you," he continued. "You need to understand that. But you're going to fear this until you experience it, so let's get it over with."

Before I could suggest a counter-proposal that didn't involve me dangling from the horse like a yo-yo, Hakk slipped off Jimbo's collar, and she took to the sky.

Five minutes later, as I held on to the horse, Hakk yelled, "Roll out, Annie! Trust the gear!"

I looked down and shook my head.

"If you don't do it willingly, I have my ways."

"It's all right!" Fell called from her bench. "I can catch you!"

As we circled, I wondered if I *really* knew her well enough to entrust her with my life. Would Hakk catch me if the line broke? Would they try to rescue me together and, say, get their spells entangled? What would happen if they crossed the streams?

I hadn't signed up for this. I was just a PI-turned-barista, not a stuntwoman. Hell, I didn't even like roller coasters.

What the hell was I *doing*? Why was I—

In that moment, as my thoughts spiraled toward terror and visualizations of pulverizing myself on impact, I remembered the blood all over Wylan's trashed apartment. The broken antler kicked against the wall. The handprint by the door, evidence of his attempt to escape.

Not even his own brother would come to his rescue. I was his last hope. And if that meant throwing myself off a perfectly good horse…

I took a deep breath, gave Jimbo a last pat, then pulled my right leg over the saddle, held on for a second as she banked, and let myself fall.

Speaking from experience, you reevaluate all your life choices when you're dangling from a flying horse, bobbing at the end of a bungee cord and hoping to avoid both the hooves above you and the ground below. It's not the sort of situation I'd recommend.

After a moment, once my internal screaming subsided to a terrified whimper, I tried to assess my predicament. Physically, it felt a bit like those swing rides at the amusement park, the ones in which you end up spinning in a circle with your dangling legs at an angle to the ground. Hakk seemed to be yelling something below me, but I was too preoccupied to pay attention until Jimbo started to descend.

"Get your feet under you!" he shouted. "Try to land upright!"

Clinging to the cloth-covered portion of the cord, I positioned my legs like I'd seen skydivers do on TV, hoping I wouldn't be swept into Jimbo's path as she touched down. Suddenly, the ground was rising up to meet us, and I felt the shock through my legs as my feet hit the dirt. I leaned to the left, trying to simultaneously run from the horse and avoid her left wing before her hooves pounded down, then sprinted along on my tether while she executed a graceful landing. As she stopped, I grabbed the saddle and held on to steady myself, then decided to hell with it all and released my grip, when I promptly sank into a puddle at her feet.

"Not bad," said Hakk, strolling over to meet us. He pulled a sugar cube from his pocket and rubbed Jimbo's nose as she took the treat, then glanced down at me and asked, "You going to sit there all day?"

"Just…give me a minute," I muttered.

"Eh, you're fine," he said, and pulled me off the ground. With a check of my harness, he ordered, "Saddle up, kid. Let's try that again."

By the end of the week, after too many fake midair falls and a spectacularly twisted ankle, I had sufficiently satisfied Hakk with my aerial performance to progress to the next step. When we arrived Friday morning, he had already set up archery targets in the training ring. "Let's see what you can do with a bow," he said as soon as I slammed the van door. "How's your shooting, would you say?"

I grimaced. "Longbow is meh. I'm a lot better with a pistol."

"Well, then, at least we know where to begin," he said, and ordered me out to the ring.

I spent the morning shooting a loaner bow from Hakk's gear—a little big for me, I thought, but I knew better than to complain. After lunch, Hakk put me atop Jimbo for a few more hours of archery. Shooting at static targets on horseback was challenge enough, but soon, Hakk muttered at the targets until they began to drift around the ring, running from me.

"What the hell?" I demanded, lowering the bow before I could waste an arrow on a target that darted out of my reach.

"You've got a horse, kid," he said, leaning on the fence with a smirk. "Use her."

After hours of mediocre shooting, I wasn't heartbroken when Pars had to beg off that night. But as soon as I got out of the shower, I heard a knock on the door and threw on a bathrobe to investigate.

"Hi," said Fell, who'd slipped into leggings and flats instead of jeans and boots by then. She gave me a quick inspection—to be frank, the hot shower hadn't done anything to make me less red. "You can't take a painkiller until later, correct?"

"That's my healer's advice," I replied. "Why?"

In response, she held up a tube I recognized from the drug stores of home. "This feels warm on contact, then cools. Good for—"

"Muscle aches," I finished. "Hey, thanks. Where's you get it?"

"It's Keef's, actually. She rows for her school, and they get this from friends of friends with connections to the outside. My class did, too. Practically tradition," she added with a faint grin. "Anyway, massages are a part of team bonding. Since it's just us girls…" she said with an exaggerated look around my empty room.

Fell waited while I threw on a sports bra and pajama pants, and then she directed me to lie facedown on my bed. When she pushed my wet hair aside, I heard a sharp intake of breath and guessed the cause. "It's healing nicely," I said. "The scars are starting to fade."

"Is this from…"

"Yeah."

"I did that to you?" she asked, aghast.

"You didn't do anything. I was blistered, I carried you, and the blisters broke. Really, it's getting better."

"I am *so* sorry."

I turned enough to see her sitting beside me, a stricken look on her face. "You didn't ask to be abducted, and I did what was necessary to get us both out of there. The scars don't even hurt."

"But—"

"It's okay, Fell." Giving the tube in her hands a pointed glance, I added, "You know what would *really* make it feel better?"

Soon, I found myself sprawled out and groaning as she worked the contraband cream into my aching back and arms. "You're all knots," she said, digging her strong fingers into my flesh. "And you're bruised in some odd places."

"You try falling off Jimbo," I mumbled into my pillow.

"Oh, no, I'm not criticizing," she soothed. "I just feel bad that you're hurting."

"This is helping."

She grunted. "Temporarily." Pausing to squirt more cream into her hand, she said, "You're doing well, you know. Maybe you don't feel like it right now, but you've come quite a long way in a week."

"I can't reliably hit the broad side of a barn," I groused. "If my Huntsman skills are meant to be the thing that saves Wylan, then he's doomed."

"Is that what Lord ti'Dana told you?"

"He keeps hinting. Jerk won't give me a straight answer."

Fell laughed to herself and resumed the massage. "That's what farseers are like, or so I hear. I suspect his silence isn't personal."

"*Everything* about this is personal."

Her hands stilled again. "I'm sorry, that was insensitive—"

"You didn't mean anything by it," I replied, rolling over. "I'm not upset with *you*, of all people, I just…"

We regarded each other in awkward silence for a moment, and then Fell pulled me into a sitting position and began to knead my left arm. "If they'd taken Camun," she said softly, "I don't know what I'd do."

"I bet you'd do whatever you could. It's kind of amazing what you find yourself willing to attempt when someone you care about is in trouble."

She focused on her work. "When the Hunter took me, Camun didn't do anything."

"He tried to be helpful when I interviewed him," I countered, though I heard how lame that sounded. "He said he understood why your mother was keeping the investigation under wraps and that his father agreed with her decision, but he told me that he'd never forgive them if you died. It was pretty clear to me that he loves you," I continued, wincing as she found a bruise in my bicep, then joked, “Not like he lasted long on my list of suspects.”

“I love him, too,” she said, “but…”

I hesitated. “Are you, uh…rethinking the wedding?”

“Not yet. *He* probably is—he’s never been so distant with me as he has been since I came back from the lodge. Guess I’m damaged goods now. But…you know.” She sat back and squeezed out more cream, and when she spoke again, her voice was almost too low to hear. “Maybe he loves me, but he didn’t fight for me. He didn’t tell our parents to put their pride aside and start a public search, did he? He may not have liked their plan, but he *accepted* it,” she said, the word sharp and bitter. “Didn’t make a scene. And that…that’s something I’m dealing with.”

When she met my gaze, I saw the hurt in her brown eyes.

“You owed me nothing,” Fell said. “You didn’t know me. But you almost killed yourself to bring me home. And when the person who claims to love me more than life merely sat back and waited for someone else to fix the problem…”

“I mean, he *is* an accountant,” I offered.

She laughed, though the sound carried overtones of a sob. “I know, and I’m not expecting heroics, but…*something* would have been nice. And now you’re working yourself to exhaustion every day on a farseer’s suggestion that it might be the trick to saving…uh…”

“Wylan,” I muttered.

“I know his name,” she said testily. “Wylan’s obviously more than a friend to you, but I wasn’t sure what to call him.”

“Oh,” I said, mollified. “Good question. And I suppose we’re friends.”

She finished my left arm in silence, then switched places with me and started on the right. “I like to think that if I were in your position and Camun had been taken, I’d be doing what you are,” she said. “Don’t know how true that is, but it's a nice thought."

"I just wish I could *get* to Wylan," I mumbled. "If Lord ti'Dana's wrong and my shitty archery isn't the key to saving him…"

Fell gripped my hand until I met her stare. "You're trying. Even if you fail, you made the effort."

She was doing her best to reassure me, and I bit back the retort aching to spring free:

If I fail, who's to say the Hunt won't kill him?

I'd like to say that I was a champion archer by the end of the weekend, but that would be a dirty lie. Sure, I was hitting the targets with a bit more regularity, and Hakk was even talking about upping the difficulty and making me shoot from the air, but I managed only two bullseyes all day on Sunday, and both of those were attributable to dumb luck.

Fell insisted that she saw improvement, but perhaps sensing that I didn't buy it, she was nice enough not to complain when I tuned my van's radio to the one Pactlands station that played a block of human imports every Sunday evening. True, the DJ wouldn't know the top forty if the list were dropped on his desk, but the weird mix of eighties hair metal, nineties rap, aughts pop country, and the odd song in Korean helped with the homesickness.

When we returned to the mansion, we headed for the kitchen and walked in on an impromptu decorating contest. Maya and her substitute minions having made far too many sugar cookies, they'd whipped up bowls of royal icing and conscripted Rose, Scel, and Ranarma to serve as a theme selection committee and judges. To my surprise, Keef had joined them—a dark horse contestant, to be sure, but Maya was helping her with her piping, and judging by the colorful streaks on Keef's chin and fingers, she was having a fine time.

Fell took one look at the scene and laughed. "Mother let you out of the room, did she?" she asked her sister.

"I'm supposedly in the library," Keef replied, carefully coloring in a palm tree with a plastic bag of green icing. "Don't tell her, and you can have cookies."

"Join the judges' table," Rose offered, patting the empty stool beside her. "We eat the losers. Annie, hungry?"

"Shower first, I think," I told her, and headed upstairs while Fell munched a polka dotted cookie.

After half an hour under the spray, I dried off and threw on pajamas and a bathrobe, deciding I could at least make an appearance at the unending house party before crashing for the night. But as I padded toward the staircase, I glanced out a window and noticed lights in a part of the house I'd yet to visit—a greenhouse, I thought, considering the sheer quantity of glass. Curious, I wound through the hallways until I reached the door into the mansion's appendage, then stuck my head inside for a peek.

Warm and almost as humid as the bathroom I'd just steamed up, Diriem's greenhouse was at least a couple thousand square feet, maybe more. One corner near the mansion side was piled high with bags of imported potting soil and fertilizer—a necessity, considering the trees growing within. Though October had taken most of their leaves, the trees were a good fifteen feet tall, giants by Pactlands standards. Marching in neat rows down the greenhouse were raised troughs of rich soil, some empty, others covered with healthy vegetation. I recognized the nearest planter as an herb garden, while the one beside it bore a small placard labeling its contents as potatoes. The greenhouse *had* to be built atop a connection to the outside world—there was no way that it could produce plants like that without serious help in the Pactlands.

Hearing voices, I peered into the shadows at the far end of the building and found Diriem chatting with Yven.

Well, "chatting" was, perhaps, an exaggeration. Yven seemed to be lecturing, and I recognized a few of the flowers around him as his prized orchid collection.

Diriem had had Yven's entire garden brought over, I realized, spotting the wall trellis on which he grew his vanilla orchid. And like a fool, he'd stuck around long enough for Yven to begin the horticultural tour.

As I slipped out, Rose walked past, glanced into the greenhouse, and winked at me. "They're still in there?" she whispered.

"How long's it been?"

"Oh, about two hours." Quietly closing the door, she said, "Yven was worried about his babies, so Pop offered him the greenhouse this afternoon. You'd think he offered Yven his pick of the garage," she added, smiling indulgently as she shook her head.

"I didn't know Lord ti'Dana was into plants," I told her.

Rose snickered. "He's not. The garden is Ranarma's project. But *Yven* loves his flowers, and Pop wants us to move in, so he's being a good sport."

"You think so?" I asked, trying not to disclose anything Diriem had said to me in confidence.

She nodded. "Sometimes, if you know how to look at him, Pop's transparent." With a peek through the window in the door, she added, "Doesn't look like Yven has thrown up yet. I'd say this is progress." Turning to me, she said, "Come judge cookies with us. Or run interference in case Lady ti'Mal starts snooping, either one. You could use a break, Annie." When I hesitated, she wrapped her arm around mine and started tugging me down the corridor. "At least eat your dinner around other people. It's no sin to stop for a meal."

Rose had a point, and twenty minutes with the cookie brigade was good for my mental health, but still, guilt nagged me with every bite I swallowed.

Wylan was out there somewhere. Was he eating?

Sleeping? Bleeding?

And there I sat in my pajamas, stuffing my face with leftover porkchops while even Fell took a turn with a piping bag.

My dinner settled in my stomach like a rock, and I begged off and went to bed before I could scream.

CHAPTER 10

I let Fell drive us home from Hakk's place the following Friday night while I nursed a sore shoulder. A target had flown too close to Jimbo, who'd shied in surprise and thrown me, and I'd awkwardly grabbed for my tether as I plummeted, catching myself but almost wrenching my arm from its socket. Hakk had yelled at me when Jimbo brought us down, telling me I was going to hurt myself if I couldn't trust my equipment, but he'd stopped my lesson early and sat me down with an ice pack. Though the old man could be gruff, he wouldn't allow us to leave that afternoon until he was sure I didn't need to see a healer.

I kicked myself as Fell navigated us toward the portal. My shooting had improved with a week of practice, and I'd been doing reasonably well until the incident. Now, instead of another few hours with Jimbo, I was riding back to the mansion with Hakk's chastisement echoing in my head.

"You still have a healing potion, don't you?" Fell asked. "That should help the swelling. You'll be back to normal by morning."

"Not soon enough," I muttered.

She sighed. "Annie, you're allowed to rest. You *should* rest. Any decent trainer will tell you that. Hell," she said, pulling into the portal lane for Beukal, "when I was in school, just before one of our meets, our captain thought we needed another few sessions on the water to ensure we had our rhythm. She had us sneak to the boathouse well before dawn on our off days. That was fine the first two times, but we were out too long on the third morning, and our coach caught us. Yelled at us for ten minutes and swore that if we pulled a stupid stunt like that again, she'd withdraw us from competition."

While I knew Fell was attempting to cheer me up, I bristled at having my current predicament compared to a crew meet, though I tried not to let on. "It's been almost three weeks," I said as we passed through the hole in space and headed into the outbound queue for Viratta. "And there's no telling when the Hunt will ride again. I need every bit of practice I can get."

"You're doing your best."

"And that might not be enough," I said, then leaned against the window and listened to the radio for the remainder of the trip.

That night, after Pars released me for the weekend—he had to spend a *little* time with his family, after all—I waited until the late news ended, then looked up the television station's phone number and quickly dialed. The receptionist who answered sounded weary, but she put me through when I asked for Moonless Night's extension, and I crossed my fingers.

To my surprise, he answered. "Channel One News, this is Moonless Night," rumbled the familiar bass voice. If I wasn't mistaken, his Pactish bore a slight Trollish accent—whatever else could be said for him, he was a *solid* actor.

"It's Annie," I said, and hastily added, "Please don't hang up."

Morial paused, then asked in a carefully guarded tone, "What can I do for you?"

"I'd like to talk about, uh…our mutual friend."

True, he'd never so much as spoken to Wylan, but I didn't have a better cover story on short notice.

"Let me call you back," he said. "This is your number?"

"Yeah."

"Five minutes," was his only reply before the line was cut.

I took my evening potion and sat back on my bed, putting my thoughts in order as I waited for his call. Finally, just as I'd begun to worry that he'd blown me off, my phone rang.

"The station's phone calls are recorded," said Morial after my hello. "Security and liability issues."

"Is this your cell?"

"Exactly. What do you want?"

"I've been working my ass off since you walked out," I told him. "Learned to ride a freaking flying horse, and—"

"*What?*"

"Yeah, there's a guy out in Gerentrent who raises them for Pact use. Lord ti'Dana convinced him to teach me. So I've learned to ride, and he's had me doing mounted archery for the last week, and…" I forced myself to breathe, hearing my words speed up. "Just give me another chance, *please*," I begged. "I can do this, and I'm willing to put in the work, but I need your help."

"Annie—"

"They've had Wylan for almost three weeks. Rose says he's not dead yet, but—"

"*Annie.*"

"Please? One more chance to prove myself, that's all I'm asking."

I held my breath for a long moment, and then I caught Morial's soft exhalation. "Gerentrent, you said?"

"It's a ranch."

"Mm. Will you be there tomorrow?"

"All day."

"Send me the address. I'll see you around ten," he said, then hung up.

Fell and I arrived at Hakk's bright and early Saturday morning, and with Diriem's blessing, I filled him in about

Morial. "I don't know what he's going to look like when he gets here," I finished, "but if you could play dumb, that would be ideal."

Though Hakk muttered about DOI shenanigans, he agreed, and he said little when Morial's oversized SUV rumbled up the gravel drive. Morial emerged in his Moonless Night guise, nodded to Hakk and Fell, then turned to me and cocked his head. "Well? Let's see what you can do."

With Hakk supervising, I swung into Jimbo's saddle and connected the emergency cord, and Hakk removed her grounding collar as he set the targets into motion. I nudged Jimbo into the air, waited until she settled into lazy circles, then reached for the quiver hanging by my leg and nocked an arrow. The first shot wasn't a bullseye, but I hit the second ring—not prize-winning shooting but respectable. I continued flying around the targets until I emptied my quiver, and to my relief, all the arrows but one had at least struck *something* besides empty air.

I coaxed Jimbo down, and as Hakk collared her again, I dismounted and approached Morial, whose expression was impossible for me to read. "Not bad, huh?" I said, trying to discern meaning from his folded arms. "I know I've got a ways to go to keep up with the Hunt, but you saw what I could do two weeks ago, and—"

"She's been out here every day, *all* day," Fell cut in. "And she conditions with an agent most nights. Annie's doing everything she can."

"Kid's made great progress," Hakk offered, dusting off his hands. "Better than I'd imagined, actually."

I smiled at the unexpected praise, then looked up at Morial. "What do you think?"

"I'll admit that I hadn't expected to see you atop one of those," he said, nodding to Jimbo, who'd turned her attention to a patch of grass. "She seems capable of matching the Hunt's mounts."

My smile widened.

"But your shooting is still problematic," he continued. "I appreciate that you've been diligent in your training, but the skills you would need to acquire would be the result of years of dedicated work, *if* you could ever match a Huntsman's ability. Your efforts are commendable, Annie," he said as my face fell, "but yours is a lost cause. I'm sorry."

"If you would work with me again—"

He held up a hand to silence me. "I can't bring you to competence quickly enough. Neither can he," he said, pointing to Hakk, "though his work with you has been excellent. I don't mean any of this as an insult."

"None taken," Hakk murmured, though Fell's mouth had tightened to a thin line.

"I'm sorry," Morial repeated, and turned to go.

"What if the Hunt kills him?" I blurted.

He stopped for only a moment. "He made his choice when he defied the Hunter. I dare say he would prefer that you not commit suicide on his behalf," he said, then walked off without another word.

Once we heard the SUV pull away, Hakk patted my shoulder. "Want to take an early lunch, kid?"

"Sure," I mumbled, and shuffled to the barn.

Hakk worked me for a few hours after Morial's rejection, but no one's heart was in it that day, and he suggested that I go home and rest around three. As I turned onto the road, Fell, who'd been pensive all afternoon, cleared her throat. "I have an idea."

"Unless I wake up an Olympian, I don't think Morial's going to be impressed," I replied.

"A what?"

I frowned. "An Olympi…oh, right. Uh, unless I discover massive talent with a bow overnight," I amended, recalling my audience.

Fell waited until we'd rounded a bend in the road, then

said, "Pull over."

I did as she asked and waited while she raked her teeth over her lower lip. Finally, she said, "You need better archery skills, yes? Better aim, maybe a bit quicker on the draw."

"Yeah…"

"There's this necklace at the museum."

"Which one? The Museum of Fine Art?"

She nodded. "We've got a collection of magical jewelry. It's all stored in a back gallery, as much for security as anything else. Pieces are selected for their artistic merit and craftsmanship as well as their power, see? We've got some *exquisite* rings from the early years after the Pact, really fine silver work…anyway," she said, catching herself before she slipped into docent mode, "there's a necklace I remember. Gold, very delicate, about a thousand years old. I *know* it came out of one of the southern Halls, but I can't recall which one offhand. Supposedly—and the records back this up—it gives the wearer almost preternatural marksmanship."

"I can't imagine why it's in a secure gallery," I joked.

"Oh, *quite* secure. But what I'm thinking is…you know, why don't we borrow it?"

A burst of incredulous laughter escaped me before I could swallow it back. "I'm sorry, you want to *borrow* a thousand-year-old necklace for me? From a *museum*? How the hell could I borrow an artifact like that?"

But Fell merely smirked. "Leave that to me. Are you willing to try it? I know you've had difficulty with magical jewelry…"

"I've been shooting arrows from a flying horse all week," I pointed out. "Sure, I'd try it. Can't hurt, right?"

"Except your kidneys, your skin…"

"I'm in."

"Good." Nodding to the road, she said, "Let's get back to the mansion. I need to make a call."

Fell told me to meet her in the garage at seven and tell no one what we were up to, and I played along. I threw on a dark green button-up over leggings, casual enough to pass as loungewear but suitable for leaving the house, and hung out in my room after I dried my hair. As the time approached, however, I began to have doubts about the wisdom of Fell's plan. Sure, my scent neutralizer was still working—the full-body rash made that *quite* clear—and I probably smelled of nothing more notable than lavender shampoo. But the only place I'd been outside the mansion in the last three weeks was Hakk's ranch, and now Fell was leading me on a trip back to the capital.

A wiser woman would have gone to Diriem and asked about the probability of finding trouble in Beukal. I hadn't heard of death and destruction in the city of late, but that didn't mean that it was safe for me to be waltzing around the museum complex.

But the part of me that counseled caution also warned that Diriem might put the kibosh on our little excursion if he learned of it…assuming he didn't know already and would be waiting to take my van keys.

Still, if I wasn't going to seek advice from the guy on the premises who could literally see the future, my gut told me I needed to do *something* in the way of taking precautions. Dragging a bow along for the trip seemed like a terrible idea…

And then I thought of the rest of the DOL loaner weapons.

Scel had schlepped the lot into the gym for safekeeping, minus the archery gear I was storing at Hakk's. I sneaked from my room and hurried over to dig through the trio of bags, and I quickly hit paydirt. Nestled within one were the guns—mostly rifles and a shotgun, but packed in matching padded cases were a pair of 9mm pistols and another pair of .45s.

Kabno *was* generous with her toys, I mused, pawing through the stash until I found a beautiful double holster at the bottom of the gun bag. Made of supple black leather, it buckled around my hips and slung low, and a leather leg tie kept the holsters from shifting. Putting it on, I felt like I was in desperate need of a cowboy hat and an old-timey saloon, but I shoved the thought aside, loaded the 9mms, and slid them into place. The pistols were semiautomatics, not the sort of Old West revolvers that my borrowed gear deserved, but I'd sacrifice historical authenticity for a larger magazine.

Duly equipped, I sneaked downstairs and out to the garage to wait. Fell arrived right on time—and alone, fortunately. As she slipped out the door in a black turtleneck and dark trousers, I asked, only half in jest, "We're not going to break into the museum, are we?"

"Of course not," she replied, opening the passenger door of my van.

"Oh, good."

"I do have lock credentials, you know."

Shooting her a look of exasperation, I said, "Before I start this engine, are we planning to commit a crime? Yes or no?"

"*Relax.*" Fell chuckled and adjusted her seatbelt. "I've asked my boss to meet us there tonight. Let me explain the situation—I think we can convince him."

I'd met Fell's boss only once: Katoun ti'Lir, the Assistant Director of Education, tall, dark-haired, and handsome in the elven sense. He had a *definite* thing for pretty blondes like Fell, and he'd more than hinted to her that Camun wasn't a good match, but when I'd seen him, he'd been very much in a relationship.

"Does Katoun even have the authority to loan out museum pieces?"

When Fell smiled at me, her expression seemed more predatory than reassuring. "Do you know who the single largest donor to the museum is?"

"No…"

"Lord ti'Lir. So if his darling boy does something silly, I

suspect the right people could be persuaded to look the other way. Let's get going. And by the way," she asked as I began backing out, "why are you carrying *guns*?"

"Because it's dark, and the bow seemed conspicuous."

She snorted. "Not going to lie, you look kind of like a deranged cowboy."

"Whatever, pardner."

To my surprise, she giggled. "Say that again. *Pardner*."

I rolled my eyes but obliged, doing so in my best drawl. Fell clapped, and I glanced her way as the garage door opened. "You like Westerns or something?"

"Don't tell my parents, but I used to check them out of the school library when I was your age. Subtitled, naturally, but…well, they were my guilty pleasure for a while. We don't have any deserts here."

She sounded almost melancholy.

"Have you seen a real one? A desert?" she asked.

I pulled onto the driveway and headed for the road with the strange blue lighting running ahead of the van to guide us. "Yeah. When I was eight, my parents took me out to the Grand Canyon over summer vacation. I was pretty bored—it's a big hole in the ground, and there were way too many mule droppings for my taste—but in retrospect, it's pretty phenomenal. Stark but stunning. Anyway, after that, they pushed on for Death Valley. Wanted me to be able to say I'd seen it."

"Death Valley?"

"Big desert national park. Lowest point in the country, and since there's so little light pollution, the night sky is *fantastic*." I sighed and propped my elbow on the door. "If I ever get out of here, maybe I'll take another trip west. Now that I can appreciate it, I mean."

"I've never been out of the Pactlands," Fell murmured. "Think I'd like to see a desert."

"Maybe someday, eh?" I said.

"Yeah," she replied, and softly exhaled. "Maybe someday."

The museum complex was a place I'd have liked to explore, had I not been otherwise preoccupied. Located just north of the downtown district, it struck me as vaguely collegiate without being overly pretentious—lots of marble and tall windows, sure, but also a grassy quad in the middle of the four museums with an outdoor stage and plenty of rest areas. There was even a little playground for families with small children unenthused about furthering their education.

Fell kicked herself as we drove up the quiet street toward the complex. "My employee parking pass is back in my car."

I tried to recall where I'd parked on my previous visit. "There are a few street spots, right?"

"Sure, but the big visitor lot behind the Museum of Natural Science should be open," said Fell. "Safer place to leave the van, anyway."

Frankly, if someone was desperate enough to hotwire my beater van, I might have just stepped back and given them my blessing, but I followed Fell's directions and parked beneath a security light. Thoroughly disoriented as to where we were meant to be going, I stuck close to her as she set off for the side of the long building. Pink marble wouldn't have been my aesthetic choice, especially not in the quantity sufficient to cover the massive edifice, but what did I know?

"Where are we?" I asked, keeping my voice low.

Fell pointed to the cotton-candy-colored structure blocking us from the quadrangle. "Museum of Natural Science. Unfortunately, the Museum of Fine Art is on the other side of the complex, so we've got a walk ahead of us."

As we finally reached the footpath into the darkened quad, she pointed to the white marble building to our left. "Museum of History. Fine Art is straight across," she said—I recognized the green marble from my previous trip—"and the other one is the Museum of the History of

Magic."

I'd noticed that one before, designed in slate-blue marble with silvery veining that I wasn't entirely certain occurred naturally. "Sounds interesting."

"Eh." She flapped one hand dismissively. "We took enough field trips there during school that it lost whatever luster it held for me. *So* many writing assignments. But you might like it," she added. "A quick tour, at least. I, uh…I suppose you didn't have to study magical history, did you?"

"I mean, seeing as magic doesn't actually exist…"

She snorted. "Humans."

"What? Everyone who can use magic *left*."

"Fair, I guess," she allowed. "Anyway, don't let me dissuade you. Take a peek in there someday. And Natural Science and History are entertaining if you've got a weekend to kill."

I grinned. "But Fine Art…"

"Well, obviously, I think you should make multiple trips to Fine Art to truly appreciate our offerings," she said, smirking back at me. "But I might be slightly biased."

At the front of Natural Science, the footpath joined a ring around the edge of the quadrangle, while other paths cut straight across. I started to walk through the middle so as not to waste time, but Fell pulled me back. "It's kind of dark in there," she said. "Mind if we stick to the lights?"

I glanced at her, poised to point out that I was strapped like a gunslinger heading for a high-noon shootout, but then I caught the flicker of apprehension in her eyes as she considered the shadows of the covered pavilions between us and our destination. "Sure, no problem," I said, and patted her arm. "You know where we're going."

"I'm sorry, I just—"

"It's okay, Fell."

"It's not," she muttered, "but thank you."

We headed left toward the Museum of History. "Not my favorite of the four," she confessed, "but there's a wing devoted to cultural studies. They've brought in items from outside over the last centuries, and that's always a popular spot…" She paused then, as if recalling where I'd come from, and mumbled, "Probably nothing new to you. Um…"

"Believe me, there's been more than enough novelty in my life over the last year. Tell you what," I said, "let's you and me break out of here. Steal some masking jewelry, bribe our way through the portal, and I'll take you to the museums around Richmond. *Ooh*, or we could do the Smithsonian…"

"The which?"

"Bunch of museums up in D.C. It's a drivable trip. Art, history, science…we'd need a few days to see all the good stuff, and I'd need masking jewelry that didn't screw up my scalp, but we could make a long weekend of it."

Fell smiled as we passed a lamppost. "A perfect plan but for a few insignificant hitches."

"What, parking in D.C.? It's no fun, but we'll figure it out."

She laughed and seemed to relax, and we walked in front of the history museum in comfortable silence. Other than the occasional swish of a passing car on the streets ringing the complex, the night was quiet…and aside from the bite in the air, it hardly felt autumnal. I missed the crunch of dead leaves under my feet and the skeletal fingers of winter-bare trees overhead, the proliferation of pumpkins and the invitations from friends to find an orchard, any orchard, and pick enough apples to feed a family of ten. I missed coffeeshops that had the insane urge to add pumpkin spice to every item on the menu.

I missed the usual texts and calls I got from my mom at that time of year, double-checking birthday present suggestions and asking about what sort of cake I wanted. I might celebrate with my friends, but my parents always had me over for dinner at the next convenient weekend, and they insisted on topping whatever dessert I chose with the appropriate number of candles.

At least they wouldn't have to buy thirty that year.

God, I missed them.

"Once you get a free day again," said Fell, pulling me from my spiraling funk as we neared the Museum of Fine Art, "let me give you a tour. I know where the good pieces are that the public tours generally miss…"

Her voice faded, and we stopped in our tracks as a shape stepped out of the shadows about twenty feet up ahead. Another pedestrian on the path around the quad wouldn't have given me cause for alarm, but the figure in the yellow glow of the streetlight was broad and muscular, sporting an off-white tunic belted over dark leather leggings. That he was a Huntsman was made obvious by the full rack of antlers rising above his long red hair, but that wasn't what made me gasp.

I *recognized* him.

Cralf. The one who'd grabbed Fell in the park, whose scent Wylan had identified in the scraps left behind. He was bigger than Wylan, and what little I'd seen of him at the lodge didn't give me the warm fuzzies.

And judging by his sudden look of interest, he recognized Fell.

She stood two paces in front of me, frozen like a deer on the freeway, and I knew I had to act.

I stepped in front of her and pulled my right-hand gun, sacrificing the left for better aim. "No closer," I barked.

I'd expected him to call my bluff—I had no idea how old Cralf was, but he'd surely faced opponents more intimidating than me. Instead, he stiffened in surprise, then took a step back. "Who the hell are *you*?" he demanded. "*What* are—"

"Get lost. Get out of here. Unless you'd like a few new perforations, that is."

Maybe, my inner optimist suggested, this would work. I'd thrown him off for a moment, and I'm sure my appearance had to confuse him. Even if the antlers hadn't given him pause, I still looked like I was on the verge of sun poisoning, and the security lights surely weren't flattering. If I could keep it together, maybe he'd back away long enough for us to…well, I didn't know what. Running for the museum door wouldn't save us since Huntsmen could teleport—he'd beat us there. But if he thought I might present an actual challenge, then perhaps we'd have enough time to call for help.

I could hear Fell's ragged breathing behind me and willed her not to have a panic attack.

"Who *are* you?" Cralf repeated. He took a deep sniff, then scowled, and I thanked whatever mad genius had come up with the scent neutralizer.

"I'm Annie, asshole, and that's all you need to know. Back. *Off.*"

Unfortunately, Cralf recovered his footing all too soon, and he chuckled at my threat. Pulling a long knife from the scabbard on his belt, he grinned at me and cocked his head. "You think I'm afraid of you, little girl? And your friend—oh, I remember *you*," he said, leering at Fell. "When I bring you back to Father, once we've had our fun, maybe he'll give me your pelt after we hunt you down. You'll look lovely spread across my bed, no matter what form—"

I felt a sudden burst of heat behind me, and then Cralf was flying off his feet, pushed through the air by a jet of bright white fire. He slammed into the front of the Museum of Fine Art with a sickening crack, then tumbled to the ground, still aflame, and didn't move.

Keeping my gun raised at that point felt like overkill. I peeked over my left shoulder to find Fell standing there, arms extended, hands locked together one atop the other and palms facing Cralf. Wide-eyed and hyperventilating, she began to shake, and I quickly holstered my weapon and turned around. "Holy *shit*," I whispered. "You can make concentrated fire? Lord ti'Dana's display wasn't that strong…"

"Pyromancer," she mumbled. "Trained. I swear I can control it…"

Given her current state, I wasn't entirely convinced, but I told her to stay put and jogged over to see what remained of Cralf. That he was dead was no great deduction—the stuff Fell had shot at him had left him blackened and curled on himself, but equally worrying were the deformity in the back of his skull and the fresh bloodstain on the green marble ten feet above him.

Fell's footsteps padded up the sidewalk, and I turned to find her standing a yards feet away, biting her lip. "Is he, um…"

There were many things I could have said in that moment. Despite the number of sorcerers and elves I'd met in the last year, I still had only fuzzy notions of what they were capable of when provoked, and *no one* had mentioned magical napalm. Fell was an ambulatory flamethrower. But from the way she hugged herself and her jaw quivered, I could only imagine what her previous encounters with Cralf had been like. I mean, the man had kidnapped her to be used as prey—her reaction didn't exactly surprise me.

"He's not going to hurt you," I murmured, hurrying to her side. When I hugged her, she gripped me like a life preserver and trembled. "It's okay," I soothed. "It's going to be okay. He threatened us, he pulled a weapon, and you reacted. It's all right, Fell."

Once I coaxed her into taking a few deep breaths to calm down, I released her and glanced at the smoldering corpse. "Hate to ask, but what should we do with the body? Get a bucket of water and call DOL?"

Before Fell could answer, the front door of the museum burst open, and a dark-haired figure in a formal robe ran out. Backlit as he was by the warm light within the building, I couldn't see the details of his face, but I recognized Katoun's voice when he yelled, "What the *fuck* is going on out here?"

"Abduction and murder averted," I replied. "She's unhurt."

"Fellora?" He peered at us, then scrambled back a few paces as he picked me out of the shadows. "Who the hell are—"

"Questions later. Could you get some water, please?"

But Katoun's preferred panic response seemed to be shouting. "I demand to know who you are and what you're doing!"

"First problem first," Fell muttered, then gestured at Cralf. The corpse vanished, but I barely had time to goggle before another set of gestures cleaned the marble wall and repaired a fresh crack.

"I…uh…" I stammered.

"Did I do something wrong?"

"You can…*disappear* people?" I managed.

"Oh. Um…well, technically, yes," she replied, "but it's incredibly difficult to do that to a living person, not to mention illegal. Dead things are another matter."

"Good to know."

She gripped my shoulder. "The grounds staff can fix the burned grass. Let's deal with Katoun…"

Her voice faded as an unassuming golf cart sped up the sidewalk, emerging from the pathway between the Museum of Fine Art and the Museum of the History of Magic. It parked by the front door of the art museum, and as the driver, a blond sorcerer in black clothing, gathered a bag, his passenger took the lead. I wasn't accustomed to seeing gnomes dressed like they were anticipating a fight, but that one, three feet tall and sporting an elaborately braided white beard, strolled up to us in his child-sized boots with a confident swagger.

"Good evening, ladies," he said in a voice too high-pitched to sound truly threatening—though I knew damn well that you underestimated gnomes at your peril. While they might have been the size of kindergarteners, they could lift several times their body weight and outrun trained human sprinters…and this one seemed to be carrying a small firearm on his hip.

"Uh…hi," I said for lack of a better idea.

Fell just swallowed hard.

"Saw the fire," he said with a nod to Fell. "Impressive. I'd been wondering why the director told us to be here."

"The director?" I echoed.

His hand went to the gun-free side of his belt and flashed a silver agency badge. "DOI."

"We've come to fix the security cameras," the sorcerer explained, shifting the bag on his shoulder. "It seems the ones in this portion of the museum complex are glitching tonight. Unfortunate, that," he deadpanned.

The gnome pointed to the small camera mounted twenty feet up on the side of the Museum of History. "And there's the first," he told his colleague. "Boost?"

The sorcerer handed a small computer to the gnome, then muttered until the diminutive agent was floating two stories above the ground.

"Have a nice evening," the sorcerer said as the gnome began the coverup. "And, uh…try not to kill anyone else tonight, eh?"

We mumbled promises and hurried for the steps up to the door of the art museum, where Katoun watched in shock. As we reached the top, Fell said, "Hi. We need to talk."

"You…you *incinerated* that man…" her boss stammered.

"It was justified," I snapped, and pushed him toward the lobby.

Once we were inside, I pulled the door closed and turned to inspect my companions. Fell still looked shell-shocked, while Katoun's complexion seemed stuck between green and chalky. Having passed the shouty phase of panic, he was instead staring at us as though we might blast him into atoms at any second.

"Okay," I said, my voice echoing around the vaulted

hall. "Let's all breathe before we do anything stupid. You okay, Fell?"

She shot me a glance of pure incredulity.

"Are you going to puke?" I clarified.

"Not just yet."

"Good. Katoun…uh, hi. I'm Annie," I continued, raising an empty hand. "We've met, but I was undercover, so—"

"Huh?" he interrupted.

"You showed me around last month. Namia, blonde sorcerer, new in town? I asked you out?"

His jaw dropped. "That…*what*…"

"I'm a private investigator, I was looking for leads on Fell's whereabouts, and I needed to get a read on you. Nothing personal," I said with a shrug.

"You're a…a Huntsman!"

"I'm a human with a bad potion reaction, but close," I muttered. "Also, the asshole out there is the guy who abducted Fell, and he was poised to do it again, so stop gawking at her like she murders puppies."

"But…" Katoun looked back and forth between us, his blue eyes wide and a little unfocused. "You…you could have called for DOL—"

"We'd have been history by the time anyone arrived," I protested. "He overpowered her once, yeah? Why would we risk letting that happen a second time?"

"But—"

"Just shut up, Katoun," said Fell. "I need a favor."

"You're a pyromancer!" he cried. "Why didn't you tell—"

"Because it's none of your business. I'm trained, it's managed—"

"Then what was that tonight?" He ran a hand through his hair and began to pace. "We can't allow known pyros in the galleries! Think of the damage if you lost control—"

"She had *great* control," I interjected. "Didn't singe a hair on my head."

He looked at me like I'd lost my mind. "*She burned a man alive!*"

"Technically, I think he was dead once he hit the wall. Marble's pretty unforgiving. Anyway," I said as his mouth flapped open, "since Diriem *fucking* ti'Dana sent a cleanup crew, maybe you could shut up for a minute and hear the lady out, hmm?"

Katoun's cheeks began to redden. "How dare you—"

"Believe me," said Fell, "if Lord ti'Dana's offended, I'm sure we'll hear about it in due time. For now, I need to borrow the Bowman Chain."

Her boss sputtered briefly, then spat, "*Borrow*? This isn't a library! What do you—"

The rest of his protestation turned into a squeal as Fell marched up and grabbed his robe in her fists, then yanked him close. "Look," she murmured, "Annie and her friend Wylan saved my life. Now the Hunt's taken Wylan. Annie needs that necklace to get him back. And I am *not* leaving without it."

"I…I can't…"

"I don't know what Lord ti'Dana saw happening tonight," she continued, her voice dangerously low. "Maybe he just saw me attack that Huntsman. Or maybe those two agents are going to need to come up here next and deal with the cameras *inside* the building. I don't know."

"Is that a threat?" he retorted, recovering a bit of his spine.

"No. But this is me telling you that Intelligence is aware of what's happening tonight, I'm a pyro, and I need that necklace. *Now*."

"If it helps," I offered, "Lord ti'Cren loaned me some pieces when I went after Fell, and I haven't destroyed any of them yet."

"You're talking about a priceless artifact—" he began.

Fell snorted. "Nonsense. If I recall, the museum paid about twenty thousand marks for its acquisition. Hardly *priceless.* But we're trying to save a life, and time is running out, so be a dear and fetch it, won't you?"

While Katoun clearly wasn't happy with the directive, the threat of DOI involvement seemed to do the trick, and he finally stalked off toward the other end of the entry hall. Fell and I hurried after and followed him through the galleries to a small room in a quiet corner, which was lined with glass cases full of carefully displayed rings, pendants, and bracelets—even a pair of tiaras. Lips tight with distaste, he typed a combination in the keypad on the wall, and one of the cases unlatched. Katoun then unlocked a small cupboard beneath another case and crouched down to pull out a blank sheet of thick paper the size of a large index card and a pen. He printed a vague note about the necklace having been temporarily removed for preservation, popped it in the case, then gingerly handed me the necklace.

"If you lose, break, so much as scratch this…" he warned.

"I'll guard it," I said, clasping it around my neck. The chain was as delicate as any piece of fine jewelry I'd ever worn, and it linked to the tips of the limbs of a tiny golden bow. Not feeling any sort of warning tingle of magic at work, I asked, "How do I use it?"

Katoun scanned the placard. "Allegedly, hold the bow between the finger and thumb of your dominant hand and say 'Kentsia.'"

"'Begin.' It's High Elvish," Fell offered. "Easy enough." With a nod to Katoun, she said, "Thank you. Perhaps you could keep this quiet until Annie's ready to return the necklace."

He grunted. "You realize you're fired, don't you?"

"Not the worst thing that's happened to me lately," she countered, and swept from the room.

"Sorry about this. You, uh…you really are a good tour guide," I told Katoun, and quickly followed her out.

I'd barely buckled up before Fell broke down.

Unsure what to say that wouldn't sound like stupid platitudes, I rubbed her back while she hunched over in the passenger seat and sobbed, and it took a solid five minutes before she was able to straighten and catch her breath again. She shivered beside me, and I grabbed an empty shopping bag from the back, just in case her distress decided to manifest as vomiting.

"He was going to hurt us," I reminded her. "And I was ready to shoot him. You did the right thing."

"I've never *killed* anyone…"

"He'd have killed you. Took you to the lodge, didn't he? Let you get locked out there in the barn?"

She closed her eyes and took a moment to collect herself, and I was afraid she was on the verge of being sick when she said, "He visited me out there. Every day. Said he was going to convince his father to let him play with me before the Hunt rode." She paused, her eyes squeezing tightly shut. "The Hunter came with him once, maybe to be certain that I was still alive. Cralf asked him again. His father said no—it would be too dangerous to put me back in my own form. I might be able to fight, then, see? Might cause problems. And Cralf, he…he insisted that I would be a good girl. That's what he said, 'a good girl.' I wanted to rip his face off…"

When her voice faded, I said, "Not the face. Leave that for last."

"Huh?"

"If you're going to rip something off, start with his fun bits. Play with your food, know what I mean?"

She giggled, though the sound was too unsteady to be true amusement.

"Let's go home," I said, and pulled out of the parking lot. "I think we could both use a drink."

As we drove toward the portals, Fell muttered, "What am I going to tell my parents?"

"You're going to say nothing for now and let Lord

ti'Dana handle it," I replied. "Yeah?"

"How am I to explain that I lost my job? 'Sorry,'" she minced, 'things got weird. Katoun watched me kill a man, and he decided I couldn't be trusted with paintings'?"

"That's not a problem for tonight, okay?"

"Okay," she mumbled. "Annie?"

"Yup?"

"I really do have it under control. I promise. It…it's not common in elves, you know, pyromancy. Not a wild talent that runs in my parents' Halls. But they did have me trained. I won't lose my temper and—"

I reached across the gap between our seats and gripped her hand, and Fell held on to me until we'd put Beukal behind us.

Obviously, we couldn't linger in the capital. That we'd seen a Huntsman on the street strongly suggested that they were still trying to follow the scents left around Wylan's trails, and I didn't want to be within range when the protection of that morning's scent neutralizing potion began to wane. But Fell was a mess, and nothing said we had to drive back to the mansion straight away.

Since gasoline wasn't an issue in the Pactlands, we cruised the backroads for hours, popping through random portals long enough to take a look at the settlements on the other side. We drove past quiet neighborhoods and empty swaths of prairie, cattle ranches and Pact-owned farmland anchored to the outside world, sleeping small-town main streets and marshy lakes. One portal took us into a resort town in the Edoli Mountains, and I was shocked to see snow-dusted peaks after a year spent in a glorified plain. I'd traveled little outside of Beukal to that point, and so the change of scenery was a welcome novelty, even in the dark. As for Fell, she sat beside me and said little, but her occasional crying jags shortened and grew less frequent over the hours as we cruised. When I pulled into Diriem's garage shortly after midnight Sunday morning, her face seemed almost normal but for the puffiness beneath her dark eyes.

I suggested a quick nip before bed, assuming that the house would be asleep, and Fell agreed as she followed me inside. But when we stepped into the kitchen, we found Diriem waiting for us at the counter with a squat bottle and two lowball glasses at the ready.

"Sit down, girls," he said before we could stammer our excuses and flee. "You need this."

We slunk across the room and slid onto a pair of barstools, and he poured. Slightly reckless with the hour, I asked, "Patrón? Really?"

"Gran Patrón Platinum, to be precise. Annie, if I can convey to you no other piece of experience-taught wisdom, know this: don't drink cheap tequila." With that, he passed us the glasses, then gestured. A stool floated around to him from our side of the counter, and he took a seat and waited as we sipped.

"Did you find what you needed tonight?" he asked.

I nodded and opened my collar, revealing the necklace. "Katoun's not happy."

"He'll live," said Diriem, then folded his hands and waited until we met his eyes. "Your secret is safe, Fellora," he murmured. "In any case, I can't imagine a tribunal convicting you for your actions tonight…well, your actions *outside* the museum—"

"You heard?" she mumbled.

"My dear, I've already seen the recordings that absolutely do not exist. And I saw this play out a couple weeks ago," he admitted, "so no great surprise, there. Now, since young Mr. ti'Lir apparently likes his job, he won't say anything to his superiors about the necklace going missing because he would be held responsible, but Annie, perhaps you could keep your shirt buttoned, hmm?"

I nodded and drank.

"What do I tell my parents about my job?" Fell asked.

Diriem shrugged. "Tell them you quit. You want to explore your career options, and you're not satisfied there."

She smiled bitterly. "And do what instead? My job there was nice and respectable for, you know, *the heir*," she said, rolling her eyes. "And what will Camun think? We mustn't forget about *Camun's* feelings," she muttered into her glass.

I knew I wasn't imagining the look Diriem shot me.

"If I may be frank?" he began.

Fell lowered her drink and nodded.

"Camun's no fool, and he knows he has a good thing. Your mother's ideas about what would upset him have remarkably little basis in reality. If necessary, I'll deal with Noiana, but put that from your mind tonight. And honestly," he continued, "it's not a bad development that you've left the museum's employ."

She arched a brow.

"Seems a pity that a pyromancer of your ability is giving museum tours."

"You knew about that, too?" she asked, reddening.

Diriem nodded. "My agency pays attention to young wild talents, and despite your mother's efforts to keep yours quiet, your talent is no great secret at DOI. It's a gift," he said, holding her stare. "Something to be nurtured, not feared and hidden away." With that, he stood and returned his stool to its place in the line. "Well, I'll let you two drink in peace. Take what you need," he added, nudging the bottle of tequila closer to us. "I've already informed Hakk that you won't be out tomorrow until the afternoon. Oh, and Fellora?"

"Sir?"

The corner of his mouth ticked toward a secret smile. "Are you aware that DOL has an art forgery unit?"

"Uh…no, sir…"

"Mm. A niche field, to be sure. Kabno would be able

to give you the details, but I do know that their work occasionally takes them outside the Pactlands. Well, goodnight," he said, and left us to drink in peace.

Once his footsteps faded, Fell squinted at me in thought. "Is Lord ti'Dana saying I need to apply with DOL, or was that just a casual suggestion?"

"Hell if I know," I replied, and reached for the bottle.

CHAPTER 11

"Well, now," said Hakk as I shut the van door, "I see you didn't get your beauty rest, kid."

I flipped him off with a rash-covered finger as I rounded the vehicle. "Good morning to you, too."

"Afternoon, and you know that gesture doesn't pack such a punch around here, right?"

"Bite me," I muttered in English.

I didn't know if Hakk understood, but his snort suggested I wasn't totally incomprehensible.

"Rough night for you, too, huh?" he asked Fell. "What, did you stay up watching movies and lose track of time or something?"

"Something," she replied, "and best not to ask too many questions."

Soon enough, I'd saddled Jimbo, mounted up, and clipped in, and Hakk set the targets into motion. Gripping my borrowed necklace, I turned to Fell and called, "What was the word, again?"

"Kentsia."

"Right. Uh…kentsia," I told the pendant. It seemed to vibrate ever so faintly, and as I tucked it back inside my shirt and reached for my bow, I wondered if it had lost its efficacy over the centuries like a drained battery left on display.

I coaxed Jimbo into the air and waited while she settled in, watching the targets drift. Nocking an arrow, I sighted down the nearest and let fly.

Bullseye.

"Good start!" Hakk yelled up. "Try again!"

The second shot was slightly off center, but the next three were all dead on target. By the time I emptied my quiver, I'd shot more bullseyes in ten minutes than I had cumulatively to that point, and Hakk gawked at me as Jimbo landed. "What'd you eat for breakfast, anyway?" he demanded. "Or drink? I thought you were avoiding strange potions, kid."

"I am," I said, and reached beneath my shirt to show him the necklace. "Loaner. It improves my aim."

He whistled appreciatively. "I'll say. But what's all over your hand?"

"Huh?" Frowning, I dropped the tiny gold bow and looked down, only to see that my fingers were turning blue—not the bluish shade of poor circulation, but rather a shade akin to ripe blueberries. "*Now* what?" I muttered.

Fell jogged over to take a peek at the new development. "Cross-reaction?"

"Probably."

"Does it hurt?"

I gave my hand an experimental wriggle. "Not yet. They're just discolored."

Blue hands adjacent to red arms made for a bizarre sight, but I decided to keep going and hope for the best. Fortunately, the cross-reaction seemed to be limited to my new pigmentation, which had migrated halfway to my elbows by the time Hakk called it a day. I disengaged the necklace and drove us home, but the color hadn't faded by the time we returned to the mansion, nor did a hot shower do anything to reverse the effect.

Thus, I still looked like I'd dipped my arms in a vat of paint after acquiring a nasty sunburn when Kabno rang the doorbell that night.

Diriem ushered her into his office, then pulled me from my perusal of the latest leftover pastries to join them. He sent Scel to find Fell as well, but when the house manager returned, he had Fell and her parents in tow. As

Scel shut the door behind them, Lady ti'Mal peered at the diminutive white-haired woman perched on the leather couch, her short legs dangling above the floor. Kabno had eschewed a formal robe that evening, opting instead for a pair of child-sized jeans and a lilac sweater with batwing sleeves.

"What are you doing here?" Lady ti'Mal demanded.

"Good evening to you as well, Noiana," Kabno replied with a professional smile. "I actually wanted to speak with Annie and Fellora—"

"Don't you think my daughter's been through enough?"

While Fell looked uneasy to be in the DOL director's presence—Diriem's assurances aside, she *had* killed a man the previous night—she bristled at her mother's tone and stepped in front of her. "Of course, Director. What can I do for you?"

"*Fellora*," her mother began, but Fell cut her off with a quick turn and what sounded like a sharp retort. I couldn't understand a word of it, given my ignorance of the elven languages, but Lady ti'Mal looked like Fell had slapped her across the face. Pulling herself to her full height, she snapped at her daughter in turn, then stormed from the room. After shooting Fell a pained glance, her father hurried after his wife.

The door slammed in their wake, and Fell sighed as she sank into one of the chairs flanking the couch. "My apologies, ma'am. Again, how can I help you?"

Kabno's eyebrows rose. "That was, um…some *choice* vocabulary, young lady."

"If you'll pardon my bluntness, my mother has been a pain in the ass since I returned."

"I'm sure she's still shaken by your abduction—"

"Which she did absolutely nothing to resolve," Fell interrupted. "Even now, she's more concerned with the Hall's *precious* image than with me, and frankly, I've wearied of it. I'm a grown woman—I can talk to you without my parents holding my hands."

I glanced at Diriem in time to catch the directors exchange a brief look, and then Kabno nodded and gestured to the other chair. "Annie, dear, there's no need to stand. Believe me, you gain no strategic advantage by doing so. I'm quite accustomed to looking up at others."

Mumbling an apology, I sat.

"Let's keep this brief," she said. "My people are building our case against the Hunter, and we *are* proceeding. I'm prepared to pursue an arrest warrant."

"That's fantastic," I replied, and Fell emphatically nodded. "Have you figured out how to get to him?"

"Not yet," Kabno admitted. "And there's another complication. This is a political matter, as we're moving against a Pact signatory. I wish this weren't the case—"

"It shouldn't be," Diriem interjected, his arms folded. "We should be held to the same legal standards as anyone."

Her mouth twitched. "Appreciated, but that doesn't change my situation. The path to a warrant for the Hunter goes through a Forum subcommittee," she told us. "They've considered our file and report, but they want to hear from the two of you before they decide. Would you be willing to come downtown tomorrow?"

"Absolutely," said Fell without hesitation. "Annie, do you think Hakk would mind if—"

Diriem softly coughed. "I already called him. He'll see you Tuesday."

At that, Kabno cocked her head and stared at him with disapproval. "*Really*, Diriem?"

"Not to be nosy or anything," I cut in, "but just how much bandwidth are you devoting to watching us?"

He faintly chuckled. "Very little. Has Rosie mentioned the flashes to you? Unbidden bursts of farsight?"

"Once or twice…"

"Those don't go away. Let's just say that I'm not trying to fixate on you, but my farsight goes where it wants."

"Convenient," Kabno muttered.

"What are you complaining about?" he retorted good-naturedly. "You're on schedule with your blinding potion, yes? I couldn't spy on you if I tried."

"Why does that not reassure me?" With that, she slid off the couch and tugged her sweater into place. "Have them there by nine, won't you?"

"Oh, I'm to be the escort?"

"What," said Kabno with a cheeky little smile, "you didn't know that?"

Diriem saw her to the door as Fell headed upstairs to deal with her mother. As he locked up behind Kabno, I said, "She seems fun."

"A word of advice," said Diriem. "Be certain that there are at least a few people in your life who will be absolutely honest to your face and call you out on your bullshit. They're invaluable."

"You two go back a ways, huh?"

"Not as far as you might think. Kabno's only been the director at Laws for about fifty years. Middle-aged. But I'd take her over her last three predecessors combined."

As I started up the stairs to bed, Diriem said, "Annie?"

"Sir?" I asked, turning around.

"Correct me if I'm mistaken, but you don't own a robe, do you?"

"Not unless you want to count my bathrobe."

He grimaced. "*No.* How much taller are you than Rosie?"

"Uh…probably about two inches. Why?"

Had Diriem worn glasses, he'd have been regarding me from over the top of the lenses. "You're going before the Forum tomorrow, and I'm afraid that the button-down and leggings uniform will not suffice."

"Stuffy bunch, are they?"

"Well, some don't give a damn, but others will look at you like you've just spat on their shoes if you enter the chamber in anything less than a tailored robe. Let's not make Kabno's job any more difficult than it already is."

"But I don't own a robe," I pointed out. "Most of what I've bought in the Pactlands was thrifted."

"You don't own a robe *yet*," he replied, and pulled his phone from his pocket. "Goodnight, Annie. I'll handle this."

When I opened my door the next morning to look for my laundered riding clothes, I also found a long garment bag waiting on a portable stand. Assuming it was for me, I carried it into the room and unzipped it to find a sleeveless chocolate-brown formal robe inside. The fabric felt like wool to the touch, solid but light enough that the garment didn't seem like an overcoat, and the collar had been decorated with a delicate leaf-and-vine motif in emerald thread.

I didn't know whether Diriem or one of his minions was responsible for the selection, but *someone* at DOI had a knack for color choices.

Pinned to the front was a folded note with my name on it in Pactish characters. Opening it, I found a brief, unsigned message:

> *Dress, skirt, or dress trousers beneath. If separates, dark or light shirt would be appropriate. Full sleeves.*
>
> *I would recommend minimal jewelry. Remove facial piercings if possible.*
>
> *The director did not provide your shoe size, so do your best.*

Diriem's personal shopper was definitely an agency minion, then. I tried the robe on over my pajamas, and it fit beautifully, swishing satisfactorily when I made sharp turns. While I hadn't exactly packed formalwear when I fled Beukal three weeks before, I did have clean black pants and a black button-down in my closet, and a few minutes in a steamy bathroom would remove the worst of the wrinkles. Utilitarian black flats would have to suffice. As for jewelry, the only piercings I had were the ones my parents had taken me to the mall to get on my eighth birthday, and having realized just how rare earrings on non-fauns were in the Pactlands, I seldom wore more than studs around the café. I decided I could do without.

When I came down to the kitchen just before eight, I found Fell and her parents dressed and waiting. Lady ti'Mal, who'd opted for an elaborate purple brocade number, gave me a pointed once-over as I stole a croissant from beneath the cloche on the counter, then sniffed and looked away, speaking incomprehensibly to her husband. As he answered her in kind, Fell snapped in Pactish, "She's making do! Honestly, you could *help*."

"What's the problem?" I asked around a mouthful of flaky pastry.

"Wrinkles."

"I hung everything in the bathroom…"

"Don't worry," said Fell, and gestured my ensemble to presentability. "There. Much neater."

"Black with brown?" her mother muttered. "Really?"

Fell, whose deep blue robe had to have cost as much as my prom gown, cut her eyes to the ceiling as if searching for patience. "Ignore her," she told me. "You look fine."

I raised my hands for her inspection. The blue was fading, but I was still discolored from the wrists down, and my rash was in full bloom. "Don't think I'd go *quite* that far—"

"Ah, good, you're ready," said Diriem, breezing into the kitchen. His robe was black with subtle silver embroidery around the collar, a far cry from Lady ti'Mal's selection or Janon's crimson number, but he seemed unfazed by their more ostentatious display. "Shall we? We'll need to de-scent the girls' clothing before they go."

Lady ti'Mal winced. "That potion doesn't *stain*, does it?"

"Hasn't yet, Mother," Fell replied with another roll of her eyes, and marched for the garage.

To Fell's parents' dismay, Diriem opted to ride in the van with me, and he chuckled as we pulled out. "What's so funny?" I asked.

"Some people are as transparent as glass."

"You could have gone with them. I know my way to Beukal by now, and the Benz has got to be a smoother ride than this old clunker."

"True," he allowed, "but I think the younger of the ti'Mal ladies has a few thoughts to share with the elder, and frankly, I'd rather not interfere."

"Don't know why her parents had to come with us," I said as I navigated the long driveway.

"I'm glad they did."

I turned to him, frowning. "You are?"

Diriem nodded. "Apparently, Maya is teaching the fine art of baklava today, and now Keef won't have to watch her back for a few hours."

"You're sneaky, you know that?"

"I've been called worse."

At twenty of nine, we pulled into the visitors' lot behind the massive limestone building where the Forum met and kept their offices. Topped with a low, almost flat dome, the structure rose about a hundred feet above an immaculately manicured lawn and perfectly maintained flowerbeds. The entire building was ringed with a wide, covered colonnade, beneath which all manner of robed people hustled about. A few stopped and stared as we approached, and I caught the furtive glances between colleagues and hasty whispers as they noticed me.

"Ignore them," Diriem murmured. "You'll gain nothing by wondering what they're saying about you."

"I don't really have to guess," I replied, but I tried to keep my eyes fixed on the bronze double doors ahead.

The security guards in the lobby unabashedly gawked at me, but with a nudge from Diriem, they allowed us inside.

I craned my neck to look at the high ceiling, painted to look like blue sky and puffy clouds, and Diriem steered me toward an elevator. Hearing muttering behind me, I assumed Lady ti'Mal had thoughts, but Diriem said nothing until the elevator began to rise. "You know, Noiana," he began, staring at a point above her curly blonde updo, "it's Annie's first time here. There's no need to be rude if she stops to take in the scenery, is there?"

Lady ti'Mal's face was almost as red as mine by the time we reached the sixth floor, and she offered no further commentary as Diriem led us toward a hallway carpeted with a thick green runner. Wooden doors branched off the hall at irregular intervals, interspersed with pieces of decoration: paintings, small sculptures, and even a few potted palms, a true extravagance. He paused outside a set of doors, and I noted the placard on the wall beside them: TRIBUNAL COMMITTEE.

At his knock, the door opened to a pretty brunette sorcerer, who greeted him with a smile and a respectful nod. "Director ti'Dana, good morning. Director Erenani is waiting in the lounge, if you'd care to join her." She gestured down the hallway toward an open door, through which the smell of dark-roast coffee wafted.

"I appreciate the offer, Pennan," he replied, "but if the committee permits, I'd rather stay with the witnesses. They remain under my protection, and given the frequency of Huntsman sightings in the capital of late…"

The sorcerer made a face. "Understood, sir, but you don't think they're in any danger *here*, do you?"

"I know that the security team downstairs would present virtually no challenge to a Huntsman with the slightest bit of initiative." Glancing over his shoulder at Fell's parents, he added, "Lady ti'Mal and Mr. ti'Pon wished to accompany their daughter as moral support. I assume the committee will not make an exception, no?"

Pennan flashed an apologetic smile at them. "I'm afraid not. If you would please wait in the lounge, we'll bring your daughter back as soon as she's finished."

Lady ti'Mal huffed. "Now, see here, you—"

"*Noiana.*"

I'd never heard such a sharp tone from Diriem, and it stopped her protest before it could bloom. With as much dignity as she could muster, Lady ti'Mal marched off for the lounge with Janon two steps behind her, and Pennan closed the door on us, explaining that she was going to clear matters with the committee before we were admitted.

I looked at Fell, who seemed relieved to be momentarily free of them, then at Diriem. "Didn't know you had that in you."

His mouth twitched. "During my last term on the Forum, I served on this committee. I also hired Pennan. Bright young thing, excellent at her job. I won't have her abused."

"Do you really think we're in danger here, sir?" Fell quietly asked.

"Not today."

"Then—"

"Patience, Fellora."

Before her curiosity could get the best of her, Pennan returned and bade us enter, then led us through a richly appointed office suite. "Not the conference room?" Diriem asked as we passed a closed door.

"Not today. Hearing chamber."

He grunted. "Seems a little much for two witnesses."

The sorcerer shot him a knowing look. "Representative Aniap insisted."

"Of course he did," Diriem muttered.

Without further ceremony, Pennan opened one of a pair of double doors at the far end of the suite and stepped inside ahead of us. "Members of the committee, I present the witnesses requested and Director ti'Dana."

I followed her inside and paused near the door, taking in the space. The place was set up almost like a courtroom: four rows of wooden benches bisected by an aisle that led to a dais, atop which sat a long table. Seven brass nameplates had been fixed along its length, and I considered the figures seated behind the table, trying to slot them into the little I knew of the Forum.

The Pactlands' government was representative. Each of the member species was entitled to send three people to the Forum for nine-year terms, to be chosen however the particular species deemed fit. Sorcerers held elections every three years, though there was little turnover among their representatives. Elves shared the responsibility, with the Halls' lords and ladies choosing representatives from among their number. I wasn't sure how the others figured it out—I hadn't exactly made a study of Pactlands political systems—but by all accounts, the Forum seemed to work.

While the Hunter, as a signatory, had a right to representation, he had never come to the Forum or sent a son in his stead. I suspected that this was only complicating matters—after all, the accused didn't have a voice in the government.

The seven members of the Tribunal Committee weren't exactly a fair cross-section of the Forum. Sitting in the center was a tanned, hairless person with vaguely feminine features but a flat chest. I thought she might be a sorcerer until she rose slightly for a better view and I caught a glimpse of the green and purple scales below her waist—a naga. To her left sat a blond elf, a scowling brown-haired sorcerer, and a centaur, whose chair had been pushed back against the wall, out of his way. To her right sat another dark-haired sorcerer, a brunette elf, and a rust-colored troll with a black mohawk and tusks tipped with yellow enamel caps.

The committee stared at me, some with shock, others with naked curiosity, and I fought the urge to turn around and walk out. Instead, as Pennan locked the door, I spread my arms and asked, "Shall I do a little twirl?"

The naga—Kug venDar, per her brass nameplate—sank back into her coils and cleared her throat. "That won't be necessary, uh…Ms. Humphries, yes?"

"Annie Humphries."

She nodded. "My apologies, but, um…"

"Why are your hands *blue*?" the scowling sorcerer interrupted.

I checked his nameplate: Gerem Aniap.

Ah.

"Cross-reaction," I replied, holding up my arms for the committee. "This is actually an improvement. The rash is from the scent neutralizer, and the antlers are thanks to Roulette and my awful luck. Does that cover everything?"

"Are you uncomfortable?" asked Kug. "Is there something we can do? I'd hate for you to be in pain while we discuss this case."

"Oh, uh…thanks, but I'm fine. The rash doesn't hurt."

Gerem stared at Diriem, who'd taken a seat on the closest bench. "Would someone like to explain to me why such an expensive potion is being wasted on a human? She *is* talking about the potion I think she's talking about, correct?"

The elves bristled, and Kug looked shocked at the question. But before she could intervene, Diriem said, "I trust you've seen DOL's notes about the abduction of the Huntsman earlier this month."

"I have," Gerem admitted.

"And you've surely seen the reports of Huntsmen all over the capital in the last weeks."

"Your point?"

"My *point*," said Diriem, "is that they seem to be tracking scents found in proximity to the abducted Huntsman's. They didn't just go to the café in the DPP building—they went to Ms. Humphries's apartment. She hasn't left my property without that potion in several weeks."

"So why not let the Hunt have her and be done with it?" he retorted. "We've got people scared to walk alone at night because of stories of roving Huntsmen. If the

Hunter wants her so badly, why not give her over for the greater good?"

The centaur to Gerem's left recoiled, and the troll at the far end of the table snapped, "What the *hell* is wrong with you?"

Kug raised her voice above the agitated conversation to restore order. "No one is surrendering Ms. Humphries to the Hunter—"

"But why?" Gerem interrupted. "She's not our responsibility. That thing's just a damn human, and an expensive one at—"

"*Enough*," said Diriem, his voice sharp as a whipcrack, and even the grumbling troll fell silent as he stood and stepped into the aisle. "Laws has authorized the expenditure to protect Ms. Humphries *and* Ms. ti'Mal. If you have a problem with that, Gerem, take it up with Kabno. If the committee truly believes the cost is an undue waste of Pact resources—not unlike, perhaps, your vehicle allowance," he added, staring Gerem down—"then I'll absorb it."

"Agency budgets come from the same pool," said Gerem.

"I'll absorb it *personally*," Diriem clarified, moving toward the table. "Or perhaps some of the Aniap fortune could be contributed to the cause. Your father and grandfather were good men, and I'm confident that they would have supported protecting that woman," he continued, pointing to me. "Who, need I remind the committee, is underage yet pulled off a rescue DOL would not attempt, and did so at *great* personal risk. Would you like to see the healers' notes? I'd be happy to call Pateme and have her file sent."

"That won't be necessary," said Kug. "DOL provided the synopsis."

"And what do you know about what my father and grandfather would have financed?" Gerem retorted. "What, your farsight goes in reverse now?"

Diriem shrugged. "No. I don't need it. I served several terms with Ban, and he was ever honorable. Several terms more with Kereb—who, incidentally, enjoyed my hospitality in the years before the Pactlands. And as he predeceased you, I dare say I knew him far better than you could."

Gerem remained unabashed. "What do you want, old man? More commendation? A day of public groveling?"

"A modicum of decency would be appreciated."

"Gentlemen, *please*," said Kug.

Gerem snorted and looked away, while Diriem held up his hands in surrender and retreated to his vacated seat.

"Truly," she muttered, "I haven't missed having the two of you on this committee together. Now, no one is giving the human to the Hunter."

"Last time I checked," interjected the sorcerer to her right, peering around Kug toward Gerem, "we didn't reward people who kidnap our own citizens by giving them fresh victims."

The others grumbled their approval—well, besides Gerem and Kug, who seemed like she'd had less stressful mornings—and I looked at his nameplate: Mirrik Voln. Not a name I'd ever heard, but then my knowledge of Pactlands politics was scant on a good day.

"Could we at least try to maintain order?" Kug muttered, rubbing one temple as she turned to Fell and me. "All right. We've seen DOL's reports and heard from Kabno, but we want an account from you two as well. What happened?"

Fell and I shared a look, and I nodded.

"I went for a walk one morning last month. Out at Green Lake," she said softly, folding her arms as if hugging herself while she spoke. "Alone. I was a fair distance down my usual trail when a Huntsman grabbed me. He hit me in the head hard enough to knock me out."

"How do you know it was a Huntsman?" the centaur asked.

"I saw his face for a second or two. Not long enough to react, but I did see him. And his antlers."

I knew I wasn't imagining the furtive looks a few of the representatives gave me at that.

"The next thing I knew," she continued, "my head was killing me, and I was at the Hunter's lodge. I can't say how I got there, but Annie informs me they can teleport."

"Did you see the Hunter?" the centaur pressed.

She nodded. "Roughly every other day. If my memory is accurate, I was there for about a week."

"Eight days," the female elf offered.

Fell faintly smiled in acknowledgement. "Thank you, Lady ti'Ansha. My time there has its blurry moments."

Ti'Ansha. So that was the head of Yven's Hall. I didn't know how they were related, but her stunning turquoise eyes offered a clue to their connection.

"How did he treat you?" asked the troll.

She hesitated, absently biting her lip, and I wondered what was going through her mind. Lady ti'Mal had done everything in her power to hush up the details of Fell's time with the Hunter—was Fell going to be honest or keep things vague? If she didn't want to elaborate, I'd need to be careful how I answered the committee's questions...

"I regained consciousness trapped in the form of a wolf, chained to the floor inside a cage in a barn," said Fell. "And it didn't improve from there."

She'd chosen honesty, then, and I relaxed. Given the committee's lack of surprise at her answer, I assumed that some of the details Lady ti'Mal had tried to suppress had made it into Kabno's writings.

"Care to elaborate?" asked Mirrik, leaning forward in his chair.

"If you like. I had straw and water. The Huntsmen brought me raw meat, but I've never eaten meat, and the chunks were disgusting, so I starved. No one beat me, but the collar locked around my neck certainly wasn't pleasant. I had the distinct pleasure of...*relieving* myself on the floor near my bed, if you can call it that. At night, the only lantern was kept near the door, so I could barely see within the cage, let alone beyond it." She paused and closed her eyes as she breathed. "I knew they intended to hunt me," she continued. "The ones who came out to the barn made no secret of that when they spoke to me. I suppose they wanted me to be aware of the plan so that I'd run and make things more sporting. Annie freed me the night before the Hunt was to ride."

"Is there anything else you can remember?" Kug prodded, her voice gentler than I'd yet heard. "Anything done to you? Said to you? Threats?"

Again, Fell took a moment before answering. "One of the Huntsmen wanted to take me. Not in wolf form," she hastily clarified, "but as I am. The Hunter wouldn't permit him to have me for fear that I'd fight back. His son was displeased, but he never did more than touch me, and I started snapping when his fingers came too close, so…" She shrugged. "One advantage to wolf teeth, I guess."

I glanced down the faces at the table. Lady ti'Ansha looked sick, and even Gerem seemed mildly disturbed.

"And…*she* freed you?" asked Kug, pointing to me.

Fell nodded. "Sneaked in, unlocked the cage and my collar, and carried me away on foot."

The eyes of the committee shifted in my direction. "Care to elaborate?" Kug offered.

"I'm friends with a Huntsman," I explained, "and when Fell went missing and Rose couldn't find her—"

"Rose?" Gerem interrupted.

"Ti'Dana. Someone asked her to try farsight on the sly, but she was blocked. Seems like anything that goes on at the Hunter's place is hidden," I replied. "Anyway, I didn't see signs of a manhunt, and I felt bad about the situation, so my friend and I offered to help. I've got some investigatory experience, and he's got a freakishly good sense of smell, so I borrowed a masking necklace and got to work."

"A sense of smell, you said?" asked the centaur.

"He says it's almost troll-level," I told him, and cut my eyes to the other end of the table in time to catch the troll representative's nod. "You've heard about this?"

"Once or twice," he rumbled. "I've seen no reason to disbelieve it. So...you tracked her by scent?"

"I did a few interviews first, looked for anyone who might want to hurt Fell, but everyone seemed clean. Then her fiancé gave us a bag of her sweaty clothes, and we went out to retrace her steps at Green Lake. Wylan followed the trail to a tree, then smelled hints of his brother. Not a difficult conclusion to draw. So then I took a scent neutralizer and borrowed this invisibility ring—"

"And the combination almost killed her," Fell interrupted. "The ring only worked for things on her or in her arms, and so Annie carried me until she collapsed. Organ failure, blisters everywhere—"

"Humans *are* weak," Gerem muttered.

"What part of 'Annie carried me' was unclear?" she snapped at him. "We must have walked for at least two hours. What she did, in as much pain as she must have been in—"

"How bad was it?" Mirrik asked me.

I made a face. "Like the worst sunburn I've ever had, all over my body, and simultaneously blistering. The scars are fading."

The male elf, who had been silent for much of the proceedings, finally spoke. "Why do it? What did you hope to gain?"

"Gain?" I echoed. "Nothing. It just seemed like the right thing to do. And once we got to the lodge and one of the Huntsmen confirmed that they were planning to kill Fell, I couldn't *leave* her there."

He nodded slowly. "Hall ti'Mal has rewarded you, I trust."

"Hall ti'Mal has done *nothing*," said Fell, drawing out the word.

"I did get a lovely floral arrangement," I pointed out.

"That was Camun's doing. He just put everyone's names on the card. And Hall ti'Mal did nothing to rescue me," she continued, holding the other elf's gaze. "So take what you will from that."

I hadn't expected Fell to choose the nuclear option, but in fairness, the woman did have a few legitimate grievances. I didn't know who the representative was, and one of the overhead lights was reflecting off his nameplate, but as I took a surreptitious sidestep to get a better look, it popped into view: Cirral ti'Pon.

Bingo. The head of her father's Hall. No wonder Fell was so insistent—she couldn't appeal to anyone for her mother's actions, so she was pursuing pressure from outside. Perhaps above. I couldn't keep most of the Halls straight, much less put them in order of prominence, but something in Fell's delivery told me that ti'Pon outranked ti'Mal, and she was making the most of it.

"Hall matters can be addressed at another time, I'm sure," said Kug, regaining control. "Much of what we've just heard reinforces the DOL reports, yes?" she asked, glancing to her left and right at the nodding heads. "I think our next step—"

"Question."

Kug's face snapped my way, and I lowered my hand. "Sorry. Uh…do any of you know how to find the Hunter's lodge?"

"I don't," she replied, and judging by the others' expressions, she wasn't an outlier. "Why do you ask?"

"Did Director Erenani not mention Wylan? He's been taken…"

Her brow furrowed briefly, then relaxed. "The Huntsman, yes? Your, um…friend?"

"Yeah. I'd bet my life that he's up there. Rose says he's still alive, but since she can't see him, it's the only answer that makes sense. I need to get to him, make sure he's okay—"

"I just told you what the Hunter did to me," Fell interjected. "If he thinks that Wylan betrayed him, who knows what the Hunter has done?"

"Is there *anyone* on the Forum who could find him?" I pressed.

"Well..." Kug began, rubbing her chin, "perhaps there's something in the archives, though I don't know how much work that would be for our research assistants."

"We can't be concerned with one wayward Huntsman," Gerem grumbled. "The whole lot of them are a plague. If the Hunter's decided to thin the herd—"

"He helped save my life!" Fell protested. "Didn't ask for compensation. Now he's in danger, and you can't be bothered to *care*?" Reddening, she marched closer to the table and stared up at him. "With all due respect, Representative Aniap, I understand that the Hunt is dangerous. I probably understand that better than you do, to be perfectly frank. But the Forum *cannot* refuse to act out of fear. Giving the Hunter a pass because you're afraid of him—"

"I never said—"

"You didn't have to. Looking the other way now is unjust, and it endangers the rest of the Pactlands. After all," said Fell, spreading her hands, "I was snatched on a walk, minding my own business. Who's to say it couldn't happen to another?"

"And it will," I murmured.

Kug's eyes narrowed. "What do you mean?"

"When I was at the lodge, I eavesdropped on Wylan and one of his brothers. Apparently, the Hunter's grown bored of his usual prey. He wants something more challenging," I said, and gave Fell a meaningful glance before I turned my attention to Gerem. "If you let him get away with this, then what's to stop him from grabbing someone important to you?"

Before Gerem could bluster, Kug said, "I agree that something must be done. Shall we take this to the full

Forum?"

One by one, seven hands rose.

"Thank you for your time, Ms. ti'Mal, Ms. Humphries," said Kug. "Diriem, a pleasure."

"You're a terrible liar," he replied, but nodded to the committee as he steered us out.

Once the door had closed behind us, Diriem shepherded us into a tiny meeting room and lowered his voice. "It's a good step, but this will take time. The Forum isn't known for its speed."

My stomach, which had begun to unknot with the committee's vote, tightened again. "Do we have time to waste on politics?"

He said nothing and kept his face a careful blank, but his silence told me what I needed to know.

"Let's go rescue Kabno from your parents, Fellora," said Diriem, but I held back when she stepped out. He paused at the door, eyebrow cocked, and I pulled my phone from my pocket.

"Need to make a quick call," I said.

"Meet you in the corridor, then."

Before Pennan could discover me loitering, I found Pars in my contacts and dialed. "Hey, sorry to bother you at work," I said when he answered. "Any chance that you're available for a training session tonight?"

CHAPTER 12

My first words when Morial answered his cell phone late Thursday evening were, "Don't hang up. *Please.*"

He sighed deeply. "Annie—"

"I got this necklace. Don't know how it works, but my shooting has been *amazing* this week. Like, seventy-five percent bullseyes, and every other shot on target."

Silence.

"Just give me one more chance. I can do this, I can be good enough—"

"A necklace, you said?"

"It's a loaner."

"What about cross-reactions?" Morial asked.

I glanced at my left arm, which was solidly blue to the shoulder. The color always began to fade by morning, but my practice brought it right back. "Nothing serious. Please?"

Again, I heard silence on the line for a few seconds, and then Morial sighed once more. "I've got tomorrow evening off. Same place?"

"That'll work."

"I'll be there at five."

"Perfect, thank you—" I said, but he hung up before I could fully express my gratitude.

No matter. Flopping back onto my bed, I plugged in my phone and cut the lights. My aim had been nothing short of miraculous with the necklace, and it had only improved over the course of the week. Once Morial saw what I could do with a little assistance, surely he'd help me.

I'd be ready in time, whenever the Hunt rode, and then I could look for answers to Wylan's whereabouts.

Everything was going to be okay, I told myself, and drifted off to sleep, praying the nightmares would relent.

Friday morning dawned cool and overcast in Viratta, hardly intolerable for the end of October. By the time Fell and I got out to Gerentrent, however, the clouds had opened into a steady cold rain. Pactlands weather tended toward the mild and dry end of the spectrum, and having been spoiled, I wasn't thrilled about spending the day getting drenched on horseback. But there was no alternative—I couldn't practice in the barn, and Hakk was unsympathetic as usual. At least Jimbo seemed to enjoy herself as she flew around the targets, occasionally shaking her head and sending a spray of droplets into my face.

Midafternoon, the rain finally petered out, giving way to a low, sullen sky by the time Morial arrived. He wore a T-shirt and jeans that evening, not exactly a look I would have imagined on a troll a year prior, and nodded to Hakk as he approached the training ring fence. I waved from atop Jimbo, who was taking a quick aerial loop, and his jaw fell. "You said you didn't have a serious cross-reaction!"

"I don't," I called down. "It's just discoloration."

Morial rubbed his face and groaned. "Are you *trying* to hurt yourself, girl?"

"Really, it's not painful. My healer cleared me."

Well, in a manner of speaking. After seeing me on Monday night, Pars had sent Canna in his stead on Tuesday, and she'd run a battery of tests before reluctantly admitting that the cross-effect didn't appear to be killing me quite yet.

Morial didn't seem to buy my story, but he took a seat on the bench beside Fell and grunted. "Let's see what you can do, then."

I gathered my arrows and landed while Hakk reset the

targets into motion. After slipping Jimbo a sugar cube—always better, I thought, to have her on my good side, and she wasn't hard to bribe—we rose, and I readied my bow.

I shot ten times that round. Nine of them hit the bullseye, while the one to go astray landed only slightly outside it.

Grinning, I directed Jimbo back to the ground and rode toward the bench, where Fell was beaming. Morial showed absolutely no emotion, but after almost a month with Diriem, I wasn't bothered by that. "Well?" I said. "Pretty good, right?"

"Your riding was fair," he allowed. "Marksmanship has improved."

"So…"

"Dismount."

Bemused, I unhooked from the saddle and slid off Jimbo's back. My sneakers landed in the fresh mud, and I squelched around the horse to face Morial. "What now?"

"Stay there," he said, rising, and ducked into the barn. When he returned, he carried a pair of brooms, one of which he tossed at me. I caught it, trying to keep the bristles out of the muck, and Morial let himself into the ring.

"What's this for?" I asked.

Morial began to twirl his broom in front of him. "The bow is only one of the Hunt's weapons. Let's see how you fare with a staff."

I stepped back, taking in nearly eight feet of troll. "This doesn't seem fair…"

"Would you prefer we fight with knives? That can also be arranged."

"No, but—"

His broom handle shot forward, almost hitting my shoulder, and I jerked out of the way. "Less talking, more fighting, girl."

Fine, I told myself, I could play his game. If I could shoot from horseback—no, *flying* horseback—then surely I could manage to get a few hits in.

I was absolutely mistaken about that. As soon as I took up my stance, Morial's broom swung around and cracked into my right arm just above the elbow. Yelping with pain, I looked away from him, only for the broom handle to sweep behind my legs, knocking me off balance and into the mud. My head slammed against the ground, and by the time I understood what had happened, Morial had planted a heavy foot atop my chest and was pressing me down. As I tried in vain to dislodge him, he pulled a knife from a scabbard hidden beneath his shirt and held the point of the blade above my face.

"And you're dead," he said with infuriating calm. "I can either crush your ribcage or slice your throat. Perhaps stab you in the chest. Yield?"

"Yield," I gasped, and the pressure on my lungs immediately abated.

Morial stepped back and watched me pick myself up. My clothing was soaked, and I could feel the mud dripping from my ponytail. "Okay. What do we do next?" I asked.

"Nothing. You have a very long way to go," he replied, then turned and started to walk away.

"Wait!" I called, running through the muck to catch up with him. "That's it? I still fail?"

"I can't give you the training you need."

I grabbed his thick arm and pulled until he stopped and stared at me. "What about information? Will you at least talk to me? Help me figure this out?"

"I've already given you my best advice," said Morial. "Lie low. Any other plan is doomed to fail."

"You don't know that."

"I—"

"Look me in the eye and tell me that you thought I'd be riding and shooting like this in under a month, hmm?"

Morial began to speak, paused, then huffed. "You…surprised me there, I admit."

"Then maybe there are variables you haven't

considered yet. Come on," I begged, "if you won't train me, can't you answer my questions? Talk through this with me?"

He glanced back at Hakk and Fell, who watched from the edge of the churned-up ring, then pulled his arm out of my grip. "I'll return to Lord ti'Dana's place tomorrow afternoon," he murmured. "Four. I have a dinner engagement in the capital at seven."

It was better than nothing. "Thank you," I said, and let him leave.

Once the rumbling of his vehicle faded, Hakk approached and patted my shoulder. "You're disgusting, Annie."

"I know. Can you help me?"

"Sure. This way."

I followed him into the barn and waited while he ducked into a storage room. "Is there a mud-removing spell?" I asked hopefully. "Some sort of magical cleaning agent?"

"Behold," said Hakk as he emerged with a black spray nozzle in his fist, "the wonders of the garden hose. Now turn around and brace yourself—this is going to be chilly."

At least Hakk could magically dry me off.

By the time Fell and I returned to the mansion around seven, I was craving a painkilling potion to counteract the bruises Morial had given me, but Fell suggested dinner first. "You're not as sweaty as usual," she pointed out as I cut the engine. "Come on, let's raid the leftovers. The others may not have even eaten yet."

My stomach rumbled as if on cue, and that sold me. Though tired, sore, and blue from the shoulders to my fingertips, I followed Fell into the kitchen and discovered organized chaos.

"Hey, strangers!" Maya called from the counter, where she was attacking a roasted turkey with a carving knife.

Somehow, the blade silently vibrated without any apparent power source, and it slid through the meat as if the turkey were made of gelatin. "You two hungry? We're about to sit down."

Further along the counter, Makera was putting the finishing touches on a bowl of crispy brussels sprouts, while Korek was whipping potatoes. I spotted Frog hunched over a plate of what appeared to be petit fours, carefully piping flowers. As for Dili, she was on transportation duty, running back and forth between the kitchen and the larger dining table in the adjacent room. I peeked through the doorway and found Keef setting the table, and she waved and pointed to an empty chair in invitation.

Turning back to the crowd, I spotted Rose at the small kitchen table, bent over a sketchpad, and my heart clenched as I hurried over to investigate. "Any sign of Wylan?"

She looked up, realized the cause of my anxiety, and shook her head. "Sorry, no. I was in the way, and so I was just practicing…"

I glanced at the paper and found an eerily good rendering of the five cooks swarming over Diriem's kitchen. "Nice work."

"At least I'm still good for something," she joked, and smiled as Fell pulled out a chair. "Hi. I heard Morial was going out to watch you today…" Her voice faded as I buried my head in my arms atop the table. "*Oof.* That bad?"

"He's coming over to talk with me tomorrow night," I mumbled, "and that's the best I could get from him. Of course, he beat me up today, so that's really the least he can do."

"I'm so sorry, Annie…"

"Eh." I raised my head and tried to smile. "Where's Yven hiding?"

"Where else?" she replied, closing her sketchpad.

"Camun made the mistake of admitting he knows nothing about orchids, so Yven dragged him off to the greenhouse for the crash course. I think Pop tagged along to make sure they're out of there before midnight."

"Just wait," I said, smirking at Fell. "All the flowers for your wedding are going to be changed. Hope you're not in love with them."

She brushed the thought aside with a little chuckle. "Honestly, flowers are low on my list of concerns—"

"*Fellora*!"

The entire kitchen cringed at the sound of Lady ti'Mal's shout, and I braced myself as she and Janon stormed into the room. She looked presentable as ever, her curls neatly pinned up and her robe entirely too overdone for the occasion, but her eyes had narrowed to furious flints, and her cheeks had flushed almost to the color of my constant rash. Spotting her daughter, she began to yell at her—in Low Elvish, I assumed, as I couldn't understand a word of it. Fell stood and retorted in kind, and her father chimed in, managing a few words before his wife took over and practically screamed.

By then, the prep crew had stilled, and Rose pulled me out of my chair and away from the line of fire. "What's going on?" I murmured once we were safely behind the counter.

She listened for a moment more, then said, "Someone named Katoun called—"

I groaned. "Katoun ti'Lir. Fell's former boss at the museum."

"Yeah, emphasis on *former*. Lady ti'Mal's saying that he called and told her he saw Fell kill a guy..." Her voice faded as I bobbed my head. "Fuck, Annie. *When*? What happened?"

"Last Saturday night. We went to the museum to convince Katoun to loan me this," I explained, pulling my necklace from beneath my shirt, "and we ran into a Huntsman on the way. The guy who kidnapped her the first time."

"Oh, shit," she whispered.

"Yeah, I got a bad vibe from him at the lodge, and that was before Fell told me how much he kept suggesting that the Hunter let him have his way with her. I drew a gun and tried to scare him, he pulled a knife and kept coming, and she threw him into a wall. Cracked his head."

"I mean, that sounds like self-defense to me…"

"And she turned him into a crispy critter on top of it. Anyway, Lord ti'Dana sent a cleanup crew of his spooks to fix the security footage, but I guess Katoun's too damn stupid to keep his mouth shut."

Rose considered the yelling trio across the room. With both ti'Mal women having flushed to scarlet, the fight showed no sign of winding down, and I looked behind me to see Frog coax Keef back into the dining room, away from her parents' view. "What are they saying?" I asked.

"A lot of 'how could yous' and…oh, Lady ti'Mal just brought up Cirral ti'Pon?"

"He's on the Tribunal Committee. Fell told him how her folks did jack all to help her."

"Mm." She listened to the shouting, then muttered, "Sounds like he gave Janon a piece of his mind."

"Are they brothers?"

"Cousins, I think. Janon's not main-line ti'Pon, but that Hall has greater prestige than ti'Mal, so his marriage to the heir to ti'Mal worked well." After another moment of eavesdropping, Rose said, "Lady ti'Mal is telling Fellora that she's an embarrassment to the Hall, and Fellora's telling her that she's a pathetic excuse for a mother. This seems to be going well. Sounds like…*ooh*."

Fell's arms had suddenly ignited, and white flames licked along her skin from her fists to her elbows. She didn't seem worried by this development, though her parents stepped back in alarm, and her mother's tone shifted.

"She's telling Fellora to control herself," murmured

Rose. "How the heck is Fellora—"

"Pyromancer."

Her mouth moved in a silent *Oh.* "Huh. That would explain the crispy crittering…and here comes the cavalry."

I looked toward the door to find Diriem marching in, with Yven and Camun jogging behind. "Is there a problem?" Diriem asked in Pactish.

Lady ti'Mal wheeled on him, her eyes as wide as if she'd been caught with a bloody knife in her hand. "Diriem, I…it's not—"

He looked past her at Fell, whose jaw had clenched as tightly as her fists. "Easy, now," he soothed. "Let's take a moment before we do something rash."

Maybe it was the interruption, or maybe the linguistic shift broke her focus, but after a moment, Fell let the fire die.

"Thank you," said Diriem. "What's happened?"

"She *killed* a man!" Lady ti'Mal screeched, jabbing her finger at Fell. "In public! Her supervisor saw the whole thing, and he just called to inform me…"

"And Cirral called as well," Janon added. "The things Fellora said to the committee are—"

"True." Fell glared at her parents and folded her unsinged arms. "Everything I said was true. If you're embarrassed, the fault lies in the mirror, not with me."

"How could you drag family business in front of the Forum?" her father demanded. "From what Cirral said, you made us look like monsters! And you *know* your mother didn't want the details of your incident to be made public—"

"My incident?" Fell interrupted. "My *incident*?" Her voice rose with her incredulity. "You have no idea what I went through! What I'm *still* going through! I want a counselor, and I want my damn sleeping potions so I can get through one blessed night without reliving it! How is this so difficult for you two to understand?"

"You have sleeping potions?" Diriem asked her.

"I did. The healers gave them to me, but *they* poured them out!" she snapped, jutting her chin toward her parents. "So I've done the next best thing and helped myself to your liquor for the last month. Hope you don't mind."

"I don't," he replied, "but you'll have a sleeping potion tonight. I have plenty here."

"That is *not* your decision—" Lady ti'Mal began.

"Nor is it yours. She's an adult."

At that, Lady ti'Mal pulled herself to her full height and marched across the kitchen until she was practically standing atop Diriem's toes. "You're out of line. This is a Hall matter, and I'll thank you to keep out of it."

"How is this possibly a Hall matter?" he retorted. "She's traumatized, she's of age, and you're preventing her from accessing treatment. That's not your place, Noiana."

"She's not thinking clearly—"

"Gee, I wonder why?" Fell interjected.

Her mother spared her an annoyed glance before turning back to Diriem. "And her time here has only exacerbated the trouble. We're leaving. *Now*."

Fell snorted. "Make me."

Lady ti'Mal jerked as if Fell had spat at her. "I am your *mother*, let alone the lady of this Hall, and you will leave with us before you embarrass this family any further, little girl."

"No. I won't. Bluster all you like," she said, shrugging, "but we all know there's no force behind it."

The elder ti'Mal's eyes scanned the room, then landed on me and focused in. "*You*," she said, pointing a manicured nail at my face. "You've caused all this mess. You're a terrible influence, you're a…a worthless bit of *trash*, and you are not to come *near* my daughters again, do I make myself clear?"

Rose bristled beside me, but I swept my arm in front of her before she could advance on Lady ti'Mal. "I may be trash," I said calmly, "but I saved Fell's life. What the hell did you do? Heck, I got more information out of Keef than from either of you," I continued, staring at her and Janon in turn. "Say what you will about me, but that's piss-poor parenting."

"I was worried sick!" Lady ti'Mal protested. "Don't you dare lecture me about—"

"What were you worried about?" Fell interrupted. "Whether I was alive or dead, or whether I'd done something to embarrass the Hall?"

Her mother turned to her. "How can you even ask—"

"Because I truly get the feeling it's the latter. If you cared about me, you would have called upon every resource, and you wouldn't be angry that I told the committee exactly what the Hunter did to me." She paused, cocking her head. "Did Katoun tell you that the Huntsman I killed kept threatening to rape me? That was a delightful few days. If he'd been able to take me again at the museum, he'd have made sure to have his fun with me before delivering me to his father to be run down like an animal for sport. So please, by all means, tell me how I've gone astray and ruined the Hall's reputation forever by defending myself and Annie. Tell me what you'd have had me do differently."

"Not be seen with *that*, for a start," said Lady ti'Mal, pointing to me again. "Had she not dragged you out—"

"It was my idea! Annie would never have known about the museum's holdings! She's been, what, once?" she asked, cutting her eyes my way.

"Twice," I replied, "if you count last Saturday."

"There, see? She's doing *everything* in her power to help Wylan, and all I've been able to offer her to this point has been moral support and the damn necklace. I mean, *look* at Annie! She's turning *blue*!"

Lady ti'Mal couldn't deny that.

"As I've been watching her," said Fell, lowering her voice, "I've seen her push herself as hard as she can in hopes that she'll be ready to help her friend when the opportunity arises…and what I desperately wish is that you'd cared that much about me."

While her mother struggled to regain her footing, her father took the reins. "Fellora, darling," he said, "of course we care about you! We wanted you home safely more than anything!"

"So what did you do to make that happen? Just sit there and hope the volunteers figured something out? You know Annie's only twenty-nine, don't you?"

"Thirty on Tuesday," I mumbled.

"We…" Janon paused, his mouth flapping. "We did what we could—"

"I have to think of what's best for the Hall," Lady ti'Mal cut in. "If you had eloped—"

"*Stop*. Just stop," said Fell, raising her hands and shaking her head. "I've heard enough from you both of late. And you wonder why I got an apartment in the city," she muttered. "Here's what's going to happen: I'm staying here, and if there's anything I can do for Annie, I'm going to help her. It's not like I'm missing work, right? I suppose Katoun made it obvious, but I'm not going back to the museum."

Lady ti'Mal's eye twitched. "If you refuse to come home, I'll cut off your allowance."

"Please, I'm not *twelve*, Mother. You think I don't have savings? I don't need your money to get by." Turning to Diriem, who'd been watching them squabble in silence, she said, "But I could use an introduction at DOL, if you're still offering."

"*Fellora*!" her mother cried, aghast.

Fell ignored her outburst. "You're right," she continued. "I've got talent, and I should do something useful with it."

"Stop this!" Lady ti'Mal demanded, stamping her foot. "I will *not*—"

"Shut up, Mother," she said with a sigh, then walked around the table to Camun, who'd hung back and awkwardly looked on. "Full disclosure time," she told him. "I'm a pyromancer. A *gifted* one, in fact. I'd probably be better at it if my parents had given me training in more than just suppression, but I do have a wild talent. You should be aware of that."

Camun, quiet accountant that he was, simply nodded. "Thank you for telling me. I…I'm sorry if I gave you the impression that you couldn't trust me with that information."

"I'd have said something sooner, but Mother has tried to hide it all my life for fear that it would affect my social prospects. No nice boy wants a pyro, right?"

He frowned, then pointed to his chest. "This one does."

"You say that, but you should know that I did use it to kill my kidnapper last weekend."

Rubbing his chin, Camun considered this pronouncement for a moment, then asked, "Was his death painful?"

"Not for long. I threw him into the side of the museum with a jet of fire, so the impact probably killed him before he suffered from the burns."

"That's a damn shame," he replied, and pulled Fell into his arms. He started to kiss her, but Fell pushed him away, restoring the distance between them.

"You should also know that I intend to apply with Laws," she said. "Might not always be pretty. But Lord ti'Dana's right—I'm wasting my talent at the museum."

"*Fellora*," Lady ti'Mal tried again, but the two of them ignored her.

Camun took her hands and squeezed. "If that makes you happy, why should I object?"

Her brows drew together. "Seriously?"

"I love you *for* your strength, not in spite of it. Did you think I'd protest about a job change? Honestly, if it means I no longer have to be civil to Katoun…"

"I doubt he'd rehire me if I groveled," she replied with

a mirthless chuckle. "But…look, I know you've been reconsidering the wedding—"

"What are you talking about?" he asked, stunned. "No. *No*, of course not. As soon as you're ready, I'll be there."

"Really?"

"I love you, Fell, why would you think…"

"You've been so distant in the last month…"

I knew I wasn't imagining the hitch in her voice, though she was obviously trying to maintain her composure.

Camun hesitated, still holding her hands, then dared to step closer to her. "Not because I don't want to marry you," he insisted. "I…" He fumbled briefly, searching for the words, then glanced my way. "I'm embarrassed."

Fell followed his line of sight and stiffened. "Because I've been going with Annie?"

"No! I have nothing against Annie," he hastily clarified. "Quite the contrary. I…see you two go off every day," he said slowly, "and it just reminds me of how I…I failed you, and I'm sorry. I'm *so* sorry."

"Camun—"

"I shouldn't have been quiet, I should have protested, I should have camped outside DOL until they—"

"*Camun*," she said more gently.

"I realize I've been distant," he told her, "but it's not because of anything you've done. I'm ashamed, and I don't know how to make this up to you—"

It was Fell who pulled him closer that time, and her lips on his silenced his apology. "Let's make a deal, all right?" she said once they parted.

"Anything."

"Should I ever be kidnapped again, you will put up a *very* public fuss. Understood?"

"Yes, ma'am."

"Now," she said, "in all of this, has anyone bothered to make you aware of *exactly* what happened with the Hunter? He didn't just put me in a guest room for a few days."

Camun nodded. "Lord ti'Pon called my father after your committee appearance, and he told me what you two had said." Again, his eyes darted toward me. "Annie, I had no idea you were so injured—"

I shrugged. "The flowers were lovely. Thank you."

"That's hardly enough."

"Hey, I'm alive, Fell's alive—"

"And I intend to do something useful with my life," Fell cut in. Releasing Camun, she turned to Diriem and said, "I don't have any connections at DOL, and I don't know what the process looks like, but—"

"Want me to call my aunt?" Dili volunteered from the safe side of the kitchen. "She'd talk to you."

Diriem grinned. "There are worse places to begin than with the director. Dili, if you'd rather not get involved, I'd be happy to make the introductions—"

"*Fellora ti'Mal!*"

The room turned as one to Fell's red-faced mother, whose expression reminded me of a rumbling volcano seconds away from eruption. "I will *not* allow you to debase yourself and this Hall with…with *agency* work."

Rose stiffened beside me, and I caught Yven's undisguised glare before a very quiet, very *pointed* voice cut through the sudden silence: "*Excuse* me?"

Lady ti'Mal's eyes widened as she realized what she'd said and before whom. "I…Diriem, I didn't mean—"

"There is *nothing* dishonorable about agency service," he continued in that same dangerous tone. "Some of the finest minds, the greatest talents, and the hardest-working people in the Pactlands are employed by the agencies. If Fellora wants to put her abilities to good use, then who the hell are you to tell her it's beneath her?"

She sputtered for a few seconds, looking to her silent husband for assistance, then managed, "I've raised my daughters to be ladies. For Fellora to be running around who knows where, shooting at things, perhaps even being sent outside the Pactlands—"

"Sounds far more interesting than giving art tours for the rest of my life," Fell interrupted.

"You *like* art!" Lady ti'Mal cried. "Whatever happened to pursuing advanced training? Conservation?"

"Believe me, Mother," she replied with a smirk, "if Katoun's reaction is typical, no one's going to want me anywhere near flammable artwork. I can only imagine the loss, should I lose my temper…"

"We had you trained to control it!"

"Laws can offer her a better education in that respect," said Diriem. "A more complete education, I should say—they'll teach you to use your talent," he told Fell, "not hide it. Trust me, the better you understand your ability and its limits, the easier it will become for you to manage it."

"But she *cannot* join DOL!" Lady ti'Mal insisted, stamping her foot. "I won't allow it. The heir to my Hall running around with…with *inappropriate* people…I simply won't have it. *No.*"

Diriem stared at her until she ran out of steam and sullenly met his gaze. "Many years ago," he murmured, "why I was merely the heir to a throne and not…well, you know"—he shrugged—"my father told me that those who lead from the back, who send out orders but never soil their own hands, are useless parasites. They risk nothing, yet claim every reward as their right and due. They imagine themselves to be *better* than the people they would lead."

Lady ti'Mal had the grace to wince.

"My father told me that an accident of birth had placed an immense privilege and responsibility on my shoulders," Diriem continued, "and it would be my task going forward to prove myself worthy of that burden. The throne is long gone, but the burden remains, and so I do what I can for my people in the best way I know how. Everyone at DOI and at DPP," he said, nodding to Yven, "and at DOL, and at every other Pact agency takes up some portion of the burden of keeping our world intact. And before you tell me that the heir to a Hall has no business in agency work,

I'll point out that my own son was an agent. There's precedent."

"*Your* son took the draught and ran away to disgrace himself with a damn human," she retorted. "I don't need your parenting advice."

"Oh, fuck you, bitch."

Startled to hear a rare snippet of English, I turned to Rose, who regarded Lady ti'Mal with utter contempt.

"What did you say?" Lady ti'Mal demanded.

"Something that might bruise sensitive ears as delicate as yours," Diriem told her with all due sarcasm, "but believe me, I echo the sentiment. I'll let you guess. And that's another perk of agency work," he added to Fell. "Language potions abound. You'll almost certainly never master Trollish, but if need be, you can acquire enough to get by."

She grinned. "What about whatever Rose just said?"

"Come, now," he replied, smirking, "do you *really* need a translation for that?"

Tell you later, I mouthed.

"Well," said Lady ti'Mal with a sniff, "I'm certainly not going to stand here and be insulted all night. As I said, we're leaving—"

"I'm not," Fell interrupted.

"*We are leaving*," she repeated, shooting her daughter a warning glare, "and that's final."

"Do you love Keef?" Diriem asked.

She scowled, thrown by the non sequitur. "What?"

"Keef. Your other daughter, remember? Do you love her?"

"What sort of a ridiculous question is that?" Janon snapped.

"I thought you might," said Diriem. "She seems like a nice girl. Anyway, if you do love her, you *really* shouldn't leave yet."

Janon's nostrils flared. "You're threatening—"

"It's not a threat," he said softly. "It's farsight. You

realize that the Huntsman Fellora killed isn't the only one on the prowl, don't you? I know they're still searching for Fellora, but something tells me they would settle for Keef."

Lady ti'Mal and Janon shared a long look, and she finally said, "If this is a trick—"

"I would happily send you on your way this minute," Diriem told them, "but basic decency demands otherwise. So before we say anything else we might regret, perhaps I could have dinner sent to your suite."

"That will not be necessary," said Lady ti'Mal, and swept from the room, with Janon quickly falling in behind her.

Once their footsteps had faded, Fell mimed wiping her brow, and the kitchen crew nervously laughed. "I'm so sorry," she began, turning to Diriem, but he shook his head.

"You've done nothing wrong," he told her, then patted Rose's shoulder. "I think I'll have a working dinner tonight. Would you ask Scel to bring a tray whenever he has a moment, please?"

She covered his hand with her own. "Pop—"

"It's all right, Rosie."

He gently extricated himself and started to walk away, but Fell said, "You knew Katoun would tell them, didn't you, sir?"

Diriem smiled. "Perhaps. Now, you should know that I *did* have a quiet word with Kabno about certain recent events—all hypotheticals, of course," he clarified before Fell could panic—"and her expert assessment is that no tribunal in the Pactlands would punish you for defending yourself in the manner in which you did. Hypothetically, of course."

"Of course," said Fell, and nodded as he took his leave.

With Diriem gone, Fell hugged Camun, but only until Keef emerged from her hiding place in the dining room. She pulled her little sister close, and Keef mumbled, "Are you really going to try to get a job at DOL?"

"I think so," Fell replied, releasing her. "Do you have a problem with that?"

Keef shook her head. "No. Actually, I'm glad."

"You are?"

"Yeah. I, um…I kind of think I might like to work in the DPP greenhouse someday, if I score highly enough in my biology classes, and if you're at Laws, then maybe Mother and Father won't be upset with me."

At that, Rose slipped up behind Keef and threw an arm over her shoulders. "So, here's the deal. I can't get you into the greenhouse—I've still got a million trainee restrictions."

"Heck, *I've* got restrictions there, and I'm a full agent," Yven muttered.

"But once this blows over and we can go out again without sneaking around, I wouldn't mind calling my great-uncle," Rose continued.

Keef's brows knit. "Your great-uncle?"

"Teolm ti'Cren. He's an experimental botanist at Dashom Brothers, and he works with some *weird* plants. I bet he'd at least talk to you."

Her face broke into a wide smile. "*Dashom*? Really?"

"That's what he tells me. But in the meantime, do you like orchids?"

"Uh…I don't know much about them, but I saw there were a bunch in the greenhouse. Mother told me to stay out of there, so I haven't had a proper look around—"

"Want to fix that?" asked Yven with a gleam in his eyes.

"Yeah!"

"*Ah*." Rose caught him by the sleeve before he could pull Keef out of the kitchen. "Dinner first. Trust me, Keef, you don't want to take the guided tour on an empty stomach."

As the three of them headed for the dining room, Yven already animatedly briefing Keef on the highlights, Fell kissed Camun and let him lead her toward the table. "So," she asked me as I joined them, "what did Rose tell my mother?"

"Something I probably shouldn't say within earshot of your baby sister," I replied.

Fell nodded. "Mm. You know, I think I might just like her."

CHAPTER 13

After dinner wound down and was cleaned up, Yven lured Keef to the greenhouse, and Rose tagged along to prevent him from holding the kid hostage all night. Fell and Camun went to bed—Camun had a room adjacent to the family suite, separated by a lockable internal door, and he was only too happy for his fiancée, who'd been sequestered under her parents' watchful eyes all month, to join him. As for me, I hung out with Maya and the culinary grads for a time, with most of the crew winding down over beers while Maya set up to bake pumpkin cheesecake. "Halloween tomorrow," she reminded me. "It's only right that this makes an appearance."

I eyed the line of springform pans stretched down the counter, then the foil-wrapped blocks of softening cream cheese, cans of pumpkin, boxes of chocolate graham crackers, and bags of sugar and chocolate chips. "How many did you have in mind?"

She grinned. "Do you have any idea how much cheesecake Yven and Pars can put away between them?"

"I'm claiming half of one," Frog volunteered.

"And the rest of us would like at least a taste," said Makera, tightening her blue ponytail. She studied me briefly, frowning. "How are your arms?"

I pushed up my short sleeve to the shoulder. The blue reached my armpit, but if I wasn't mistaken, it had receded slightly since the afternoon. "Well, they're not rashy."

"I know it's not ideal, but they don't look *diseased* or anything," she replied. "I know several blue-complexioned nymphs in case it, you know…spreads. Or lingers. If you wanted wardrobe tips, that is."

That possibility made me uneasy, but I knew Makera was trying to make me feel better. "Thanks."

"Of course." She took a swig of beer and wiped her deep violet lips. "Honestly, some people are so strange about *skin tone.*"

"Elves do have fairly limited options in that regard," Dili pointed out. Unlike Makera's blue locks, the little gnome's pink buns were the result of a dye job, and a half inch of her natural white was peeking through at the roots.

"Their loss," said Makera. "If they can mask so easily, there's no reason that they shouldn't experiment with color, see what suits. Don't get me wrong, Lady ti'Mal is pretty enough, but blonde on beige—*boring.*"

Leaving them to debate aesthetics and lay claim to Maya's cheesecakes, I headed toward the staircase and my bed. But something drew me past the foyer and down the hall toward Diriem's office, where I found the tray of his dinner leavings sitting on the runner by the closed door. I paused, listening for movement or voices within, then reminded myself that eavesdropping wasn't a particularly wise decision in that house and knocked twice.

The door unlatched.

Pushing it open, I spotted Diriem sitting behind his desk with a laptop and a cup of what smelled suspiciously like Earl Grey. "Did you need something, Annie?" he asked, glancing up from the screen.

I shook my head. "Just, um…checking on you."

His expression remained neutral, revealing nothing.

"Since you missed dinner. And after everything with Fell's parents tonight," I said, cringing to hear myself babble, "and…uh…" I fumbled, trying to find the words that magically wouldn't make me look like an idiot, but I only managed, "That was shitty what she said about your son. Um…"

"So you came to ensure that I wasn't brooding in the

dark?"

"Uh…maybe?"

He smiled faintly and nodded toward the leather couch in invitation, then gestured at the door to close it.

"I'm sorry," I said, sinking onto the cushion, "I didn't mean to bother you—"

"You're not. If I tell you something, will you refrain from sharing it with Fellora for now?"

"Sure."

Leaning slightly toward me over his desk, he said, "I didn't run off to hide in here because I was so overcome by the things Noiana said."

"Oh…"

"Don't get me wrong, she insulted me in my own home, and I'm not *thrilled*. But this is me being petty."

I frowned, bemused. "What do you mean?"

Diriem sat back in his chair with a smug little smile playing on his lips. "Social politics at work, dear girl. Allow me to set the scene for you. Hall ti'Mal is respectable, but it's a middling Hall at best. For instance, the only reason that Fellora's marriage to a ti'Grell isn't scandalous is because she's the heir apparent, while he's merely the third child. Barring a freakish accident, Camun will never be a lord in his own right, so it's not a terrible thing that he's marrying down to Noiana's eldest. Do you follow?"

"I think so," I replied. In all honesty, my knowledge of scandalous elven marriages extended only so far as recognition that hooking up with humans was a quick way to get yourself in a heap of trouble, and that Rose and Yven's engagement raised eyebrows for *multiple* reasons.

Fortunately, there was no pop quiz. "All of that is to say that since Noiana recovered from the shock of abandoning their home on short notice, she's been trying to turn this extended stay to her benefit," he continued. "After she emerged from her suite, that is."

"I haven't noticed her around that often…"

"Because you've been preoccupied and busy elsewhere.

I've tolerated far too much of her presence of late, and frankly, I won't be upset to see Noiana and Janon drive away."

I grimaced in sympathy. "She's annoying when she's alone, too?"

"Well, let's put it like this: on their second day here, she suggested that I either send the rest of you back to the city to fend for yourselves or keep you in the staff quarters. Didn't want to associate with the riffraff, you see, and since you had the run of the house, she felt rather put upon."

My shoulders tensed.

"But once I made it clear that I wouldn't be locking you in the attic for the duration, her tone changed. The way she's tried to flatter me, you'd think I'd converted the house to a plague ward."

"Thanks for deigning to share your air," I deadpanned.

Diriem snorted. "Five of my current guests have given my cook an unexpected break and kept every platter in the kitchen piled with pastries for the last month. You tell me which group you'd rather have around."

"If you're still on the fence, Maya's making pumpkin cheesecake as we speak."

"Mm. I *have* heard rumors."

"They're accurate, but if you want to see for yourself, you may have to fight off Yven."

He grinned. "The boy's still scared of me. I'll sneak a piece. But back to Noiana—she's been trying to ingratiate herself to me for weeks, probably hoping that I'll continue our association and thereby improve her standing. Perhaps she thinks I'm a useful idiot susceptible to her transparent praise, or perhaps she's just that desperate. Either way, she clearly doesn't think much of me beyond what I can do for her, and tonight, after all that work, she let her façade crack."

I cocked my head. "Would we call that cracking, or would we call it crumbling into tiny little shards?"

"Let's go with yours. So, Noiana was upset, but she'll cool off. Once she comes looking for me in some hasty attempt to smooth matters over, all she'll hear is that I went to my office alone and haven't been seen since. And then she'll panic in earnest," he said with a quick waggle of his eyebrows.

"Weeks of work blown with one tantrum," I replied. "Yikes."

"Oh, it's worse than that. While I don't usually bother, I can exert *considerable* influence over matters like invitations when I'm of a mind. Invitations in elven circles, at least," he clarified, "which are the only ones Noiana cares about. She still has an underage daughter to present in a few years. Should I tell the right people about her behavior tonight, I could make her…what's your phrase? Ah, yes, 'persona non grata,'" he said, his accent unplaceable.

I considered his secret little smile, the expression of one who knows the punchline already and is waiting to see how others react. "But you won't."

"No. Keef doesn't deserve to be shunned. That said, a few hours of stewing might do her parents good."

Nodding, I pushed myself off the couch and started to go. "This conversation never happened. Glad she didn't upset you."

"I wouldn't go that far."

"But you said—"

"*Most* of my sudden seclusion is for show," he explained, "but it's…you know, it's not pleasant having my son thrown in my face."

"Scandal?" I guessed, hoping I wasn't about to step in it.

"Shame."

Though I tried, I couldn't hide my confusion. Rose had said that Diriem had been nothing but welcoming to her, but if he was embarrassed by what her grandfather had done…

"I'm not ashamed of Caradin," he said, as if reading my mind. "I've *never* been ashamed of him. But you heard Camun tonight, yes? Ashamed he didn't do more to help Fellora?"

I retook my seat. "What could you have done, other than lock him in his room for the rest of his life?"

"Not a damn thing that would have worked." Diriem leaned back in his chair and swiveled a quarter-turn, then contemplated the ceiling as he spoke. "I knew what was coming for him before he did. One of the problems with farsight. For decades, I tried to work out a harmless alternative that wouldn't end *there*," he continued, and pointed to a heavy wooden bookshelf across the room.

Following his finger, I noticed a modest brass urn squatting among framed photographs. I couldn't tell the subjects of the pictures from where I was sitting, but I assumed that the urn was Caradin's.

"Never managed it, obviously," he murmured. "Several variables complicated matters, but the biggest problem was that he *wanted* his fate. The happiest years of my son's life were those he spent with Rosie's grandmother and her mother, and I had no right to take them from him."

"And then Rose brought down a drug ring," I pointed out.

"True. But even now, knowing how many lives Inade ti'Cren ruined, if you gave me the choice between seeing him incarcerated and having Caradin alive and well…"

His voice faded, and I tried to fill the gap. "That's your kid. You're allowed to be selfish—"

"Not as a farseer." He sat in silence for a moment, staring at the plaster above us, then said, "We knew it would be futile to go to the Forum and ask for an exception to be made for him. If I'd had my way, Caradin would have brought his bride here and raised their daughter in this house. But since the Forum would never have permitted a human to remain, Caradin had no choice but to take the draught."

"Couldn't he have just sneaked out?" I asked. "Skipped the part about the death potion?"

"You might think so," Diriem replied, an edge of bitterness in his voice, "but we both saw what that alternative looked like. In every permutation, he would have been discovered and given the choice—and he wouldn't have simply returned here after his wife died. He'd have wanted to stay there for Joss, and eventually, he'd have been found out."

"But wouldn't he have had more years that way?"

"Certainly. However, there would have been a massive scandal, and Inade would have started keeping watch on Caradin's family as a source of potential leverage. In that scenario, he would then have learned of his own grandson once Joss and Henry met, and he'd have killed them all. Rosie would never have existed." His chair squeaked as it bobbed back and forth. "We took the best of the bad choices and dealt with it. But as much as I know on an intellectual level that going to the Forum and pleading for Caradin's life would have only made matters worse, part of me will carry the shame that I said nothing until the day I die." He sighed softly. "I'm sorry, Annie, you didn't need to hear this—"

"No, it's okay," I insisted, but my stomach clenched as I considered the problem his account had brought to mind. "Um…question."

He gestured for me to proceed.

"Fell said that she'd go to the Forum for me. If we can get Wylan back, and he wants, uh…a relationship…she said she'd go to the Forum if I want to stay here. Assuming DPP ever finds an antidote to Roulette. Now, Morial was pretty pessimistic about my chances with the Forum, but…"

Diriem considered the ceiling for a moment longer, then sat up and swiveled back toward me. "I'm sure Fellora meant the offer, but if she believes she could sway the Forum on your behalf, then her mother has been grossly overstating their family's influence."

My heart sank. "So…"

"Do you want me to be vague in a way that could be construed as reassuring, or plain? I believe I know which you'd prefer, but I'll give you the choice."

"Plain."

His smile, fleeting though it was, seemed genuine. "Very well. The only reason the Forum is currently tolerating your and Maya's continued presence in the Pactlands is because of the risk you pose to us if you were expelled in your present condition. Early on, there was a suggestion raised that we give you memory potions, make you forget everything, and send you home as you are. More rational plans prevailed—"

"Because we'd probably end up buried in some top-secret government lab?" I interjected.

"That was the compassionate angle. The pragmatic one was that no one is still entirely sure of how Roulette works, and we can't guarantee that a memory potion will behave properly in your system right now. Easier and safer to keep you here."

"Generous," I muttered.

"If it makes you feel better, the decision wasn't purely a risk calculation. The discussions in which I was involved often circled back to the unfairness of further victimizing the two of you by sending you out to fend for yourselves. In the end, there were simply too many good reasons to keep you here. The Forum speaks with one voice when it makes law," he added with a wry twist of his mouth, "but the representatives are hardly so unified."

I thought of the Tribunal Committee's dueling sorcerers: Gerem Aniap on one side, Mirrik Voln on the other, and poor Kug venDar stuck between them, trying to maintain order.

"With that said," Diriem continued, "once a cure is found—"

"*Will* a cure be found?"

He gave me a long look over his desk. "Assume I speak in hypotheticals. Once a cure is found, there will no longer be a need to keep you here. The Forum will insist upon memory potions, and you'll be returned to Richmond."

I knew DPP had given the unaffected guests from Maya's ill-fated Halloween party a memory wipe and sent them home, but it hadn't really hit me until that moment that they'd do the same to us. Everything I'd experienced in the Pactlands, the places I'd been, the people I'd known…*poof.*

"It's already been almost a year," I replied, my thoughts swirling. "What if it takes DPP, like, ten years to figure it out? Twenty? What if it's fifty years from now, and I'm eighty years old? They're just going to erase my whole life and show me the door?"

"Annie—"

"What am I supposed to do? Live in limbo and hope they find a cure before I'm an old woman?" I pressed. "If I can find Wylan, and if this thing between us turns into something more…"

"It would still be illegal," he said gently.

"Maybe he wouldn't care," I protested, my eyes pricking. "Maybe we'd be together anyway. On the sly."

He sat there for a moment while I stewed, then absently rubbed his forehead. "Assuming that you and Wylan were to have a relationship and the Forum were to learn of it, that wouldn't constitute grounds to allow you to stay, no matter how long your relationship lasted. And since your release will necessarily come with a memory potion…"

He didn't finish the sentence, but I saw with painful clarity where he was going. "They'll make me forget him."

Diriem nodded.

"If I were here for fifty years, if we were together all that time…they'd force me to forget him?"

"If Wylan decided he couldn't live without you, then perhaps an arrangement could be made," he replied. "They could alter his memory at the same time they did yours and give you a false shared past. But for that to happen, Wylan would be required to take the draught."

A death sentence.

I rested my head in my hands and stared at the rug while I absorbed that.

"I am of the firm belief that exceptions should be made," Diriem said after a time, "especially for someone who rescued one of our citizens at great risk, but I don't speak for the majority. I'm not even a representative at the moment. All I can tell you is that the Forum will not carve out an exception for you. Morial wasn't wrong about that." He waited until I looked up, then held my stare as I tried not to cry. "Does this change your mind about pursuing the course you've been on for weeks? Even if you find Wylan, you won't be allowed to keep him."

"No," I whispered.

Again, I caught a brief glimpse of his smile. "I didn't think so."

With a curt nod, I swallowed the lump in my throat and rose again. "Morial's coming here tomorrow afternoon."

"Glad to hear it."

"You don't sound surprised."

He gave me another pointed look and spread his hands.

"Farseer, right," I muttered, and turned to go. "Good night, Lord ti'Dana."

I was almost to the door when he said, "Diriem."

Pausing, I glanced over my shoulder and found him watching me from behind his desk. "Excuse me?"

"I have lingering doubts as to your sanity, Annie, but I respect what I've seen thus far. It's Diriem. And good night."

Touched but too worried about Wylan's future and my own to dwell on the gesture, I walked upstairs alone, hearing the faint echoes of laughter from the kitchen, and flopped into bed. In my predawn nightmares, I clung to Wylan's hand as he dangled from a cliff, but he slipped from my grasp over and over until the alarm rescued me from my invented precipice.

As the hallway clock chimed four on Saturday afternoon, I paced the foyer, waiting for Morial's arrival. It was Halloween, I mused—fitting that I should be waiting for the doorbell.

Not for the first time, I recalled that had I stayed home to pass out candy on the previous Halloween night instead of party at Maya's, I'd never have been stuck in the Pactlands with a damn rack of antlers and shoddy career prospects. But while that thought used to make me bitter, my reaction had shifted in the last months. After all, had I not been dosed with Roulette, I'd never have met Wylan—and in all likelihood, Fell would be dead. Sure, things would be simpler in that alternate universe, but I'd seen people change their faces with a muttered word, traded paperback thrillers with a faun, and watched an elf torch a guy without breaking a sweat. I'd never have experienced *that* back in Richmond.

And someday, I'd be forced to forget it all…

The doorbell interrupted my circling train of thought, and Scel strode into the foyer to admit the visitor past Diriem's protective barrier. Opening the door, he nodded and stepped back a pace. "Mr. Night, good afternoon. You're expected."

There was, I thought, more art than science to applying honorifics to troll names, but if Morial took offense at Scel's attempt, he didn't show it. With a murmur of thanks, he ducked through the door and noticed me loitering by the wall. "Annie."

"Morial," I replied.

"You'll forgive me if I don't remove the mask. I'm dressed for dinner," he said, gesturing to his deep red robe, a beautiful piece decorated with gold embroidery around the collar and down the front, "and I'd rather not be buried in my own clothing."

"Understood." I pointed to a hallway, then started off in that direction. "We've got a sitting room reserved."

He followed me and settled onto the couch with an alarming creak while I locked the door and took one of the adjoining armchairs. The windows were shaded against the afternoon light, giving the place an additional degree of privacy. Scel had ensured that the coffee table between us was set with a pot of tea and a few of the kitchen crew's latest cookies—iced bats, I noted, and wondered how Maya had explained that to the others.

"So," said Morial, crossing his legs, "what did you want to know?"

"For starters, I guess, how many Huntsmen are in Beukal?"

He shrugged his broad shoulders. "Difficult to say. I've seen a few, always from a distance. They don't seem to be targeting me, and none have approached. I assume they're still seeking you and the elf."

"Well, presumably, since 'the elf' had to barbeque one last week."

His orange eyebrows rose. "What do you mean, *barbeque*?"

"You know Cralf?"

Morial grunted. "Unfortunately. The little worm was troubling you?"

"He's the one who grabbed Fell in September. Saw us downtown and thought he'd try his luck. Didn't know Fell's a pyromancer."

He whistled low around his tusks. "Cralf was never my favorite. A stupid boy who thought far too often with his lower head, as I recall."

"I see you're not weeping at his demise," I said.

"Should I? I've not spoken to him in centuries. No great loss to me. But I trust you wanted to talk of more than just killing my brother," he continued, leaning back against the cushion.

"How long do you think they'll keep searching for us?"

"Difficult to say. Until Father finds something more interesting on which to fixate, I suppose, but there's no way of knowing what will ultimately distract him. How long do you plan to keep hiding here?"

"That's still up in the air," I replied, declining to mention Noiana's aborted flounce out the door. "Wylan told me a bit about the Hunt, and I've heard snippets from others. Can you confirm or deny, fill in the gaps?"

"That depends on the answers you seek, but I'll hear your questions."

"Okay." I propped my elbows on my knees and steepled my fingers. "The Hunter's ancient, right? No one knows where he came from?"

Morial nodded. "Father was never born. He manifested. *When*, precisely, I can't say—he never gave me a date, but I suspect that dating wasn't a concept at the time."

"Where did he come from?"

He paused, considering the question. "There are…other magics than the ones taught and employed here. *Older* magics, more primal. They can't be dissected and quantified and theorized to death—they simply are. You understand them innately."

I frowned but didn't interrupt him.

"The cycle of hunter and hunted is one of the oldest," Morial continued. "The hunter hunts his prey, then becomes the prey himself to something stronger. It's life and death in a constant dance, and those are powerful forces. Father emerged from that cycling power."

"And then he created all of you?"

"Eventually. Not at once. I don't know when Father settled into his current form, and he may have made companions for himself in the distant past. Again, I was never his confidante, though I know for a fact that I'm not his eldest son."

"Dare I ask?" I replied. "Wylan's eighty-nine…"

Morial winced. "He's practically a babe."

"And you?"

That he had to stop and think about the answer should have told me enough in itself. "More than eleven hundred," he finally answered. "Precisely how much more would take some calculation."

"Shit," I muttered. Morial made *Diriem* look young.

He grunted. "Humans."

"But…all right, help me out," I said, moving on. "He created you…why, exactly?"

At that, Morial shrugged. "Companionship, maybe. Must be a lonely existence after a certain point. Anyway, he gave himself a band of followers to ride with him…an extension of himself, I suppose."

"And he's always in charge?"

"Absolutely. Father does not tolerate disobedience. I should think I'm proof of that," he added, barely smiling. "A few of us have had our moments, going out to see the world beyond the Hunt, but seldom for more than a season or two at a time. Everyone returns when the Hunt rides. That's non-negotiable."

"Why?"

"Because Father demands it. The ride is our purpose," he explained, "and all else is inconsequential by comparison."

"I don't mean to ask dumb questions, but what *is* the purpose of the ride?"

To my surprise, Morial didn't laugh in my face. "It's complex," he said, running a hand over his chin, "but at its most basic, that ride is the reason Father exists. It is, in miniature, the eternal struggle between predator and prey, played out again, and again, and *again.* He's drawn to the ride, and to a lesser extent, so are we."

"Because of some ancient magic?"

He nodded. "Something that I sincerely doubt they teach the younglings here."

I considered that for a moment, mulling over the

information Morial had given me. "If you're drawn to the ride," I said, "but you've been kicked out of the Hunt, then how do you—"

"I've lost my mount, but I can still hunt," he replied. "That soothes the itch, so to speak. I slip off every few months and take to the woods." He glanced toward the wall, as if studying something in the distance. "Never do I feel more alive, more *complete*, than when I hunt. It is, after all, what I was created to do. Wylan would say the same."

"So…hypothetically, what would happen if the Hunter didn't ride?"

Morial's eyes flicked back to mine in an instant and held my stare. "I don't expect you to understand this, but one does not fight old magics," he murmured. "One may find ways to work around them, but they can't be confronted head-on. Not without dire consequences. The Hunter *must* ride."

I didn't avert my gaze. "Let's say he were arrested, tried for attempted murder, and incarcerated. What then?"

"*If* the Forum could find a way to hold him, and I'm not convinced that they could, it would be catastrophic. Not only in the Pactlands, but in the outer world. There must always be a Hunter, and the Hunter must ride."

"And by 'catastrophic,' you mean…"

"Annie," he said with a hint of exasperation, "you're suggesting dismantling one of the primal magics. The underpinnings of the whole damn system. I can't predict everything that would occur, but I wouldn't be surprised if the little spells that hold this place together collapsed in the wake."

I wondered if anyone on the Tribunal Committee had considered that possibility. Moreover, if what Morial was telling me was accurate, then what was the point of going to the Forum? They couldn't afford to lock up the Hunter, and Fell would never have justice.

Nor would Wylan…assuming I could find him alive.

Pushing that thought aside, I tried to focus on the

opportunity at hand. "Okay…let's talk about the ride itself. Walk me through it, will you?"

"If you like." Morial shifted on the couch, crossing his legs in the other direction. "Father chooses the day and time. It's obvious when he's preparing—we can feel it—but he seldom gives confirmation until the day before. There's often feasting in advance."

I recalled how restless Wylan had been in the days prior to our trip to the lodge and the party we'd found upon arrival. "When does he tell you where you're going?"

Morial squinted in thought. "He doesn't, exactly. Not in words. But when I was with the Hunt, I just knew where we were bound when we set off. Even now, when the ride commences, I can feel its destination. Like a beacon, I guess. I'm sorry, it's difficult to be more precise with one who's not experienced that pull…"

"It's fine. How long does the ride last?"

"That's up to Father. I rode on hunts lasting a night and on hunts lasting a week. Depends on the prey he follows. He chooses that as well. Deer, bear, foxes…"

I smirked. "Humans?"

"Those, too. Elves. Trolls on occasion. He likes a challenge."

"Not sure if I should be flattered or horrified."

He chuckled low in his throat. "Perhaps a bit of both. Anyway, once he selects the prey, the Hunts rides after it. Everyone searches, but we all know to hold back and allow Father to shoot first once the initial target is found."

I cocked my head. "Why's that?"

"First blood."

"Huh?"

"Right," he muttered. "Father operates by the rule of first blood: he who draws it first has marked the prey as his own. Even if someone else delivers the killing blow, the prey belongs to the one who first wounded it. Do you follow?"

"Yeah…"

"Well, considering who and what Father is, he would be *exceedingly* cross if a Huntsman tried to claim first blood on the first target of the ride. If I've not made it clear, Father doesn't tolerate insubordination."

As Morial spoke, I recalled my hunting trip back in September. "Wylan kind of brought that up with me."

"Did he?"

"When he took me hunting. I shot an elk in the rump, it ran, and by the time I caught up with Wylan, he'd killed it. He asked me if I claimed first blood."

"I'm not surprised. That's the Hunt's code." He considered me briefly, then asked, "Did you claim it?"

"Of course not—Wylan did all the work. We ended up splitting everything. He cleaned it and gave me half the meat."

"Was that elk the first target of your hunt?"

I nodded. "He told me to take the first shot, and I flubbed it, and then he helped me shoot straighter…what?" I asked as Morial's eyes widened.

"Step back and view this from my perspective," he replied. "A Huntsman offered you the first shot at the first prey, and though you only annoyed your elk, he offered the carcass to you under the rule of first blood."

"Basically…"

"Annie, that…that's a *great* show of respect. You understand that, don't you?"

I grimaced. "Uh…"

He sighed and rested his head in his palm. "The idiot boy's so young, he probably didn't realize how clueless you are. But believe me, what he did with you was not casual."

I decided not to mention how Wylan's lips had felt when they locked on mine once we got back to Beukal, which had also been far from casual. But as I thought of Wylan's actions in the woods with me, a sudden crazy idea burst to the fore.

"What if I were to claim first blood?" I blurted.

Morial's heavy brow furrowed. "Come again?"

"If I were to ride along with the Hunt, figure out what they were tracking, then shoot it first, I'd have the right to claim first blood. If that's so important to the Hunter, then maybe he'd be willing to give me Wylan in exchange. What do you think?"

"I…think that's reckless and quite possibly insane."

"But do you think he'd abide by the rule if I were the one to shoot first?" I pressed.

"Probably," he admitted with clear reluctance. "But he would be furious to be so disrespected. *If* he were willing to make the trade with you, then you would need to pray to whatever gods you trust that the protections on this house hold fast."

"But you think he'd do it?"

Morial sighed. "For the sake of the ride…yes, I imagine Father would be willing to trade quite a lot to claim first blood. On the other hand," he continued before I could cut in, "should you shoot and miss, and should he notice you, he'd probably kill you on the spot. Whatever weapons you carried would be useless against him. Father's practically invulnerable."

I said nothing.

"Little girl," Morial said quietly as he slid to the edge of the couch and leaned toward me, "you've pushed yourself beyond reasonable limits all month. You're still bearing traces of yesterday's rash except for your arms, which inexplicably continue to be *blue*."

I pushed up my sleeve to show the discoloration line, which by then had receded to my elbow. "It's fading."

He ignored my protest. "Is Wylan *really* worth this? For all you know, he's perfectly fine at the lodge."

"No way in hell is he fine," I said, vehemently shaking my head. "If he were able to contact me, he'd do so. He wouldn't leave me worrying like this. And yes, he is *absolutely* worth it. Every bit of it," I said, staring into his brown eyes and imaging their true amber hue beneath the mask.

"If he's half the man you think he is," Morial replied, "then he wouldn't want you to risk yourself like this for him."

"I've risked little yet. And I have one more question for you."

"Ask it."

"Will you tell me when and where the Hunt rides next?"

His face twisted. "Annie—"

"You're the only chance I have of finding them. I can't sense the ride—*you* can. I'm not asking you to go with me or help me," I hastened on before he could object. "Just give me the damn coordinates. That's all I want from you."

Morial sat in silence for a *long* minute, his face blank but for the occasional twitch in his jaw. Finally, he said, "You realize that this terrible plan of yours has zero room for error, yes? If anything goes wrong, you'll be killed. If everything goes right, you may still be killed."

"I'm aware. Will you tell me where to find the Hunt?"

"Wylan wouldn't want you to do this."

I shrugged. "Wylan doesn't get a vote. Will you do it?"

He pushed himself from the couch and straightened his robe. "I'll think about it."

"Morial—"

"I said I will think about it. Good evening, Annie," he added firmly, and strode from the room.

CHAPTER 14

I woke from restless, dream-plagued sleep around four Sunday morning and rolled over to look at my phone.

November first. One year in the Pactlands.

One whole *freaking* year.

I darkened the screen again and flopped onto my back, but my mind was already churning and none too thrilled about the possibility of slipping into whatever predawn nightmare was next in the queue.

"Goddamn it," I muttered to the silent room, then crawled out of bed and headed for the kitchen, using my phone to light the way through the sleeping mansion.

I wasn't shocked to find Maya sipping white wine at the counter, her wings hanging limply over her tank top. "Morning," she said, lifting her half-full stem in salute. "You, too, huh?"

"It hit me." I pulled another glass from the cabinet, and Maya slid me the bottle of chardonnay she'd opened as I took the stool beside her. Giving myself a generous pour, I raised my drink in my still-blue hand and smirked at her. "Happy anniversary to us."

"I feel like there should be diamonds involved," she replied, and clinked her glass against mine.

"Frankly, I'd settle for antler removal." I took a sip of wine, savoring the taste before I swallowed. While I didn't recognize the label on the purloined bottle, I suspected that it hadn't come from the grocery store.

"So," said Maya once I'd sampled the vintage on offer, "two days until the big three-oh."

"Yippee," I muttered.

"Eh, thirty's not bad. I survived it," she said, grinning. "What do you want to do to mark the occasion?"

"Well," I began, "I'm thinking heavy drinking wouldn't be the smartest idea, though Fell would probably join us—"

My ringing phone shut me up, and I yanked it off the counter, fearing who might be calling me in the middle of the night. Praying that I'd see a DOL name on the ID—maybe even the long-silent Detective Venanu—I flipped the phone over and blinked at the readout.

Ice settled in my stomach as I took the call. "Yes?"

"It's time," said Morial. "The Hunt will ride by dawn."

"Where?"

"Annie, are you sure—"

"*Where*, damn it?"

He sighed. "I'll take you there. How soon can you be at that ranch?"

"Give me an hour."

"Fine. I'll meet you there."

He hung up without another word, and Maya's eyebrows rose as I jumped off my stool. "What's going on?" she asked.

"The Hunt's about to ride. I've got to move."

"Oh, *shit*." She downed the rest of her glass in one quick gulp. "How can I help?"

My cleaned clothes were waiting in their sealed bag, as I hadn't gone out to Hakk's on Saturday, and I dressed once I gulped a scent neutralizing potion. By the time I'd pulled my hair back and checked the progress of my telltale rash, Maya had returned from the gym, where I stored DOL's bags of loaner goodies. "Here," she said, thrusting an armored vest into my hands. "Cover the important bits."

The vest was only slightly too big, and Maya, who'd also brought up the spray bottle of neutralizer from the garage, took pains to douse her hands before touching me to adjust it. She waited until I strapped on the double holster I'd worn to the museum and fitted the loaded pistols snugly inside, then made me turn in a slow circle as she spritzed potion over every inch of my borrowed gear. "Want me to wake Frog?" she offered. "Just to make sure we got everything de-scented?"

"Morial can verify that," I replied, and shoved down the impulse to hug her. After reaching beneath the vest and my shirt to ascertain that the necklace was in place, I let Maya open the door and hurried for the staircase, then almost bumped into Diriem as I ran around a corner.

"Whoa," he said as I caught myself before plowing into him. "You're up early, Annie."

"It's time. Morial called."

"Mm." He gave me a brief inspection, then nodded. "Bound for Hakk's, I assume?"

"He's meeting me there. Uh…look," I said in a rush, "in case something happens and I don't make it back, thank you for everything."

Diriem smiled tightly. "It's been my pleasure. I wish you good hunting today, Annie."

"Thanks." I hesitated, then asked, "Any chance of a little last-minute farseer advice?"

"Not from me—this is the time of potentials. But I'll ask Rosie to be on standby today. You have your phone?"

I patted a pocket in my vest.

"Good. Call her when you need a pickup. I'm sure she'll be watching for you. Oh, and take the extra potion," he added, pointing to the spray bottle in Maya's hand. "You'll want to be thorough with your horse."

Maya passed it to me, and I tried to smile at them both, though I'm sure it looked strained. "Well, uh…thanks. I'll be seeing you, I hope."

I was halfway down the stairs when I heard Maya call, "Annie, wait! This isn't a great idea—"

"I don't have time for a better one," I replied, not

daring to look back, and ran for the garage.

Diriem must have called Hakk while I navigated to the portal out to Gerentrent, as he'd dressed and had Jimbo saddled by the time I drove up to the barn. "Your buddy's not here yet," he said as I slammed the van door and checked my guns. "Come on, kid, let's get you ready."

"I brought scent neutralizer for Jimbo," I began, holding up the bottle, but Hakk shook his head.

"I already got a dose down her. We'll spray her tack and the rest of your gear before you leave."

He helped me into my harness, then liberally misted the potion over the horse, my safety equipment, and my DOL bow and quiver. Satisfied that we were sufficiently doused, he allowed me to mount to the damp saddle and clip in. Jimbo nickered and turned her head, and I patted her neck to calm her.

As the rumbling of Morial's SUV echoed over the property, Hakk murmured, "You two come back alive, okay? The healers can patch up quite a bit, but corpses are tricky."

"Going to do my best," I replied, fighting my mounting nervous nausea.

When Morial joined us, he was still masked but had abandoned his formal robe for a loose-fitting black shirt and trousers. A matching knit cap hid his stripe of orange hair, and he'd applied a darkening pigment to his tusks. He appraised Jimbo and me for a few seconds, then approached, took a deep sniff, and closed his eyes. "I can't smell either of you," he declared after consideration. "Annie, are you *sure* you're not in pain?"

"It's just a rash," I replied. "And why the hell did you *drive* out here? I know you guys can teleport."

Morial stiffened, then glanced at Hakk, who shrugged. "Diriem knows I can keep my mouth shut," Hakk told him, "but come on, someone had to give me a good reason why Moonless Night was involved in this mess."

He grunted but let it go. "Nervous energy, if you must know," he told me. "The Hunt's riding—I can't help it."

"Fair," I said. "So where are we going?"

"Outside and north of here. Do you know of a city called Ottawa?"

"Uh…I mean, there's the one in Canada, but I've never been…"

"And you won't be going there this morning. There's a large preserve to the northwest of the city." He glanced at the sky, then at his watch. "We don't have long to get in place. That far north, the sun should rise in perhaps an hour and a half, but the Hunt may ride before then. Are you ready?"

I nodded. "Yeah."

"Are you certain? There's no shame in being sensible," he said, looking me in the eye.

"I said I'm ready."

He nodded curtly, then took the spray bottle and covered his hands with potion before untying Jimbo and gripping her reins. "Just to be clear, I hate everything about this plan."

"I hear you," I said, unhooking Jimbo's grounding collar. The horse shook her head and fluffed her wings, anticipating a flight, but I rubbed her neck until she calmed. Once she settled, I did my best to smile for Hakk, then turned to Morial. "We're wasting time. Let's do it."

He muttered something inimitable with mere human vocal cords, then told me, "Hold on."

Having teleported with Wylan, I knew what to expect, but that didn't mean my stomach *liked* it when the ground seemed to drop from beneath me. Before I could consider that perhaps I shouldn't have made the jump while on horseback, Jimbo had spread her wings to compensate, and she landed without stumbling. She looked around, probably surprised to have traded the barn lamps of Hakk's ranch for twilit fog, and stamped her feet as if to reassure herself of the solidity of the forest floor.

Morial had dropped us in a clearing, but beyond the silhouettes of conifers, I could make out little of our surroundings. "Where are they?" I whispered.

"Listen." He cocked his head, and I held my breath until he said, "They've not arrived yet, but they'll pass this way. There's a system of lakes to the northeast of this point, and this clearing lies along the usual trail. Once the Hunt chooses a target, they'll flush it in this direction." He paused, listening again, then cleared his throat. "If I were you, I'd stay low until they pass. Use the trees and the fog to your advantage. If you're quiet, they may never sense you down here."

"And they'll be above?" I asked

"They'll ride around treetop level, but they won't come down until it's time to claim the prey. Try to avoid being shot," he said, then released his hold on the reins. "Last chance, Annie. I'll take you with me if you're having second thoughts."

"No, thanks," I said, hoping I sounded more confident than I felt. "We've got it from here."

Morial stepped back and gave me a final look. Just as I imagined he was going to try to talk me down once more, he murmured, "Good hunting," then vanished.

That was it, then. This was on me now…well, and on Rose, assuming she was tracking me and knew of a nearby portal. I sure as hell couldn't have pointed to the nearest one, let alone a sign of actual civilization. Then again, since I was sitting atop a creature out of mythology and looked kind of like a red-faced, blue-armed woodland demon, perhaps that was for the best.

"You okay, girl?" I asked Jimbo.

She snorted in reply and began to nose at a patch of weeds.

Though I was grateful not to have landed in the middle of a blizzard, I shivered in the saddle. The temperature had to be hovering around freezing, and I wore only a cotton shirt beneath my armored vest. I'd forgone gloves, too, not thinking about the weather outside the Pactlands—not that I'd have wanted to shoot with them on, but they'd have been nice while we waited. Still, there wasn't anything I could do about it, so I settled for tucking my hands beneath my arms and thinking warm thoughts.

After a time, I pulled out my phone to check the time. It had somehow picked up a Canadian network—good news, though not entirely surprising—and put the hour at close to six. Reluctant to waste the battery, I tucked it away and patted Jimbo, who continued to graze on the little remaining vegetation. Her hair was slick from the fog, and I leaned over the side to wring out my own ponytail, which had begun to drip down my back.

Suddenly, far in the distance, I heard voices—male, certainly, though I couldn't say how many, nor could I make out what they were saying. But I knew in my gut that I wasn't overhearing a group of Canadian campers out for an early-morning hike, and so I gathered the reins. "Come on, girl," I said, nudging Jimbo in the sides. "Let's get out of here."

Jimbo wasn't overjoyed to leave her snacking, but another nudge coaxed her into flight, and we climbed until we were deep in the fog and well above the treetops. She banked almost soundlessly as I listened to the nearing voices, and as they crescendoed, I urged Jimbo to fly higher. She acquiesced, and while she flew in slow circles, I noticed the shapes that passed below us in the fog, barely lit by the lightening sky. The Hunt's horses flew silently, but the Huntsmen called to each other, giving me a vague sense of their location. They'd spread out in a fan, and I imagined that they'd be in position to cut off escape once their prey reached the water.

Jimbo looked at me as they passed, and I guided her into following them, staying just above the pack and out of their sight.

On we flew through the mist. I reached beneath my

shirt and triggered my necklace, though I didn't yet nock an arrow—I had no idea what the Hunt was pursuing, and I didn't want to shoot one of them by accident with my numbed fingers. But as we neared a short rise, I pulled ahead of the Hunt just in time to catch a glimpse of the ground through a break in the fog. Below me, sprinting for its life, ran a deer. I thought it was a doe at first, but then I saw its antlers.

Its *broken* antlers, little more than jagged stubs where its rack should have been.

A cold chill hit me as I realized with almost preternatural clarity what I was seeing.

Wylan wasn't riding with the Hunt. He wasn't locked away back at the lodge.

He was being *pursued.*

The fog thickened again, but I reached for an arrow and sped along the buck's path until I spotted another gap in the cloud cover. Taking aim, I yelled, "*Wylan*!"

The buck raised his head toward my voice in alarm, which was all the confirmation I needed.

I released my arrow, and it embedded itself in his right rear flank. As Wylan stumbled, I sent Jimbo down for a landing, then unclipped myself when I was still a few feet above the ground, swung out of the saddle, and jumped.

My landing wasn't exactly graceful, but I didn't break anything on impact, and I quickly righted myself. As my horse landed by the shore of the lake ahead, I pulled my phone from my pocket and shone the flashlight on Wylan. His amber eyes gleamed, though they were wide with fright, and I said, "I'm so sorry. *Stay down.*"

His sides heaving, he sank to the dirt and lay still.

I turned at the sound of rustling branches to see an enormous black horse landing a few yards away from me…and then, approaching through the mist like a monstrous creature in a nightmare, strode the Hunter.

While I knew I had to stand my ground, every instinct bellowed at me to run. He was a foot and a half taller than me without considering his antlers and twice as broad, a musclebound figure with long, dark hair and braids in his beard. If he felt the cold in his sleeveless tunic, he didn't show it. Fleetingly, I thought of trying to blind him with my phone, but prudence dictated that the better course of action was to draw a pistol and level it at his chest.

"That's close enough," I said.

Even with the fog and the low light, I could tell he was pissed. Anger almost seemed to radiate from him as he drew nearer. "Who the hell are you?" he demanded—in Pactish, at least, though his deep bass did nothing to soothe my nerves. "*What* are you?"

He wasn't just angry, I realized—he was shocked. Maybe he didn't know about Roulette. In that case, finding himself confronted by an apparent Huntsman he'd never created had to throw him for a loop.

"I'm Annie Humphries," I replied, trying to keep the tremor from my voice, "and first blood is mine by right."

By then, the rest of the Hunt had landed, and some of them had dismounted to see what the fuss was about. I kept them in my peripheral vision, focusing on the biggest threat.

Cocking my pistol, I said, "Stay where you are. The buck's mine."

I heard a few sharp gasps from the Huntsmen at that.

The Hunter stared down at me. He didn't reach for a weapon, but then again, he didn't exactly *need* one. "You cannot kill me," he rumbled.

"Maybe not, but I know how to make you hurt."

"What do you want?"

"Only what's mine," I said. "The buck. And I'll even give you a little something for him."

"Oh?"

I nodded. "A word of advice. If I were you, I'd keep my goons out of Beukal." Tilting my head in feigned confusion, I asked, "Haven't you wondered where Cralf is?"

That, at least, seemed to unsettle him, though he held his ground. "Cralf…has yet to return."

"And he won't. Sometimes, Pact justice is swift. Now, if you'd like to raise a stink about it, the Forum would *love* to talk to you about what you did to Fellora ti'Mal."

"Who?"

"That elf you were going to hunt a few weeks ago? Remember her, big guy?"

He said nothing at first, and when he spoke again, he almost growled. "*You.* You stole her from me."

As much as I wanted to flee at the sound of that voice, I planted my feet and tried to pretend I was bigger. "I took something you had no right to possess. You broke Pact law—and since you're a damn signatory, I would think you'd know that abducting other citizens to fucking *hunt* them is illegal. You had no claim to her. But *I* have a right to this buck, and I'm keeping it."

The Hunter's muscles rippled as he folded his arms. "Fine. Strike him dead."

"I'll do it when I'm good and ready. Maybe you should find another deer to hunt today."

I held my breath, praying that my bluster would work. If it came to it, I supposed I could shoot him in the crotch…

He turned to glance at the Huntsmen behind him, then looked back at me and shrugged. "You want that useless creature so badly? Very well. He's not worth fighting for. But I warn you, girl," he said in a low tone that sent a shiver racing up my back, "this is not over."

I stood guard over my prize and watched while he and the rest of the Hunt mounted up and took to the sky. Only once their voices faded did I de-cock the pistol and holster it, and then I knelt beside Wylan.

Up close, I saw that he was covered with moisture from his run through the fog, and he seemed far too thin. His eyes still looked wild, and I stroked his head to try to calm him—he had to be in pain from the arrow sticking out of his hindquarters. "It's me, it's Annie," I murmured. "I'm going to get you to the healers, okay? I'm so sorry about shooting you, but I didn't know what else to do…"

I looked up at the sound of footsteps and found that Jimbo had returned unharmed, and judging by the motion in her mouth, better fed. "You're not going to like me," I told her, "but I need your help." Turning to Wylan, I asked, "Do you think you can stand? I know it hurts, but I can't lift you by myself."

Slowly, he eased himself to his feet, though his injured rear leg shook when he tried to walk. I coaxed Jimbo closer, then tried to figure out how I was going to sling him over her back. But perhaps there was something more magical to the horse than just her wings, as she considered the situation for only a few seconds before lowering herself to the forest floor and snorting.

"You're the *best* girl," I told her as I helped Wylan straddle her backside. "And the prettiest. And I will buy you a whole box of sugar lumps when we get home, okay?"

When Jimbo stood again, Wylan's hooves dangled a few inches above the ground. I had nothing with which to secure him in place, so I settled for rubbing Jimbo's neck while I stood beside her and called Rose.

She picked up on the second ring. "Annie! Holy *shit*," she said in emphatic English, "what were you thinking? He could have swatted you into next week!"

"Yeah, I'm sure my nightmares will remind me all about it," I replied, "but y'all can yell at me later. Where's the nearest portal? Wylan's hurt, and I can't take Jimbo up while he's barely balanced on her."

"You're in luck. There's a portal about a twenty-minute walk north of you. Follow the lake, and I'll guide you in."

"Really?"

"I'm sitting here with Pop, a map, and an open line to the portal attendants. Yes, I'm sure."

"Okay. Let me mount up, and we'll be on our way."

Patting Jimbo, I said, "It's just a little walk, girl. Can you do that for me?"

She didn't protest when I swung into the saddle, and she took her time picking a path through the forest while I rode with one arm flung back over Wylan to hold him in place. I tried to avoid his neck, which seemed to have been rubbed raw in patches.

With Jimbo's pace, it was more like a half-hour slog to the portal, a massive lightning-blasted pine at the center of a little glade. While I waited, an opening appeared in the air by the tree, quickly enlarging to the size of an eighteen-wheeler, and I nudged Jimbo through.

Fortunately, the portal attendants on duty that morning had been forewarned, as no one batted an eye when we walked up to what seemed like a tollbooth within a large building. "Uh…hi," I said to the centaur on duty, "I need a healer—"

"This way, please," he interrupted, coaxing us off to the side, and another attendant took his spot. As I dismounted, the portal opened again, admitting a passenger car.

"Morning traffic," the centaur grumbled. "Even on the external portals, it's always the same."

"I really do need a healer," I insisted. "I shot him—"

"Eh, that's not life-threatening," he said, peering around Jimbo's head to inspect Wylan's injury. "Painful, sure, but he'll live. And don't worry, DOL's on the way."

I held Jimbo's reins, hoping she wouldn't get any bright ideas about bolting into traffic, until a line of black SUVs and a white cargo van screeched into the portal building. First out was Detective Venanu, whose green ponytail flew behind him as he ran toward us. "What happened out there?" he demanded. "Did you locate—"

"Transformed, just like Fellora," I cut in, pointing to Wylan. "He needs a healer, *now*."

The nymph's face scrunched as he considered the patient. "They *shot* him?"

"No, that was me, and I'll explain later. Healer first."

"But—"

"*Healer*!" I shouted, my voice reverberating around the room, and a few of the portal attendants ducked into their booths.

Detective Venanu raised his hands in placation. "Healer. Okay," he said, and turned to call for the rest of his team. "We've got a big one! I need trolls!"

As the agents quickly assembled a stretcher, I helped Wylan slide off of Jimbo and rubbed his head. "It's going to be all right," I whispered. "Everything's going to be all right. You're safe now."

The detective wouldn't let me accompany Wylan to the healers, and in turn, I declined his suggestion that we have a debriefing interview. "Call me when Wylan's ready for visitors," I said, swinging onto Jimbo's back. "We can talk later."

He scowled up at me. "The director will want—"

"She knows where to find me, and I've got a promise to keep."

With that, I clicked my tongue and guided Jimbo out of the building and into the warmer morning light of Beukal. Pulling my phone from my pocket, I called Rose again, then said, "Hey, let me talk to Diriem, will you?"

"Y'all are on a first-name basis now?" she teased.

"Actually, yes. Please?"

A few seconds later, he came on the line. "How's the patient?"

"In DOL custody. I need a favor."

"Name it."

"Could you please tell me where the closest grocery store is, then give them a call and, like, buy a box of sugar cubes for me? I'd do it myself, but I didn't bring any cash."

"Sugar cubes? Uh…certainly," he replied bemusedly, "but why—"

Jimbo whinnied at the sight of the capital's glass spires winking in the sun, and Diriem muttered, "*Ah*. Yes. There's a market about a two-minute drive from the portal building. Just follow the main road. I'll make the arrangements."

And thus it was that I returned Jimbo to Hakk around eight that morning, having taken her through the external and internal portals, for a long flight across Beukal, and for a few laps around his ranch before she landed. "She's eaten about half of this," I said, extending the sugar box to him as he ran up, "and the rest is hers. Also, she could probably use a bath."

"What happened out there?" Hakk asked as I unclipped and slid down. "Did you find your Huntsman?"

"Yup." I took two steps before the ground began listing, and Hakk steadied me so I wouldn't fall into the dirt. "Hey, do you think you could spot me some water and maybe a sandwich before I go?"

He guided me to a bench, then said, "Sit still. I'm calling Diriem. You're not fit to drive."

"I'll be fine," I protested, "I just need…" I noticed then that my blue hands had begun to tremble, and I frowned up at Hakk. "Um…"

"I'll get you a sandwich in a minute, kid," he said, and gripped my shoulder to keep me seated while he called the mansion for a pickup.

CHAPTER 15

DOL wouldn't let me see Wylan until my birthday two days later.

The officer who met me in the tower's parking garage seemed taken aback by my appearance, and I sighed as I straightened my shirt. "The rash is from scent neutralizer, and the blue is fading. Neither condition is contagious. Shall we?"

Though there had been no reports of roving Huntsmen in the capital since the Hunt rode, Diriem was taking no chances, and he'd insisted that I drink up before leaving the house that afternoon. I didn't mind—getting ambushed by the Hunt was low on my wish list—and if a little redness was what it took to get me in to see Wylan, I could pay that price.

The officer, a sorcerer, escorted me to the elevator and punched the button for the twentieth floor. "The infirmary is being heavily guarded at the moment," she said as the elevator rose. "Director's orders. You should be safe."

"Has anyone mentioned the part about how the Hunt can teleport?"

I caught her quick grimace. "Yes. We're doing our best. There's a constant guard on the patient's room." Eyeing me, she explained, "I mentioned that because your belongings will be searched before you're admitted."

The only thing I had on me besides my wallet, keys, and phone was the opaque plastic box in my arms, and I opened the lid to reveal the quarter of a chocolate cheesecake inside, Maya's surprise to me that morning.

"It's my birthday cake," I told the officer. "Brought some to share with him."

She leaned closer and caught a whiff of the dessert. "Oh, my…"

"You'll want to visit Mangia Due once it reopens. You know, the café in the DPP tower?"

"Lucky DPP," she muttered.

When we stepped off on the twentieth floor, I found half a dozen officers just between the elevator and Wylan's room. A few of them gave me sharp looks before seemingly recognizing that I was authorized to be there, and I wondered how bad the Hunt's presence in the capital had been over the last month. One of their number patted me down and opened my wallet, and as she peeked in the cake box, Canna emerged from an office, her dark hair tied back and her purple lab coat fluttering in her wake. "Annie," she said, and gave me a quick, tight squeeze. "How are you feeling?"

"Can't complain. How's Wylan?"

She crooked a finger and beckoned me into an empty examination room, then closed the door and leaned against the counter with her arms folded. "We think he's still in shock. He's not speaking yet."

"But you got him back to his—"

"Oh, yeah, he's in his original body. He's just not talking. Do you have any idea how long he was stuck like that?"

I could only shrug. "Might have been most of October."

"That's what I'm afraid of. The mutism is probably temporary. Could be a trauma response, or it could simply be due to the fact that he spent a considerable time in deer form."

I mused, not for the first time, that quite a few things taken for granted in the Pactlands would be absolutely insane elsewhere.

"How is he otherwise?" I asked.

"Intact. Some signs of cuts and bruises, but most are old. He's got some abrasions around his neck—he may have been collared. I think he scratched himself a bit on that last run. No broken bones. And we got that arrow out of his bum without issue. A bandage and some healing potion, and he'll be fine. You couldn't have shot him in a better place."

For that, I had only the necklace to thank. As cold as my fingers had been, I was grateful to have avoided shooting him in the heart.

"Now, he does seem thin," Canna continued. "He was dehydrated on arrival, and we've been running an IV for the last two days—some fluids, a couple potions, the usual. He doesn't seem to have an appetite yet, which isn't *great*, but I'm not ready to insert a feeding tube. My guess would be that he was starved recently."

I thought of Fell's cage in that dark barn and wondered where they'd kept Wylan. "What can I do to help?"

Her face softened. "A visit should do him good. Other than that…" She grimaced. "Once we have a better idea of his psychological state, we can put together a treatment plan, but for now, I think it would help him to see a familiar face."

I nodded and followed her down to Wylan's room, bracing myself and trying to think sunny thoughts. Canna rapped twice on his door, then opened it a crack and peeked inside. "Hi, Wylan. Didn't want your lunch, eh? Well, we'll just leave it there in case you change your mind. I've got someone to see you out here—feel up to it?"

I couldn't see past her, but whatever response he gave was apparently agreement, as Canna stepped aside and opened the door a little wider. "Come get me if you need anything," she whispered, and I plastered on a smile as I walked in.

"Hey, you…"

My mask of positivity crumbled as Canna closed the door behind me. Wylan looked *gaunt*. His cheeks had lost their fullness, and his large eyes seemed almost sunken in his face. The healers had propped him on pillows and angled the head of the mattress upward, presumably so he could eat his untouched meal, and he looked lost in the clean white bedding. Someone had washed his long brown hair, but it had dried in odd waves and snarls. No one had approached him with a razor, however, and Wylan sported a couple days' growth. His left arm was connected to the IV stand by a length of plastic tubing, which delivered a slow drip from the bag of burgundy fluid above his head—a healing potion, I surmised.

But what hit me immediately were his broken antlers. The left was perhaps an inch tall, while the right might have been a hair longer at its highest point, but both stumps were jagged, a far cry from the rack he'd sported only a month before.

"I'm so sorry," I whispered, putting the cake box on the counter. "How are you?"

He tried to smile, but his eyes filmed, and the quiver in his jaw betrayed him.

"Hey." I sat on the edge of his bed, and Wylan wrapped his arms around me. "It's going to be okay," I murmured, hugging him in turn as he shook with silent sobs. "You're here, and you're safe now, and you're going to get better. It's over."

My shoulder was soaked by the time he pulled away and swiped at his eyes, and I took his hand as he sank back into the pillows. "Let me apologize again for shooting you in the ass," I said. "I swear, it was the only thing I could think to do in the moment…"

He didn't speak, but his grip on my hand tightened and released in a quick two-beat pulse.

"Forgive me?"

Wylan nodded, then frowned. His free hand reached up and brushed against his stubs, and his face fell again.

He had to have been missing the weight, I realized, thinking of my own miserable first weeks with antlers.

"Don't worry about that right now," I told him. "You've got to focus on getting your strength back, all right? Canna says you're not eating."

He sighed and shook his head.

I gently freed myself from his grip, then stood and retrieved the cake box. "Can I tempt you? Maya made chocolate cheesecake for my birthday."

His brow knit, and he pointed to me.

"Yeah, my birthday's today. Still underage around here, but hey, I'm creeping toward my metamorphosis into an old fart," I joked.

Wylan reached up to cup my cheek in his palm, then flashed a small, weary smile.

"Thanks. So how about trying a little cake for me, huh? It's practically a health food."

Though he patted my cheek, he shook his head.

"Okay, fine," I said, rolling my eyes, "but I'm leaving it here in case you get hungry. You know Maya doesn't make bad cake."

I slid the box into the minifridge beneath the counter and returned to the bed. "Fell's been with me for the last month. Fellora, I mean," I clarified. "She's very grateful for everything we did, and I'm sure she'll want to tell you herself once you're feeling up to it. And she's fine," I added. "Mostly. Nightmares, but she's physically whole. You'll get there soon."

He took my hand again, then lifted it and frowned as he studied it.

"The blue's a cross-reaction—and it's just temporary discoloration," I assured him as his eyes widened in alarm. "Really, it stops above my wrists now. I borrowed a necklace that makes me a better shot, seeing as I'm still kind of shit with a bow. And stop worrying," I said as his look of panic shifted toward consternation. "I feel fine. Canna's been monitoring me all month."

Wylan squeezed my hand again and shook his head.

"That's nothing," I insisted. "The invisibility ring was a

million times worse. That said, I'd have put it on in a heartbeat had I been able to get to the lodge."

His headshaking grew more insistent.

"I would have! I didn't leave you to suffer on purpose—no one could get me there! I'd have come for you, Wylan. You know I would have, right?"

Slowly, he began to nod, and his eyes filled once more.

"I've been trying to find a way to reach you," I said, my throat constricting, "and riding after the Hunt was the only thing I could do. But if anyone could have opened the way, I'd have been there weeks ago. Rose has been watching, trying to see something, and she said you were still alive, but…"

I felt my face crumble, and Wylan sat up to hold me in turn while I tried to wrestle my tears under control. "I'm sorry," I mumbled into his shoulder, "I've just been so fucking scared, and I didn't know what they'd done to you, and there was so much blood at your apartment…"

We held each other there, alternately crying and consoling, until Canna stuck her head back in the room. "Annie, honey? I think Wylan could use some rest."

Reluctantly, I freed myself from his arms and stood. "I'll be back tomorrow, okay?"

He nodded.

"Don't forget that cake. I almost had to fight off a troll to get it out of the house."

He pressed his hand to his chest and faintly smiled, and I loitered by the door until Canna tugged me into the hallway, promising us both that I could return in the morning.

I let the escorting officer take me back to my van, then pulled out onto the street and found a spot to park away from the deck, where the reception was better. Chiding myself to get it together, I called Morial's cell and waited through three rings.

When he answered, he sounded unsure. "Hello?"

"Hey, it's me," I said, leaning back against my seat.

"Do you have a minute?"

"*Annie?*"

"Yeah?"

"You're *alive*? Wait, don't go anywhere…"

I heard the sound of squeaking furniture, then footsteps, muffled voices, and a slamming door. "Sorry, I wanted to take this somewhere private," Morial said. "Recording booth is soundproof. Now how the hell are you still alive?"

"Dumb luck? Grace of God?"

"Meaning?"

"Your dad blinked first."

He sharply inhaled. "So you did speak with him? Did you learn anything about Wylan's whereabouts?"

"Yeah. The asshole turned Wylan into a deer and was running him down."

A long pause stretched on the line, and then Morial murmured, "Father must have been *furious* with him. I've never heard of him attacking one of us like…like *that*…"

"Well, he ended up riding off after something else. I shot Wylan first and wouldn't give him up."

"You…" He groaned. "Annie, tell me you're somewhere safe."

"I'm heading in that direction. But listen—"

"No! Get moving! He will *not* forgive that insult—"

"I'm de-scented. Listen, Wylan's at DOL, and he's not okay. Not eating, not talking. I think your father starved him. The healers just kicked me out for the day, but I'm coming back tomorrow morning. Would you come with me? Please?"

"I…um…"

"I realize you don't know Wylan, but he's your brother, and he's hurt, and I don't know how to help him," I said in a rush. "I'm not sure the healers have it entirely figured out, either. Please, I wouldn't ask, but I'm afraid…"

My voice broke, and Morial waited until I steadied myself before finishing the thought: "You fear he'll do something rash?"

"I don't know. If he wastes away or cuts his own throat, what's the difference in the end? Please? You've been through this, I haven't—"

"What time?"

I softly sighed with relief. "Is nine too early?"

"No, that's before I'm due at work. I'll meet you at the tower. And why don't I hear an engine?"

I turned the van back on and pulled into traffic. "Better?"

"Marginally. Get back to the mansion, girl."

"Wow, the way you're carrying on, I'd almost think you cared."

"Tomorrow," he muttered, and cut the call.

Switching into my contacts list, I quickly punched the button for Diriem, who'd left for the office shortly before I headed downtown. "Hi. Need a favor," I told him.

"One within reason?"

"Maybe. Can you convince Director Erenani to let me bring someone else to visiting hours?"

The officers on duty Wednesday morning looked up at my companion with wide, starstruck eyes. "You're—" an elf began.

Morial nodded. "Moonless Night. Good morning, sir."

The officer's face split in a broad grin. "Oh, my brother's going to *die* when he hears about this. He was in the 1978 junior melee finals."

"Really?" Morial replied with what sounded like more than mere politeness. "The Thunder?"

"Blaze," he muttered, grimacing. "He was carried out on a stretcher. His leg—"

"Oh. *Oh*, yes, I remember that one. Well, tell your brother they played admirably, and I do hope his leg healed well."

We made it through security after a handful of

autographs, and I glanced up at Morial as we headed for Wylan's room. "What happened in '78?"

"The Thunder," Morial murmured, "were then led by Dancing Ripples in the Stream at the Spring Rain. She's gone on to have a career as one of the most celebrated players in the history of the sport. And at the '78 junior finals, when that poor idiot elf made a run for the goal, Dancing Ripples grabbed him by an ankle and swung him around her head. Almost tore his leg out of its socket, and when she threw him, he broke instead of bouncing."

"And *why* do you let kids play this?"

"Because it's fun," he protested.

I grunted my disbelief, then knocked on Wylan's door and popped my head inside. "Hey, you. Is now a good time?"

Wylan's breakfast tray sat untouched on the bedside table, but he was sitting up again, and he nodded and beckoned me in.

"Great. I brought a friend," I told him, then stepped inside and waited as Morial followed.

Wylan's brow knit as he considered the troll beside me. Unlike the officers on the floor, he obviously hadn't grown up watching Moonless Night's sports reports.

"Just a second," I said, then locked the door and nodded to Morial. "Please?"

He sighed and played with his ring until the mask dropped away, leaving him swimming in his formerly tight shirt and dress trousers.

Wylan gasped and started to scramble toward the far side of the bed, but I ran over to stop him before he could dislodge his IV. "It's okay, he's not going to hurt you," I insisted, grabbing his arm. "Wylan? Wylan, look at me."

He met my gaze, and my heart broke to see the terror in his eyes.

"This is Morial," I said softly, motioning him closer. "He's here to help."

The look of fright turned to confusion, and Wylan

pointed to him in query.

"Father told you I was dead, yes?" Morial asked him. "To *him*, perhaps. He banished me from the Hunt years ago. I live here in the city now."

A look of comprehension crossed Wylan's face as he turned back to me.

"Morial helped me find you," I told him. "He couldn't get me to the lodge, but he worked with me on my shooting, and he knew when and where the Hunt would ride."

As Wylan considered that, I glanced at Morial, who seemed faintly surprised by my sketchy account. Seeing nothing to be gained by mentioning how he'd given up on me just then, I nodded, and he dipped his head in understanding.

"We don't want to overwhelm you," I said to Wylan, "and I'm sure the healers will kick us out soon, but I thought Morial might have some insight that they lack."

"The first thing is that you need to eat," Morial told him. "You're not helping yourself by starving in bed. Get up, put food in your stomach, and the rest will follow." He glanced at the breakfast tray with its bowl of congealed oatmeal and made a face. "I mean, I understand not wanting that garbage, but can we bring you something?"

Wylan hesitated, then pointed to the minifridge.

"This?" I asked, retrieving the cake box.

He nodded, and I plucked the fork off his tray. "You want a plate?"

Morial glanced inside, then shook his head and pushed the box toward Wylan. "He doesn't need one. Start eating, boy. Annie, why don't you leave us for a bit? Let us get acquainted."

Wylan paused, fork embedded in the cake, and I mumbled, "Uh…I mean…"

"*Please*," said Morial. "I swear to you, I won't hurt him, but we need to talk."

I didn't want to leave again, especially not so soon after

arriving, but I *had* requested his assistance. "Is that okay?" I asked Wylan. "I'll come back tomorrow morning."

He gave Morial a long, cautious look, then nodded and gripped my hand.

"He's here to help you," I said, squeezing his hand in turn. "I'll see you first thing Thursday. Want me to bring breakfast? You know Maya wouldn't mind sending takeout."

Wylan grinned at the offer, and with more than a few misgivings, I left him alone with his brother. I didn't know how they'd get along, but considering that Morial was the only member of Wylan's family who hadn't recently tried to hunt him down, I figured that was as decent a start as any.

I cannot begin to describe how amazing it was to sleep through the night after a month of troubling dreams and predawn alarms. Sure, we were still hunkered down at Diriem's place, and now I was on the freaking Hunter's shit list, but Wylan was relatively safe at DOL. Just knowing that he had a bed and a team of armed guards gave me the necessary peace to begin catching up on the hours of sleep I'd missed of late.

Still, my body had begun adjusting to its schedule, and so I was clean, dressed, fed, de-scented, and out the door well before eight Thursday morning. But as I started toward Wylan's room, Canna appeared from around the corner and pulled me aside. "My office," she murmured, and I followed her through the corridors until I reached her space: small, windowless, and painfully institutional in décor but for the many pictures of her four kids and the taped-up exemplars of the older girls' artwork. She closed and locked the door, then whispered at the ceiling until a bright flash briefly enveloped the room.

"What the heck," I yelped, closing my eyes against further assault.

"Privacy spell," she replied, hoisting herself onto the edge of her metal desk. "The walls are thin in this unit."

I risked a peek at the world and found it restored to its usual artificial lighting. "What's going on?"

"Well, after I heard that Moonless Night, of all people, had come to visit our resident Huntsman, I mentioned it to Pars, and he told me who that troll *really* is. Yven couldn't keep it to himself."

"Seriously?" I muttered.

Canna shrugged. "Those two have been best friends for decades, and I doubt they have many secrets from each other. It's damn lucky that Rose and I get along. Anyway, *I'm* not going to say anything to blow Moonless Night's cover, but since he got here ten minutes ago, I thought you might want to see what they're up to."

"Here's here already? He didn't tell me anything about coming back…"

"What can I say? Men." With that, she muttered briefly in the direction of a blank patch of off-white wall, and in seconds, a live feed of the interior of Wylan's room began to play. "We keep security cameras in the patient rooms," Canna explained. "Normally, they're not monitored, but if we think something's awry, we can access them. And it looks like he's unmasked again…"

Morial, sporting oversized sweatpants and a T-shirt that looked more like a tent on him, had pulled up a rolling stool beside Wylan's bed while Wylan methodically ate his breakfast. Judging by Wylan's expression, I figured he'd have plenty of room for the bag of croissants I'd carried in with me.

"I will be frank with you," Morial said, "because anything less would be insulting. Father won't take you back. Ever. Have you heard of Gigron?"

Wylan nodded. "He died, yes?" he asked, his voice a rasping croak.

"He didn't just *die*. Father killed him when he begged to be allowed back in the Hunt. Or one of our other brothers may have killed him, I can't say. I found his corpse."

"No one ever told me the details."

"Probably because you're young yet. Or perhaps they'd prefer to forget his fate. That doesn't matter, though. What you must understand is that this is your life now, and you'll need to be strong and make the best of it. Pull yourself together and find a way forward. You're only delaying the inevitable by lying in that bed."

"You know, I *did* just spend a month in the wrong body, caged in the barn, being nearly starved before the others tried to hunt me down," Wylan retorted. "I've had better days. My limbs are still weak—"

"I don't doubt it," Morial replied, not unkindly, "and you have my sympathy. But the Hunt has been stalking this city ever since they snatched you, following your trails. People are on edge. There's been a lull in sightings in the last few days, but there's no guarantee that they've given up the search." Leaning closer to the bed, he added, "And you know Father won't allow Annie to go unpunished forever."

Wylan dropped his fork and pushed the remnants of his tray aside. "How is she? Truly?"

"Well, the blue discoloration seems to be subsiding…"

"Be serious."

"I am," Morial replied, unruffled. "She has been…a force. Persistent. Refuses to listen to sensible advice."

"I still can't believe you led her to Father."

"I almost didn't. But she told me about your hunt, and…well, it's obvious how you feel about her."

"Then why would you put her in danger like that?" Wylan cried.

Morial stared him down. "Because she feels much the same about you. Because she's been guzzling scent neutralizer in order to learn to ride a flying horse and strong-armed a museum employee into loaning her a necklace that makes her a more accurate shot but turns her blue on top of the potion rash. Because she *has* shown improvement in several disciplines through sheer stubbornness. She's being housed at a secure location for her own safety, but she has worried about you. In truth, she would have gone to the lodge weeks ago had I been able to convey her there. That's not an exaggeration."

Wylan closed his eyes and muttered under his breath.

"Has anyone mentioned that Cralf almost got her? He caught her with that elf in the museum complex. Apparently, Annie tried to defend them with a *gun*."

"She did *what*?" Wylan demanded.

Morial nodded. "Or so Lord ti'Dana says. We spoke the night before the ride. He encouraged me to give Annie a chance."

"I'm going to kill him—"

"*Peace*, little brother," said Morial, gripping Wylan's wrist. "He's farsighted. Perhaps he knew something I did not."

Or perhaps Diriem had been bluffing, I thought, but held my tongue.

Once Wylan calmed, he asked, "How did they escape Cralf?"

"The elf broiled him alive. Frankly, I think he had it coming."

Neither seemed entirely heartbroken by their brother's demise.

After a moment, Wylan murmured, "Annie shouldn't have risked herself."

"But she did," Morial replied. "For some incomprehensible reason, you mean a great deal to her, and you're alive because of that." Pushing himself from his stool, he said, "If she were anything else, I'd counsel you to marry her and start over here, but…" As Wylan's forehead furrowed, he explained, "Human, remember? The law is rather clear about that."

"It's a stupid law," he muttered.

Morial patted his shoulder. "Do me a favor and don't kill yourself before you're at least fully ambulatory again, hmm?" Glancing at his watch, he said, "I should go. Annie will be here soon."

As Morial masked up, Wylan asked, "Why do you keep your antlers so short? Wouldn't your mask cover them?"

He rolled his eyes up toward his false stripe of orange hair as if he could see over his jutting brow. "It would," he replied, his voice restored to its famous timbre. "But they never regrew after Father broke them."

Wylan froze where he sat, staring at his brother.

"I'd suggest you file down what's left," Morial continued. "Even them out and remove the rough edges unless you just want to rip up your bedding."

"Never?" he mumbled.

"You'll adjust. Until tomorrow," said Morial, then quickly took his leave.

I turned from the projection to Canna, who'd watched in silence. "What do you think?"

"He's making progress. Speech is a great sign."

"True. How long should I wait before I go in there?"

"Eh, give it another thirty seconds," she suggested. "Let Moonless Night get to the elevator."

Poking my head into the hall, I waited until I heard the elevator chime and the doors close, then slipped into the corridor and made my way to Wylan's room. With a brisk knock, I let myself in and started to greet him, only to find him trying to get out of bed. "Here," I said, hurrying to his side, "lean on me."

"I can do it," Wylan protested.

"You're wobbling like a ninety-pound sorority girl after a frat party, and you've got to take *that* with you," I said, wheeling the IV pole from around the bed. "Come on," I coaxed, wrapping my arm around his back, "let me help before you hit the floor."

I'd thought that Wylan needed to use the toilet. Instead, once we shuffled into the attached bathroom, he leaned on the sink and studied his reflection in the little mirror, then shuddered and glanced away.

"Wylan?"

"I'm broken, Annie," he whispered.

He didn't resist when I eased his hands off the sink and hugged him, holding us both upright as he shook in my arms. "I don't care."

"You deserve—"

"I don't care," I repeated. "It's good to hear your voice."

He pulled back just enough to look at my face. "I thought I'd never see you again…"

There was no need for him to elaborate. My lips met his, and I felt his hunger and desperation as he pressed my back against the sink and kissed me.

I knew we shouldn't go further. For one thing, the poor guy was still tethered to his morning bag of fluid, and I didn't trust him to walk on his own. For another, we were dancing dangerously close to the fire.

But I told myself that whatever cameras DOL had hidden in their infirmary surely wouldn't extend to the bathrooms and explored Wylan's face and neck until his wobbling knees gave out.

He looked up at me from the tile, flushed and lightly panting. "I told you I'm broken."

"Maybe," I said, kneeling to help him back to his feet, "but you'll mend."

CHAPTER 16

Not until Sunday did Wylan and I learn that he was homeless.

"Your apartment building's manager is a twitchy little man," said Syvin, who'd stopped by DOL to visit Wylan that morning with an offering of strong coffee. "He started bleating about throwing you out before the evidence technicians had finished in there. Your belongings are in boxes at DPP," she explained as his shoulders slumped. "I made sure that the techs got it all…well, except the broken furniture. You had a crate in your den that didn't make it, but the techs packed the rest and got the blood out of your bedding."

I offered to drive to DPP and bring back his clothing—after nearly a week in infirmary pajamas, Wylan was ready for a change—but Syvin wouldn't hear of it. "Annie," she said, giving me a look of reproach as she pulled out her phone, "you're still skulking around on scent neutralizer, and I have minions. I may as well put them to good use."

When she stepped out to intercept the agent on delivery, I sat beside Wylan on the rumpled bed and took his hand. "You can stay with Maya and me until you figure out what you want to do, okay? Once Diriem lets us move back to the apartment, I mean. He says I'm to take you out to his place after the healers release you."

"Why?"

"Safety. He's not entirely convinced that the Hunt has stopped prowling for now, and his house is protected.

House," I repeated, and laughed to myself. "The place is enormous. And I don't know what sort of magic went into those mattresses, but let's just say our apartment has lost whatever luster it once had."

"At least you have one," he muttered. "I can't impose on you—"

"It's an invitation, not an imposition. Maya won't mind. The couch isn't great, but I'll ask about getting a futon, if that'll work."

Wylan grunted. "I'm not one to be picky at the moment. The floor would suffice—"

"Absolutely not." I leaned over and kissed his cheek, the most I could risk in case of snooping healers. "Were you planning to shave for tomorrow? I'll pick up a razor if you need one."

He ran his free hand over his week's growth. Frankly, I thought it suited him, but I wasn't about to suggest additional changes to his appearance. "Thought I might keep it for a time," he replied, then hesitated. "Unless you think it's—"

"It's great. Definitely more impressive than anything I could grow," I said with mock solemnity.

He snickered and kissed me in turn, and I might have suggested sidling off to the bathroom had Syvin and the physical therapist not arrived and kicked me out.

The healers discharged Wylan on Monday after breakfast—one he supplemented, as usual, with a bag of Maya's "get well soon" goodies, which Canna tolerated as long as she could sample. Right on her heels came Detective Venanu, who, having been barred from the unit all week, hustled us into the elevator up to the director's suite on the top floor for an interview. I was certainly underdressed for a trip to the penthouse in a potion-misted button-down and leggings, while Wylan had opted for his old lace-up tunic and the pair of jeans I liked the most, though they hung more loosely from his hips after his month away.

The executive conference room was fairly ordinary, as such places went, but for two features. First was the seating: the long wooden table was ringed with black leather chairs in a variety of sizes, including a stack of plush floor mats at one end. The chair at the head of the table could have accommodated a preschooler, and a built-in step gave its presumably short occupant a boost up to table height. The second feature, however, was what kept my attention: a long bank of windows around two walls that offered with a spectacular panoramic view of the capital. Thirty stories might not have been a record-setting height in most cities, but in Beukal, the DOL tower was a veritable skyscraper.

I was standing as close to the glass as my antlers would permit, trying to orient myself against the roofs and street grid below, when Kabno walked in. Detective Venanu straightened immediately, but the director waved him to the table and climbed up into her chair. "Join us, won't you?" she asked Wylan and me, patting the tabletop as the detective opened his computer. "Or stand, if it makes you more comfortable. I don't mind."

I pointed to Detective Venanu's laptop. "Is this being recorded?"

"Naturally," said Kabno. "Is there a problem with that?"

There was definitely a familial resemblance between Dili and her aunt—aside from their tiny stature, the two women shared pale blue eyes and thin lips—but while Dili pulled her pink hair into a variety of creative styles, Kabno had kept hers its natural white and tucked it into a professional bun. Her simple eggplant robe was child-proportioned but contributed to her air of gravitas, and the way that the detective, though almost twice her size, instinctively deferred to her reminded me that she was not a gnome to be trifled with.

"No, ma'am," I replied before Wylan could weigh in. "Just making sure before I say something stupid."

She smiled. "Understood. For reference," she continued, raising her voice for the microphone, "this is being recorded on November ninth in the four hundred eighty-third year of the Pact, approximately eight-fifteen in the morning capital time. Speaking is Kabno Erenani. Present with me is Detective Kov Venanu of Major Offenses. This is the joint interview of Annie Humphries and Wylan…um…"

"It's just Wylan," he offered.

"Very well. Wylan, could you please tell us what happened on the morning of October fourth?"

He looked to me for clarification, and I explained, "When you were taken."

"*Ah*." He slowly exhaled and tucked a loose strand of brown hair behind his ear.

It didn't take a seasoned interrogator to sense his discomfort, and Kabno was no amateur. "A complicated question, I'm sure," she said soothingly. "Let's start at the beginning. If there's something you absolutely cannot bring yourself to discuss, we'll work around it, but the more you can tell us, the better our case. Kov, could you get our guests some water, please?" she added, and gave the door a pointed glance.

The detective rose and slipped out, and Kabno murmured, "Better?"

Wylan nodded. "I'm sorry, I—"

"Don't apologize. These interviews aren't easy for anyone. Now, I was there for Ms. ti'Mal's, and I suspect I have some idea of what you're about to tell me."

She stopped talking, letting the silence stretch while Wylan fidgeted. Finally, as I was about to say something, *anything*, to break the tension, he began.

"I awoke in the night to find six of my brothers in my apartment," he said, his voice quiet but steady, and kept his eyes trained on his hands. "I don't know when, but the sun had yet to rise. They surprised me in bed—I think they were hoping the ambush would be sufficient. But I had enough presence of mind to fight back."

"We found blood," said Kabno.

"I'm not surprised. Seven Huntsmen in close quarters, and six on one…I know I gave a few injuries, but I took more than I delivered. I was disoriented and tried to run for the door—I was going to take myself to DPP once I shook off their hands."

"How were you planning to get there?"

Again, Wylan turned to me for assistance, and I said, "Teleportation."

"That," he agreed. "But I couldn't do it until I freed myself. If I'd jumped with them touching me, they'd have been carried through as well."

I thought of Wylan's bloody handprint by the door and tried to push the image from my mind.

"There were too many of them," he said, clenching and unclenching his fists. "One of them finally hit me in the head hard enough to knock me out. The next thing I knew, I was home."

"By 'home,' you mean…"

"The lodge. My father's house."

"And where is that located, exactly?"

Wylan chuckled incredulously. "I don't know how to answer that. It's within the Pactlands, but perhaps not entirely?"

"Like a pocket within a pocket?" I suggested.

"Maybe. That's as good a description as any."

"And how does one get there?" asked Kabno.

"One does not unless one is of the Hunt. We're the only ones who can find it…or, well," he amended, "*they* are the only ones. I used to know the way—it was as simple as knowing up and down. But I can't feel it anymore. Father banished me," he mumbled. "I'm sorry, I'm not trying to be difficult—"

"You're doing very well," she replied with a little smile.

"Now, for clarity, when you say 'Father,' are you referring to the Hunter?"

"Yes."

"Thank you. Let's go back to that morning. What happened when you woke at the lodge?"

Wylan's shoulders tensed. "I was in one of the barns, actually. It's near the main building. There are cages within, and I was penned inside with a chain locked around my neck."

Her pale eyebrows rose. "Chained?"

"To the floor. I remember I was bruised and cut from the fight. Father and some of my brothers were there. Witnesses, I guess. Father began to interrogate me about how Fellora managed to escape. He was convinced that I'd had something to do with it, and he wanted a confession."

"What did you do? Could you not teleport out?"

"I said nothing at first, and no, I couldn't leave. I tried, thinking the chain would simply come with me, but Father had anchored it somehow. The area around the lodge was created by his will," he explained. "I'm not surprised that he could keep me there."

Kabno nodded. "What happened next?"

"I didn't want to confess," Wylan murmured, "but Father told me he would extract the truth from me however necessary, beginning with my legs. He would break them, and if that failed, he would *remove* them. So I…I gave him what he wanted."

I reached over to rub his back, and Wylan flashed a weak smile of thanks.

"What did you tell him?"

"I said I'd freed her. That I'd sneaked out during the drinking the night before the ride and returned her to Beukal. I said that her abduction was illegal and I couldn't sit by and allow her to be hunted."

The director stroked her chin. "That's not precisely what happened, is it?"

"No," he replied. "I never left the lodge that night. It

was Annie who found Fellora and carried her out—I drank with the others until nearly dawn. The only thing I did to help was get Annie to the lodge in the first place."

"But you didn't tell the Hunter about Annie?"

Wylan emphatically shook his head. "*No.* He'd have abducted her, too, if he didn't just kill her on sight. I couldn't put her in danger like that," he said, turning to hold my stare.

"Did he believe your confession?"

"Eventually. I tried to make it convincing—and what's more plausible, that I went rogue after spending a few months in the city or that I sneaked an invisible, scentless human into the lodge and wished her luck?"

"It's okay," I murmured, feeling his muscles bunch beneath my hand.

Kabno gave him a moment before she resumed. "What happened after that? Were you incarcerated in the lodge?"

He laughed briefly, a harsh bark that carried not a trace of amusement. "No. Father told me that since I'd stolen his prize before the last ride, I could take her place. I was no longer one of them. He unlocked the cage..." Wylan hesitated, slowing his breathing, then said, "Two of my brothers held me still while Father broke off my antlers. Broke them into pieces, actually, and kicked the leavings into a pile. I got to look at that for the rest of my time with him."

The director waited, letting Wylan set the pace. I took his hand, and he squeezed it so hard, I almost cried out.

"Father did to me what he did to Fellora," he told Kabno. "Only he left me in the form of a buck instead of a wolf. And I remained chained in that cage until the Hunt rode."

"I was afraid of that," she said, and steepled her fingers. "Ms. ti'Mal said that she was given food and water during her captivity, though in light of her dietary preferences, the food was inedible. What about you?"

Wylan grimaced. "A few of my brothers—and I'm not

naming them in case this recording should ever fall into Father's hands."

Kabno motioned him on.

"They gave me fresh water every day or two, and they sneaked me some of the horses' feed. Hay, mostly. Never much, not enough for Father to notice."

"Did they try to help you escape?"

"No. Father would have done to them what he was doing to me. I don't blame them," he said, though I thought I detected a note of hurt beneath his superficial businesslike tone.

The director nodded and considered Wylan briefly before resuming her interview. "You said you were kept out there until the Hunt rode?"

"Yes."

"Which was…"

He could only shrug. "I lost track of the days, so I couldn't tell you."

"The morning of the first," I volunteered.

"All right," said Kabno. "What happened then?"

Wylan absently ran a hand over his infirmary beard. "I heard the revelry in the lodge the evening before, so I suspected it was coming. In the night, Father unlocked my cage and put a different chain around my neck…like a leash, you could say," he explained. "They mounted up and took me with them to a forest. I know the place decently well, but it was dark and foggy, and having barely eaten all month, I wasn't thinking entirely clearly. Father told me they'd give me ten minutes' head start, then unchained me and let me go." He sighed. "Part of me wanted to stand there and let him get it over with. I was exhausted before I began. But something told me to run, and whatever part of me controls my limbs decided that it wanted to live. I…I ran for my life," he said simply, "though I knew I was heading into a trap. I thought perhaps I could swim to safety, lose them in the fog. But then I heard Annie call me and looked up, and she was flying overhead."

Kabno's gaze briefly locked with mine before it returned to Wylan. "Did she help you escape?"

"Shot me in the ass," he replied, squeezing my hand again, "for which I'm eternally grateful…"

His voice drifted off as Detective Venanu returned with a couple bottles of water. Sharing a knowing glance with the director, he slid them across the table to us and took his seat.

"Wylan, why don't you take a minute?" Kabno suggested. "Annie, let's go back to October fourth."

I frowned. "What do you want to know?"

"Well," she replied, folding her arms on the tabletop, "since Diriem has been stingy with certain details, why don't you go ahead and tell me everything?"

It was past nine by the time the interrogation wrapped up, and Wylan looked exhausted.

"The plan," Kabno told us, "is to eventually bring formal charges against the Hunter for kidnapping, assault, and attempted murder, both for Ms. ti'Mal and for you, Wylan. What I'd like to know is whether you'd be willing to testify against him."

He froze, his eyes uncertain.

"Of course," Kabno smoothly continued, "this doesn't need to be decided at the moment. You've had quite an ordeal. Think about it for a few days, then give me a call with your decision, hmm? Diriem knows how to reach me."

Detective Venanu assured us that Wylan's belongings had already been loaded into the back of my van, and I helped Wylan out of his chair and tried to subtly steady him as we headed for the exit. But before we could leave, Kabno asked, "Annie, a word in private?"

"I can do it," Wylan whispered, and I let him wobble out the door with the detective in the lead.

Once their footsteps faded, the director slid down from her chair and walked over to me, palm extended. "Don't you think it's time you returned that necklace the museum so generously loaned you?"

I smirked down at her. "Is that what we're calling it? A loan?"

"Whatever could you mean?" she replied with feigned bemusement. "Katoun ti'Lir was very helpful in organizing the loan on short notice."

"Okay, I *know* that 'helpful' isn't the term I would use."

"A pity, since I intend to give him all the credit in my communications with the museum director."

Seeing the predatory edge in Kabno's smile, I was suddenly very glad to be on her good side. "He's a real prince," I said, unclasping the necklace, and deposited it in her hand. "So generous."

"And I'm sure he'll try not to take the credit," she replied, tucking the necklace into her robe's inner pocket.

"Thank you for the loan as well," I said. "The gear, I mean. It's all back at the mansion, and I could drive it in—"

"I'll collect it in my own time. We'd be in a terrible state if DOL couldn't afford to do without a few guns and bows." Kabno considered my face for a moment, then stepped back and crossed her arms. "I'm going to tell you something that may sound insulting, but I mean it solely as a compliment."

"Uh…okay…" I stammered.

One corner of her mouth curled. "I *truly* wish you were anything but human. I'd hire you on the spot."

I cocked my head. "Thank you?"

"Seriously. Do you have any idea how ineffective Kov looks right now? The man's a highly commended detective, and yet you're the one running around finding our missing persons."

"Private investigator," I replied with a grin. "What can I say?"

She snorted. "Just put my mind at ease and get back to Diriem's place before a Huntsman grabs you, eh?"

Wylan was quiet on the drive out to Viratta, and I hoped he would sleep. Despite a week's recovery, he still tired easily, and I knew the interview had to have been draining. But he managed to stay awake, watching the rolling grasslands go by as we approached the mansion and making only the odd comment on the scenery until I pulled into the garage and cut the engine.

"Annie?" he said, reaching for me.

I unbuckled and gripped his hand tightly. "Everyone's been great except Lady ti'Mal and Janon, and they're probably still sulking in their room. You've got nothing to worry about, okay?"

"Thanks, but I wasn't overly concerned about that. Annie…" He paused, choosing his words. "Why did you do it?"

He'd been silent while I'd related the events of the last month to Kabno, and I wondered how much or little Morial had told him. "Because I didn't want you to die. Good enough reason, or should I come up with something more dramatic?" I joked, trying to lighten the mood.

Wylan didn't bite. "Morial was right. You had no business confronting Father—"

"Do you wish I hadn't?"

"No," he allowed after a moment, "to my shame, because he could have killed you."

I shrugged. "He was going to kill *you*, wasn't he? I don't regret my decision."

"But if you'd been hurt or worse because of me—"

"That was my choice to make," I said, and leaned over to kiss him while we still had the privacy of the vehicle. "I'd do it again."

"*Why*?" he demanded, staring into my eyes. "I'm not worth that risk."

I held his gaze. "You are to me. Now come on, let's get you inside."

We left his things in the van for the moment, and he didn't protest when I walked close to him in case of stumbling. As I opened the door to the house, Scel appeared from around the corner in a sweep of dark robe. "Ah, Annie, excellent timing," he said, and nodded to Wylan. "You must be our new guest."

Wylan blinked. "I…um…"

"This is Scel Curain," I told him. "He runs this joint. Scel, Wylan. He's kind of wiped out," I told Scel, "so is there an empty room we could use? Or I could put him in mine for now…"

Scel shook his head. "No need. His room was readied not fifteen minutes ago. Lord ti'Dana suggested leaving the bed turned down, and"—he squinted in appraisal—"I believe I know why. It's the empty room adjacent to yours in the tower, Annie. Would you like assistance?"

"Thanks, but we'll manage. Wylan's clothes and gear are still in my van—"

"Ranarma can spare a few minutes of his vacation to bring them in," he replied with a grin, and beckoned for my keys.

I asked him to pass along my thanks to his nephew, then helped Wylan upstairs and through the corridors toward his waiting room. Scel had left the door cracked—considerate, I thought—and the first thing I noticed on entry was the vase of flowers on the table by the window, a nice touch. A selection of snacks and two bottles of water sat on the tray beside them, just as I'd found on my first night. The main difference between our rooms, however, was the bed. While his appeared to be every bit as plush as mine, Wylan's bed had a headboard and had been pushed against the wall—a normal arrangement for anyone who didn't have to deal with a rack, but surely foreign to him. I decided not to draw attention to it.

"Sit down," I said, coaxing him to the edge of the bed,

and waited while he slipped off his boots. "I'll draw the curtains. Get some rest, and I'll wake you for lunch, all right?"

Before Wylan could answer me, I heard running footsteps in the hallway outside, and then Fell's head popped around the doorframe. "You're here!" she said, panting. "Scel said you'd just come…"

Wylan pushed himself back to his bare feet and raised a hand in greeting. "Fellora, yes?"

She nodded, then hurried into the room and hugged him. "Thank you," she said as Wylan, startled at the sudden touch, relaxed. "*Thank* you. I'm so sorry…"

He patted her back, and she released him. "Nice to finally meet you," he said with a little grin. "Perhaps we could compare notes later…"

"Oh, yes. Of course," Fell replied, stepped back as if just registering the turned-down bed and the weariness in his expression. "How are you feeling?"

"Better than I've felt of late…"

"But you could still do with a nap," I said, and tugged the curtains together, throwing the room into shadow. "I'll meet you downstairs, Fell, okay?"

"Absolutely." Whatever else could be said for her, the woman could take a hint. "By the way, the kitchen team is making a *massive* dinner. I do hope your appetite is back," she told Wylan, then let herself out and closed the door.

Once we were alone, he sank to the bed with a sigh, and I pulled aside the blankets until he relented and stretched out. "Sleep," I told him, covering him up. "They can't get to you here. You're safe."

"Annie?" he mumbled.

I bent and kissed his forehead. "I'll be down with Maya or Fell. *Sleep*, Wylan."

By the time I cracked the door open, his breathing had quieted, and I walked off with a lighter heart to see what state of chaos the kitchen might be in.

As neither of Fell's parents joined us for dinner, the mood was cheery, and the table practically groaned beneath the weight of the spread that Maya and her crew had thrown together: a roast chicken, whole fish, way too many starches, perfect vegetables, and enough bread for a small bakery. A peek at the line of covered dishes in the kitchen had given me hints as to the scope of dessert. Diriem took pains to keep the alcohol flowing, even presenting Frog with a large bottle of troll-strength beer that he forbade the rest of us from sampling for health and safety reasons. Though people joked and laughed—the kitchen minions in particular had a never-ending stream of friendly barbs for each other—they seemed gentle when it came to Wylan, and no one asked him questions about how he'd spent the last month or what had become of his antlers.

For his part, Wylan was perkier than I'd seen him in days, and he flashed genuine smiles during the meal. But he only picked at his food, and Korek eventually got up and returned with a cup of tea for him. "That's nothing fancy," said the faun, "and if you want something with espresso, I'm your guy, but it should help your digestion."

When dessert wound down and most of us were uncomfortably full, Maya turned to Diriem and said, "As lovely as this has been, and as much as I'm going to miss this place, I do have a café in the city that's been closed for weeks. Now that Wylan's back, is it safe for us to return to Beukal?"

He sipped his wine and briefly considered the ceiling. "If you can bear it here, I'd feel better if you stayed a few days more."

"Oh, I'm not complaining," Maya hastened to reassure him.

Diriem grinned. "Neither am I. Still, rest assured that I'm not trying to hold you captive. My visions remain somewhat muddled at the moment, but I *believe* the worst of the threat is over for the immediate future. If things proceed as I assume they will, I'd say you could be back in your own bed by the weekend."

"You don't think the Hunter's coming after Annie?" asked Fell.

"Not yet," he said, slowly shaking his head. "In time, perhaps, but he doesn't seem to be in the mood for immediate action. I don't believe he quite knows what to make of you," he told me, "and his ignorance may keep you safe for a while longer. Of course, should a threat materialize, you'd be welcome to return."

I smiled in thanks.

Just as Korek began taking orders for after-dinner coffees, the doorbell rang, and Diriem calmly put his napkin aside. "Good timing," he said, glancing at the ornamented clock on the wall. "Wylan, would you come with me, please?"

Hesitantly, Wylan rose from the table, and I joined him, intending to explain my presence as insurance against falls if Diriem protested. But our host made no complaint, and so we followed him through the mansion and into the foyer to find that Scel had already admitted Syvin and another faun, a dark-haired man I didn't recognize, who carried a large bag over his shoulder and gawked at the architecture in silence.

"Good evening, Director," said Syvin. "I hope we're not interrupting."

"Not at all," he replied. "A private space, perhaps?"

Curious, I shepherded Wylan toward a sitting room, but Diriem held me back while the two fauns and Wylan stepped inside. He closed the door, then motioned for me to follow him down the hall and into another empty room. "The fellow with Syvin is a horn specialist," he murmured. "She suggested bringing him out here once Wylan was released from DOL."

"Morial doesn't think his antlers will regrow—" I began.

"I have no reason to doubt him. Specialists like Syvin's friend work in the faun community—they break their horns on occasion, and a professional can grind them down properly to keep them manageable while they grow. Considering the state of Wylan's antlers, Syvin though he might want to at least even them out."

"And he doesn't need an audience for that," I said, understanding my exclusion.

"I shouldn't think so. Give them ten minutes, and I'll check."

Diriem's estimation was spot-on. When we returned to the sitting room, the specialist had already packed his bag, and Diriem escorted him and Syvin back to the foyer. Left alone with Wylan, I found him standing with his back to the room's lone mirror. His antlers had been reduced to rounded-off stubs, evenly matched but almost lost in his hair. If he'd kept his pointed ears covered, he could have passed for human at a distance—well, until he looked up at me and the room's lamps triggered his eyeshine.

"Are you all right?" I asked.

He shook his head.

"Is there anything I can do to make it better?"

"No. But I'll be fine," he insisted, and let me help him toward the door. "Not like I have a choice in the matter."

Slowly, we made our way to his room, and I watched while he flipped on the lights. "I'll come to bed in a little bit, and I'll be next door if you need me," I said. "If you fall or get hungry or something, just yell. The walls aren't entirely soundproof."

"You needn't worry," Wylan replied with a tired smile. "This bed really is quite nice—I doubt I move before dawn."

Shortly before eleven, his terrified screams ripped me awake, and I bolted in to find him on the floor, tangled in the bedding and caught in the throes of a nightmare. He flinched when I touched him, but with a hard shake, he woke and blinked blearily at me, his eyes glowing in the light from the corridor lamps. "Annie?" he whispered, panting.

I knelt on the rug and held him until his tremors subsided, and he spent the rest of the night in my bed, occasionally whimpering in his sleep until I woke enough to mumble reassurance that he wasn't alone.

With no sightings of the Hunt in Beukal for the rest of the week, Friday morning was deemed the end of Diriem's extended house party.

First to depart were Lady ti'Mal and Janon, who dragged Keef with them almost before she could finish breakfast. Her sister stopped her in the kitchen, hugged her fiercely, and told her to call *anytime*, while Rose promised Keef that she'd talk to her great-uncle and see about setting up a greenhouse tour. Keef skipped off all smiles, while her much dourer parents told Fell they would be in touch for wedding planning.

Fell sighed when the garage door closed behind them, and Camun wrapped his arm around her shoulders and pulled her close. "Better?" he murmured.

"Much. Hey," she said with a sly grin, "just wondering, but have you ever considered eloping?"

The two of them left soon thereafter, bound for Camun's apartment in the capital. While Fell had her own place, she wasn't yet keen on staying alone, and her fiancé was only too happy to continue their slumber party. Fell thanked Diriem profusely on their way out, and he assured her that she'd be receiving a call from DOL about a job interview.

Having heard from Pateme ti'Tam that Mangia Due was cleared to reopen on Monday, Maya was in a hurry to get back to Beukal and see what had become of her restaurant—and to her delight, she wasn't going alone. Diriem, it seemed, had had a quiet word with his DPP counterpart about the menu at the mansion that month, and Pateme had agreed to keep Korek, Dili, Makera, and Frog on full-time. I didn't know if this development heralded the end of my tenure behind the counter, but I wasn't heartbroken. My ten-year plan had never included pulling shots, and I was glad that Maya finally had a team she could count on for more than making sandwiches and working the register.

While Yven was relieved to be free to report to the office, I learned during breakfast that he wasn't exactly heading back to his apartment in Beukal yet. "We're not that far from the portal, and I'll be making the trip to DPP pretty regularly, anyway," Rose confided when he slipped into the kitchen to brew more coffee. "I think this place has grown on him."

"I can't imagine why," I deadpanned.

She chuckled. "He actually offered to pay rent last night. Pop was shocked."

"He thinks Yven's that cheap?"

"No, he just didn't imagine that Yven would expect a rent schedule. Pop told him that as long as he's with me, he's family, and that's final." Grinning, she added, "Since Pop has given Yven free rein over the greenhouse, at least I'll always know where to find him."

"And Diriem gets homemade vanilla extract out of the deal," I teased.

"*Naturally.*" She leaned closer and lowered her voice. "Pop likes you, Annie. I don't think he fully understands you, but he's intrigued. If you two wanted to stay, I know he wouldn't mind."

As much as I appreciated the offer—and regretted the loss of the guest bed—something told me that Pateme would be miffed if I didn't return to my DPP-funded apartment, where I could be housed conveniently close to the Roulette research team. Wylan and I were the last to leave that morning, and as he and Ranarma loaded all of his possessions back into the van, I pulled Diriem aside and said, "Thank you for everything. I don't know how many strings you've pulled on my behalf—"

"It's been my pleasure," he replied. "You have my

number—use it as needed, yes?"

I nodded. "Probably goes without saying that your money's no good at Mangia Due."

"I'd try to lure Maya to DOI, but Pateme would kill me. Never spoken to a man so thrilled by the prospect of having pastries on the premises."

"Didn't think he cared so deeply."

Diriem smirked. "Pateme can hide his feelings well when he's of a mind to do so, but once you've known him long enough, he's not difficult to read."

By lunchtime, with Maya busy shopping for her long-neglected restaurant kitchen, I'd made up a couch bed for Wylan and organized a plan of attack for cleaning the apartment after our extended vacancy. While Wylan had grown increasingly ambulatory over the last days, I ordered him to take a nap while I dusted and swept, and he didn't fight me. His sleep had been fitful all week, and his healing body needed whatever rest he could get.

Fortunately, there would be therapy in his future. Syvin, who'd warmed to Wylan since he helped bring Fell home, had called on Thursday night to offer counseling through DPP. "We have a good team," she'd told him. "And since you're still on the agency payroll, there's no reason why you shouldn't take advantage of it."

With much encouragement from me, Wylan had accepted the offer, and his first appointment was set for Monday afternoon. I had no idea what therapy looked like in the Pactlands, but I hoped it could help calm his nightmares. While I didn't mind sharing my bed, I knew it embarrassed Wylan when he screamed himself awake.

Once the place was relatively tidy, I stepped out to hit the nearest market and restock our depleted pantry. I returned about an hour later with my arms full of grocery bags and found Wylan awake. "Let me," he insisted, taking my load, and I went back to the van to grab the rest. The two of us made quick work of the unpacking, but as I folded up the bags for later, I glanced up in time to see

Wylan catch a glimpse of himself in the mirror we'd hung beside the table, then quickly look away.

Telling him I'd be right back, I slipped off to my favorite secondhand store and rummaged through the outerwear until I found a decent black knit ski cap. When I presented it to Wylan, he turned it over in his hands, studying it, and I said, "I know what it's like to hate your reflection. I don't know how to make this better for you, but maybe you wouldn't feel so awful if you couldn't see the stumps."

"Maybe," he mumbled, then tugged the cap into place. I made a few adjustments—having never worn a hat before, Wylan didn't quite have the hang of it—and he walked over to the dining room mirror to see the result.

His eyes welled as he stared at the glass, and I pulled him into my arms as he silently cried. "I'm sorry," I murmured after a moment, "I thought that would help…"

"It's fine," he lied, and forced himself to smile as stepped back to look at me. "I'll get used to it."

I cut my eyes to the pantry closet, then realized that cooking was the last thing I felt like doing that evening. "Want to go out for a walk, maybe get something to eat? If you're up to it—"

"Absolutely."

I told him he didn't need to wear the hat, but he insisted it was comfortable and set off with his ears and the remains of his antlers covered, a passable sorcerer to anyone on the street.

It was strange being back out in the open after a month in near seclusion. Freed of my daily scent neutralizer, I'd finally lost my rash, and the last of the blue tinge had left my fingertips—I looked closer to normal than I had in weeks, or at least not like the victim of a bizarre dermatological emergency. But the stares I'd come to know and loathe in the months before my vacation had returned with a vengeance, something I'd picked up on during my brief shopping trips that day and tried to ignore.

As we walked down a crowded block, people gawked, crossed the street, and ducked into open doors to avoid us. I spotted more than a few people conversing in agitated whispers nearby, and seeing a mother turn her body to pull her baby out of my line of sight left me feeling monstrous.

Apparently, for the good people of Beukal, my absence hadn't made them any fonder of the freak in their midst.

Noticing the reaction of the other pedestrians, Wylan took my hand and pulled me closer to his side. I glanced up and smiled, trying to disguise my true sentiments, and resolved to enjoy the evening. There was a nice park not too far from my apartment with plenty of benches—we could take a stroll in the pleasantly nippy afternoon, rest as Wylan needed, then hit up my favorite local restaurant for dinner. I'd last seen the nice couple who ran the place on the morning of Wylan's abduction, and given my regular appearances prior to that, I suspected they'd have questions.

As we neared a popular downtown bar—still quiet, given the hour—a pair of elves stepped out, blocking our path. "Stop right there," the shorter of the two ordered, and I took in their neat red shirts and black dress pants. Bartenders, I suspected, not bouncers, but having seen Fell in action, I had no desire to antagonize them.

"You," the shorter elf said, pointing to me as his companion folded his arms. "What's your business here?"

"Uh…going to the park?" I replied, taken aback. "Excuse us—"

"Sir," he said to Wylan, not budging, "are you being held against your will? Do you need assistance?"

While I'd heard that people in the capital had been on edge with the recent spate of Huntsman sightings, I hadn't appreciated how that would manifest.

Wylan, confused, told the men, "No, of course not. We're just walking."

"Are you *sure*?" our inquisitor pressed. "Why don't you step inside with us for a minute, hmm?"

At that, I released Wylan's hand and slowly raised my empty palms. "I'm not what you think I am. I'm going to pull out my wallet, okay?"

The shorter elf scowled, but his partner dipped a curt nod.

"Annie," Wylan muttered, "what are you—"

"Just a minute," I said, keeping my tone light, and fished my wallet from my purse. Opening it, I held it up for the elves, revealing my DPP non-agent ID card. "I'm not a Huntsman," I said. "Did you hear about the Roulette potion last year? I was exposed. If you need proof, I can give you the number for the chief deputy at DPP, and she'll vouch for me."

The elves appeared to waver as they leaned closer to look at my card, and I worried that I'd have to drag Syvin into the affair before they finally relented. "All right, then," the shorter elf said, retreating a pace. "Sorry for the confusion."

"Have a nice evening," the other offered, and they stepped aside to let us pass.

I didn't tuck my wallet away until we'd put a full block between us and the bar, and as tense as I was, I almost jumped when Wylan put his hand around my waist. He said nothing for the rest of the walk, but he led me straight to a bench and held my hand as I again tried to fake a *this is fine* smile.

"They're afraid of the Hunt," he murmured.

"Looks like it."

He sighed. "It wasn't this bad before…"

"Sounds like it's been a weird month in Beukal. I'm sorry, do you want to go home?"

"Why are *you* sorry?" he asked, brow furrowed. "I'm the thing they fear, but you're the one suffering." Squeezing my hand, he said, "Sometimes I forget about that potion. You've been trapped here—"

"Hey, we're not in a contest to the top of the misery heap," I replied.

"Still." Wylan leaned closer, his eyes softening as I held his gaze. "I…I want you to know that you're beautiful, Annie. Even if they stare, even if you don't feel like it…you are."

I smiled in earnest and cupped my free hand against his cheek. "You are, too."

He chuckled. "I wouldn't go that far—"

"The beard's a nice touch. And in case I haven't made it clear, I'm really glad you're back."

Wylan gave my hand a last squeeze before standing and pulling me to my feet. "Want to walk?" he asked, nodding to the path that wound around the Pactlands' stubby little trees.

"Yeah," I said, ignoring the joggers who darted *far* out of our way. "Yeah, that'd be nice."

We took our time in the park, then lingered over dinner. Maya had texted me to let me know that she'd be out late at the café, and as the nice restauranteurs not only welcomed me back but told off a table of sorcerers who'd started to give us a hard time, we were in no rush to get home. By eight, though, Wylan was flagging, and my thoughts had started to drift toward my bed—my *disappointing* bed, but a mattress with clean sheets nonetheless. It had been a long day.

But not ten minutes after we returned to the apartment, just as I was heading toward my room in search of pajamas, the doorbell rang.

Wylan tensed on the couch, but I motioned for him to sit still and went to the door. "If this is Diriem warning us to get out of town," I muttered, "I'm going to be pissed. I've already unpacked…"

When I opened the door, however, I found a troll on the welcome mat. Green-skinned, with a sandy blonde mohawk, uncapped tusks, and an implausible ruffle-front floral-print blouse, she looked down at me and nodded.

"Sorry for the late visit, Ms. Humphries. May I come in?"

"Uh…yes, ma'am," I replied, stepping back from the door. Though I'd had minimal interaction with her, I recognized Gentle Breeze, the chief of DPP's Interdiction side. The role seemed like a good fit for her—I mean, personally, had I been growing illegal plants in my basement, I'd have hated to find myself confronted by more than eight feet of troll, no matter what she was wearing.

Wylan relaxed slightly when he saw who'd arrived—Gentle Breeze wasn't exactly a regular at the café, but she came around enough to leave an impression—and he stood as I closed the door. "Is something wrong?" he asked.

"Nah." She folded her muscular arms and waited until I slid closer to him, then said, "I've come with a proposition for you two."

Wylan and I shared a look, and I took the lead. "What sort of proposition?"

"Well, correct me if I'm wrong, but the café's now got five actual cooks. Frankly, I'm not the only one who thinks your talents might be better used elsewhere."

I frowned. "What do you mean?"

"How would you two like jobs higher up in the tower? Say, with my people?"

"*Interdiction*?"

Gentle Breeze shrugged. "We're a mixed group. I've got a decent idea of what a Huntsman's capable of, and you're pretty damn scrappy. I respect that."

A job in Interdiction sounded leagues better than my gig behind the counter, but I still couldn't quite believe the offer. "But…Director Erenani said she couldn't hire me…"

The chief snorted. "That's DOL for you. *We* do our own thing. Now, sure, it may be unorthodox to bring on a human and a freaking Huntsman, but I've got a good feeling about this, and Pateme approves. What do you say?

Trial basis? We could get you in training and see how things work. I mean, hell," she added, nodding to Wylan, "I *know* you'd qualify on at least a few weapons, and I could use a nose like yours."

It wasn't perfect, but nothing was. And life could have been so much worse.

I looked at Wylan, saw a sparkle in his eyes that I'd very much missed of late, and turned back to Gentle Breeze. "What time do you want us on Monday?"

ACKNOWLEDGEMENTS

Hello again! Thank you for coming along on this journey with me. If you've made it this far, I think you'll like the final installation in Annie's story, *Hunted…*

My thanks go to the Novel Chicks for their feedback and friendship and to Adam Domby for his many excellent suggestions. Much appreciated, y'all.

And yes, here's to you, Mom and Dad.

ABOUT THE AUTHOR

When not writing fiction, Ash Fitzsimmons is an appellate attorney and an unrepentant car singer.

Find her online:
www.ashfitzsimmons.com

www.ingramcontent.com/pod-product-compliance
Lightning Source LLC
LaVergne TN
LVHW091030080826
845145LV00002B/431

* 9 7 8 1 9 4 9 8 6 1 5 7 0 *